Readers love
M. KING

Filth

"M. King writes eloquently about the feelings of despair and loneliness a person feels when they are born in the wrong body… I highly recommend this book."

—The Novel Approach

"*Filth* is not a romance, but it is one hell of a love story! One to marvel at and be envious of."

—Boys in Our Books

"…engrossing and beautiful. Reading it was an almost voyeuristic experience."

—Pants Off Reviews

Breaking Faith

"Although brilliantly written, with stunningly well-drawn characters, and a very compelling plot, this book was difficult to read… I couldn't put it down, and I thought about it for days and weeks after I read it…"

—Dear Author

By M. KING

Breaking Faith • Passing Shadows
Filth
Light and Water
Tonight or Else

Published by DREAMSPINNER PRESS
www.dreamspinnerpress.com

Light and Water

M. KING

DREAMSPINNER
PRESS

Published by
DREAMSPINNER PRESS

5032 Capital Circle SW, Suite 2, PMB# 279, Tallahassee, FL 32305-7886 USA
www.dreamspinnerpress.com

Light and Water
© 2016 M. King.

Cover Art
© 2016 Brooke Albrecht.
http://brookealbrechtstudio.com
Cover content is for illustrative purposes only and any person depicted on the cover is a model.

ISBN: 978-1-63477-458-1
Digital ISBN: 978-1-63477-459-8
Library of Congress Control Number: 2016903151
Published August 2016
v. 2.0
First Edition published by MLR Press, 2011.

Printed in the United States of America
∞
This paper meets the requirements of
ANSI/NISO Z39.48-1992 (Permanence of Paper).

I stood in Venice, on the Bridge of Sighs;
A palace and a prison on each hand:
I saw from out the wave her structures rise
As from the stroke of the enchanter's wand:
A thousand years their cloudy wings expand
Around me, and a dying glory smiles
O'er the far times when many a subject land
Looked to the winged Lion's marble piles,
Where Venice sat in state, throned on her hundred isles!

—Lord Byron, "Childe Harold's Pilgrimage."

CHAPTER ONE

VENICE WAS sinking, so people said. Year on year, inch by inch, descending into its own sumptuous decay. Dan stood at the open window, camera in his hands, and looked out across the terracotta-tinted wedding cake rooftops that led down to the Piazza San Marco, kissed orange and gold by the dawn. It was impossible to believe, because nothing this beautiful should ever change.

He didn't normally get up so early. In fact, after the nightmare of a flight from Heathrow, he was surprised he was conscious at all. Three hours of purgatory, with some ghastly child doing a foot drum solo on the back of his seat, should have left him so tired he'd have been dead to the world until midmorning, at least.

Last night, arriving late at the hotel, he'd done nothing but dump his bags and pass out on the bed, barely bothering to undress. Yet the magic of Venice must already be working on him because he'd woken feeling good, eager to get out there and explore.

Dan rested his head on the window frame, the painted wood still cold from the night's chill, and looked out at the vaulted arches and pillars of the Palazzo Ducale, stained purple against the cloud-fringed sky.

His friends had said he was mad to come here on his own, but they hadn't understood. Chris, who probably had the distinction of being Dan's oldest friend—and would have pouted at being called that—had said it was like going to Paris to go trainspotting. "It's the capital of romance, you prick!" he'd wailed. "You can't just… just go and walk around taking *pictures*!"

Dan raised the camera and reeled off another succession of shots of the dawn. Each frame would be just that little bit different, catch a slightly altered tone or fleeting bounce of light. He paused, holding the camera strap in his teeth as he fiddled to fit a wider-angle lens.

What no one realized was that this time was all his. It didn't matter if it was a working holiday. Any pictures he took out here were for him—not for yet another arrogant teenage girl's modeling portfolio, or some foul-mouthed celebrity chef's new cookbook. It was all about what *he* wanted to do, what *he* wanted to see… and after the past couple of months, independence was valuable to Dan.

He glanced at his watch, wondering how early it was worth striking out for San Marco. Funny, really, but time didn't seem to matter here. Even the seconds passed grudgingly, as if they preferred to linger, charmed by some strange glamour. He zoned the camera onto the ruffled horizon, pricked by the shapes of a hundred tiny churches and ancient *palazzi*, wrapped around with the dusty, orange-gold light. Out there, beyond the rooftops, the hazy canals glittered, gleaming ribbons that snaked through the city.

Dan bit his lip. It felt like the place was calling, beckoning him. Sure, he'd only just arrived, but he couldn't wait to get out there and start to learn its secrets, to touch the crumbling stucco and stonework and find its hidden places.

He knew that was silly. He'd read all the magazine articles that tutted about the state of the city's economy, the property prices pushed up by rich incomers and an unsustainable level of tourism, until the Venetians themselves could neither afford nor abide the place. Dan supposed he should feel guilty about adding to the problem, but he'd been looking forward to this so much, and for so long, that he couldn't feel bad about anything.

He shivered a little as the cool air brushed his bare arms. He'd chosen one of the quietest times of the year to visit, right between the February *Carnevale* and the Venetian high season, which ran pretty much from mid-April to October and picked up again in time for Christmas. It meant fewer crowds, comparatively, but chilly, damp days and cold nights. Not as if that fazed him—England was hardly renowned for its sunny climate.

Dan turned from the window, changed the camera lens over again, and zipped his kit back into its case before setting it on the square, pine-effect hotel vanity, along with the tripod and the bag that held spare batteries and memory cards.

Paul had always said they'd come here together. Venice, Florence, Rome… just do that whole Italian tour thing, take six weeks away from it all and spend the summer pretending they were gap-year students again, with no responsibilities and no worries. Obviously, Paul had never actually done half the things he'd said he would do—although they had gone to Magaluf one year. The weather had been scorching hot; too hot to do anything, really, except lie by the pool and read cheap spy thrillers. The room had been nice, however. Great air-conditioning.

Dan ran his fingers through his hair, finding it stale and sticky with recycled plane air, then stretched his arms above his head, linked his fingers together, and let the tension creak slowly out of his back. A shower would be nice. He shucked off the T-shirt and boxers he'd slept in and padded through to the pristine white bathroom.

It wasn't that Paul had hurt him. He was sure of that. Not... hurt. Sure, they'd had arguments, and sometimes the fur had really flown, but it hadn't been *that* vicious. Dan had hated the casual, arrogant insensitivity that Paul could be capable of, and the self-centered egotism he seemed to cloak himself in as he glided through the world, but he'd never been truly awful. Maybe it was the price to be paid for being with someone who was so used to success, or at least to getting his own way, and Dan supposed he'd been as much to blame for just giving in and letting it happen.

For every small thing that had drummed on Dan's nerves like summer rain—every pouting disagreement over a restaurant menu, every bout of complaining or bitchy drama over nothing—he'd reminded himself that it could have been worse, and that most of the time it was good. He'd let the routines that bound them together knit back over the cracks, and it had been routine that killed things. In the end, perhaps they'd just grown too used to each other.

They'd met at one of the self-consciously hip and trendy cocktail-slinging bars Chris insisted on dragging Dan to, and for weeks nothing else had mattered. Paul had been everything he thought about, slept, and breathed. They hadn't known each other well enough for Dan to judge whether or not he'd even liked the guy, but Paul had made him moan, made him cry... made him think he could be in love.

Dan fiddled with the shower controls, catching his breath as first icy, then scalding water hit his chest. Sure, they'd had good times. The sex had always been good, often great. Sometimes mind-blowingly incredible. The trouble was, there had never seemed to be much else besides it, even though there should have been... even though he'd tried to make himself believe there *had* been. Paul worked for an art gallery, and they should have had that common interest to share. They had the hundred little details of life that jumped out and made it seem like they might be happy ever after, but eventually he and Paul had found they had less and less to talk about, and less and less to care about.

What had hurt most was the feeling of not being able to stop it all sliding away. It became somehow awkward to share the same space and despite the bewilderment of his friends, Dan had slowly come to realize that he wanted out.

Chris had said he was crazy. To him, Paul had been Mr. Perfect, the amazing boyfriend. Drop-dead gorgeous, glitzy job, and shiny car, and he'd said and done all the right things: all the things that made him sound wonderful, and made Dan doubt his own sanity when he felt things start to fail.

At the time, it had been impossible to explain. In the time since, Dan had tried to rationalize it. Maybe he was grasping at straws, but it felt as if Paul belonged to clubland, to the weekly round of hookups that followed a few too many vodkas and a few too many hormones. Wonderful relationships could start like that, but something about what he and Paul had shared died if you took it out of the dark. Dan wished he'd seen that at the start. It had seemed so different then, as if they'd really made the leap into something real and long-term, and he was sure he'd wanted it. However, as time wore on, it became painfully apparent that wanting things to work just wasn't enough. It certainly wasn't enough to mean he could face the thought of looking at Paul over the breakfast table every day for the rest of his life, trying desperately to think of something new to say that wouldn't end up fading into the same cycle of argumentative friction and recrimination, followed by needling boredom.

Dan reached blindly for the complimentary sachet of hotel shampoo and wrestled with the little plastic packet. He'd thought he'd found the right guy; they'd lasted three years, hadn't they? Longer than David, who'd taken his virginity and his heart at sixteen, then left him to go to university; almost as long as Luke, who'd promised him an eternity, but only managed to deliver four years before moving on to greener pastures and a family in the suburbs. So, Dan thought, he'd been wrong. Again. What was new?

Still, it could have been worse, he reflected, finally winning the war and squeezing the shampoo out into his hand. Endless indifference might leave a soul hollow, but it didn't cut like true cruelty.

Dan massaged the shampoo into his hair, sniffed, and wrinkled his nose. Great. He was going to smell like an elderly auntie's knicker drawer. So much for packing light. He would have to buy some essentials for the week.

He'd left Paul not long after Christmas… about three months ago now. Perhaps *he* had been the cruel one, but Dan reasoned that if Paul cared as much as every breathless "I love you, Danny" he gasped when he came indicated, then it would hurt. It would hurt so badly it would knock the breath out of him. Paul would have reacted somehow; fought against him, fought *for* him, maybe. Anything except that small, sad shrug, and an anemic "Okay, if you think that's best." Simple. Passive. Amicable. Infuriating. And yet Dan still dreamed of his touch, still dreamed about being fucked until he ached from being held so hard, sore from beard burn, wet with kisses.

His soapy fingers slid over his body like other hands, other lips on his skin, as he closed his eyes, letting the warm water flow over his face and ears, drowning out everything beyond his own head. Chris kept trying to push him back into the game, setting him up on date after date; some excruciatingly embarrassing, some tepid, others almost bearable. None of them made it easier to connect. "Dry spell," Chris had said, trying to cheer him up. "Nothing to worry about. You'll get your mojo back."

Dan had been tempted to tell him exactly where he could stick his mojo, oldest friend in the world or not. Instead, he'd smiled, said nothing, and booked himself a holiday. Time out, time away… somewhere completely different. You couldn't get much more different than Venice, right?

He stepped from the shower, contemplating the vast stretch of time before him, islanded and perfect. No one looking over his shoulder, no responsibilities, and no ties: it was going to be wonderful.

Dan tossed the once-fluffy and now damp hotel towel onto the floor and picked through his luggage. He slipped on fresh briefs, relishing the feel of crisp, clean cotton, and flicked through a couple of the guidebooks he'd slipped into his case. So much to do, so much to see. He could have made an itinerary, but this was time made to be wasted.

He smiled to himself as he slid on a pair of old, comfortable shoes, stuffed the deep, secure pockets of his worn jeans with photocopies of his passport and papers, and pulled on his beloved tan leather blazer. He'd had it for years, bought from a Camden flea market and now so vintage its elbows were thin and shiny, and the leather had developed a rich patina full of good memories and lazy summer afternoons.

Dan gave himself a brief but critical glance in the mirror, popped a stick of gum in his mouth, and ruffled his damp hair, leaving it lying in dark honey waves at his temples. He'd do. He just wanted to get out there and get hopelessly lost, to spend the day walking and discovering unexpected, unsought treasures. The Falk map he'd bought at the airport suggested, perhaps optimistically, that it would be easy enough to explore the city if he stuck to one district at a time, and Dan was prepared for the challenge.

He checked his watch against the clock in the room—almost eight fifteen—picked up the camera bags, and left, humming cheerfully under his breath as he jogged down the winding stairs of the small, family-run hotel. Golden sunlight spilled into the reception area from tall windows. Piles of complimentary leaflets and allegedly easy-to-read maps stood by the front desk, all crammed into a single, overstuffed stand.

Dan paused to take a look, picking up fliers for smaller local galleries, studios, and museums that the guidebooks didn't even mention. Then, of course, there was the Murano glassblowing… his mother collected glassware, and would never speak to him again if he didn't bring her something back. Dan snagged a leaflet showing how to get to the factory on Murano Island, and as he glanced at the pictures of various colorful vases and mirrors, he noticed another leaflet pushed in behind the first. The bright logo caught his attention, as did the picture of the tanned, well-oiled dancer beneath it, airbrushed muscles rippling and digitally enhanced eyes smoldering.

Dan's fingers lingered over the edge of the leaflet. Club Commodoro. Well, it figured, given the little white hat perched atop the dancer's ebony curls. Still… there wasn't any harm in checking out the nightlife, was there?

The concierge was a well-spoken young Venetian whom Dan had seen at check-in late last night, and he'd been exhaustingly eager to impress even then. Maybe he was the owner's son, or nephew, or something. Now he noticed Dan and breezed to the end of the desk, smiling, to say good morning.

"Ah, Signor Wright! You have good sleep, I hope? You are taking your breakfast in the hotel, or to go out?"

"Hm? Oh… yes. Thank you." Dan slid the brightly colored leaflet into the stack of others he'd picked up. "Um. I thought I'd go out. I've heard so much about the coffee rooms on San Marco, I thought I'd take a look."

"Oh, *sì*! *Sì, signore.* Piazza San Marco is very beautiful in the mornings. Many excellent café. Grancaffè Quadri, it is very good. They open in 1775, so plenty of time to get the coffee right, yes?"

Dan smiled obligingly as the young man started a drawn-out story about how coffee was originally brought to Venice from Istanbul, and how the coffeehouses that had sprung up in the Piazza became legendary hotbeds of scandal and political intrigue. Politely, Dan listened to how the great Casanova had slipped between the carved panels and frosted glass lamps of the cafés, evading the doge's guards and the threat of the bleak, damp prison cells at Piombi, and felt his morning sliding slowly away.

"…and then, while you are there, you must see the Basilica di San Marco, of course. And the Museo Archeologico *e* the Museo Correr— very, very beautiful paintings! The Palazzo Ducale is worth the time you spend to queue. Will you spend all your day in the Piazza and the Canale?"

"Probably not… I thought I'd just go exploring. I had been planning to go to Castello, or maybe take the water taxi out to Burano."

The concierge frowned. "Burano? Eh, there is nothing in Burano, signor. Just old men drinking grappa and grandmothers making lace. It's a long way just for one or two pretty houses. Castello isn't bad, there's plenty to see, but if you ask *me*, signor, all the big *palazzi*, all the most beautiful churches, they are not in Castello." He shrugged. "You want to see the treasures of Venezia; you should stay here in San Marco, or go to San Polo, or Dorsoduro, across the Canale…. Dorsoduro is nice. There is the Galleria dell'Accademia—it has many great paintings and works of art. Very… uh, *come si dice*? Funky." He gave a little wriggle of his shoulders. "Many artists, sculptors. Lots of old *palazzi*, *chiese*, beautiful buildings. You must go to Chiesa dei Carmini, is wonderful church. You will make many beautiful photograph, signore!"

"I hope so." Dan patted his camera bag. "I'm due to go up to Cannaregio tomorrow, to the Spanish synagogue. They're letting me take some pictures."

"*Sì?*" The concierge's face lit up. "This is very good, signor… they have just finished rebuilding. So much history there. You must go to the

Madonna dell'Orto, and to Santa Maria dei Miracoli, also. Very famous, beautiful *chiesa*." He smiled shyly. "I am getting married there, at Santa Maria, in two months. My Giulietta."

"Congratulations," said Dan dutifully, wondering if he was going to get out of there any time before midday. "I'll bear what you said in mind."

"*Sì, signore*. You should see the Rialto too, *e* San Polo. For your shopping, the Rialto is best. My cousin, Stefano, he has a shop in the Ruga. Very nice jewelry. You find him, you say Italo send you, he will give you very nice price, all right? Here, I show you best way for to go."

Dan passed over the map and let him mark where the various churches, gallerias, and family businesses were to be found. He hid a resigned sigh. He'd been hoping to get out without being caught, but for all he knew, the kid was on a commission and needed the money. Besides, it paid to get someone who knew where things were to lend a helping hand, as Venice's streets and canals, where they actually *were* numbered or signed, had most likely been codexed by a madman. The travel guide had warned him of this, but Dan hadn't been prepared for how true it really was. Digits leapt between odd and even, sequences and logic forgotten… although there probably wasn't much point in relying on logic in a city built mostly on water.

After what seemed like hours, he got away.

"You have a wonderful day now, Signor Wright." The concierge beamed widely at him. "This is beautiful day in the most romantic city in Europe. Who knows? You might meet a beautiful *signorina*, eh?"

Dan smiled uncomfortably, thanked the guy, and gave him another tip just to shut him up. Outside, in the cool, crisp air, he breathed deeply. He had been right: it was the quality of light. Like the reflections of blue tiles in a swimming pool, or leaves above a woodland creek, it made the whole place shimmer slightly. Of course, it could just have been the sense of expectation that hung over the city. Hundreds of thousands of people, all coming to Venice and expecting it to meet the image they'd imagined: the fairy-tale city guarded by four winged lions, poised like a beautiful swan upon the water.

Venice was quieter now than in much of the year, and even more so in the morning. As he walked through the narrow pathways that led from the hotel down to Piazza San Marco, Dan had only to deal with straggly crowds of tourists instead of the gridlocked mass he'd been warned to expect during much of the year.

He let his fingertips brush the rough brickwork and stone of the tall loggia he passed, pressing back against the walls to allow for the crush of foot traffic on narrow walkways. There were few enough parts of Venice you could get to on foot, so people made the most of them. The sun rose higher now, warming the city gently, waking it like a lover. He breathed in the cool, damp, slightly salty air, and smiled.

The great, wide expanse of the Piazza San Marco, seen fresh for the first time on foot and on the level, took Dan's breath away. Despite the gaggles of people that thronged the square, the scale and sheer openness of the space was impressive, palpable. It was so much louder here, but the scale of the place let the sounds echo and float above the crush. Not even the mangled cacophony of noise from the cafés, *trattorie*, and shops for tourists could detract from the sense of timeless perfection here. Anchored by the Basilica di San Marco rising at the far end in a mass of Byzantine domes and tangled, ornate arches, the massive campanile and the broad walls of pilastered and balustraded Renaissance buildings were something entirely set apart.

Two tall white columns, complete with the heraldic winged lion of St. Mark, and the figure of St. Theodore, rose from the paving, topped by pigeons. The birds congregated in their thousands in the arches and window ledges above, and on the intricate black iron streetlights, their cooing battling with the clink of china and the bustle of waiters. Some hardy diners were taking breakfast outside, braving the faint chill and the extra cost of paying for a table, with their coffee and croissants. Some looked like tourists, others seemed like native Venetians, unfolding their copies of *Il Corriere della Sera* and trying to carve a small window of peace amid the bustle.

Farther away to the left, the *piazzetta* led gently down to the water, a once-symbolic gateway to the city so perfectly framed that Dan almost regretted not arriving by boat so he could have experienced it the way the architects had envisioned. It must have been wonderful back in the days of the Grand Tours, even with the chaos and crowds… and he'd have given anything to have his first glimpse of the city laid out that way. Pure romance.

Dan, his back wedged against the front of a high-class gift shop, took out his camera and reeled off fifteen or so shots of the view toward the Basilica, then of as much of the piazza as he could get in without changing lenses, and another twenty of the view out to sea, where the city's wonderful improbabilities joined together; the light, land, and water fused in a perfect band of hazy blue. The gift shop was one of more than a dozen that peppered San Marco and its surrounding side streets, and he couldn't help but notice the display of *Carnevale* masks in the window.

They were just as improbable as the city itself—ridiculously expensive artistic confections, drenched with history and meaning, brand-new yet ancient, and incredibly beautiful. The traditional half masks or *colombina*, bowed shapes covering the eyes and bridge of the nose, came in so many styles. Rich fabrics and textures burst everywhere, from the *losanghe* patterns of deep-colored velvet and harlequin cloth edged with thick gold brocade, to intricate macramé, tiny veins of gold and silver leaf threaded through with ornate floral designs. There were *naso* and Scaramouche masks, with their long, beak-like noses, painted in bright reds and gleaming gold, and the bone-white, polished *dottore* masks, similar in style but with the darker connotations of the old plague doctors, who had worn them centuries before, for scant protection from sickness.

Stick masks, their delicate barley-twist handles striped like the city's piers, held serene, perfect faces with hollow-cut eyes and crystal accents, mouths forever painted into cherubic pouts. Crests of raven-black feathers sprouted from heavily decorated *piume* masks, while the traditional Venetian *bauta*, with their molded, blank features in plain white and black, leered out from between the mischievous, cheeky grins of brightly colored, crackle-finished *diavolo* and jester faces, decorated with bells and sinister smiles.

Aware he was grinning like an idiot and not caring, Dan zipped the camera back into its bag and decided to contemplate his next moves over breakfast. He gravitated toward the Grancaffè Quadri, bought an espresso, and a warm, freshly baked croissant, and slotted himself into the crush between the rather oppressive mirrored walls and overwhelming panel work, probably very little like the original eighteenth century designs. He ate his *croissant con marmellata* standing up, with the rest of the patrons who hadn't wanted to pay double for a table, and tried very hard not to get apricot conserve all over his chin.

DAN PASSED the morning in San Marco, content to let the life of the place wash over him, and to be a tourist among other tourists. He did all the expected stuff—queued up to see the Palazzo Ducale, took the tour that showed the duality of its pink-and-white fairy-tale façade, its gilded public rooms and the stark, white offices from which the city had really been run—and for once found himself happy to be lost in the crowds.

He enjoyed watching them. There were Swedish, Spanish, British, Australian tourists… Italians too, on day trips or weekends from the south. Tour groups filed obediently after guides like flocks of awestruck sheep with cameras. Children grizzled, failing to see the finer points of the city's beauty. There were women carefully adhering to the dress codes that said no one could visit the churches and Basilica with bare shoulders, arms, or knees, and men, young and loud, old and quiet… all extremes and all kinds of people.

Dan saw one or two clutches of young Italian guys out on the town, all perfect hair and teeth and metrosexuality, and smiled to himself. Perhaps it would be worth it, despite the crowds, to come back in the summer and sit on the Lido, watching half-naked beautiful people frolic in the surf. He doubted it, but the option was always there… like the electric moment between checking a guy out and seeing whether he smiled back or not, the few precious seconds of delicious uncertainty that signaled the game.

He shook himself. Chris would poke him in the ribs and tell him to put on a tighter T-shirt and see what the nightlife had to offer. Chris would have looked at that flier by now.

He slipped the paper out of his pocket when he stopped for a coffee in the Museo Archeologico, a Renaissance confection of incredible proportions, all pilasters and porticos in white stone grayed with time.

He sat in the overpriced coffee shop, drinking another espresso, the thick crema silky on his lip, and looked at the flier. Club Commodoro was obviously new; it proclaimed itself Venice's first and best gay nightclub, although it didn't say much about the quality of the venue, given the lack of competition. There wasn't much information available, except the bar's location and opening times. Dan tucked the flier back into his pocket, thinking no more of it. After all, this was time for him. If the weekend ritual of dressing up and hitting the clubs had become depressing at home, left him feeling old and unattractive, what would be different here?

Dan finished his coffee, wandered back through the Museo's floors, winding his way past the silent marble figures, and left after an hour or so, feeling languidly cultured and a little hungry. He made his first tourist error when, slipping into a small *trattoria* off the Zattere for lunch, he didn't realize that he'd turned up in the traditional workmen's break that ran from twelve until one. The place was tiny, squeezed in between a copy and print shop and a dry cleaner that appeared to be permanently closed, and from behind the counter an unseen radio babbled some kind of discussion program in Italian way too fast for Dan to follow.

The midday special was a huge bowl of pasta and half a bottle of red wine, which Dan ordered and ate surrounded by middle-aged guys in construction boots and dusty overalls. He tried not to stand out too much, with his Marc Jacobs cologne, Ben Sherman shirt, and bags of expensive camera equipment. No one commented, although he wouldn't have understood it if they had. He smiled to himself and decided it was definitely one to jot down on the postcards.

After he'd eaten, Dan started the walk out to Castello, one of the city's less glamorous districts. It had once been a center of the shipbuilding trade, with thousands of *arsenalotti* on hand, able to construct a galley in a matter of hours. No longer a city-state bent on political domination and power, Venice now had no way to support a navy, and the mystical marriage of La Serenissima and the sea had lapsed.

Dan wandered aimlessly through the *sestiere* as the sun grew warmer, unable to believe his luck as he stumbled on perfect view after perfect view—old houses with window boxes on their balconies, terracotta-red render and soft brick cradled by thick, balmy light, making the whole scene look as if it had been sketched in chalks. Quiet canals crisscrossed with little bridges were still, only a few launches and private boats bobbing in their moorings, sending gentle ripples across dark water that might otherwise have been a mirror.

He lost himself that afternoon, traipsing through the endless narrow backstreets where buildings seemed to meet above him, old wooden shutters blind to the sky. Here and there, he found a deserted square or garden, a quiet place where the city's pulse thrummed distantly, washing over the gray-blue paving stones and the dark greens of neatly clipped olive trees. He sat on a bench beside a tiny church that was closed for renovation, watching birds circle in the sky, high above, while an old woman shook freshly washed linens out of her apartment window, pegging them to a line that ran right across the canal. From within, Dan could hear the indistinct, tinny noise of a game show on a television.

He took pictures of the cloth billowing white against the sky in that perfectly clear spring light; pictures of the scaffolding and the gantry holding up the church; pictures of the olive trees, so close it was hard to see anything among the leaves. Finally satisfied, or at least needing to change his memory card, he slung the camera bag across his back and set off again.

He stopped on the way back to the hotel to do some postcard and gift shopping, and after battling his way back through the Rialto and the Mercerie, Dan was staggering slightly under a pile of mass-produced idiocies: beautifully drawn and photographed, gate-folded postcards for everyone he knew would want one; cheap but nonetheless attractive sculptures of the lion of St. Mark, a gondolier (with detachable gondola, pole, and straw hat), and a Pulcinella, the *Carnevale* figure; for his sister's kids, plus laminated wall chart maps and apparently historical sealing wax kits that looked suitably messy and entertaining; and a gondolier's hat for Chris, which he would probably wear while drunk and singing extremely bad fake opera.

Exhausted by the time he got back to San Marco, Dan was disappointed slightly to see the Piazza coming to life with the impending evening. Restaurant musicians and street orchestras competed not just with each other, but also with the piped music of *trattorie* and clubs, and the tourists that thronged in placid groups by day, unchained from their guides, now pinballed all over the place in loud, irritating numbers. Dan slipped up a side street to a small *trattoria* he'd spotted that morning, perhaps feeling a little too smug at remembering where it was. He ordered *bigoli con l'anara*, a Venetian pasta special with duck sauce (or at least, sauce made from *parts* of a duck), and followed it up with *sgroppino*, the sweet, sticky treat made from lemon sorbet and fruity, sparkling Prosecco.

After more coffee, Dan was getting a second wind. By the time he got back to his hotel, he was wide-awake and buzzing. It could have been the caffeine, the wine at lunch, or the thought that, just over twenty-four hours ago, he had been stuck in the stuffy London office of *Calypso*, the magazine Chris worked on, being diplomatic and polite to the editor when he'd have preferred to tell her where to stick the changes she wanted made to his most recent submissions.

Here, Dan didn't need to pretend. Tonight, this was his time, his place, lost between worlds and without responsibilities. He went up to his room and stowed all the crap he'd bought in his case, promising himself he really would write those postcards sooner than the day he was due to travel home. He emptied his pockets onto the nightstand, including the handful of crumpled fliers, the one for Club Commodoro among them. Dan picked it up between two fingers and looked again at the two-dimensional stud on the flier, wearing nothing but a silly hat, a white jockstrap, and a bottle of baby oil.

Well… maybe he did deserve some fun. A few drinks, maybe a dance, maybe more. A little bit of freedom. Why the hell not? He narrowed his eyes, then dropped the leaflet back to the nightstand. If he didn't go tonight, if he didn't make the most of this sudden sense of liberation, he wouldn't go at all.

After a quick shower, he rummaged through his luggage for a fresh shirt and, pulling on a bright blue tee, glanced at his reflection in the mirror. He wouldn't bother shaving. Let there be a touch of stubble and some raw machismo. Dan grinned crookedly at himself and set about tucking the essentials into his pockets. He didn't need much: condoms, lube, gum, photocopies of his paperwork, and the minimum amount of cash.

He shut the rest of his personal effects into the nightstand, and cast an eye around the room. Would he really bring anyone back here? His stomach tightened at the thought, part in excitement and part, he was surprised to find, in a stab of anger at Paul or, at least, at the memory of him. They'd been at their best in bed, and it was hard to forget. Worse, it awoke in Dan the cold and gnawing fear that, whatever else was out there, it wouldn't be as good.

In that moment, he hated his ex-boyfriend, both for that, and for the way that just thinking about him, even now, made his throat tighten as fast as his underwear.

CHAPTER TWO

THE FLIER gave general directions to the Commodoro. The club was on the mainland, at the edge of the old industrial district of Mestre, and getting there was going to be a little more complicated than Dan's initial excursions into the city. It seemed worth it, though; he *was* here to explore as much of the place as he could, wasn't he?

Mestre was, Dan's *Rough Guide* said, a hinterland to which the native Venetians who couldn't afford to renovate their decaying houses had long ago fled, but never bothered to gentrify—where La Serenissima kept her factories, new housing estates, and office buildings. Perhaps, in one way, more of the "real" Venice than all the old *piazzette* with washing lines and grandmammas combined. *The webbed feet under the swan*, thought Dan, as he walked down past San Marco to the *vaporetto* stop that the tiny printed map on the flier showed as Rialto C. All around him, the city blazed with light, shining in the dark.

Venice's ancient waterbus had once literally been a "steamship," but was represented now by an old and crumbling fleet, all owned and operated by a single company. As Dan discovered, the boats skimmed the water like floating lawnmowers, plowing temperamentally through the canals with a series of crunching roars from their engines, hulls pitching with the erratic quivers of cherry blossoms in a hailstorm. Irreplaceable Venetian institution the *vaporetto* might be, but he actually missed London cabs.

Dan got off at Piazzale Roma, took a moment to breathe deeply and regain his land legs, and looked about him for some glimmer of a street sign, or at least the suggestion of a timetable outside the sprawl of the nearby bus station. Even late into the evening, there were still regular buses heading across the Ponte della Libertà for the mainland, and the flier he had stuffed into his pocket promised an easy trip there and back again… presuming he could find the right bus to get on in the first place.

Remarkably, there were a couple of taxis idling not far from the ranks of parked buses, and Dan decided that might be his safest option, instead of ending up in completely the wrong place just because he'd misjudged his request stop. After a bit of pantomiming and mispronunciation, he managed to convey to the tired-looking and rather surly driver that he wanted to go to the Via del Commercio, and Dan settled into the car's gray leather upholstery, playing out a thousand scenarios in his head. They varied from getting to the bar, having a great time, and hitting it off with a tall, handsome Italian count who owned a medieval *palazzo* and a string of sports cars, to the question of whether a foreign tourist being mugged and murdered would make the newspaper headlines or not, and how long it would take his family to report him missing.

The journey was surprisingly quick, despite the traffic, though there was something a little unnerving about the low, flat width of the bridge. It stretched over the water like a recently unearthed causeway, and Dan couldn't shake the feeling it was somehow impermanent, another piece of make-believe in a fantastical place. He knew that was ridiculous. The bridge had been there since 1933 and though its name was different now, changed to reflect the freedom the city found once *il Duce* was no more than a bitter memory, it was as much a static landmark as anywhere else in the place.

Dan's laconic taxi driver deposited him at the wrong end of the Via del Commercio for the club and, he suspected, overcharged him for the privilege, but Dan didn't complain. He began his walk, pressing through the fluorescent glow of the streetlights, through the dim streets and the inevitable nighttime drunks and party people. It was relatively early, barely eleven o'clock, but he could hear the thump of distant music. He followed his ears, past the shops, hotels, and restaurants, their comparative modernism strange after the city's ancient façades, and found the place he was searching for in only a few minutes. Club Commodoro was subtle, by nightclub standards, the street door leading to a small booth front-of-house, brightly lit, where a stocky middle-aged guy sat behind the narrow desk. He smiled at Dan, the three gold earrings in each ear shaking slightly as he tilted his head to the side.

"Arcigay card?" the guy asked with a heavy Italian accent.

"Sorry?"

"You need card to get in. If you don't have, it's fourteen euros, and you fill in this form," he explained, pushing a clipboard and pen across the small counter ledge. "There's an English version. You English, or American?"

"English," Dan replied, wondering if it was really that obvious. He peered at the form. "Why the card?"

The guy shrugged. "Safer. Hey, it's a good deal—this card gets you in all the clubs."

"I thought this was the only one in Venice?"

"It is, but you can go to Padova, Milano… wherever you want. All good. So. You going to have card, or not card?"

"I will. Thanks."

Dan filled in the form, signed, paid his money, and accepted the little oblong of card printed with the Arcigay logo.

"Show Francesco at the bar your card, you get three drink entitlement all free. Three drink only. Bar and disco downstairs, upstairs for the video room and the cabins, all right? Enjoy."

He buzzed Dan in and the door opened. Club Commodoro turned out to be everything its advertising promised—fresh, cosmopolitan, sensual, and tasteful. Well, about as tasteful as it could get with the bar staff and the dancers wearing nothing but white jockstraps and sailor's caps. The security was tight but discreet, the lighting low but clear, and the music flowed as freely as the booze. Dan breathed in deeply, taking time to adjust to the room, the smells and sounds of the place. It reeked of sandalwood incense, with a faint undertone of disinfectant.

The barman, Francesco, stamped his entitlement card and gave him a huge, gleaming smile that went extremely well with his huge, gleaming pecs. Dan sipped his vodka tonic and tried not to drool or stare too hard at the ivy-leaf tattoo that curled down over the man's left collarbone and onto the great muscular slab of his chest.

The night was still infant and the club wasn't too crowded. A few patrons lingered at the bar, flirting with the staff. Every so often two men might pair off, leaving by the front door or disappearing up the stairs to who knew what hidden pleasures. Dan's eyes followed them, and he was amazed to find he was nervous. Stupid—it wasn't as if he'd never been anywhere like this before.

By the time he ordered his third vodka, he was feeling more relaxed. He'd made an assault on the complimentary bowl of mints and the complimentary bowl of condoms, both equally cheerful in brightly colored wrappers. The bar had started to fill up, and though no one had really caught his eye, it was definitely a varied crowd. Italian, French, Dutch, German, American, and Japanese voices could all be heard under the beat of the ever-louder Europop, as the DJ brought the room up a notch. Dan had tired of ogling Francesco and turned to watch the dance floor instead, the lights and the rhythm and the pervasive scents of sandalwood, sweat, and skin all swirling in his head.

The atmosphere grew closer, and Dan wasn't sure whether to blame the booze, the club, or the want pressing up in his own body. It seemed clear that, for most of the men here, this was a place where daytime rules were suspended. The hazy, sickly fragrant air lay heavy with adrenaline and expectation, the buzz of people lost in their own enjoyment. Italy, a country split in two by its own conflicting morals, the unbearable pressure of its past and future, its sinners and its saints, certainly knew how to forget about everything, let its hair down, and have a good time, even if it would have to go to Confession with a hangover in the morning.

There were dancers, oiled and amazing, each with a ridiculous but incredibly sexy white sailor cap, bumping and grinding against each other, and the coat check had started checking more than just coats for some patrons. The floor filled up now—shirtless men and shameless men, hands sliding over slick flesh and bodies pressing together in the crush. The music thumped louder, filling Dan's chest, every beat a command, a primal impulse.

Each body in the crowd was a flicker in an infinite flame, and when Dan joined them, he was the self he was in dreams… conscious and feeling, but without thought. He was working purely on sensation, thinking only in color, shape, and touch. Hands and skin sought, found, and united, breaths becoming collective sighs, articulated desires.

He found himself face-to-face with a young blond man, tall and tanned and built like a model, moving hypnotically before him, his expression unreadable behind a glossy sweep of hair. Dan let his eyes glide over the long legs that met in a promising bulge, even draped in loose white pants, the slim waist and lithe torso encased in a simple vest, low enough to show off plenty of light musculature and even brown skin. The lights picked out the pale scattering of hair on his arms and chest, coloring it blue, green, and purple, though the white of his clothes glowed, unearthly and pure in the dimness.

They danced against each other, the blond looking steadily into Dan's eyes as he rubbed subtly and excruciatingly against his body. Dan gritted his teeth, his nipples tight and sore against the suddenly rough, imprisoning fabric of his clothes. He reached out, his hand meeting one bronzed, slim arm, sliding up against skin and cotton in a hum of electricity. They danced, touched… swayed around each other in anticipation, until the blond hooked two fingers into the waistband of Dan's pants and drew him close enough to kiss: a long, intense exchange that was both exploration and negotiation.

"I have room," he said, his English hard and jagged. "Not far. You come?"

Dan nodded, quietly relieved. He preferred a little privacy. The other man's thick accent only added to his appeal. He wanted… *needed* this. Now. Wordlessly, Dan let the blond lead him out of the club, through the small car park, and then on through the grim, gray streets of Mestre. They passed two cross streets, then the blond took his hand and pulled him around a corner and down a flight of steps to what turned out to be a basement flat.

Dan had been determinedly avoiding the kind of pointless small talk that, in another place or time, he might have made, but he did notice the pile of mail on the doormat, the cat basket in the hallway, the clash of tastes in pictures on the walls, and the firmly shut doors that suggested this was space shared with at least one other person. Flatmate? Mother? Lover? Waiting for the blond to lock the door and lead him to the bedroom, he started to wonder who the guy was. It didn't last long.

The door shut behind them and the light flickered on, revealing a small room with a single bed, a chair, computer, and desk, a chipped white sink in one corner and a pile of clothes on the floor. It was soon a larger pile of clothes, four hands fighting to remove two pairs of pants, two shirts, and underwear that might as well have been on fire.

As they tumbled onto the bed, Dan rolled the blond over, raising himself up until he could see the full length of his body. He ran an appreciative hand over the long, athletic chest, dipping his head to trace his tongue along the line of crisp blond hair that ran down to a nearly flat belly. The other man winced, his body tightening. Dan wrapped his hand around the smooth cock, short but thick, which strained to greet him. It nestled, with a pair of low, heavy balls, in a thatch of hair deep gold against completely white skin. He traced the stark tan line across the blond's cute butt that spoke of summers spent in Speedos, and he was excited more by that band of pale flesh than by all the flawless expanse of bronzed muscle. Secret. Hidden. Shown only for him….

Yeah, right.

The blond groaned softly, his breath hissing through his teeth, and wriggled impatiently. Dan stilled his hand and, in stilted Italian, asked him what he wanted.

"*Nel culo*," he murmured, lifting his leg to curl around Dan's hips. "Inside me."

Dan smiled. That suited him just fine. Releasing the blond's cock, he reached down beside the bed for the condom and lube he had in his pocket. He caught his breath as a hot, wet tongue suddenly latched onto the back of his neck, tracing an urgent line across his skin.

"Hurry up!"

The blond squirmed impatiently. Dan's hands shook as he tried to uncap the lube, his chest tight with anticipation. The blond edged back, settling into position. He placed a pillow from the top of the bed beneath his hips, hoisted up his knees, and spread his legs wide. He stroked himself slowly as Dan slipped one, then two fingers into him, seeking and twisting until he saw pleasure flush the young man's face. After a few long moments, torture when he was so ready for it to be hard, fast, primal, Dan withdrew, relishing the gasp of disappointment from the blond. Panting, he tried to swallow his desperate need, concentrating on filling the blond slowly, inching in until his head thrashed on the pillow, his pretty hair mussed and his eyes rolling heavenward as he stifled a long moan. Dan bit his lip.

So, green eyes. He'd wondered.

He lifted those long, lithe legs onto his shoulders and fucked as slowly as he could stand, the most infinitesimal movement grating on his nerves, too much to take for long. His hands slipped under the blond, massaging and spreading the globes of his butt. Fire beat in his belly, his cock twitching impatiently in that hot grip.

Dan growled deep in his throat, stifling the dirty talk and the groans of pleasure he would have liked to make in consideration of the flatmates he didn't truly know existed. God, it felt good. It would feel even better if the guy would do something other than just lie there and try not to yell, but you couldn't have everything. The demon on his shoulder tempted Dan to see what it would take to make the blond scream, and the thought excited him. He picked up his pace, holding the man's knees higher and thrusting deeper, faster. His blood pounding, eyes blurred, Dan batted the blond's hand away from his red, throbbing cock.

"Turn over," he rumbled, half helping, half pushing him onto his hands and knees.

Dan gripped his hips hard and heard the blond moan as he pushed back in. He began his assault again, harder, deeper, thrusts growing faster and more erratic as he fought the inevitable climax, so desperately needed, so wanted, but not… yet. Dan dug his nails into that perfectly white, pristine flesh. The blond panted and moaned beneath him, stifled groans and growls as he pushed back on Dan's prick, hungrier with each thrust, hand pumping his cock. The walls seemed to suck in on them, the room filled with the wet slapping of skin on skin, their hard breathing, and the small, stifled gurgles and grunts of pleasure. Dan gave the blond a ringing slap on the ass and slammed his hips against him two, three more times before coming so hard he nearly lost his balance. He pulled out sooner than he meant to, collapsing beside the blond on the mattress.

Dan peered blearily at the other man, whose scarlet, sweat-beaded face and sticky, wet stomach spoke of as much satiation as his own, and smiled. The blond shot him a strange look, part lust and part venom, then slid back in a cat stretch, and paused for a moment before carefully sitting up and getting off the bed. Dan watched his body as he picked his way across the floor. He no longer felt such raw hunger, though it was certainly interesting, and Dan enjoyed a small flush of embarrassed pride at the red half-moon crescents so very visible on those pretty asscheeks.

He was wondering how long his mark might stay there when he realized the blond was picking up his clothes. He turned to face the bed, looking haughtily at Dan, then wiped his belly and cock with Dan's blue shirt and threw it at him, along with pants, shoes, and underwear.

Wordlessly, the blond jerked his head at the door, then took a packet of cigarettes from the desk and padded over to the window, which he opened, still casually naked, then lit himself a smoke. Dan stared for a moment, then dressed, pulled on his newly stained shirt, checked his pockets, and quietly left the flat. There wasn't much point in doing anything else.

The cold night air hit him as he climbed back up to the street, and he stopped for a moment to get his bearings. Somewhere, a train rumbled past. Light rain began to spatter the pavement, sleeting drops visible against the orange glow of the streetlights. Slowly, Dan started to retrace his steps, the rain either cold with reproach or his face hot with embarrassment. He didn't ask himself what the hell had just happened, or why. Confusion, anger, and disappointment whirled in his head, all numbed by a shot of practicality. The whole grubby fumble had taken less than fifteen minutes. Feeling all at once dirty, humbled, and wholly exhilarated, Dan started back down toward Via delle Macchine in search of a late-night bus back to Piazzale Roma.

He'd got what he wanted, hadn't he? A simple, animal, no-strings fuck. He'd proved whatever he needed to prove to himself. It would have been nicer to make a night of it (had he really been that bad?), but there was still plenty of time to take another bite at the proverbial cherry, and Dan's mind skimmed briefly over all the things he'd liked to have done with that pliant, sexy body, and all the things he'd hoped its owner would do to him, even if he did seem to be a little fucked-up.

He passed the third cross street, following the thumping music, and Club Commodoro loomed to his left. It sounded as if the night was really ramping up, and Dan realized, if he went back in, probably nobody would even notice the sticky, drying stain on his shirt. Who even needed a shirt, he thought, remembering the coat check.

As the postcoital euphoria drained from him and the rain grew harder, Dan couldn't quite bring himself to go back inside. It was like lying in bed on a weekend morning, trying to recapture the lost landscape of a dream. He shivered, watching a couple leave by the same door he had, passion spilling under the orange glow of the streetlights. It was amazing they could walk at the same time as doing that, he mused.

His immediate itches had been scratched, and there was always tomorrow night… wasn't there? Dan sighed, wiped the rain from the end of his nose, and wished he had a coat. A pale sliver of waxing moon shimmered weakly on the greasy asphalt near the bus stop, catching on the myriad colors in oil stains. Dan stared at the reflections and waited glumly for the bus.

At least they ran twice an hour until the morning, so he didn't have to wait long.

The long yellow shape coasted to a halt, and Dan climbed on board, grateful that the driver understood his pronunciation on the first try. Dan took his ticket, folded into a seat, and tried to pass as unnoticed as possible. He was increasingly aware that he smelled of sex and sandalwood, and the stain on his T-shirt couldn't look anything but suspicious.

At least it was dim on the bus, but for streaks of streetlights and the passing glare of other vehicles, and few other people were aboard: just an elderly drunk, hunched into his own seat and humming quietly to himself, and a handful of young hotel workers ready for the graveyard shift. Dan knew he looked out of place, but he didn't much care.

He was wet, chilly, and tired of the night.

CHAPTER THREE

THE NEXT morning, Dan woke later than he meant to, the dreamscape of his night too full of strange, sickeningly pitching swirls that smelled of sandalwood and semen. He opened one eye very carefully and found the sun streaming through a chink in the heavy drapes, so he swore at it, reluctantly peeled himself out of bed, and headed for the shower.

He picked his T-shirt off the floor, took it with him, and rinsed it out under the hot water. As he hung the wet garment over the radiator, Dan wondered what that blond would be doing this morning, but thought it wiser to sweep all traces of the night out of his mind. The hot water pummeled the groggy ache from his neck and back, and he started to feel better, although it didn't last long. The fleeting sense of recovery was soon replaced by the feeling that he'd done something very stupid.

The wonderful memory of the freedom on the dance floor, of acting purely on instinct and impulse, of rutting with a complete stranger who shared nothing with him except desire, started to pale in his waking mind. His sensible side found itself nudged by unwelcome thoughts about the dangers of roaming unchecked through foreign cities… and foreign men's beds. The idea of going back to the bar shriveled in the morning sun like a soft, pallid thing, and scuttled back under the rock of the night.

Dan dried himself briskly. The towel knotted around his waist, he went to his luggage and took out his camera, concentrating on checking the charge and spare batteries. Last night had been about temporary release. If he went back, it would still be about that, but what would it be when he went home? Would he go back to the same old routine, doing his hair just so, wearing the right clothes, hoping every prince he took home would stay that way and not turn into a frog by morning? Maybe he should just have stuck with that in the first place. Maybe it was easier that way. If you got your disappointment over with by ten a.m., you weren't involved enough to be too hurt.

He skipped breakfast and got himself down to the *vaporetto* stop at San Marco, where he spent several minutes trying fruitlessly to understand the timetable, at least in relation to the service that was actually running. It was more by luck than judgment that he caught the right boat to Cannaregio, but Dan stopped worrying about it once he was aboard, and the journey skimmed by in a blur of grays and blues, with cold air ruffling the water. The ghetto stop was marked in both Italian and Hebrew.

He'd read about the area. It dated back to the sixteenth century, when the Venetian doge had decreed that a small, grubby island in the smelting district should have the dubious honor of becoming the world's first ghetto, the word itself taken from the Venetian for foundry. It was a smaller community now, and so the Chabad's representative had responded enthusiastically to Dan's e-mail, happy to let him take his pictures and show them wherever he might find an audience.

Dan got off the *vaporetto*, instantly feeling the change in mood. Not drawn in chalks, but charcoal, this was a different place. Eventually (and only once he stopped trying to find it) he found the Via Vittorio Emanuele, Venice's broadest thoroughfare. It was deserted and, because it had started to rain again, slightly depressing. Somehow, though, Dan found he liked the way the rain blew in across the buildings and gave the street a slight oily sheen underfoot. He photographed the Holocaust memorials on the Casa di Riposo Israelitica, the home for the aged, and found that the weather lent them even greater dignity. Something always seemed wrong about a monument to suffering when seen in the sunshine.

For a moment, Dan wished someone could be here with him. Someone he could talk to, share it all with, and who saw the world the same way. Despite the misgivings of the morning, he couldn't really regret last night, but he still found himself painfully reminded of why it hadn't been enough. He set his jaw and turned his attention to tracking down the Spanish synagogue.

It turned out to be a great big yellow stone building of tall, beautiful arches and grand proportions, and it had, as the concierge at his hotel had said, recently been refurbished. Dan found it rather disheartening to learn that the new women's gallery had been added at street level, simply because the female congregation had an average age of around seventy-three and were starting to find stairs a trouble. Helena, the friendly and knowledgeable guide he spoke to, told him that most of the Venetian Jews moved to New York sooner or later.

Helena was a round, pleasant woman with a comforting, crinkled face and large plastic-framed glasses, and Dan listened with interest as she told him the history of the *sestiere* and helped him set up the photos he wanted to take. Back in the day, in the times of persecution and ostracism, Venice had walled them in with water, placed guards on the bridges, let people out only for the three sanctioned occupations of textile trading, banking, and medicine, and only then if they wore the yellow circle on their clothing, a badge that prefigured another, more horrible marker. Emancipation had come first with Napoleon, but freedom lagged behind for another seventy years, until Venice broke from the Hapsburgs and joined the rest of Italy.

During the war, the Nazis had lined up Jews to deport to camps just there, in the square where the rest home now stood. Had he seen the memorials? They were by the sculptor, Arbit Blatas. One was called *The Last Train*. The rest home housed less than ten people now, and poor Mr. Ottolenghi couldn't look at the reliefs without bursting into tears like a child at the thought of his uncle and aunt being taken away. Of course, the community shrank a little more every year.

Dan was moved by it, as much as by the Holocaust memorial, and impressed by the quiet strength he found there. He took a few shots of Helena, standing in the foreground of the new women's gallery in her navy blue cardigan and huge glasses, and spoke politely with the rabbi, thanking him for his permission to photograph the building, its places, its people, and its imperfections.

He wandered slowly through the ghetto in the light, fine rain, troubled and lost in the web of past and present, old and new: the double lives of the city.

Afterward, Dan caught the *vaporetto* to Murano. He thought about the lacemakers, the shipbuilders, the old and dying. Somehow that sense of impermanence wasn't depressing. It wasn't that he could only see the beauty of it, the strength and the calm and the wisdom; he also saw an optimism that said that the spirit would live on, even as these things, these places, these people, were lost.

He hoped he wasn't being naive.

As the rain grew heavier, Dan ducked into the glassblowing factory tour, and whiled away the wet weather learning more than he ever thought he'd needed to know about the craft. Still, the images were powerful: strong, dark figures in the furnace half-light, black against the red glow of molten glass. The fragility of the pipes and the beautiful twisted shapes they made seemed impossible. He was able to take a few photographs and, at the end of the tour, managed to buy a pair of pearl, enamel, and glass earrings for his sister that he knew would suit her, yet she would probably never wear, and a convex mirror set in an elaborate glass mount for his mother.

Back at the hotel, Dan laid the mirror carefully into his case and went downstairs for a meal of grilled fish and crisp white wine in the hotel dining room. He ate quickly, enjoying the food but preoccupied with the thoughts scratching at the back of his mind. He was having a great time; Venice was wonderful. Everything he'd expected, hoped for. The word "but" dangled precariously at the end of the sentence, hovering over his mind like a black bird. Dan stayed at his table until nearly ten thirty, when the kitchen closed, then retreated back to his room.

THE THIRD day of his holiday dawned sunny, and Dan woke feeling that the solemnity of yesterday, though not forgotten, could well be exchanged for some fun. He took breakfast in the hotel, picked up a free newspaper from the stand in the dining room, and, finding himself unable to work out more than one word in three, turned to flicking through the pictures he'd taken over the past two days, deleting the worst frames and checking batteries and memory cards.

After breakfast, well fed, watered, and ready to go, Dan shouldered his camera bag and set out for Dorsoduro, with the promise of art galleries, studios, and some artistic impulse shopping. He walked down through San Marco, feeling he knew it like a native, and decided he didn't need the map to tell him where the Ponte dell'Accademia was.

After a couple of false starts and wonderfully wrong turns, which led him into narrow alleyways peppered with shuttered windows, medieval balconies, and dark, mysterious archways, which then burst back into dazzling bright sunshine after only a few rough, cobbled feet, Dan found his way to the bridge. It took him nearly twenty minutes to cross it because every step seemed to present a new photograph, another view that he had to capture.

The Grand Canal, laid out beneath the pale old stone of the bridge, was everything he'd hoped for. The city stretched away to the horizon, beautiful in and for its flaws, draped in the impossible blue of the sky.

Gondolieri, with striped shirts and sometimes less than wonderful voices, poled the water and bellowed fragments of opera at their fares, while the commuter water taxis purred by, and the *vaporetto* roared and rattled on its route. Dan watched the traffic, enthralled. He watched a few of the *gondolieri* taking a break by their loosely moored gondolas, just sitting, sharing a cigarette, and dangling their toes into the water.

Eventually he wandered on, crossing the bridge through to the comparatively empty walkways of Dorsoduro. The concierge had not been wrong: old, empty houses loomed out of the *vie*, all blank windows and stucco streaked with damp. There was a certain sleazy elegance to the place, at odds with the glossy feel of the main promenade, the Zattere. Dan's fingers itched with the desire to start framing up pictures, and he yielded to those impulses for the morning.

For lunch, he hauled in at a pizzeria that overlooked the Canale and the ponte. Unable to believe either his luck or the view, he stood for a minute, watching the light gleam off the water, and the people and the boats pass by. A friendly, good-looking waiter with sandy red hair and pale skin inflicted the normal Venetian litany about nice food and nice prices on him, but gave him a table and a menu. Dan ordered pizza, salad, and wine, so relaxed in the warm sunshine he might have been there all day.

As he waited for the equally relaxed service, Dan pulled out the crumpled newspaper he'd picked up earlier. He studied the front page for a while, trying to fool his stomach into thinking about something other than food, and realized that he really had overestimated how far a few phrase books and some evening classes would take him in Italian. Beaten once again, he refolded the paper and set it on the table, smiling as the waiter brought his wine. Dan settled back in his chair, glass in hand, wondering idly what the highest point this side of the Canale was, and whether he could get up there to take a wide-angle panoramic shot or three. At first, he didn't notice the mellow voice and the gentle clearing of a throat behind him.

"Scusi? Posso prendere in prestito il suo giornale?"

Dan turned in his seat and found himself looking at the not-at-all-uninteresting crotch of a baggy, crumpled, pale suit. He blinked and raised his gaze. The Italian was edging past to the table beside his. He was tallish, broadish, and smiling, displaying even, white teeth set against light olive skin, and he had thick, dark hair, wavy and slightly receding.

"Um. *Mi dispiace.*" Dan swallowed, feeling not just like a complete idiot, but a complete idiot with terrible pronunciation. "*Non parlo molto italiano....*"

The man sat down, hand extended in a gesture of apology, but his eyes not leaving Dan's face.

"Oh, I am sorry. Your newspaper... I wondered if I can borrow...?"

"Of course. Please, take it." Dan passed him the paper. The tables were set quite closely, making the most of every inch of the spectacular setting, which meant he and the stranger were seated almost side by side, angled down the gentle camber toward the Canale.

"Molte grazie." The Italian smiled again graciously and peered at Dan with dark, hooded eyes. "Pardon me, but you are inglese, no? English?"

"Yes, on holiday." Dan grimaced. "Is it very obvious?"

"A little." He shrugged kindly. "Your accent, *naturalmente.*"

"Uh-huh... and the fact that my Italian's awful, right?"

The man shook his head, demurring politely, but with an amused glint in his dark eyes. He was rather attractive, in a slightly disheveled, unexpected sort of way. No wedding band, Dan noticed, inwardly reprimanding himself for checking. That meant nothing, of course.

The silence between them seemed to stretch out into minutes, though in fact it lasted merely seconds. It felt wonderfully and strangely comfortable. Neither looked away, but neither spoke.

"You shouldn't worry." Another of those ready, dazzling smiles. "It is a very nice accent. And the English gentleman is welcome everywhere, *sì?*"

"Well, that's good to know." Dan smiled back. Ah, flirting. Now, *this* was familiar ground. "As long as you *are* a gentleman, I suppose," he added, with a flick of his eyebrow.

The Italian laughed—a pleasure to watch. Dan guessed he couldn't be much older than his early thirties. He looked young, despite the rising forehead. A shadow of dark stubble played around his jaw, and Dan dragged his attention away from it, only to be distracted by the long, supple fingers that rested on the arm of the man's steel chair.

"So, do you live here?" he asked, sipping his wine.

"Ah, no... I, too, have holiday. I come from Lunigiana. Pontremoli." The Italian extended one of those graceful, square-palmed hands. "*Mi chiamo* Cesare."

"Dan…. Daniel."

Dan tried to ignore the thrill of contact as they shook hands across the tables, but a certain electricity pulsed in Cesare's warm, firm touch. The Italian gave a slight backward tilt of the head, regarding Dan with those dark, heavy-lidded eyes.

"First time in Venezia?"

"Mm-hm."

"Ah! They say La Serenissima is like a beautiful woman. You see her once, you are intrigued, so you must see her again, and before you know it—mah!—" Cesare struck his palm with the backs of his fingers. "—you are her slave." He gave a self-deprecating little smile. "We say things like that a lot in Italia. Is strange, but I have come here many times now, and I think it is true. You fall in love with the place. But… I don't know if I think Venice is like a woman." He shrugged. "Maybe. Certainly, she never shows everything she's got at once, and she is at her most beautiful when it's dark."

He chuckled and Dan joined in, partly because he'd found it funny, and partly because he found Cesare's mouth extremely compelling.

"It is a very beautiful city," he said. "Water and light."

"*Prego?*"

"The canals, the way they reflect the light… it's like the whole city shimmers."

"*Ma guarda!*" Cesare seemed delighted with the description. "That is very true. You are a poet, a writer?"

"No, no. No, I'm a photographer, actually. I work freelance. Commissions, for books, magazines… sometimes, if money's tight, I do portraits. Y'know. Modeling, the occasional wedding…."

"*Sì?* An artist, then." Cesare raised his own wineglass in salutation. "I am impressed. I studied art once, but now I am a schoolteacher, which I don't think is an art at all. You know how they say? Those who can, do. Those who can't, teach."

Dan grinned. The wine warmed his mouth, full and fruity. "Oh, no. Not at all… my sister works with children; I know what a hard job it is. What age kids do you teach?"

"*Scuola elementare*, so they start at six, and I have them for five years. Not always the same class, but, *sì*, that age. *Diavoletti*, sometimes, but… I do my best." He grew quieter for a moment, and his gaze flicked to the tabletop before returning to Dan's face. "So, what made you want to come to Venezia, Daniel? Are you here alone?"

Dan's gut flipped, perhaps for no good reason other than the wine he had been drinking on an empty stomach. This was the crossroads, then. Go on, he told himself, you're on holiday. Give it a shot. What's the worst that can happen?

"Yes. My… partner and I split up just before Christmas."

He paused, trying to judge Cesare's reaction to that wonderful, ambiguous word, which could imply so much, so succinctly. Did it make the same kind of sense to someone for whom English was a foreign language? He watched as the Italian inclined his head slightly, raising his glass to his lips, his eyes never leaving Dan's.

I know you, they seemed to say. *I have found you.*

"I am sorry to hear that," Cesare said, in a tone that suggested he was so sorry he might just punch the air in jubilation.

Dan's pulse quickened a little. He'd forgotten how much he liked this game.

"I'd always wanted to see Venice," he continued, "so I thought I'd take the opportunity. A bit of time just for me, you know? For some fun. So far, I definitely haven't been disappointed."

"You have been to Santa Croce yet?"

"No, not yet. I've seen some of Cannaregio, and Castello… and San Marco, of course. I've just been wandering about, really, taking it all in. I thought I'd have a look around here this afternoon, maybe take some more photographs."

"Ah, then you will like Dorsoduro very much," Cesare assured him as the waiter brought Dan's lunch. "The Galleria, the Guggenheim collection… there are many excellent small studios, also. But you must go to Santa Croce, to the Museum for Modern Art. There is a photographic exhibition there this month; also one here in Dorsoduro, in San Vio. You know there?"

"No, I'm afraid I don't. Where…?"

"Not far. Three cross streets that way, to the right, then left, and over the bridge. You can't miss it. Local artists, views of Venezia… very nice."

"Well, thank you. I'll make sure to have a look." Dan chewed at his pizza. "You certainly know your way around the city."

Cesare shrugged. "*Un poco*, perhaps."

"You said you've come here a lot?"

"*Sì*. I live near Pontremoli… to the west, not far from Pisa. Is really quite a short trip, and I like Venezia. The history, the art… is nowhere like it. I come one time, years ago, with a friend." He held Dan's gaze for a moment, making sure he understood. "The friend, I no longer see. But Venezia, I come back to!"

Dan smiled. As the waiter reappeared with Cesare's food, Dan motioned to him to set it on his table.

"Look, please… why don't you join me? There's no sense our taking up two tables, not when I'll need to grill you for all the best shortcuts around the city."

"*Grazie, Daniel.*"

Cesare moved tables, his hand resting briefly on Dan's arm as he passed. In closer proximity, his scent was delicious, like citrus and spices. Cloves or pepper. Dan poured himself another glass of wine and started to suspect that he should know better than to entertain the thoughts that had started to gyrate across his brain.

"I just can't get over how beautiful it is here," he said, watching Cesare address a *panino* stuffed with some kind of seafood. "But, P-Pontremoli, you said? Near Pisa?"

"The town is Pontremoli," Cesare explained. "But we say there, Pontrémal. It is in the Lunigiana area of the *comune di Massa-Carrara*. Toscana," he added helpfully.

"Tuscany? Oh, I see." Dan nodded, mentally catching up. "Of course. There's some beautiful country there too, isn't there?"

Cesare looked thoughtful as he chewed. "In its way, yes. We too have much history, much that is good. Very different to here…. Pontremoli is very old town. In the Middle Ages, the pilgrims would come there before Roma, so we have many old *chiese*, like Venezia, but nothing of the… *eccitazione*. The *palazzi*, the rich men's houses you see in Venizia, there is nothing of that in Pontremoli." He smiled. "Very strict, very boring, but I wouldn't be anywhere else."

"You've always lived there, then?"

"Oh, *sì*. I was born in Pontremoli itself, then when I was a boy we moved to a village not far from the town. Gravagna Montale. Is very beautiful there. I went to school in Pontremoli, and I went to the Istituto Magistrale there, to do my training to teach. Now, I am working at a nice school close to Gravagna. I have never live anywhere else," he added, rather sadly. "And I have only been out of Italia a little. Never to

England. I learn my English as a boy, and now from Rosemarie—she teach English at my *scuola*. I don't know if I speak well?"

"You do. Your English is excellent," Dan assured him, adding in the privacy of his own head that the thick accent and occasional mangled word just made it sexy.

He picked at his salad, enjoying watching Cesare smile. He had a way of starting to blush ever so slightly that made Dan want to flatter him more. He tried to resist, tried to remind himself that the point of this vacation was time out, time for him. It wasn't supposed to be a weeklong cruisefest.

"I'd be happy if my Italian was half as good, but I've always been awful at learning languages. Do you have any tips?"

"Maybe," Cesare said thoughtfully, "what you need is practice with Italian speaker. Not too easy to learn from books, but from *conversazione… sì*. Much better."

"That's a good idea."

Dan sipped his wine. Cesare appeared to be thinking something over; his gaze tracked from Dan's face back to his own plate over and over. Eventually he spoke.

"I am more than happy to talk to you, Daniel. If you would like."

Dan smiled, a little gleam of triumph in his blood.

"That's very kind of you. I'd love to hear your advice on Venice… what to see, where to go. What to do, and so on," he added, watching the smile spread from Cesare's lips to his eyes.

He'd made up his mind, Dan decided. He wanted this man.

They talked more as they ate and drank: of the city, of their interests, and of things of no real consequence. Dan displayed his appalling tourist Italian, much to Cesare's amusement, and Cesare himself proved to know a lot about the art and architecture, and didn't seem to get bored when Dan talked about cameras. He recommended a series of galleries, churches, *palazzi*, and studios that were worth visiting, and after the meal, Dan professed complete idiocy and said he'd never find the studio in San Vio that Cesare had recommended on his own.

Cesare smiled and said he would show him.

They left the pizzeria together and headed into Dorsoduro's network of backstreets. Chatting all the way about this or that point of Venetian history or architecture, Cesare led Dan to the gallery.

It was pleasant, with a range of works by artists from across the Veneto region: not the sickly, mass-produced tourist artwork, but real, honest stuff that spoke of things beneath the surface, of an Italy whose history included dark years... pain, poverty, and loss as well as beauty and light. Dan fell in love with a landscape in oils that reminded him of a van Gogh, all yellows and oranges and browns, undulating curves and hot skies, and bought it, along with a small stack of prints from local artists, carefully chosen after agonizing deliberation.

Cesare stayed, lingering with him all the while, talking with passion and sound knowledge about the art. Dan was glad of it.

His presence, just close enough, was exciting.

CHAPTER FOUR

DAN WISHED he'd stayed on water at lunch instead of sinking almost a whole bottle of house red. He'd be thinking more clearly. They visited the Peggy Guggenheim Collection, wandered through the Nasher sculpture garden and, inside the pink-and-white fairy-tale house, got completely distracted by rooms hung with Surrealist and Cubist masterpieces, as well as African masks and the strange, meltingly colored paintings they inspired. They took a moment to rest their weary feet, sitting on a white leather couch that, judging by the photographs on the wall, Peggy herself had used when the room was her private library.

"These, I think, are beautiful," Cesare said, of the Kandinsky paintings opposite them.

"He was inspired by music, wasn't he? Tried to paint the rhythms and the patterns."

Dan looked at the gashes of primary color on the canvas, the hatchings, and lines and shapes that were not things in their own right, but made a damn good job of making you think of other things. He remembered Club Commodoro, the dance floor, becoming a part of something real and yet unreal, and he worried that he blushed when Cesare looked at him, his gaze lingering a little too long. It wasn't the first of those looks.

"*Sì.*" Cesare gave him a small, encouraging smile. "Not what something is, but what it feels like."

Dan looked at the painting again, if only to avoid those gorgeous eyes. He hadn't thought about abstract art quite like that before. Three years of art college taught you to analyze a painting, and maybe taught you how to bullshit your way through an artist statement, but perhaps it also helped you forget how to really *feel* your reactions... how to respond without thought or context. He squinted, trying to understand what Cesare meant, and it certainly seemed clearer. If you looked, and stopped trying to see, the whole world opened up to you.

After the gallery, they passed by the Chiesa dei Carmini, a great Gothic church that was mostly closed for renovation, as approximately half of Venice appeared to be at any one time. Dan took some steep shots of the exterior, playing with the way the late afternoon shadows fell on the few ornate carvings to adorn the simple red brick façade. He took some of Cesare, who professed to be camera shy, when he wasn't looking, and thought how elegant he was, how photogenic.

He no longer doubted two things. First, that he had to have this man, and second, that Cesare felt the same. The whole afternoon and the early evening stretched behind them, a perversely extended foreplay that served only to torture and tantalize. They seemed not to even need words to explore each other's thoughts and desires, and the flirting continued under the sight of a thousand Catholic martyrs. Light and water conspired to fill Dan's vision with nothing but his handsome companion, made the air between them vibrate with an increasing tension. Yet, Cesare hung back.

He intrigued Dan… capable of teasing him almost to distraction, but never quite naming what he wanted. As if it could all be innocent, a misunderstanding. A couple of times, Dan wondered if he really had ever shown interest, or if perhaps if he'd had second thoughts. At those moments, Cesare would brush closer to him, guiding him by the elbow to the particular fine points of a piece of architecture, a statue of some obscure saint whose life story he knew by heart… and his touch would linger, fingers firm and questing, curving to hold Dan's arm, his body just a little closer than necessary, his face barely inches away, and his breath warm on Dan's neck.

The anticipation was all part of the game at first, though as the afternoon turned golden and hazy with the sun, expectancy became frustration and started to wear on Dan's nerves. Cesare was pleasant company, but the tension had started to get too heavy. As he raised the camera to his eye, trying to frame the campanile, Dan felt Cesare's presence behind him.

"I feel very guilty for taking up so much of your afternoon," he said, realigning his viewfinder.

"It has been my pleasure."

Cesare's voice purred by his ear and sent prickles down Dan's spine.

"Still, I'd like to find a way to thank you," he said. *No more games.* "I'm sure we could find something I can do."

The sun caught the windows of the church, turning them to molten gold. Dan heard Cesare's breathing change.

"I could buy you a drink," he continued, turning his head just a little, holding Cesare's gaze for just long enough. "Or dinner. Or, maybe... *maybe* we can think of something."

There was a long pause. Dan thought he'd overstepped some kind of invisible line. He waited for the excuse, the deferral, expecting at the very most a dinner date that would leave him with a hard-on and no phone number. Then Cesare spoke.

"My hotel is not far from here," he said, his voice low and strange. "I have some very good grappa I bought from a vineyard nearby. I wonder if, perhaps, I could offer you a glass of grappa, Daniel?"

Dan smiled, leaning into him, breathing in that gorgeous scent of oranges, grapefruit, spice, and musk... too subtle for cologne. What was it? Shampoo, shower gel, his skin? He tilted back his head, planning only to murmur toward Cesare's ear, not plant a kiss on him, though nervous tension still stiffened the man's body. Maybe it was to do with the number of people milling around them; maybe it was just anticipation.

"You certainly can," Dan said quietly. "And I'll say yes."

THE HOTEL was near, modern, and bland. Anonymously well appointed. Dan followed Cesare, unquestioning, not caring about the surroundings, his pulse humming. Strange, he thought, that this should be so much more nerve-racking than Club Commodoro. But then, that night, he'd gone looking. No uncertainty, no element of surprise. Meeting someone out of the blue like this.... God, he hadn't done this for ages. Was that why he was so on edge?

Suddenly, what had seemed hypnotically distant all afternoon slid into sharp focus, and Dan found himself worrying about whether his deodorant had held up, whether his breath was all right, and if he still had a condom in his wallet.

The foyer was wide and bright, its corners filled with potted palms and its walls covered with historical prints of Venice, framed in black plastic. Cesare led him past the gallery of images and down beige-carpeted corridor after corridor, each indistinguishable from the last.

He stopped abruptly, fumbling in his pocket for his key card. The door was the last on the right, just before the fire exit. Dan noted it, uselessly trying to make some kind of mental map.

"*Prego.*"

Cesare ushered Dan into the room, that same tone of jangling nerves in his voice, his face tight and pale. Dan stepped inside. He heard the door close, felt Cesare's presence just behind him. He set the painting he'd bought, wrapped in crisp brown paper, down by the door, along with his bags of camera equipment, and took a look around. It wasn't a bad room—light and airy, if slightly too neutral for his taste.

For a moment he wanted to laugh at the absurdity of it. They were two strangers, sharing nothing more than a few hours' companionship in a foreign city and a flicker of attraction, yet making such a big deal of it. Why take so seriously something that was supposed to be fun?

Perhaps, Dan realized, because in any other place he probably wouldn't have gone to the hotel. He tried to drown that thought quickly. Cesare had moved to the bland and faceless dressing table by the window. Three bottles of Bassano grappa, one of the Veneto region's most famous exports, stood on it. He opened one, fetching two glass tumblers from the bathroom and filling them with the clear liquor.

Cesare offered him one of the glasses, and the expression on his face made Dan's chest hurt. He looked terrified, a lost boy, his eyes crying out from a man's face.

Dan took the glass, mouth dry, wondering why in the hell Cesare would be that scared. He sipped the liquor, but Cesare gulped. It was fiery, heavy on the tongue and long on the palate. Strong stuff to be tossing back like water. Dan could spot Dutch courage when he saw it.

"Look, it's really all right," he blurted. "Nothing has to happen that you don't want."

Cesare shook his head and tossed off the rest of the grappa. "I'm sorry. It's just… I wasn't expecting for this. It is… a very long time for me."

"Like I said—"

"No! No, you must not think that I don't want…."

Tentatively, Cesare put the glass down and reached out his hand. His fingertips brushed the lapel of Dan's jacket, as if he didn't believe the figure before him was real.

"Please."

The word was whispered, a prayer that could have cut through steel. Dan set his glass down by Cesare's and stepped closer, closing that small distance that had separated them since they met.

No defenses, no proprieties in this pale, dull room.

He took Cesare's jaw lightly in his fingers, stroking the shadow of coarse stubble with his thumb, enjoying the roughness of it, and the tremor his action caused. Touching Cesare's lips lightly with his own, not demanding, not rushing, Dan waited for him to respond.

It was worth waiting for. Cesare kissed him slowly, a tentative exploration. His body pressed through the burdensome fabric of clothes, matching Dan's own desire, but the kiss was unhurried, almost ridiculously chaste. His pulse hammered, but he knew that he would never have wanted it to be different.

He moaned as the kiss deepened, Cesare's tongue slipping along his, tasting of grappa and the warmth of cornfields. He was aware of the crisp smoothness of Cesare's hair in his fingers, the hardness of his body, the wet heat of his mouth… and very little else. When Dan pulled away, a soft cry of disappointment broke from Cesare.

"Tell me what you like," Dan murmured, his fingers working on the other man's shirt buttons.

"You," Cesare answered fatuously, diving in to kiss his neck, inhaling his scent.

Dan smiled and opened up Cesare's shirt. The hair on his chest was thick, but not overly abundant, covering the upper part of his torso and pecs, half hiding large, flat nipples that tightened to the gentlest of touches.

"*Sei troppo bello… dio mio, Daniel! Come mi tocchi….*"

Dan shuddered as Cesare's voice teased his nerves, even as his teeth grazed his earlobe, his neck, his jawline. He wriggled out of his leather jacket, pulled Cesare's shirt and jacket off in one muddled, crumpled mess that he dropped unheeded to the floor, and backed him toward the bed. Cesare's legs folded as the mattress hit the backs of his knees, and he sat heavily. Dan pulled his own T-shirt off and smiled down at Cesare, bare-chested and tousle-haired, as he began to unbutton his jeans.

Face flushed and eyes wide, Cesare stared at the hard bulge in front of him, gaze flicking back up to Dan's face for reassurance. Dan edged his jeans past his hard-on and let them fall to the floor, resisting the temptation to shove every inch he had down Cesare's throat… something to do with all the pseudovirginal nervousness, he decided. Too sexy for words. He knew there were questions he ought to ask, but the words were leaden on his tongue.

"We might as well get stripped, yeah?" he said instead, uncomfortably aware that it wasn't exactly the height of romance.

Cesare was sitting with his fingers bunched in the bedclothes, his suit pants, shoes, and socks still on, and at first he didn't seem to hear him. Dan slipped his thumb beneath the waistband of his briefs, enjoying the way it transfixed him. He teased for a few moments more, enjoying what he could do to this man just by slipping off his underwear. Cesare's breath rattled in his throat as Dan tossed away the briefs, knelt down, and slowly removed Cesare's shoes. He reached out tentatively to stroke Dan's hair as he carefully rolled off first one sock, then the other, running his fingers over a well-shaped, clean pair of feet. Dan slid his palms up Cesare's calves, knees, thighs, loving the way his legs spread for him, his arousal evident through his pants.

He took the Italian's mouth in another hard, determined kiss as his fingers worked on the belt buckle and zipper. Cesare lifted his hips, letting Dan pull off his underwear and pants, his body tense.

Dan pitched the last of their clothes to the carpet, bringing his hands back to trace the contours of Cesare's body, the thickness of his shoulders and his broad chest. He stroked his hands down Cesare's torso, feeling the crisp hair give way to softer skin. His body was that of an active man, but not an athlete: a broad frame padded by solid flesh and muscle rather than washboard abs and slablike pecs. Cesare inhaled sharply, his thick cock hard enough to knock against his stomach.

The floor getting painful on his knees, Dan climbed up onto the bed, reaching for him again. It seemed to galvanize Cesare. He crawled up the covers, hands shaking as he traced gentle fingertips across Dan's body, as much wonder as desire in his face.

"Go ahead," Dan prompted gently, the calm of his voice belying how much he wanted to be touched right now, how much he wanted to be held, gripped. "It's okay. You can take your time."

Cesare smiled shyly at him, dark eyes deep and foggy with lust. Wordlessly he dipped his head, working his way over Dan's body with teeth, lips, and tongue, exploring and tasting at a leisurely pace. It soon seemed painfully slow, and Dan raked his heels against the bedclothes as Cesare's tongue twisted in his navel.

All right, definitely not that *virginal.*

Cesare moaned against his skin, little vibrations that thrilled through Dan as hot breath skimmed his hip and a broad, square palm cupped his balls, giving him such excruciating pleasure as that full, talented mouth brushed the side of his waist.

Dan squirmed, wanting more. He marveled at the way Cesare was finding hot spots that even he had all but forgotten about, and though he was certain he hadn't kissed anyone this much since college, he did nothing to discourage Cesare as the Italian crept up his body, arriving in his arms again. He was bolder now, lips firmer on Dan's mouth, his tongue seeking and teasing, the heat and weight of his body pressing close to Dan's side.

"*Sei così bello*," Cesare murmured, breaking the kiss, his breathing shallow. "*Mi fai impazzire....*"

Dan caught his breath, trying hard not to lose it just listening to that voice. He shut his eyes, not daring to look at Cesare's face. Their bodies cleaved together, rubbing and chafing in their damp heat as one sentient creature. He felt Cesare tweak dreamily at his nipple, his cock caught against a firm, hairy thigh. Dan growled, deep in his throat. Perhaps it was the air here, or perhaps that they'd spent the whole afternoon leading up to this, here, this space between times, between lives. Perhaps it was just Cesare, in all his contradictions, so tense but, oh, so hot under his hands.

"C'mon. Tell me what you like," Dan repeated, Cesare's lips on his collarbone, tongue working on the sculpted hollow of flesh in slow, agonizing circles. He knew, if this went on too much longer, it would all be over before the fat lady got out of the dressing room, much less sang. "What do you want?"

Dan shivered as Cesare's hand curled around his cock, his grip gentle, almost timid, but so exciting.

"*Ti voglio*," Cesare murmured, barely audible, tugging gently at him. "I want you. This. *Il tuo ucello*," he chanted softly. "*Il tuo bell'uccello...* your beautiful cock."

His voice was hypnotic. Dan hissed between his teeth, stilling Cesare's hand with his own.

"Mmm. You can have it, I promise. Have you got condoms?"

Cesare tensed against him. Dan opened his eyes to see the Italian's puzzled frown.

"Daniel, I am sorry... I never thought to need—"

"It's all right." Dan disentangled himself from their embrace, leaning over the edge of the bed for his jeans and the one remaining free rubber he'd tucked into his wallet at Club Commodoro. "I think I have."

He muttered a silent thank-you to whatever deity was listening when his fingers closed on the wrapper.

"You are, y'know, all right?" Dan asked as casually as he could, feeling Cesare fidget against him as he heaved himself back onto the mattress. He noticed Cesare's look of confusion and wished he'd never said anything. "Just asking," he mumbled awkwardly. "I mean… you know."

"*Sì*." Cesare's hand rested lightly on Dan's chest as he started to open the condom wrapper. "I am fine. I… *come si dice*? Not many men," he explained, blushing furiously. "But, always safe. Um. Daniel?"

"Hmm?"

"Please…. Not *nel culo*. I-I have been long time, and—" Cesare stammered, going even redder. "I don't…. Will you fuck me, *fra le coscie*? Between my thighs. It will still be good for you. Tight. *Prometto*."

Dan frowned, trying not to show the twin disappointment and embarrassment burning inside him. It wasn't as if anyone owed him a right to any specific kind of sex, of course, but it still came as something of a surprise. He'd not even asked, just assumed… like the fucking idiot he was. But Cesare was still gazing pleadingly at him, his body begging. Dan's cock throbbed, and the more complex emotions of the moment soon went away.

"Sure."

"*Grazie*," Cesare whispered.

His arms wrapped around Dan's neck, his cock strained between their bodies, and Dan thought how attractive it was, how elegant, arching, yet powerful. He struggled to draw his attention away, wanting to taste him, take him, wanting everything at once. No. There'd be time for that later. A man for whom encounters like this were as rare as they seemed to be for Cesare wouldn't let him go that quickly, he was sure. Strong hands skimmed over his back, shoulders, biceps, neck, through his hair, as if Cesare wanted to learn him by touch. The sensations melded until nothing existed but blank and burning desire.

Cesare turned over, adjusting himself on the bed. He glanced at Dan over his shoulder, for a moment looking as if he'd get all overcome with nerves again.

"There is some sun cream on the nightstand, if you want."

Dan found it and, with fingers slippery and gentle, massaged those broad thighs until the crisp curls of dark hair grew flat and wet. Cesare moaned appreciatively, squeezing his legs together as Dan's fingers dipped into the dark crevice between them, brushing against his tight balls. When on earth had he last done it like this? Had to be years, at least. Well, they did say holidays were about rediscovering yourself and trying new things.

Still... sun cream. Dan suppressed a smile. Not latex-friendly, but definitely one of those ordinary household products he would never look at in the same way again. He rubbed his thumb over Cesare's perineum, enjoying the rough gasp he gave, and the way his whole body twitched like a bird breaking cover.

"Ready?"

"*Sì*, very much. I want... I want to feel you. *Tutto il tuo corpo, sopra di me.*"

"All right."

Dan hoisted himself up the mattress, an arm either side of Cesare's head. Years of swimming and running had given him a long, lithe figure, but he was far from a featherweight. Cesare moaned, giving a long, low, guttural groan as Dan slid slowly into place. Starting an unhurried, steady rhythm, toes crunched into the sheets, propelling himself forward, he rubbed himself against Cesare's body, losing his senses in delicious friction and slick penetration, the feel of hot skin and the sound of Cesare's low voice rumbling against his chest. His legs clenched around Dan's cock convulsively.

It felt better than Dan remembered. Liberating.

The heat of his arousal spread throughout his body, more than just focusing on cock and ass. Like his skin was a glove over his soul. He lowered his head, face in Cesare's hair. Oranges. Cloves. Pepper and cornfields. He hadn't a clue what Cesare was saying, but, God, Italian was a fucking sexy language. Dan's cock nudged between Cesare's cheeks, and Cesare cried out, humping back against him as it chafed against his shaft and balls. It was hard to believe he'd ever seemed nervous, though he clammed up a little when Dan changed his angle, sliding up tighter against his ass. Dan pulled back. Maybe Cesare had never done it like that, or had some kind of history that way. Dan hoped not, for his sake.

However, whether it scared him or not, he obviously liked it. Dan pushed down on him, crushing his body to Cesare's, rubbing his hands over those powerful shoulders, tracing the outline of his ribs, the narrow gully of his spine. He wanted to go further, to take all of him. It was what he'd expected, what he'd waited for. Frustration burned in his belly. So good, but not enough. He wanted more. Dan rubbed his face against Cesare's neck, licked, then nipped at his nape. Cesare bucked under him, his voice as taut as his body.

"Ah! *Non ne posso più.... Abbracciami, amore!*" He gasped, his fingers knotted in the sheets, knuckles white with an intensity that Dan hadn't expected to see.

Dan screwed up his eyes and stopped breathing. The climax took him by surprise, and it didn't seem to be his voice that cried out, strangled and hoarse, in the blank and neutral room. He reared back, pushed away from it as he finished, aware of Cesare's crumpled moan. He turned over, flushed and eager, reaching for Dan with so much of his earlier hesitancy forgotten he almost seemed a different man. Cesare's touch spoke of a need that bordered on desperation.

His cock, trapped, rubbed between them, grazed Dan's belly and painted his pleasure on it, shivering with need. Recovering his breath, Dan closed his hand around that thick, handsome shaft.

Cesare breathed hard, ragged, struggling to last, and Dan's touch broke the final thread. Neck arched back, Cesare wheezed a silent scream and came, messy and relentless. He stared up at Dan, flushed and gasping, his eyes so open to him, so flooded with pleasure. They were such a clear, luminous brown. It frightened Dan to feel that, in that moment, he could have reached inside Cesare and plucked out his heart.

Dan let him go, allowing him to relax, whimpering with the last tremors of aftershock. Fuck, he was hot. And how long had he been waiting for that? Weeks, months, or more? Somehow unsettled, Dan disentangled himself. He swung his legs off the bed, heading for the bathroom and coming back with a damp towel. He opened the window, then crawled back onto the bed and cleaned them both gently, Cesare's limbs heavy in his hands. He rolled over for Dan, pliant and sated, though a small moan of protest did escape him. Dan guessed that, though he allowed his body to be wiped clean of the mess, he would rather have lain in it, his badge of pride and achievement.

Still, Cesare didn't look like he was about to argue. After that, Dan wasn't sure either of them could be capable of anything except sleep. Cesare smiled lazily up at him. Somewhere, beyond the open window, the waters of the Canale lapped, and a gondolier was massacring "Nessun Dorma."

"All right for you?"

"*Era incredibile*," Cesare murmured, his fingers flexing optimistically against Dan's soft cock. "*Daniel... stiamo insieme stanotte?* Will you stay with me tonight?"

Wordlessly, Dan nodded. Seemingly relieved, Cesare exhaled softly, his eyelids drooping as he relaxed against the pillows, everything apparently right with his world. Dan watched him fall asleep, the marks of his kisses, his touches, still raw on that fair olive skin. He felt an uncomfortable, protective pull toward this man, in all his contradictions: his easy, confident charm, his brittle nervousness, his passion, and his tense reticence. It confused and disoriented him.

Dan pulled the coverlet up, as if there was any danger Cesare would get cold in a mediocre hotel that insisted on heating all the rooms to jungle temperatures. Slowly, as silently as he could, he slipped out of the bed and started hunting for his clothes, one eye on Cesare. He turned and mumbled a little but didn't wake.

Quietly, swiftly, Dan dressed and slipped from the room.

CHAPTER FIVE

VENICE, FOR all its reputation as a city of unresting delights and languid, sensual momentum, apparently closed early. Dan jogged down the steps outside the hotel into a gray-blue evening dusk, checked his watch, and found it was barely seven o'clock. Unfortunately, and unlike most of the rest of Italy, this meant it was the dinner hour: no lingering late-night *cena* for your average Venetian. He blinked, squinting about him in the unfamiliar *sestiere*. The hotel had once been an old *palazzo*, all Renaissance curlicues and archways, but had been converted by a less than gifted architect. The modernized parts of the building seemed uneven, and the metal letters that spelled out "LOCANDA" sat stark, ugly, and gray against the yellow stone. It stood on an intersection of two *vie*. To the right, the building overlooked a canal that Dan was pretty sure led back down to the Grand Canale. Or perhaps to a maze of other canals and anonymous walkways.

Dan exhaled. He was, he decided, an idiot. He certainly felt like one, not to mention a bit of a slut... or a lot of a slut. What the hell had happened here? He thought of the day, not long before he left London, when he'd had lunch with Chris at a local sushi bar. "I'm not going there to pull," he'd protested, when Chris teased him about the gay holiday guide he'd been reading and the "most romantic city in the world" thing. "I'm just going for some me time." Ha! He'd never be able to tell Chris about this. First Club Commodoro, then picking Cesare up in a pizzeria... hell, had that been tacky?

Whether he thought it tacky or not, Chris would never let him live it down. Not in a million years.

Dan tried not to think of Cesare waking up alone, though he might have tired himself out enough to sleep for a while yet. Dan hadn't seen anyone come like that for a long time, not since he'd given in to a (now ex-) fuck buddy's whining and tied him to the bed with silk neckties and blindfolded him before doing kinky things to him with a feather duster. It might have looked silly in Dan's opinion, and not done anything for him at all, but it was fantasy fulfillment, and Jonathan (or Jeremy? Dan could no longer be sure of his name, and he mourned the loss for a very brief moment) had done an extremely passable impression of a spastic fire hose. Not to mention, Dan remembered with satisfaction, being only too happy to repay him with regular and exquisite blowjobs for a fortnight. It was amazing what playing to a fantasy could do, even, he supposed, if that fantasy was nothing more than a simple human connection.

Dan shook himself. There was no harm in it, though. Was there? It was just a holiday. And he'd played safe, hadn't he? His stomach growled again, impatient and demanding. He gave up pacing the walkway, trying to peer into the sea mist that was starting to roil into the city's tidal waterways.

"Shit," he muttered, the word echoing in the damp air.

A little way along the narrow canal, Dan heard the tinny thrum of an outboard motor. A boat came into view, its shadowy outline illuminated by the dim wink of a halogen lantern. He craned his neck to see through the mist. He'd been lucky: it was a water taxi. He walked to the little landing at the end of the hotel's frontage and flung out an arm, feeling faintly ridiculous. He obviously looked it too, for the taximan cut the engine and looked quizzically at Dan from under a heavy pair of eyebrows as the boat drifted to the jetty.

"Er. *Scusi. Può aiutarmi?*" he tried. "*Dov'è il negozio più vicino? Panettieria? Salumeria?*"

The boatman winced but nodded, and demanded an enormous fee. Dan spent a few minutes haggling while the taxi owner, clearly recognizing the advantage he had over the foreign idiot, tapped his authorized taxi number smugly. Eventually they settled on a figure.

"Nice price, signor," he said with English pronunciation even worse than Dan's Italian.

Dan sighed and scrambled into the boat.

IT WAS almost half past nine when Dan got back, substantially poorer and wondering if it wouldn't have been easier to just find an *osteria* or *ristorante* that did takeout. Probably cheaper, at any rate, and definitely quicker. What on earth was Cesare going to think if he woke to find himself abandoned? Dan winced at the thought of the sorrow in those dark eyes… or maybe anger. He'd have reason to be pissed off, wouldn't he? It was so stupid. What should have been a nice gesture had turned into an odyssey, and now Dan just felt ridiculous. He hadn't even asked what Cesare liked to eat. Hell, maybe the guy had allergies. That would be typical of his luck with men, Dan mused: try to do something cute, and end up poisoning someone.

He slipped through the hotel's foyer, past the younger, professional crowd gathering in the bar for *cicheti*, Venice's answer to antipasto or tapas, and counted the corridors until he was reasonably sure he had the right room. Dan knocked softly on the door, marshaling the half a dozen clever things he'd tried to think of to say.

The door opened a little, and Cesare peered at him from the gloom within: sleepy and looking a little confused. He'd showered, put on a white T-shirt and a pair of gray boxers. Dan's mouth turned dry, all those words lost and useless. Cesare's lips curled in the smallest of smiles. He reached for Dan's wrist and drew him back into the room.

Closing the door behind him, Cesare pressed Dan against the painted wood and kissed him. No curses, no complaints. He hadn't said a word, much less asked a question. His mouth was warm and enveloping, tasting more strongly of grappa. A glance to the nightstand confirmed that the bottle of Bassano had been considerably emptied.

Dan lifted the grocery bags he carried between them, part explanation and part shield.

"Supplies," he said, as Cesare broke away. "I don't know about you, but I'm starving."

Cesare took the bags from him and investigated the contents.

"*Che volpe!*" he exclaimed, finding treasure after treasure.

Dan had bought something of pretty much everything: little tubs of pasta salads, dressed chicken, noodles, bread rolls, and individual pats of butter, chilled cans of *caffè latte* and a bottle of Prosecco di Conegliano, together with an assortment of disposable cutlery and a bag of *bussolai buranelli*, the little ring-shaped Venetian butter cookies. He always found it hard to walk past a sweet bakery.

"I hope you didn't mind my slipping out like that."

"I knew you'd come back." Cesare smiled, waving a dismissive hand. "You leave all your camera things."

Dan looked at his camera and tripod bags, placed neatly by the door, together with the brown-wrapped painting he'd bought at the studio in San Vio.

Ah.

He hadn't thought of it like that. He left Cesare to unpack their picnic dinner and went for a quick shower, pretending he didn't feel quite as stupid as he did.

When he came back, the room was dim, except the flickering of the TV, showing an old black-and-white film. Cesare had laid out the food on the bed, folded back and tidied since their exertions. He sat propped up against the headboard, the Prosecco open and two glasses poured. The TV screen highlighted his face in profile, the high planes of his forehead and cheekbones in sharp relief against the dark shadow of stubble on his jaw. Dan thought how much he'd like to photograph him, properly set up in studio with decent light conditions… among other things.

"You're sure you wouldn't rather have gone out for a meal?" he asked, his voice filling a silence whose depth he hadn't appreciated.

Cesare's head snapped round, as if he'd been in some private reverie, and he looked Dan over hungrily before he smiled, shaking his head.

"Of course not! *Prego.*" Cesare passed one glass of wine to Dan and held his own up in a toast. "Is maybe not fine crystal… but it is better, here, with you. *Salute!*"

Dan laughed, embarrassed.

"*Salute,*" he echoed, taking a mouthful of wine.

It fizzed against his palate and tongue. Dan found the sensation surprisingly exciting, as if everything was heightened, every nerve and sensation pushed to the limit. He swallowed, resisting the urge to laugh.

Cesare looked at him, very seriously, and held out his hand. "*Vieni.*"

Dan smiled, unable to refuse him anything at all when he looked so solemn.

CESARE SWALLOWED, his whole body floating on tightly wound nerves and grappa. He couldn't quite believe he'd found courage enough for this… any of this. Certainly not to be here with someone like Daniel, and to be putting on such a show of confidence—crazy! He didn't feel confident at all. He looked at the man before him, and he still didn't seem real. He was so beautiful… a shade under six feet tall, a long, lean body, neither really slim nor heavily cut with muscle, but well proportioned and trim. Sandy brown-blond hair grew in tufts in his armpits and in crisp scatterings across his body, trailing down his belly to the fold of the towel, a hated fabric that Cesare suddenly wanted to rip away and utterly destroy so that nothing might keep him from that body in all its perfection.

He shivered at the memory of Dan's cock, so hard and hot, slipping between his legs, pressing against his most secret places as Dan fucked him, loved him with that beautiful rod. And that he was interested in *him*... unbelievable. A happy miracle, but crazy all the same. Cesare smiled, feeling heat rise to his face as this beautiful man accepted the hand he held out, his silly gesture of—what?—supplication? Daniel's touch electrified him. Ridiculous that this innocent clasp of fingers could do so, Cesare thought, when already they had touched in much more intimate ways. Yet he shivered at the contact. The way he clambered onto the bed, with his glass held out to the side, his smile and the grace, the mesmerizing economy of his movement, it could drive a man insane. Cesare's gaze tracked over every inch of his body, and Dan seemed to enjoy the attention.

He opened the towel slowly, displaying his heavy cock with a pride not altogether serious, but teasing and playful. It stirred a little under Cesare's inspection; the sight of it, he was pleasantly surprised to find, made his mouth water. Thick, set against loose balls, the delicate skin of his most sensitive parts only a shade or so darker than the rest of him. It looked... appropriate, Cesare thought, so much a part of Dan. So natural and unstudied. Freckles flecked the top of his chest and arms: close-knit, almost like a sort of marbling to the skin. Cesare wondered if the sun brought them out and lost himself in thoughts of Daniel shirtless in the summertime, or as good as naked on the beach, the sliver of a swimsuit protecting his modesty.

Not that he was modest, not in the sense of self-consciousness. Far from it. That much Cesare thought evident, and it intrigued him. Never before had he encountered such a sense of freedom in someone... and it couldn't have been more attractive.

DAN WAS aware of how closely Cesare watched him. He reknotted the towel, then flopped down against the pillows, took another gulp of wine, and nearly burst into renewed hilarity when Cesare reached across to pop an olive into his mouth. The salty little fruit burst between Dan's teeth, but Cesare's touch still traced his jaw, his neck, unwilling to relinquish him.

They ate in comfortable, companionable, wonderful silence, never quite apart but never quite pushing over the line back into full foreplay. Dan hadn't a clue what the film was about: his abilities in conversational Italian didn't stretch that far. Two guys were arguing and a beautiful woman kept bursting into photogenic tears, so it might have been some kind of love triangle. Or possibly a murder mystery. He didn't really care, not with Cesare next to him, smelling so good and looking so tempting, picking at a bread roll. His bare foot stroked Dan's shin gently, almost absentmindedly, and the weight beside him on the mattress, the scent and warmth of Cesare's body, became ever more distracting.

"So," Dan said into the quiet, "why did you come to Venice?"

He knew he didn't need to ask. He could simply have rolled over and given the rest of the night over to the wordless language of bodies. There was no pressure to make put-yourself-at-ease small talk. Not here.

"Why?" Cesare echoed, turning his head to look at Dan, that familiar, clear honesty in his eyes. He smiled, not a trace of bitchiness in his voice. "When there are other cities to go to, you mean? Roma, Padova, Firenze… places with big gay culture? Places to go for…." He waved his hand expressively, trying to capture a meaning. "…fucking?"

It surprised Dan. He'd thought Cesare would tense up again, reject any kind of personal question… certainly not that he'd go right to the point of the matter.

"I suppose, yeah. Hang on, no. I didn't mean I thought you were just here for—" He sighed. "I mean, you said that you came here with someone once. I know it's none of my business, but… I just wondered, I guess… what the story was, if there was one."

"You remember what I say? That's nice." Cesare smiled and pressed a kiss to the point of Dan's shoulder, reaching across him for the wine. "*Sì*. There was a man. I met him in Pontremoli. He had an uncle who died and left him an apartment here in Venezia. Castello, not far from the Navy Museum. Have you been there?"

"Castello, yes, but I didn't know there was a Navy Museum."

"No? Is very good. You must go there, Daniel." Cesare sipped his wine. "So. We would meet at the apartment, perhaps once a month. Tito wanted it that way and I… *ehi*, I just said yes. It was easier for him than for me, I think. He had a wife, and two little girls. I didn't know at first. When I did find out… ah, I was *stupido*. I thought, you know, *è amore*.

I kept meeting him." He laughed softly. "I started carrying golf clubs in my car, and I told everybody I had taken up golf."

"Did they believe you?"

"*Sì*." Cesare smiled, leaning against him. Dan wished he'd take the T-shirt off, wanting skin on skin again, contact and satiation.

"Then what happened?"

"Ah… I thought I could—*come si dice?*—that I could handle it. Then Tito bought me a watch."

"A watch?" Dan reached into the paper sack for a *buranello* and bit into the crisp cookie, letting it crumble against his tongue. "That doesn't really sound like a deal breaker to me."

"No? It was an expensive watch. Swiss. Handmade."

"Wow."

"*Sì*. And he asked me to go to Roma with him. He said it was a business trip. I wouldn't go. I felt guilty, said that he should spend his money on his wife, his children… not me." Cesare took another swallow of wine, memory clouding his face. "He went to Roma without me, and when he came back, it was only for to pack his bags."

"Pack his bags? Why?"

Cesare drained his glass and stifled a belch, his face mellowed with alcohol and sex, his gaze semidistant as he wandered through the misty landscapes of the past.

"To leave his wife e bambini. He said he was moving there, that he was sick of lying… of hiding. He said I should come too, but I wouldn't. I felt so bad for what he had done. Leaving her that way, and the girls… and I was scared. Scared of going to Roma, of living the way he was talking about."

He held out his glass for Dan to fill again.

"This was several years ago. I was much younger than him. Perhaps I saw more… there was still a lot of violence. Abuse. The police, as well as—" Cesare's mouth twisted. "—other people. Things are better now, but… it is still not easy. It was hard then. Sometimes, dangerous, and that made me scared. But it made Tito angry. He went to Roma. He got involved with the running of Arcigay, you know? The gay rights group. I went to visit him just one time there. There was a… a protest, a rally, *sì*? We went. I thought it would be all right if I stuck with Tito, but things got bad. The police arrested a lot of people."

Dan frowned. "That's awful. Did you—?"

Cesare wrinkled his nose. "They did not charge me with anything, but it was a horrible experience. Maybe I was too scared, but I said I would never do it again. The *carabinieri* were… not friendly."

"They beat you?" Dan winced, unable to stop himself picturing a series of terrible vignettes. "That's appalling!"

"No, no. No beatings. It could have been much worse. But it was frightening. I never saw Tito after that," Cesare added reflectively, his brow creasing a little. "I was angry when he didn't come to get me, and I went straight home to Pontrémal. I wanted nothing more to do with protests, or politics, or Tito. He sent a letter, and said I was a coward. He used to write, sometimes… he said he would never forgive me for letting him down. We lost touch after a little while."

Cesare took another sip of wine, resting his head on Dan's chest. At a loss for words, and full of a sense of protective sorrow, Dan reached up and stroked his hair, enjoying the scent of what he now knew was shower gel, that tantalizing, brief smell of citrus and musk. The little intimacy didn't seem strange to him, and he kissed the top of Cesare's ear, feeling him exhale contentedly.

"He sold the place in Castello," said Cesare, quietly. "Although, I think, for a while, when I took holidays, I went to Venezia to see Tito, even though I knew he wasn't there. But… each time I went, I find something more of the city that I like… something more that is a thing *I* see, not him. So, after a time, it was no longer for him, but for me that I come. You understand?"

"Yeah." Dan leaned his cheek against the crown of Cesare's head. "I think I do."

"Hmm." Cesare chuckled. "Is funny. I used to go to Padova, Firenze, Bologna… all those places, *sì*? For… you know. This is the first time I ever meet someone in Venice."

"I should feel honored, then."

"Maybe." Cesare tipped his head farther back, until he was able to peck Dan on the lips. "*Forse è il destino*, eh?"

Dan smiled. Fate could indeed be a funny thing. Cesare sat up, turning himself over so that he rested on his elbows, giving Dan his full attention. His glass of wine still clasped in one hand, he ran his fingers lightly over Dan's chest, sketching out maps and poems and who knew what else on his skin.

"It has been a long time," he admitted, flicking his thumb across Dan's nipple. "I don't go to those places anymore… I think I spend my whole life pretending, Daniel. At home, at work… you know? So it feels like, if I go to a club or a sauna, I am still pretending. *Sì?*"

Dan nodded. The expression in those eyes was enough to break a heart. Suddenly, his own childhood, his youth, and his growing pains seemed a pale attempt, devoid of drama. His blessings seemed to haunt him, left strewn about his life unheeded and uncounted, like so many unwashed socks on a bedroom floor. He wanted to reach out for Cesare, but he didn't dare.

Cesare bent his head, trailing tiny kisses across his chest like a slow fall of rose leaves.

"For so long, I don't talk to anybody," he said between touches, eyes darting up to Dan's face again. "I didn't… you know. So, thank you."

He fell to tracking his lips across Dan's body again, moving inexorably down, down toward the towel that was still knotted across his waist. Dan tensed, taking Cesare's glass from him and wriggling back against the pillows, making it easier for him.

"You—oh, that's good—you don't have to thank me, you know," he said as Cesare's hot breath grazed his stomach. "Really. I… mmm… wanted you. Ow!"

He flinched as Cesare's teeth tugged at his treasure trail.

"I'm sorry… but you make me very happy to hear that, Daniel. *Che bello…. Fammi sentire quanta voglia hai di me, sì?*"

"Huh?" Dan grunted as Cesare unknotted the towel. The cool air skittered across his hardening cock, and he was in no state of mind for translations. "Wha'?"

"Show me, Daniel. Show me how much you want me," Cesare murmured, dipping his head to kiss Dan's thighs.

Dan's eyes fluttered closed and his lips parted as Cesare's tongue traced up the inside of his thigh. The Italian made a small, satisfied noise in the back of his throat as if he really relished the taste of Dan's skin. His lips tickled the sensitive cleft that joined leg to hip and Dan wriggled a little. His stiffening cock brushed against Cesare's cheek, maybe seeking out his flesh, demanding to be touched.

Some kind of communication obviously went on between it and Cesare, some kind of pidgin language that Dan didn't need to partake in, because Cesare grasped his dick tentatively in one hand and pumped once, twice. Dan's hips lifted, encouraging him, so he continued, watching it come to life. He seemed entranced by the soft foreskin, almost pretty in its delicacy, the glossy, dark head that slipped from it, the veins that wrapped the thickening shaft. Dan was sure Cesare must be able to feel his pulse flutter against that large, square palm.

His broad fingers slid over Dan's thigh, raising chills where the curled fuzz of hair parted for him. Dan hauled himself up on his elbows. He needed to see this, to watch properly as Cesare bent his head and flicked his tongue gingerly over the pouting head. He paused at Dan's sharp intake of breath and peered up at him, questioning. Dan reached out, his hand on Cesare's head, fingers brushing the rim of his ear, guiding him gently without pressure or demand.

Dan probably smelled of salt and musk and the faint traces of the complimentary hotel soap…. Cesare would taste all of it. He pressed his mouth to Dan's cock again, massaging the soft skin with his bottom lip. Obviously he didn't have a problem with it.

Dan winced as Cesare sucked again on the head of his dick: a jagged, intense, and all-too-brief pleasure. A moan escaped his lips when Cesare took him deeper, pumping the base of the shaft with his hand, his warm mouth a swirling pool. Dan lifted his hips, wanting to thrust against his face, but he held back, knowing that, despite the irritation of Cesare's subtle stimulation, he shouldn't push it. Not yet.

Cesare bobbed over Dan's cock, and his free hand moved between grasping Dan's hip and toying with his balls. His own arousal apparently grew more intense with every moment. He breathed harder, shorter; dark noises of want hitched in the back of his throat. Dan knew it all too well… the knowledge that he'd made another man so hard he ached, that he would make him come, make him lose himself in a shapeless mass of color and sensation that would fill him like a drug.

Yeah, that felt good.

Though Dan didn't mean to think of his ex, he couldn't help but remember how good Paul had looked when Dan had sucked him. Looking up from that strange vantage point just south of his belly, seeing the whole of his body laid out, how he'd sweat and tremble and lose all of that überbutch attitude crap he used to carry.

Dan wondered if Cesare saw him the same way now, open and defenseless, or if he'd be so hung up on the *how* of the act he forgot the why. His hair was so soft under Dan's fingers… no trace of coarseness or graying, despite the way it receded a little at his temples. He seemed so young sometimes. Absurdly so. Dan supposed it must be the way he wanted to please, the way that—even now—he seemed desperate to give a porn star blowjob, trying to take Dan's shaft down to the base as if he could impale himself on it. Of course he couldn't. It was too much, and he pulled back, gagging and mortified.

"Don't worry, it's all right," Dan murmured, rubbing Cesare's neck. "Take it easy."

Cesare took a few deep breaths and tried again, once more almost choking himself.

"Use your hand again. It's okay… use your hand, and you won't try to take more than you can manage. Like—oh, yes, you've got the idea…."

Dan leaned on one elbow and watched Cesare suck inexpertly but energetically on the first inch or so of his cock. Very endearing but also unbearably frustrating.

"Hold on," he said eventually, unable to take it anymore. "Stop, just for a minute."

Chastened, Cesare obeyed, giving Dan room to move around on the bed, his slick cock hard and glistening like a jewel. His heart went out to this man, in all his inefficiencies, his desire to stretch past the boundaries that didn't seem to be ones he'd have chosen for himself. *Culture?* Dan wondered. Maybe religion.

Good thing he didn't have to hang around for the panicky morning after.

He switched them around, enjoying Cesare's pliancy beneath his hands, the want that flushed his face. The remnants of the bag of *buranelli* dropped to the floor in an unheeded rustle of paper, falling among the empty food containers from their makeshift meal. Cesare reached for him, seeming confused for a moment until he realized that Dan was lying down beside him, preparing to return the favor. Cesare opened his mouth to speak, but when Dan took him between his lips, all that emerged was a strangled gasp and a succession of short, panting breaths.

His eyes closed for a moment until he regained himself. Cesare adjusted his position on the abused sheets, grasped Dan's thighs, and held him tight enough to capture his rod, snaking his tongue around it, tickling and laving at the hard flesh. Dan moaned around Cesare's cock, sending vibrations through him that made him cry out but thankfully not bite down.

Dan flexed his toes on the sheets, wriggling against Cesare in the hope of encouraging him to do something more adventurous with his hands. Leading by example, he massaged Cesare's ass as he sucked, feeling the earthquake within the man already starting to build. That wouldn't do at all…. Dan didn't want to relinquish his new toy so quickly. He sucked deeply at the base of Cesare's shaft and pressed two fingers to the sensitive strip behind his balls, delighted at how easy he was to bring to the brink and back again. Dan had a feeling that, once everything locked inside there started to come out, it would be a torrent almost impossible to stem. He flicked his tongue across the wide, thick head of Cesare's cock, teasing him before taking it deep into his mouth again.

Cesare, his forehead pressed against Dan's thigh, groaned. He'd slowed the pace of his own ministrations, apparently finding it difficult to concentrate.

"*Sei un diavolo!*" he murmured, his breath whispering against Dan's flesh.

Dan pressed down on the base of Cesare's shaft and backed him away from destruction. The Italian's soft whimper and the twitch of his hips told Dan that, even with all the evil little tricks in the world, he wouldn't hold out much longer. It seemed a shame not to make it memorable for him.

Dan looked up and caught sight of the Prosecco on the nightstand.

CESARE, THINKING Dan had signaled a break, reluctantly relinquished his cock. Panting, he still clasped Dan's legs close to him and his cheek rested on one firm, peach-fuzzed thigh. He peered up the bed as he felt Dan move, and frowned at the sight of him swigging wine from the bottle.

"What—?" he began, but then Dan dipped his head and engulfed him.

Cold liquid washed over Cesare's cock like ice. Bubbles burst in tiny beads of fire and Dan's tongue, like an arrow, sought out the sharpest pleasure at the underside of his shaft. Cesare yelled even as Dan, unable to hold both the wine and him in his mouth for long, spluttered, swallowed, and resumed a more conventional method. He winked at Cesare, indescribably appealing in that moment.

Definitely devilish, Cesare decided. He'd never before *imagined* that… oh, Holy M—did he want to do it again?

Dan stifled a laugh and moved to take another mouthful of wine. He raised his eyebrows, questioning, holding the liquid in his mouth. Dumbly, Cesare nodded, clutching at the sheets. *Maiala della miseria!* It felt like nothing he could ever have envisioned, and he gasped, light-headed. It was everything: wet and sharp, cold and hot, so very, very good. He didn't look, didn't know how Dan could avoid choking on the wine and, with such the smallest of pauses, take his cock back so soon into that sensuous, incredible mouth. He didn't *dare* look.

Maybe there would be nothing to see. Maybe he'd tumbled into darkness, and the whole world had vanished except for Dan's mouth, chilled with the wine, then warming around him in the strangest, most wonderful way.

Cesare moaned softly, his hips thrusting against the movement of Dan's head, long, rhythmic strokes, firm and deep, threatening to pull his soul out through his cock. Dan's hands massaged his thighs, his buttocks, playing with his balls, consuming him in dizzying, deep-seated pleasure, then he felt a gentle, wet pressure on his perineum, sliding back between his cheeks. He gasped, moving against the sensation, trembling as Dan lapped at his shaft, crying out at the indescribable satisfaction of a finger sliding into him, then slowly seeking, then rubbing inside him, pushing him further to the edge with a thousand tingling kisses.

All thoughts of Dan's cock, hard and wet and just beside his head, were impossible to act on as Cesare came, mesmerized by the sight of Dan taking his slick, shuddering cock in his mouth again and again as he shot, losing his load onto that seeking, eager, ruthless tongue, blue eyes staring into his, goading him on, milking him dry.

"*Basta*… please… enough, Daniel," he croaked, whimpering as his wet flesh slipped from Dan's lips, so sensitized that even the air was painful. "*Fermo! Oddio… mi ucciderai! Ehi, sei venuto?*"

Cesare raised himself up on one elbow, peering at Dan's cock. Still hard, still… impossibly hard. That wasn't good. He couldn't possibly do anything about that. Not now, when it took so much effort just to breathe.

"It's okay," Dan assured. "I can take care of it."

"No… no. Please."

With considerable effort, Cesare pulled himself up until he was level with Dan. He wrapped a hand around his shaft and stroked him, leaning up against Dan's body, barely able to support himself, enervated and exhausted. Dan smiled and covered Cesare's hand with his own, showing him how to squeeze just a little more, make him just a little hotter. Cesare let him take charge, happy to touch him however he wanted, and ready to drown in the new-mown-hay scent of his skin, musky with sweat and sex.

Dan tilted his head, surprising Cesare with a kiss. He hadn't expected to taste himself so strongly or for it to be so... changed. It wasn't unpleasant. In fact, flavored with the wine, and with so much else besides, it was better than he could have imagined. He kissed Dan with renewed fervor, quickened his pace, and before long Dan murmured against his mouth, fidgeting and bucking. Cesare leaned his cheek against Dan's shoulder and watched him come like a lava flow, scalding his hand with the knowledge that he had pleasured this beautiful man, that Daniel was here, and real, and enjoying him. Cesare crawled down the bed, licked him clean and bound each taste, each scent, each quiver of his softening cock to memory.

This—this man, this pleasure—would be forever.

CHAPTER SIX

THE DAWN slipped over Venice like silk, quietly iridescent, at least for some. In other rooms, other places, cleaners and maids were working. On the islands in the lagoon, cemeteries were tended, graves dug, market gardens irrigated, and returning fishing boats greeted by those with a day's work of gutting and filleting to do.

Dan woke with the sun well up in the sky and the curtains still closed, and found Cesare gone. A note on hotel stationary had been left on the pillow, though it took some minutes to find it, as he'd rolled over and managed to get it stuck to his cheek.

Daniel—a presto. TVB, C.

He puzzled over it while he made himself an insipid cup of coffee with the sachets of instant yuck and the white plastic kettle the hotel supplied. The "see you soon" bit he understood, but what the hell was TVB? Dan shrugged to himself and drank the coffee, feeling a little mean for being grateful that he'd woken up alone.

It was good to have… space.

Dan walked to the window, checking out the view as he wondered what would be in store for today. He thought about dressing now, leaving quietly and drawing a line under what had happened, but it was impossible. Cesare's face stalked his mind: pale and terrified, drawn and serious, flushed and lustful, flooded with pleasure. He thought of his touch, his mouth, the way he was when he came, so totally open and without defense.

It was that which Dan found unnerving.

A Friday night hookup at home was essentially two people rubbing their bits together in the expectation of getting off. Maybe everyone involved pretended it was more most times, but pretending was all it was. That didn't feel like what had happened, though.

Dan shook that thought. It wasn't a safe one to have. And besides, what kind of man laid himself open to every fuck the way Cesare had? He swallowed the remnants of the coffee and wrinkled his nose in distaste.

Maybe it was just that he didn't expect another chance. Poor guy was obviously holed up so deep in the closet he could see into Narnia.

Then again, who *did* expect a chance encounter to end up like that? Dan thought of Club Commodoro and the blond, amazed to find those memories seemed so distant. He was even more amazed to find he actually felt guilty about it now; that he could do that, when Cesare… no, Cesare had probably never thought he had that kind of freedom.

Even so, they must put something in the water out here.

Dan couldn't remember the last time he'd come four times in one night, especially when the sex had been so utterly tame. No, that wasn't fair to Cesare. All right, so he was edgy about anal, but a lot of guys didn't fuck that way. Dan thought of his thighs, slick and hot; the enthusiasm he showed for learning how to use his mouth properly… the intimacy of their bodies pressed close together, mouths united not just in kisses but breathing, sharing the same air. It certainly hadn't happened in a while. And besides, it had been—good? No. Better than that. Something other than that. Good was one decent orgasm—maybe two—and not being thrown out before breakfast, or at least until after a small pit stop. It didn't cover the sleepy, after-midnight oral of their last bout, Cesare sucking him off twice without stopping, sending him spinning through the stars until he thought he'd fall off the planet.

That was… something else.

Dan put the cup down next to the kettle and padded into the bathroom.

CESARE SLIPPED in through the foyer, trying not to catch the eye of the pretty girl on the front desk. Clad in a green cotton sundress and a polite smile, she reminded him of his sister, which was at that moment painful. He pushed all thoughts of Eugenia from his mind and walked briskly along the corridors to his room, heart pounding with each step. He clutched the brown paper bag of goods to his chest, fumbling with his key.

Cesare breathed deeply as he entered the room, trying to detect the scent of sex, a man's sweat-musk that filled his life so rarely, and left such a void behind it afterward, only empty rooms and shadows.

The bed was empty, rumpled, but the drapes and window had been opened. He shot a glance to the bathroom, ridiculously relieved to see the steam curling from under the door. If *he* had gone, perhaps it would all have been a dream.

Cesare smiled to himself, which faded as he cast an eye over the bed. Thinking practically, what if the maid found stains? The heat of a blush shaded up around his neck… it made him think of when he was a boy, and his mother had found the evidence of his nocturnal activities on his bedding. She had made him scrub each one clean in the scullery sink and recount his deeds to the heavy-breathing silhouette of the priest at Confession.

He had never fully trusted Father Vaccaro, who was, of course, a man of God, so not as other men, and who should, Mamma said, inspire awe and a little fear, for how else were the faithful to be dissuaded from sinning? Even so, Cesare remembered the small, dark space of the confessional smelling of greasy furniture polish and tobacco, and he remembered hearing Father Vaccaro's deep, rumbling voice in reply to the words he choked out weakly, his voice squeaky and breaking, his palms wet.

Cesare remembered the cold terror when the priest asked him why had he committed this sin of the irregular motion of the flesh? The *act*, that was indeed a mortal sin, but were they not also sins to willfully lust after another, to let his mind weaken and dwell in impure thoughts, and to bear lust in his heart, like a maggot in an apple?

Cesare had tried to stammer out some kind of response, to say he didn't know, but to lie before the representative of God was an unconscionable sin. His whole youth, Cesare reflected as he set to making the bed, had been a paradox. He had known what his body and his heart begged for since he was barely adolescent. He had also known that to think those thoughts was wrong and to act upon them would be even worse.

He smelled the pillows and sheets as he straightened them, trying to bind each sensation to a memory that would sustain him through everyday life and frustration. Lost in reverie, he vaguely registered Dan leaving the bathroom and padding naked to the chair on which his clothes lay.

Cesare remembered considering, in that icy, terrifying moment in the confessional with Father Vaccaro awaiting his response, that he should confess his desires and try to exorcise the male bodies that stalked across his teenage libido like colossi. Yet he had also considered, in those achingly long seconds, that if he did confess, he could not truly be penitent for it. What was there to be sorry for in love? For love it was. He might have been young, but he had been wise enough to know that. He understood that spying on girls at the swimming baths with his friends might be exciting and naughty enough to make his *uccello* harden, but that only seeing Carlo Antonelli with his shirt off at soccer practice made his head light and his heart quicken.

No. If he claimed that he repented, he would give a false confession, a terrible thing, and because Father Vaccaro would admonish him, give him penances to make and prayers to say for his soul, *that* would lead him into the equally mortal and infinitely worse sin of hating God.

Cesare remembered clasping his hands together, feeling as if the smell of the confessional would choke him. Tears had welled in his eyes as he told the priest that he was inspired to commit impure acts by a neighborhood girl, Maria, who had long dark hair and firm breasts. He never gave the priest her name but spun stories around her, using her to cloak all the secrets he kept.

It seemed to satisfy Father Vaccaro, who would settle against the grille and try to wheedle details from him: What precisely were his thoughts? What did the girl do to inflame them? Were her breasts big and heavy, like melons, or small, like peaches ripe with juice? And Cesare would recount lie after lie, compounding his sins with the stories he created but enjoying the role of clandestine showman even as he prayed privately for forgiveness.

"Hi."

His head jerked up at the sound of Dan's voice. Cesare exhaled, speechless. Dan was even more beautiful in the daylight. Cesare's mouth turned dry, his mind full of sensations and things no words could ever be big enough to express. He swallowed, watching Dan's sly grin as he bent over to pick up his underwear, showing Cesare his tight, pale ass, dusted with sandy hairs, and—briefly—a glimpse of the clean, pink flesh between the two cheeks.

"Oh!" Cesare leaned against the bedpost.

Dan peered over his shoulder as he pulled his boxers up.

"I wondered where you'd gone. By the way, what does TVB stand for?"

Cesare blinked owlishly at the paper bag he'd set down by the bed. He remembered writing the note, but he'd almost forgotten those three little letters. They embarrassed him now, seeming so silly and juvenile:

something a teenager might text to a sweetheart. It was too familiar, too soon. Too much.

"Oh, that? Uh, *ti voglio bene*. Just… I would see you soon."

The lie was only a small one, and perhaps Daniel didn't know enough Italian to spot it. Cesare couldn't be sure, but he hoped so. He knew English people didn't use terms of endearment quite as freely as Italians, and the thought of trying to explain just why he'd scrawled that rather cavalier message of affection filled him with dread.

Cesare gestured to the things he'd bought, hoping to distract Dan— maybe to distract them both—from the note. "Here, I got these for you. I am a little late, I think. You have already shower. But… *prego*."

DAN CROSSED to him, taking the brand-new toothbrush, razor, and expensive, aromatic shower gel that he offered from the bag. He smiled, partly at the outrageous gesture of the purchases, and partly at Cesare's morning attire. The crumpled suit was gone, replaced by dusty brown chinos, a light blue shirt, and an old gray sports jacket.

Does everything except this man's birthday suit need pressing?

"You didn't have to do that," Dan said, grinning delightedly.

"I wanted to. You don't mind?"

It might have been a sudden streak of mischief, it might have been pity, or it might have been a reaction to being shopped for. Dan cupped his hand behind Cesare's neck and kissed him, eliciting more enthusiasm than he might have expected. Cesare moaned into his warm, wet mouth, rubbing his face against the morning stubble on Dan's chin. The toiletries he'd bought, clasped between them, dug into Dan's chest with sharp plastic corners.

Cesare was breathing heavily when they parted. He looked embarrassed; Dan guessed it was because such a small action could leave him so obviously aroused. The Italian cleared his throat.

"Are you… uh, are you hungry, Daniel? I-I was thinking, perhaps we could have *prima colazione* together. Before you…. That is, I don't know what plans you have today… but…."

"Mm, good idea. I'm starving," Dan said, rescuing him from mangling his sentences any further and choosing to gloss over anything after breakfast. No sense in planning too far ahead. "Can't think what I did to work up such an appetite."

Cesare's color ripened to a nice deep pink around the ears. "*Monello!*"

Dan tilted his head. "What's that mean?"

Cesare smiled. "Nothing."

"Hey… I thought you were supposed to be improving my Italian?" He folded his arms and struck up a pout.

Cesare laughed. "All right. It means… how would you say? A… a boy who is naughty, I think. Not wicked, but—"

Dan raised an eyebrow. "Just you wait. You don't know how wicked I can be."

Cesare smiled again, lust in his eyes. Dan took the toiletries from him and went back to the bathroom to shave. Cesare was still smiling and, Dan thought as he snapped the plastic safety guard off the razor, would quite possibly be smiling for months to come. That image pleased Dan. He liked the idea of being somebody's private sex god. And, he reminded himself as he winked at his reflection, there was no harm whatsoever in that.

Last night had been great, and it was just sex. He needed it, Cesare needed it, and what happened in Venice could stay in Venice.

No one got hurt.

He'd just finished up in the bathroom when a soft knock on the door presaged room service. Dan heard Cesare conversing with the waiter in Italian, too fast for him to follow, and tactfully hung back behind the door. It riled a part of Dan to do so, but he let it slide. This wasn't his hotel room, his country, or his rules. He strode out nonchalantly after Cesare shut the door and called to him, pretending he'd just finished in the bathroom.

Cesare was setting out the breakfast on the dressing table by the window. He'd turned the TV to an Italian news channel and pulled round the room's two tatty velour armchairs so that they could sit in comfort. Dan's stomach rumbled in anticipation. Cesare seemed to have ordered one of almost everything the hotel had to offer. The tray groaned under the weight of rolls and pastries, a coffeepot that could probably have served ten people, and enough cream and sugar to clog the arteries of a small country. It smelled fantastic and they ate hungrily, the faint lapping sound of water drifting up from the canal below the window.

Cesare helped himself to a poppy seed roll, liberally buttered, and picked at it as the background babble of the TV and the sounds of the city washed over them. Dan supposed he should start making his excuses and go. He finished off the last of the *croissant con crema*, seeing as it looked like Cesare was a savory breakfast person, and thought harder about going. There was a lot to see. Photos to take. He was aware of Cesare's foot, shoeless and clad in a thin cotton sock, resting against his ankle. No footsy, no pressure, just the gentle weight of his presence.

"Where will you go today?" Cesare asked, apparently nonchalant.

Dan shook himself out of whatever dreamland he'd drifted into. Had he forgotten, in a few short seconds, what that low, mellow voice sounded like? It was as if he'd never heard it before.

"Um. I-I don't know, really," he said.

First hint. Get your stuff and get out. He swigged the last of the coffee from his cup and replaced it on the tray.

"Oh. I thought I might go over to Sant'Erasmo."

Dan glanced at Cesare, who appeared to be looking out of the window. The sky was the impossibly clear azure of spring, a sign of hope for the months ahead.

"Where's that?"

"Is one of the islands. North of the Lido. Venezia is built on more than a hundred islands, all around the lagoon. Sant'Erasmo is very beautiful… it used to be called Isola Alba, the Island of the Dawn, because of the pale sands. Is a very nice beach. Much nicer than the Lido, and less crowded. You can see the Torre Massimiliana, the big tower there, for miles, and there are very good markets. They grow fruit and vegetables there. They don't taste the same anywhere but Venice. Many artists go there, for all the views of the lagoon. Painters, poets…." Cesare shot him a sly sideways glance. "Photographers."

Dan laughed. He couldn't help it. It might have been amusement at the way Cesare looked at him, it might have been relief. Either way, Cesare laughed too.

"*Che volpone*, eh?" Cesare wiped a tear from his eye. "I don't think I am very subtle. But, I would like it if you come. If you think is not a good idea, then—"

"No, it's a great idea. I'd love to," Dan said, realizing that it was true. He was in no hurry at all to say good-bye, no hurry to tuck his night with this man away in a little labeled box of memories.

"I am glad." Cesare smiled shyly. "I would very much like to see you again, Daniel. I-I am very happy that I was brave, at the pizzeria."

"Hmm?" Dan quirked an eyebrow.

"*Sì*. I never thought I would have the nerves to talk to you... but I did."

Dan noticed a triumphant gleam in his eyes. Sexy but kind of endearing as well. As if it had really meant something to Cesare. He smiled and tried to work out whether he'd been chalked up as an achievement or a miracle.

"I'm glad you did too. It's made my holiday a lot more interesting."

Another light tinge of color in Cesare's cheeks rewarded him. Standing, trying to hide his embarrassment, Cesare moved to his case and found a pen, tearing a scrap of paper from an academic year diary.

"I will give you my number, Daniel. Just in case. The boat for Sant'Erasmo stops at Fondamente Nove... is the number 13. I don't know, where is your hotel?"

"It's near San Marco. I know... touristy."

"No, is very *centrale. Prego*," he said, handing Dan the paper. "I just think, you will want to go back there first, *sì*?"

"Clean clothes might be nice," Dan conceded, although a little reluctantly. Part of him didn't want to leave this comfortable room; part of him was worried about agreeing to something that was essentially a date, making that step up from one-night stand to holiday fling.

"Then, when you are ready, I will meet you on the bus, perhaps? They go every hour."

"All right." Dan added his cell number to the paper, tore it in half, and passed it back to Cesare. "That's my number, in case you need it."

"*Grazie*."

"I'll get going, then." Dan stood, feeling slightly awkward. "Thanks for breakfast, and... everything. You'll let me buy you lunch, won't you?"

Cesare smiled. "I would let you do anything, caro."

He meant it, Dan realized. It wasn't just the glib, flirtatious remark it seemed, despite the way Cesare's eyes brightened so enticingly.

"Hmm... I might just hold you to that," he warned with a smile. Dan stretched, feeling the warmth of the sunshine and of Cesare's gaze, on his skin. "I'd better get going."

"There's no rush."

There was, thought Dan. He felt it more the closer they drew. Cesare's lips brushed his, almost clumsy for a moment, then firm, familiar, warm. They pressed against each other, less urgent now, but still hungry, until

Dan wasn't sure whether he was being kissed good-bye or convinced to stay. All he knew was that at that moment, in the honey-colored air and the neutral room, with the sounds and glamour of Venice at the window, he didn't want to go, ever again. But it was safe to feel that, wasn't it? Safe to be in these strong, comfortable arms, because when the week ended, he'd be going home.

A LITTLE over an hour later, Dan finally left Cesare's hotel. He walked slowly back through the winding footways and narrow bridges, now coming to a dead end at the wall of some derelict *palazzo*, now finding an unexpected canal, the tang of salt on the air with the high tide that washed through the city, cleansing and renewing the water.

Small private launches and ornate gondolas bumped gently together in their moorings, and the sun was warm on his back. He took his time, unfazed by the wrong turns, until he found the Ponte dell'Accademia and, from there, the route back to San Marco and, at last, his own hotel.

Dan changed briskly, wrote a couple of postcards, fiddled with his hair for longer than was strictly necessary, and ended up almost missing the *vaporetto*. He showed his weeklong pass and stumbled aboard, looking for Cesare among the crowds of passengers, patchworks of bright colors, and sunglasses, listening for his voice amid the chatter of a dozen languages. Dan had started to suspect that Cesare wasn't there, when he felt a tap on the shoulder. He turned to find Cesare smiling and looking every inch the handsome patrician Italian as, with a hand on Dan's arm, he kissed him on both cheeks.

Dan caught his breath. There was a lot going on behind the scenes of that harmless little bit of continentalism. Steadying himself on Cesare's wrist as the boat roared and juddered down the Canale, he marveled at the confidence Cesare exuded among all these people. Was this really the same man who'd shied away from having breakfast with him in public?

"*Ciao*, Daniel. I am glad you made it."

"Of course," he said, still a little wrong-footed.

Cesare guided him to the side of the boat so that the great landmark of Sant'Erasmo—the vast red brick and stone Torre Massimiliana—became visible over the glittering blue of the lagoon. He could see it rise into the sky, the sandy cliffs tumbling to a white-flecked ocean beneath.

"Wow," he murmured, snapping a few frames as the tower got larger, filling the horizon.

"I thought you would like it," said Cesare, leaning on the rail beside him. "It is not a truly beautiful building, like the rest of Venezia, but is *importante. Come posso spiegarmi?* Imposing, yes? It used to stand guard over the whole lagoon. These days, they use it for conferences, retreats, and things. I don't know what's on the program this year, though."

"Why the Maximillian Tower?" asked Dan, squinting through his wide-angle lens.

"For the Archduke Massimiliano. He sheltered in the fortress once... I don't remember when. Maybe 1850, I think? It was when Venezia was still a republic. The Austrians were a powerful presence here, perhaps because of all the, uh, money... the taxes that come with controlling a port, *sì*? That tower was once the fort that protected the whole of Venice."

"Really?" Dan raised his eyebrows. "It looks so small from here."

Cesare just smiled.

They got off the ferry at Chiese, one of the three stops running along the island's inner shore. The *vaporetto* deposited its passengers and puttered off on the rest of its route, the dark water churning in its wake. Across the lagoon, the brightly colored houses of Burano were just visible through a pale ring of dispersing mist, and stretching down to the water, mudflats ran in long stretches of streaked gray and brown.

While Cesare checked the timetable, muttering something about not wanting to be stranded forever, Dan breathed in the clean, sweet air. As Venice banned cars, even where it was possible to drive one, the whole place lacked the choke of exhaust and smog common to other cities, and that faint tang of salt on the air did hang over the buildings, but Sant'Erasmo seemed different. He could smell wild thyme and sunbaked dirt, not the conflicting aromas of a hundred *trattorie*. Salt, water, and charcoal. And Cesare, beside him.

On Sant'Erasmo, maps were something that happened to other people. As the island was nothing more than a narrow strip of land a few miles long, tossed into the sea like a discarded slip of apple peel, it was perhaps pointless to chart it. They found the church that named the ferry stop, which Dan snapped dutifully, thinking its bulbous, white, arching walls to be a little like the huge concrete eggs Salvador Dalí had housed in his gardens.

The most noticeable thing about the place seemed to be the skyline. The island was flat and so were its horizons, the clear, cloudless blue uninterrupted by bell towers, *palazzi*, hotels, and all the other plaster and stone monoliths of civilization to be found stretching toward the heavens in the city.

They headed down a track beside the church, which led away from the shore and across the island. Cesare slid Dan a sideways look and seemed to be about to ask him something when, behind them, a bicycle bell rang and three tourists whizzed past, all nylon backpacks and the whiz of tires in the breeze. Stepping out of the way, Dan and Cesare looked at each other as the bikes passed.

"I remember now," Cesare said dryly. "You can hire bicycles here."

"Not a chance," Dan affirmed, and they laughed, walking closer together as they tramped along the grubby track.

"It's like Norfolk," he said as Cesare lingered politely by his shoulder, out of the light, waiting for him to finish taking a wide shot of the flat landscape.

They followed the narrow track: shallow lagoon waters to one side, flanked by mudbanks and flats, wading birds picking through the sludge on long, pin-like legs. To the other, grasses and scrub gave way to allotments and market gardens beyond, now just a palette of greens and browns, but—in the summer—something that must be wonderful to see. Colors bled through each other, layers of subtle texture in the thin light, the whole view like a well-executed watercolor.

"Norfolk?" Cesare echoed.

Dan straightened up. "It's a county, a region in England. Just east of Cambridge. The northern part's full of old canals and waterways, but the people there call them Broads, so it's known as the Norfolk Broads. It's very beautiful, like this... the countryside's very flat, so you can see for miles. And you can never quite tell where the sky ends and the water begins."

"You know that place well?"

"A bit. It's a tradition for a lot of British people to go to Norfolk and take a holiday on the Broads. Mum used to take my sister and me... we'd rent a boat and go for a week." Dan grinned, memories fresh in his mind as he fastened the camera back into its bag. "In the summer, you can hardly move for people on boating holidays. Only trouble is, that's the only time most of them ever *go* boating, so the whole place is clogged up with people who are terrible at it." He slung the camera bag back over his shoulder. "Like me."

"Oh, I am sure you are not that—"

"Yes, I am." Dan cut across him with a smile. "Believe me. We used to come up from London every August, and I used to spend half the week stinking of duck shit and blanket weed, because every year, Mum would make us take turns at driving the launch, and every year I'd end up steering us into the bank. Then she'd give me a pole and tell me to push us out again and, every bloody time, I'd manage to fall in. It's just not one of my strengths. Edith was way better at it."

"Edith?"

"My sister. She's three years older than me. I don't know… maybe it was just because of that, but she's always been the practical one."

Cesare smiled, asking him a few more idle questions about childhood holidays and places that probably seemed as exotic to him as the backstreets of Napoli did to Dan.

"You'd like England, I think," Dan said as they were rounding the track past the island's small, neat cemetery, heading toward a modern housing development that faced the opposite shore. The buildings were a visual shock after the city: small and red roofed, but recognizably new. It was almost an affront to the eye to see something less than a century old.

He bit his lip. Cesare had fallen silent. How had that sounded? He hadn't meant it to seem like an invitation, but perhaps it had. Or did he just wish it had?

Dan brushed casually against him, nudging Cesare's shoulder with his own.

"If you ever do visit, give me a call. I'll show you the sights."

Cesare nodded, and he smiled, a promise made in thin air that absolved them both.

They walked on, turning the heel of the island between fields and the muddy shoreline of the lagoon. It was eerily quiet, the salt air on the breeze, but the waves too distant to be more than a pale echo.

Dan knelt in the dirt, taking more long shots of the mudflats, hoping to catch the play of light in the stains of water, or the elegant feeding of birds. Rowing boats, old paint peeling on crisp hulls, and names no longer legible on their worn sides, were drawn up on the mud below, and he showed Cesare, through the camera, how the shadows could be made to paint depth and color upon them.

"You have such a talent," Cesare said admiringly as Dan finished off the shots. "Were you always interested in photography?"

"Oh, since forever, yeah." Dan stood, brushing the dirt from his knees. "It was the only lunchtime club at school where you could play with chemicals. You know? Back in the days before digital. Developing pictures the old-fashioned way?"

He mimed swishing prints around in a tray until Cesare grinned, signaling understanding.

"*Che simpatico!*" Cesare teased. "But what was it, really, that start you?"

"I don't know." Dan shrugged. "I suppose I like to have a record of things. People, places… what interests me is how we see things. I can take a picture of how I see something, what it makes me feel and what it means to me… it'll never be the same as anyone else's. Hell, it won't be the same set of things I think and feel if I come back and look at it in five years' time."

He looked toward the tip of the island, where the fort and the Torre Massimiliana rose among the dunes.

"Everything changes. So, for me, it's about making something that lasts, when so much just… blows away."

There was silence. Dan glanced back at Cesare and smiled. "What?"

Cesare shook his head, his expression soft. "You are very special, I think. Your gift. To make people feel things… to inspire them. It is rare."

"Thanks," Dan said, humbled.

The Torre Massimiliano and the restored fort provided some interest, although it had fallen victim to the Venetian curse of erratic opening times. They made their way past a small *trattoria* covered with swarms of local day-trippers and island dwellers perched at picnic tables, down to the muddy slope of the beach. There, waves lapped at the shore, blue-green and chilly. Boats were drawn up, small day launches taken out just to moor by the refreshments. A few people were about on the sand: families with children, picking their way through flat pebbles and flotsam, ankle-wet in the tide; couples strolling the undulating dunes; and one or two clusters of teenagers passing dog-eared cigarettes as they stood among the scrubby grass.

Dan alternated between long, wide shots out across the lagoon, entranced by the light and the play of boats on water, and views up to the ruined fortifications that ringed the island, all steep, geometric angles and decayed military grandeur.

"Do you think you will sell them?" Cesare asked.

Dan knelt in the sand, trying to get the right shot of a half-collapsed buttress. "What, these pictures?"

"*Sì.*"

"Maybe." Dan scrambled up, brushing the sand from his knees and wondering how, in these and so many other situations, sand got into places you didn't even know you had. "I hope so, anyway. Even if I can't get an exhibition going, I should manage something from stock image royalties."

He took off his shoe and hopped up and down on one leg, shaking sand out of the sneaker, making Cesare laugh. Dan grinned.

"*Prego?* This... stock image?"

"You can make decent money out of stock photography. See... this island, all of this—" Dan waved a hand expansively as he slipped his shoe back on. "—if I take good pictures, I can sell them through agencies, websites, and then if someone in a book or a magazine or something wants a picture of Sant'Erasmo, they go to the agency, they decide to use my photos... I get a percentage royalty, and if you have enough good pictures with enough agencies, it adds up. Of course, I do other stuff too. I think I told you."

"*Sì.* Your models, and weddings."

"Mm-hm." Dan stooped, sliding his shoe back on and pivoting experimentally on the toe to see if all the sand was out. He winced. "Yeah. The weddings. Actually, I've got one coming up, in April. After I get... back."

The word dropped hollowly to the ground. Cesare lowered his head and looked away, out to the froth-rimmed ocean, and Dan cursed himself inwardly.

"They're always a nightmare," he continued doggedly. "You just can't please everybody all the time. There's normally at least one huge family row going on, and then the bride has an argument, either with her mother or the groom, and she ends up crying and looking puffy and you... you just have to do your best to disguise it."

Cesare grinned, and Dan chuckled, relieved that he'd managed to make the man crack a smile.

"Still, it pays the rent. The mortgage, in my case. Which I need to do, since Paul f—Um. My ex," he clarified, seeing Cesare's face. "He used to pick up some of the bills. I only took out the mortgage on the flat because I thought we'd share it. Y'know. I could manage with somewhere smaller, but it's got a roof garden. You don't give up outdoor green space in London without a fight." He smiled uneasily. "And I do love it. Look… d'you want to get something to eat?"

Cesare followed his gaze up to the *trattoria* and nodded.

"*Sì*. Good idea."

They started walking slowly back up the cliff path, the waves beating against the shore with lazy rhythm, punctuating the conversation like heartbeats. Dan talked aimlessly about developing film and digital imaging, and gulls cried overhead, wheeling black against the blue sky.

"I've got to put something about this on the postcards for the kids. My niece and nephews," he explained. "Lauren's nine, Jack's seven, and Liam's four, going on forty…. He's got a map up on the bedroom wall. Any time anyone goes somewhere and he gets a postcard, he puts a pin in the map. Bright kid. They all are."

"You are close?"

Cesare was looking at him with a strange light to his expression. It seemed wistful, yet bitter. Almost like jealousy, he thought.

"Yeah," Dan said, unsure if he should have done.

"Ah." Cesare nodded, pursing his lips together glumly. "They sound… nice."

He said nothing more after that, and Dan felt it was an issue he shouldn't press, although he wasn't sure if it was mentioning Paul or Edith and the kids, that had cast such a shadow over Cesare's face.

They sat on rickety chairs at an equally rickety table, drinking extremely cheap red wine and looking out over the lagoon, talking tourist talk about the local food and drink as a cool wind washed across the island.

"Venezia has the best food in late spring, I think," Cesare said, seemingly back to his old self. "Here, they grow the *castraure*… um… *come si dice*? Artichoke. Purple artichokes… oh, *che bellissimo*! Only place to get them. Late April to June, you go to a good *ristorante*, there is nothing better. And the *moeche*… the little softshell crabs, *sì*? Is very good."

"Oh, stop it." Dan groaned. "I'm starving."

He peered around, hoping to see their food arriving. A lot of the day-trippers were heading back toward their boats or past the networks of ditches and canals to the ferry stop at Capannone. Old men remained, chattering away in the island dialect and nursing cups of wine. The occasional figure on a bicycle passed on the track behind them. Dan's stomach growled remorselessly.

Cesare, fiddling with the tableware, smiled indulgently at him. After a moment filled by another of those silences that fit so easily between them, so comfortable and familiar, he cleared his throat and, with a small frown, began to speak.

"W-when do you go back to England, Daniel?"

"Hmm? Oh. Um…. Saturday."

"Ah," said Cesare. And nothing more.

Dan tilted his head. "Why? What were you thinking?"

"Hm?" Cesare turned his face toward the lagoon as if he was watching the little boats that bobbed on the water. "Oh… I was just thinking. Is nothing really. Just that it would have been nice if we had time to know each other better, *sì*?" His gaze flicked back to the waiter and the impending arrival of dinner. "*Certo.*"

They had ordered a Venetian specialty that Cesare promised was good: a kind of thick stew with beans, scallops, and little pieces of pasta noodles in it, well seasoned and delicious.

"I know what you mean," said Dan as he fell on the food like a vulture. "But… well, I don't know. I'd like to, y'know, to keep in touch, if you want. I understand if you'd rather not, if—"

"No! No, please. I would like that. Very much."

Cesare's voice was low, like a lover's whisper in the night, and it seemed to Dan that the table was little more than a cobweb between them. He recognized, uncurling in the pit of his stomach, that tugging, insistent desire to make love to this man again, to make him weak and to make him burn.

"Good. Because, you know, if you want to talk, or you ever need a friend…."

"Thank you."

Cesare reached out across the table and squeezed his wrist. For such a brief gesture, it seemed to last a very long time.

They ate while watching the waves and the wading birds, and listening to the conversations lapping around them. Dan felt, oddly, less like a tourist than he had at the *trattoria* on the Zattere, and it cheered him to find that Cesare found the island dialect as undecipherable as he did. When he paid, he found a badly printed stack of fliers on the counter for the forthcoming spring and summer program at the Torre Massimiliano. Folding it into his pocket, Dan smiled. Peace conferences, reiki workshops, and celebrations of tolerance.

It looked like Italy's little market garden island had big ideas.

CHAPTER SEVEN

THEY CAUGHT the *vaporetto* back into the city from Capannone, enjoying the relative warmth of the late afternoon and watching white-capped ripples slap at the boat's hull, the lagoon seeming choppier than when they'd set out.

Venice welcomed them back with open arms, a thousand sights, smells, sounds, and colors apparently laid on just for her guests as the waterbus progressed up the Canale, crawling the interminable length of different stops. Tired, but relaxed, Dan asked Cesare what he wanted to do.

"There is a *chiesa* I know, in Rialto. They have a concert… it starts—" He glanced at his watch. "—half an hour or so. I had thought perhaps I would go, but… I don't know if it is the kind of music that you like?"

"I like a lot of different things," Dan said, contemplating the good side of a few hours spent sitting down. "Is it church music, then?"

"Not quite. *Musica antica.* Old kind… sixteenth century, medieval music." Cesare gave a self-deprecating smile. "Not exactly fashionable, but it is very beautiful. So is the *chiesa.* They have altarpiece by Titian."

"Damn." Dan smiled. "You know just how to twist my arm, don't you?"

It took Cesare a moment to follow the joke but, when he got there, he laughed.

"Then, you really want to, *si*? I was afraid you would think I am… what, boring?"

"No, of course not," said Dan as Cesare led him through the first of many winding side streets and porticoed shortcuts. "Someone with no time for history would have a lousy holiday in Venice."

Besides, he thought to himself, it seemed pretty obvious that Cesare had planned this to cap off the day, and he wasn't about to wreck the gesture. Not to mention the fact that his feet would thank him for the time off.

THE CHURCH of Santa Maria Gloriosa dei Frari was, like a lot of Venice's churches, not beautiful in the fairy princess sense. Built mainly of Gothic red brick, with few ornaments to the exterior, it loomed over the surrounding streets like a frumpy bridesmaid at her skinnier, prettier sister's wedding.

Inside, however, the very quality of the air changed. The high altar, with its enormous, long windows, commanded the senses. The paintings pressed down from every wall, heavy with old, rich colors and deep shadows, while the wooden pews smelled strongly of beeswax and turpentine polish, each one gleaming dully with the sheen of an ancient patina. Footsteps echoed on the stone floor, and the whole place felt deeply sacred: not like a museum, but a place of living, breathing worship. The furniture polish smell mixed with that of fresh flowers and candle flames, with a hint of incense left over from Mass.

Dan had been brought up with a very vague Church of England Anglicanism. He was used to entering churches solely for weddings, christenings, funerals, and the occasional Boy Scout meeting, and the thick atmosphere started to make him feel uncomfortable. Cesare, on the other hand, seemed completely at home in the dim light, the flicker of candles, and the ambient hush of voices.

He smiled at Dan and led him to sit where a small audience was gathering, near one of the side chapels. It was all very informal, more like a school recital than a paid event, the distinction made only by a collection box that passed between the patrons. Dan, following Cesare's lead, tucked five euros in and passed the box along, watching a young woman cross the nave, whispering to a priest who presumably had something to do with the church. She wore a long velvet dress in a dark burgundy color almost the same as her heavy red lipstick. A black lace scarf was tied around her long dark curls, and she held a musical instrument that looked like a lute.

She moved to the front, a respectful distance away from the white-clothed altar, and rested one foot on something a little like a classical guitar stool. She took a deep, solemn breath and began to play. The lute-like thing made a melodious, smooth sound, winding up through the church in soaring, light arpeggios, sweet and full. When she started to sing, it was in a rich, round voice, a low contralto that made the hair on the back of Dan's neck and arms stand up. He couldn't understand the words, but that didn't matter. It was beautiful. He barely felt Cesare's hand touch his at first, but gradually he became aware of the weight of it gently grazing his.

Dan blinked, looking down stupidly at where his hand rested on the wooden arm of the pew. Cesare glanced at him in the dim light, a question in his eyes and his hand lightly caressing Dan's knuckles. Dan gave the merest quirk of a smile and squeezed his fingers.

It startled him that Cesare would do that here. If a church didn't count as a public place, Dan wasn't sure what did. He didn't allow himself to dwell on the question, though.

Whatever the reasons, it was good.

They listened as the young woman worked her way through a whole repertoire of Renaissance madrigals and beautiful songs, and applauded along with the rest of the audience when she finally finished.

Just like at a school recital, people milled around aimlessly in the church afterward. Cesare showed Dan the altarpiece, and in the warm glow of the candlelight, he understood at last how to look at those great big oil paintings from another age. Galleries had it all wrong; good lighting and air-conditioning weren't what you needed, rather the flicker of flames and the smells of beeswax and old wood. The colors gleamed like jewels on the clothes of the holy figures. Even Dan, who had never seen reason to bother God much since he must be so busy already, felt something strange leap in his chest. Not belief, but the wish for belief, the ache that wanted to pour trust and love into this kind of beauty. He turned to Cesare to ask about what the painting was really showing, and the look in his eyes as he gazed at the altarpiece was both fascinating and terrifying. Dan had never seen such complete conviction in anyone's face, such total… what? Awe? Respect? Love? Dan stayed quiet, and when they left, the cool night air hit him hard, leaving him feeling dizzy and vaguely nauseated.

He wasn't concentrating and didn't expect it when Cesare, having promised he knew a place where they could eat, led him into another cross street, away from the main walkway, and kissed him.

"What?" Dan broke the kiss, unprepared and confused.

"I'm sorry." Cesare stepped back from him, looking hurt. "I just wanted—"

"No, I… It's all right." Dan brushed his fingers down Cesare's arm, wishing he hadn't pushed him away but still feeling as if he was treading water in strange currents. "Where's this *osteria*, then?"

"*Vieni.*"

Cesare headed off again, cool and quiet in the night, showing no sign of upset. Dan followed, getting his head together. The *osteria* was a little gem: old-fashioned gingham tablecloths, full-bodied wines, big plates of hearty food, and a crackling radio playing a local station that churned out tinny Italian pop and rap music.

Dan felt better by the time Cesare had them settled at a table, food and wine ordered, their privacy guarded by the fact they sat at a corner table, away from the rest of the throng.

"It was an incredible performance," he said. "The concert. Thanks for taking me."

"My pleasure. I am glad you liked it."

They talked about music for a while, regaining some of the easy conversation that Dan was thinking of as usual between them. It emerged that, in this, as in films and books and a lot of other things, they had similar tastes, and Dan felt the void opening up before him again.

"Well," he said, taking a running jump toward it, "I've never enjoyed church more than tonight, anyway. D'you—I mean, Italy's obviously a very Catholic country—d'you go to church?"

"*Naturalmente.*" Cesare twirled his fork expertly in his tagliatelle. "It is very important to me."

"So, you consider yourself a Catholic?" Dan tried, feeling his way around the edge of the question he wanted to ask as if trying to find out whether a particular part of an unfamiliar beach was quicksand. "Despite… no. You consider yourself a Catholic *as well as* being gay?"

Damn, he thought, seeing Cesare wince ever so slightly at the word. That riled Dan, but he resisted the urge to make a big deal out of it. The man had been clear from the start about not exactly being a Pride-march poster boy.

"*Sì.*"

Cesare devoted his attention to his plate once again, and Dan thought the conversation was closed until Cesare's gaze slid back up to meet his.

"The church has been wrong about a lot of things, Daniel. Ah, what do you…? *Sì*. Birth control. Holy wars. Burning heretics… is not new. Yes, what they say is wrong. I believe that. But I don't believe that makes the church itself wrong. I am a Catholic—I go to Mass, I make Confession, I try to live my life well. But I don't believe that loving the church… loving God… means I must suffer for being who I am. I have no argument with God, no great pain I bear." He smiled. "If it is with anyone, then it is with other people. But people—even priests—are not all of the church. Do you see, Daniel?"

Dan chewed thoughtfully, grappling with the idea. After a moment he nodded.

"You can be both in the eyes of God. Okay. But not in front of other people?"

He'd overstepped the mark, he was sure. He fully expected to be shouted at, sworn at—at least for Cesare to say something sarcastic. Cesare looked at him for a long time, his expression unreadable. After a while the tightness around his mouth gave way to a small smile, and his eyes softened.

"Ah," he said, pointing at Dan with his fork. "I see, Daniel. You... you want to know why? Why I hide in the... *come si dice*? Closet."

"I'm not being accusing," Dan said hurriedly, not believing it himself but not sorry for bringing the question up. "Or judgmental. I just wondered... if you don't mind talking about it."

Cesare gave a little unishoulder shrug as he addressed the rest of his tagliatelle.

"Do you?" Dan prompted.

"No. No, I don't mind." Cesare laid his fork down, noting with apparent amusement that Dan, less adept with long, complicated types of pasta, was still struggling with his. "It is simple, I think. I make a choice."

"Choice?" Dan frowned. "To hide? You used the word," he added quickly.

"A choice," Cesare corrected, "not to make trouble. I have lived in Lunigiana all my life, and it is not an open place. Tradition, *famiglia*, church... all those things. I love those things, but... I also knew how I was different. When I went away to school, to do my training for teaching, I met another boy, the same as me. *Era bello...* we had a nice time, but it was over soon. When I came back, I was busy with work, with studies...."

He gave a small, implacable shrug, silencing all the things that danced on the tip of Dan's tongue.

"I knew what I wanted was not what was expected of me. Not a marriage to a nice girl and a house in the village... but there was no one in my life, no one nearby the same, so it seemed useless to complain. Once or twice, I thought about it, but they were different times, Daniel. Harder times. It was a risk and then, of course, I started to work at the *scuola*."

Cesare took a long swallow of wine, his face clouding.

"Italia is not a forgiving country. Especially places like Lunigiana. It still happen sometime... a man who work with children, especially. Somehow his name will come in the papers, and boom! There is a problem. He loses his job, his reputation... just because of dirty whispers. Nothing true."

Dan's heart dropped. He remembered that not a year before, a gay head teacher at a London school being subjected to a whispering campaign by bigoted parents. The man had resigned rather than face being dragged through the right-wing elements of the press. Accusations always flew: less often pedophilia, these days, than some trumped-up story about public indecency, or the implication that, because a man was queer, his whole life must be bound up with alcohol, anonymous sex, and hardcore drug abuse. Everyone knew half a dozen similar stories.

Even Chris, who was going to laugh so loudly when Dan told him about this trip, had once been reprimanded by a very stern flight attendant for being "indecent" on a late-night flight into Heathrow. He'd fallen asleep with his head on his then-boyfriend's shoulder and, as he'd said at the time, "If she thought *that* was indecent, the poor girl needed to start getting out more."

"I didn't want that," Cesare was saying, "for me, or *mi famiglia*. There was Tito, of course... I told you about him. It convinced me, for a while, that I was right... I made myself believe it, because I was scared. I came to think that I didn't need somebody, that my life was full enough. And, of course, the Internet is a wonderful thing."

He offered to refill Dan's glass but Dan declined, still a little cross somehow. It wasn't his place to push Cesare, he knew, and he understood the reality they were talking about, but he still prickled defensively. Cesare's fears seemed to belong—*should* have belonged—to the past. Dan wanted to believe that, wanted to give in to feeling irked by this perceived fear and self-sacrifice, because it shouldn't have been necessary anymore. That wasn't Cesare's fault, of course, and maybe it was stupid to feel angry at him, but Dan still struggled with it... struggled with the existence of everything it made him think about, perhaps.

Cesare emptied the last of the bottle into his own glass and stared mournfully at the ruby liquid. He smiled, a small twist of his lips, wry and humorless.

"It is not that I stayed frightened, Daniel. Do not think that. I made my decision, you know… I was so, so tired of it all. I wanted to change, to say, this is me. But, Massa-Carrara is a very traditional province, and Lunigiana is a traditional, country area. I never thought that *mi famiglia* would stop loving me, you see—not for a minute. Mamma would still love me. She is a *donna italiana*. You would have to cut out her heart and bury it before she can no love her *bambino*, eh? Even if he hurts her. Papà… he would be ashamed, disgusted, perhaps. They are older, they think a different way." He shrugged. "My brother Gianni would not like it. He is very… traditional, maybe you would say. Also, he is not married yet, and everyone would start complaining only to him to marry, instead of both of us."

He smiled again, more genuine now, perhaps seeing humor in something to which Dan was blind.

"They love me," Cesare repeated, "and I have never stopped loving them. So, unless there was a good reason, I did not want to make a big announcement, and have people give Mamma bad looks every time she go to the stores, have Father Morassutti come to the house to talk to her because her son is the *frocio del paese*."

He wasn't looking at Dan anymore. His fingers played up and down the stem of the wineglass moodily, a frown creasing his brow.

"It is not fair, I know. But, I made my choice, not to hurt her… not to hurt Papà, my brothers and—" Cesare's voice thinned a little. "—Eugenia, my sister. Not to give them more to worry for me, when, because there was no one in my life, it did not seem… *come si dice*? Not worth the discussion. I think, eh, what does it matter? I tell myself again, and again, it does not matter if there is never someone, though that… no, I never quite believe that."

Cesare gave a short, mirthless laugh, and it hurt Dan beyond words to see that his eyes were wet. He blinked hurriedly.

"Then, it is almost now two years ago, Eugenia…. She was coming back from her holiday, with her husband and their *bambina*, little Elisa. She was only two—a little angel—and the car crashed on the autostrada."

Dan couldn't stop the images that formed behind his eyes, the terrible imaginings of how it must have been.

"They cut my sister from the wreckage," Cesare said, his voice flat and careful, "and it took her nine days to die. Tomaso, her husband, break his arm, his leg, and have bad… in his head, yes? Stunned…." He waved a hand vaguely, lost for the English word.

"Concussion," Dan supplemented, late and numb. He had his own collection of painful memories, echoes of which Cesare's story set into motion.

"*Sì?* Concussion. *Sì.*" Cesare drained his glass. "Elisa… she looked so small. So many machines, you know? She go the day after Eugenia. I was there, every day, in the *ospedale*… I thought it would kill Mamma. Papà try, but he couldn't be strong enough for her. I was." He lifted his chin a little, as if touched by some remembered pride. "I was strong, for them both. They needed me, and I was there. Gianni, he was working in San Marino, and Matteo, my other brother, he and his wife *e bambini* lived in Pisa then. Every day, I was there. I was there to take my parents home, and to arrange the funerals…. They needed me to be the son they wanted then. They still need me, although things are getting better. But… do you see, Daniel? I chose. And I chose for them, not for me."

He finished abruptly, his eyes dark and damp. Dan shook his head and touched Cesare's hand lightly where it lay, cold on the tabletop, and wanted so much to hold him. He was surprised, even shocked, when Cesare gripped his fingers back, holding his hand and giving him a weak smile across the table. Dan was confused; he understood the gesture's importance, but not quite what it meant, coming after that revelation.

They ate the rest of the meal quietly, conversation kept carefully light and neutral. Cesare insisted on paying the bill, and Dan let him without putting up quite all of the argument he'd wanted to. Afterward, as they walked through the dim loggia and toward the lamplit Canale, glittering in the dark like a jeweled snake, Cesare leaned close to him and kissed his cheek. Dan exhaled softly, so full of good food, good wine, and the comfortable companionship of this man, that he was already walking on air. His hand sought Cesare's, and for a little while they walked like that together. People passed by, oblivious, and when Dan and Cesare stopped to gaze down at the water from a little balustraded stone bridge, Dan rested his head on Cesare's shoulder.

"Come back with me tonight?" Dan asked, his words soft in the night air.

Cesare seemed to shiver lightly beside him. "Yes… of course."
"Good."

CESARE STOOD by the window. The maid had left it open, and now the sharpness of the night air played across his skin, the temperature of the room cool enough to raise gooseflesh. Venice twinkled away into the distance, a thousand tiny lights in the dark, and a collage of sounds drifted up from the piazza. Music, overlapping and tinny with distance, the laughter of dozens of different voices, the ever-present tang of salt on the breeze… he'd remember them all, as part of this moment.

He looked up with vague surprise at the sound of the door clicking shut. Daniel leaned against it, his palms flat to the wood behind him, a wolflike smile on his face. Somehow, Cesare still couldn't believe he was here, couldn't *expect* to see him when he turned around. He supposed something of that showed in his face, because Daniel crossed the room and kissed him, laughter bubbling out of him like the joy of giving an unsought present.

Cesare kissed him back—deeper, harder—his fingers coming to cup Daniel's face, slip up through his hair, and skim the side of his neck. Daniel exhaled as they parted, somewhere between a sigh and a chuckle. Cesare's hand slid under Daniel's shirt, caressing the warm flesh of his abdomen. The infinite possibilities of bodies spread themselves out into the future, made frustrating by the knowledge that they also had their limits, and that—right now—there was also the limit of the night. Cesare felt the urge to rail against time and space because he couldn't do everything, he couldn't live forever, and he knew that there was, even with this man, only one life and one chance.

"It's cold," he whispered, his voice thick and husky. "How big is your shower?"

Daniel looked stunned, apparently thinking for a moment.

"Um. Uh, yeah, right…. Definitely. This way."

Cesare couldn't have imagined that it would feel so good, standing under the jets of hot water, the conjunction of soap and bodies. He suspected he was too gentle, barely more than tickling Daniel, and steering away from all the places that really did need washing: his shyness precluded that. Even so, Cesare enjoyed it. His *uomo bellissimo* looked impossibly sexy with water running off his nose, eyelashes, and chin, coursing down his cheeks and plastering his hair to his skin.

In return, Daniel washed him, traced every contour and valley of his body, surprising him with lips, tongue, and fingers. He got to his knees and, crouching awkwardly in the cramped stall, addressed Cesare's stiffening cock. He moaned as Daniel's tongue slid up his inner thigh, almost losing his balance on the slippery tiles, and before anything had really begun, it became obvious that it would have to continue somewhere safer. They rinsed down and got out of the shower, wrapping themselves first in fluffy hotel towels and then each other, collapsing on the bed in the clammy heat of still-damp skin and impatient lust.

Daniel took Cesare in his mouth again, deeper than before, and seemed to relish the way Cesare's thighs trembled as he tried to hold back. The heat of embarrassment rose briefly to Cesare's face; what this man could do to him! He clung on to the headboard for support when Daniel made him kneel on the bed, not understanding until Daniel slipped beneath him and took his cock down to the root, encasing him fully in the wet warmth of his mouth. Cesare gasped and tried to pull back; Daniel had guessed the intensity of how his climax was building, inevitable and uncontrollable, and that made him vulnerable.

He closed his eyes, unable to watch as Daniel sucked the life and the soul from him, barely feeling the hands on his lower back, supporting him as he slipped back onto the mattress.

"One day," he murmured from somewhere within the pillows' incredible softness, "I will learn to do that."

"How about tomorrow?" Daniel teased, leaning in to kiss him.

After a few minutes, Cesare drew the covers up over them. Daniel shifted his weight a little, angling his body so that Cesare could play with his nipples. Cesare bent his head to suck, nibble, and bite, his hand wandering to Daniel's crotch and his hard cock. He stroked and kissed, lost in the sensations and the patterns of their breathing, winding around each other in the dark cocoon. The room wasn't so chilly now, but it was nice to be beneath the covers together, private and intimate and warm. He could feel himself getting hard again already… what was it that this man did, to give him stamina he hadn't had since he was twenty-three? Cesare rubbed his cock alongside Daniel's, gasping with the feeling of pressing their most intimate, most sensitive parts together, wishing that somehow they could just be one. One cock, one ass, one mouth.

Feeling both, loving both… a kind of conjoined pleasure, Cesare thought, stupidly aware of how ridiculous the idea was. A moment later, Daniel gave a soft moan and came on his stomach. Cesare held him, sticky and delighted, so completely content that he was convinced that if he fell asleep, he would never wake again.

CHAPTER EIGHT

DAN TWISTED in his sleep, a full bladder pushing him reluctantly toward wakefulness. He gave a small, contented sigh, aware of the warmth of skin around and beneath him. As he opened his eyes in the gloom, he realized that his head rested on Cesare's chest.

He lay still, not breathing, disinclined to move. Cesare's arm was around him. He felt good and smelled of musk and spice and sex, product of their panting night. Small cramps and deadened places twinged in Dan's right arm. It lay across Cesare's waist, his fingers curling reflexively where they brushed the sculpted hollow of his lower back.

Cesare stirred a little, his lips barely moving as he mumbled something into Dan's hair. Their legs were entwined, and the needle pains of more cramps gnawed at Dan. He tried to move, sending Cesare shifting and mumbling in protest, and so Dan stopped and waited for him to settle again. He let his fingers stroke the broad expanse of Cesare's back, turning his head just enough to watch his face. He looked so comfortable, so peaceful, so… right. The thought laid icy fingers on Dan's throat, and suddenly he felt deceitful, as if he was trying to steal something that he couldn't, he mustn't take from Cesare. Not now. Not here.

Carefully he pulled himself from the bed, brushing his fingers over Cesare's arm as he went to the bathroom. Not bothering to turn on the light, Dan groped his way through some brief ablutions by the dim moonlight that seeped through the curtains. He pissed, then sluiced his face with warm water, squidged some toothpaste onto his finger and pushed it around his mouth, swishing minty foam into the crevices, trying to remove the tastes of sleep and discomfort.

Cesare stirred, reaching out across the mattress. His hand met the warm pillow and the rumpled sheet but no skin, and Dan watched as Cesare blinked and then raised himself up on one elbow. He seemed suddenly alert and, yes, even afraid, until he registered Dan's presence by the bathroom door. Cesare smiled sleepily at him and Dan's heart swelled.

"Hi," he said, padding back to the bed.

"*Ciao, bello.*"

Cesare reached out his hand and Dan took it as if accepting the first dance. It surprised him when Cesare sat up, pulled him close, and kissed him, slow and thorough. Dan knelt astride his lap, his arms around Cesare's neck as those strong, elegant hands cupped his face. Cesare moaned softly into his mouth, fingers now sliding through Dan's hair, tongue silky, insistent and enduring. They broke as Dan was growing breathless, but didn't part, Cesare exploring the planes and angles of his face: the hardness of cheekbones and jawline, the roughness of stubble, the yielding warmth of cheeks and lips, the corded flesh of his neck, the intricate, sensitive whorls of his ears.

"*Ho tanto bisogno di te, caro,*" Cesare whispered, letting the slick nub of Dan's earlobe slide from his lips. "I want you so… you feel what you do to me?"

"Mmm." Dan squeezed Cesare's firm waist with his knees. "Yes. I feel it. And I want it. Fuck me?"

Cesare looked surprised.

"You want…?"

"Yes. Do you mind?"

In answer, Dan felt Cesare's hands on his spine, hips, cock, butt, stomach… and his mind was nothing, blank and burning except for the feel of those lips and fingers.

"Oh, God… enough," he said at last. "Lay back. I want to see your face."

He should have known that would be a mistake. Cesare obeyed, letting Dan lean across him for the condoms and lube on the nightstand. He closed his eyes, biting his lip and holding back. Cesare growled as Dan slid the condom onto his full, straining cock.

Dan breathed deeply, rubbing himself over Cesare's hardness, focusing on his own arousal, trying to ignore Cesare's rough gasps, his fingers clenching at the sheets as Dan took him, so slowly, with such control. When Cesare cried out, Dan knew it was because he could feel himself completely enveloped, fully embedded in a tight, hot embrace, his cock dancing like a live thing. Sure enough, Cesare's shaft swelled within him, hard and throbbing.

Dan worked his hips slowly, undulating with leisurely precision, accepting the erratic bucking of Cesare's body, guiding them both into a steady rhythm.

"Shh… that's it," he murmured, fingers trailing over Cesare's ribs. "Like that. That feels good, doesn't it?"

Cesare whimpered. "Oh, *così! Così, dai…. Daniel, sei tanto bello! Non fermarti, è meraviglioso.* You move like…. Is like waves…."

Dan stroked his cock as Cesare writhed beneath him, loving what he could do to this man, loving the way he felt, the way he looked and sounded, the eroticism of that accent, those words, playing his nerves like bowstrings. Cesare's fingers caught at Dan's body as he rode him, dark eyes wide and imploring.

"You like that? Yes," Dan hissed mischievously, wanting to see how far he could push Cesare, half wanting him to push back, to obliterate himself in someone else's complete loss of control. "I know you do. I do…. So good. C'mon… fuck me harder with this big cock of yours… that's it. I know you need to. Want to. More… oh, God!"

Dan cried out, throwing his head back. Cesare had pushed himself up, steadying himself with a hand on Dan's shoulder and the other braced against the bedpost, and sweating and panting, drove up with shorter, harder strokes.

"Don't stop… anything, just don't… oh," Dan murmured hoarsely.

Cesare's hand covered his, a blur on his cock, taking him further than he ever could himself, until he broke into a million pieces.

CESARE JUST concentrated on trying not to yell. All he could see was that body, the toned litheness of a runner, the way the muscles flexed in Daniel's hips, his thighs, his belly, as he did… *that*… his long fingers curled around the burnished serpent of his cock, hard and glistening like the idols of Priapus, the old Roman god.

He didn't blink, didn't take his eyes from Daniel's face, burning into his memory every detail as that perfect mouth opened and closed, a frown of concentration appearing on his brow.

At the peak of it, Cesare stopped breathing, though his lungs screamed for air. Daniel's body clenched his cock so tightly he feared it would be cut off, and it took every ounce of his self-control to keep going, keep moving as Daniel exploded around him in sighing, swearing bliss. Cesare marveled at him, his power, his wildness, the intensity of his enjoyment… almost not noticing his own slow, painful climax as it crept up on him, tipping him over the brink he had been clinging to, a dark star of needlelike pleasure that held him like a vise.

They stayed locked together for a few moments, both trying to breathe, to swim back through the fog to some kind of reality. Cesare gasped for air, his burning forehead resting on Daniel's neck, his chest and stomach branded, sticky but proud.

"*Angelo mio*," he whispered, wincing as he slid his tender, shrinking flesh from Dan and slipped off the condom. "*Era incredibile. I have never.... Le tue mani sono dolci. Sei bellissimo.*"

Daniel gave him a bleary smile. "S'not half-bad, eh?"

"*Sì*," Cesare murmured, still breathless.

There were more words he wanted to say, that he was about to say, but he stopped himself just in time because in the dark hotel room, he knew they were cheap.

THE DAWN came late, stealing over them as they slept. Dan woke first, aware of a coolness in the air, a draft from the open window. Cesare stirred a little as he got up, rolling over to usurp more of the covers. Dan smiled and went to the bathroom.

He stared at his reflection as he shaved, considering how and when things would end. They would have to. That was awful, uncomfortable knowledge, but it was true. He either had to break it off now, suggest that they see no more of each other, or carry on writing, speaking to Cesare once he got home, a kind of acquired pen pal with extra baggage. That was fine, but it would leave them both with reminders of these times, memories constantly touched and constantly resurfacing, and he worried that Cesare would be badly affected by that. Dan kept thinking of their meal at the *osteria*, after the concert, and of the story of Cesare's sister, his baby niece, and what he had given up to be there for his family.

Back home, Dan would have dismissed him as a self-made martyr, talked about it with Chris or Edith and probably even have made unkind jokes. He'd have rolled his eyes, had Cesare been English, and said how awful it was to have to put up with his drama queen performance for the price of dinner. Dan had endured enough bad dates to know how to make a good monologue out of one, but here, things were different. The actions and the lives of London were not those of... where was it? Pontremoli. What he saw when he looked at Cesare was not a masochistic wannabe, a gay martyr, but a man genuinely suffering, and not just on account of his sexuality. That was a sobering thought.

It reminded Dan vaguely of a girl he'd been at school with when he was around eight years old. She'd had a small, tight, pinched face, greasy brown hair, and baggy clothes, and he couldn't remember if he'd ever even known her name. She was quiet and faded into the background most of the time, until one of the invariable schoolyard bullies pushed her too far and she'd snapped, and in a whirlwind of red-faced fury and spite, kicked the bigger boy so hard she'd dislocated his knee. After that she faded back into the background, and Dan couldn't remember a thing about her except that a year or so later, there had been a special announcement made by their teacher to the rest of the class, telling them they had to be especially nice to… whatever her name had been… because her mother had just died.

This had amazed the other kids, who'd never known she had a mother. They'd never seen her, never heard… the girl… speak of her. They'd never really heard her speak at all, come to that. Eventually it had become common knowledge on the playground that the girl's mother had been housebound. Motor neurone disease, they were told. The family couldn't afford a mobility vehicle or adapted car good enough for her to attend the various school fetes, fairs, and events, so she'd stayed away. There was no father; a nurse came in to help, and there was the girl's grandmother, who moved in when things got really bad. The other kids had all listened to this, pronounced with great wisdom from the lips of ten-year-old Steve Kinnear, who had known everything about everything as long as it wasn't schoolwork, and each one of them had felt a blistering welt of guilt inside themselves. Dan especially, as he remembered, because he knew what living through your parents' divorce was like, although he'd been tiny at the time it happened to him.

The worst of it was, in the cool morning light, Dan still couldn't remember her name, though she looked back at him from the mirror of memory, red-eyed and tearful. He couldn't remember, and even after he'd found out about her mother—and the years the girl must have spent going not to a home but a sickroom after school—he had made no great effort to be her friend. Those who care, he thought, those who choose their families, even when they think they have no choice, are forgotten. In turning from the opportunity to escape, they wreck their chances of being able to… and they may never have that chance again.

Something was welling in his chest for Cesare, and he hoped to God it wasn't pity.

The worst of it was, really, that he couldn't even begin to imagine how he would say good-bye.

IT RAINED again that day, which curtailed most of their walks around the city, and Dan felt less inclined to suggest holing up in the hotel room with nothing but some spare towels and a bottle of champagne. They went out for breakfast. Again, he thought that Cesare was afraid to be seen with him in the somehow official setting of a hotel; outside, in the city, in the labyrinth of Venice's ancient and ever-growing heart, they were anonymous. He tried not to let it bother him and didn't even think about raising the subject with Cesare, but once or twice Dan caught himself feeling a few pangs of irritation.

Cesare mentioned, over the first proper coffee of the day, the Querini Stampalia and its modern art foundation, off the Campo Santa Maria Formosa. Dan said he hadn't been and that settled the morning. It was wonderful, but how easy it was to spend time with Cesare was worrying Dan… not that he'd had plans, of course. The whole point of the vacation was to take time out, to breathe easy and go with the flow.

The Querini Stampalia had exhibitions of modern art on the upper floor, a strange contrast to the sixteenth, seventeenth, and eighteenth century treasures below, but a refreshing one. Dan learned a lot about modern Italian art and thought and art, and even more about how widely read Cesare was for an elementary school teacher. Confronted with bright, abstract pieces that bent space and color before them, he talked fluidly and with unshakeable optimism about how the twenty-first century was going to be great for Italy: a new dawn, where being a more integral part of Europe would see an end to the poverty there had once been in the south, as well as the corruption that was, frankly, everywhere. A change in ideas, he said.

They had lunch in an *osteria* that might have managed to call itself rustic if it had been thirty miles or so outside of the city or even just on the mainland. As it was, it served rough red wine and relatively inexpensive food, for Rialto, and that was exactly what the stomach needed to escape the pervading, clammy damp of Venice in the rain. It didn't seem possible to Dan that his holiday was already more than half over.

"So," he said, apropos of little, "what are you doing when you get home?"

Cesare looked up from his *pastissada*, eyebrows raised. "Back to work, for me," he said with a smile. "The teacher only rest when the children take a vacanza, *sì*?"

"I thought they only got holidays just so you *could* take a break?"

Cesare grinned. "Ah, if only it was so…! No, we are worked—how do you say in English?—to the bone."

"Hmm." Dan tore off a hunk of crusty fresh bread and buttered it thickly. "In England, the thing teachers complain most about is the paperwork. Do you have a lot of that? Lots of administration you have to do?"

"*Sì*… there is always paperwork to do. Sometimes, more papers to take up my time than children, especially…." Cesare trailed off and shook his head. "No. You make me talk too much, Daniel."

"Especially what?" Dan prompted. "C'mon. Tell me."

Cesare's lip twitched, and his gaze dropped.

"There is one of the boys I teach. He is… autistic, yes? His name is Niccolò. Niccolò Misseri. There is so little I can do for him… even if I could maybe help, just a little, but I have always to be teaching to the other children, thinking of them. So much I cannot do because—so they say—is unfair to the others. So Niccolò has to suffer, all for the paperwork."

Dan watched the story—the anger at the injustice—spill out of him. It seemed very fitting that it should rile him that way. Something very… Cesare about it.

God, but he'd miss this when he got home. Dan dropped the thought like a hot bullet. He curled his mouth into a small smile instead.

"That isn't fair. But I bet you do everything you can."

Cesare chuckled mirthlessly.

"Do you know, Daniel, sometimes I don't think I do. I really don't."

After lunch, they meandered through the *campi* and *calli* that they'd frequented earlier in the week, with the vague idea of heading toward the Basilica della Salute and catching the waterbus back to San Marco. That kind of expedition, of course, took time. It amazed Dan that the places he thought he recognized, thought himself familiar with—Santa Maria Gloriosa dei Frari, San Polo, and even the Peggy Guggenheim Collection—held so many new sights and so many details he'd not noticed before.

Something about it felt wildly and deliciously circuitous. The white Baroque stucco of Santa Maria della Salute itself just added to that sensation:

an insane conglomeration of domes and pedimented arches with icing sugar statues and gold leaf, twinkling in the sun. Nothing seemed real, and it was maddening. Spectacular, breathtaking… and maddening.

It seemed only right that the *vaporetto* should deposit them back at San Marco, barely a few minutes' walk from where they'd started. Dusk had fallen; the customary tinny hubbub of the piazza spilled out into the streets. Dan hadn't realized it had grown so late.

The moon was up, heavy and yellow. Its pitted heart shone down on the cobbles, ironing out the unevenness of the night. It was ridiculously beautiful—sumptuous and romantic to the point of feeling staged and false. Cesare noticed it too. He grinned at Dan, nodded at the pale-washed *palazzi* across the canal.

"All this… is almost too much, eh?"

Dan nodded, a little afraid to speak. Cesare hung back, watching the water. Dan was glad of it; to touch him now, talk, or try to ask a question would have been awful. Even so, he couldn't remember wanting anything as much as the promise of taking Cesare back to his hotel tonight. The sooner the better. He didn't care if he did turn out to be digging his own grave, getting himself in deeper every time he touched the guy. There would be plenty of opportunities to worry about that when Dan got… home.

He tried to leave that thought outside in the chilly night air, where it belonged, and let the doors slam behind them on their way up to his hotel room. He didn't want to think about it, didn't want to admit to it, and, damn it, he intended to ignore the whole deal for all he was worth.

Dan would have liked to have made it last that night. The thought of stretching every moment of it out into an eternity of brink-teetering, tooth-shattering bliss held a certain appeal… but it wasn't to be. Cesare got all caught up in that incredibly appealing coyness of his, the sea mist wound around them like a silken tie, and it was all either of them could do to get upstairs before the earth cracked open and swallowed them both.

Even so, Dan wanted there to be something special. Something Cesare could remember him by. He backed Cesare up to the patchy velour armchair by the window and pushed him gently until he folded into the upholstery, his breath rough in his throat. Swift and wordless, Dan knelt in front of him and pulled open his fly. He made each action determined and purposeful, just bordering on a little rough.

Cesare leaned back in the chair; lust and uncertainty jostled for space in his eyes, his breathing short and tense as he lifted his hips. Dan grinned wickedly as he slid those crumpled beige pants down, letting them settle at Cesare's ankles, and pushed his thighs apart. His white underpants still constrained the weight of his cock, its hardness already visible, a tempting outline through the thin cotton. Dan lowered his head and skated his mouth close to Cesare's skin—not quite close enough—so the heat of his breath just grazed the sensitive strips of his thighs. He worked his way up at a leisurely pace, pleased that Cesare seemed to understand the game. He stayed quiet too, nothing but half-choked gasps and little fidgets against the velour.

Dan paused for some unkind torture at the juncture of Cesare's leg and groin, teasing the flesh and laving the smooth, tight expanse of cotton. He moved his mouth across the fabric, his tongue a hot trail, the weave rough against it the harder he pressed. Cesare shifted and whimpered, his cock responding to Dan's attentions so much that the jockeys must have begun to pinch. Dan shaped his mouth around the thickened silhouette of the shaft, running up and down it over and over until Cesare squirmed.

His underwear had grown damp and taut, and Dan enjoyed the sight of him writhing against it, half-dressed and half–out of his head. He fought the urge to yank the fabric down and finish the job properly and, instead, pulled off and backed away. His own pulse climbed, and the mixed flavors of Cesare—that blend of salt, musk, and a slight hint of soap—and the astringent, dry taste of the cotton filled his mouth. Those clear brown eyes held his as Dan reached down and lifted the hem of his T-shirt, raising it slowly.

"Don't touch," he said, seeing Cesare's hand move instinctively to his crotch.

Uttering the first words either of them had spoken since the door shut behind them, his voice seemed loud in the room, echoing back over the busy sounds of the night that floated up to the window from the piazza below.

Dan pulled off his shirt, tossed it aside, and let his hands drop to his fly.

CESARE SHIVERED in the cool air. It felt, somehow, so incredibly dirty to sit here like this, half-naked and fully exposed. He watched as Daniel swiftly shed his clothes in a swirl of cloth and fluid skin, and admired the way he moved, the decisive, quick work of fingers on buttons, the soft rustle of cotton on skin... all the while transfixed by the look on his face. Once he'd stripped completely naked, Daniel knelt back down before him. Those blue eyes never left Cesare's, that devilish mouth curled into a half smile.

Silent promises choked the air. Cesare gripped the arms of the chair so hard his knuckles whitened. He couldn't remember ever being this hard before. Perhaps it only seemed that way because his underwear still compressed him so. He shifted against the pinch of it, and he knew it amused Daniel by the way his smile broadened and the way he caught his bottom lip between his teeth.

Still, neither of them spoke. Mixed snatches of music and laughter, the tangled noises of San Marco, coiled past the window. Daniel touched the uncovered band of his thighs, brushed his fingers up toward Cesare's aching cock. He ran his thumb beneath the elastic of Cesare's underwear, no longer teasing as badly. Cesare caught his breath as Daniel eased the fabric down so unbearably, gloriously slowly and let his hard, moist flesh find its way into the cool air. Cesare watched, entranced: his *uccello* stood out, proud and demanding. It wavered a little, as if unsure what to do next... seeming so out of place, so conspicuous against the white tails of his shirt.

His breath grazed his lungs; each second seemed to take such a long time to pass. Then Daniel leaned forward and just snatched the fat head of Cesare's cock into his mouth, like some favorite treat, some hard-won prize. Cesare inhaled sharply and bit down on the expletives that bubbled behind his lips. The silence intensified things between them; free from the distractions of words, the picture they made stayed imprinted behind his eyes. His clothed body against Daniel's terrible, powerful nakedness. Not the way things usually worked, Cesare had to admit, but then so much about this man had turned him upside down.

He almost cried out when Daniel's mouth moved down to his balls, all hot breath and wet heat as his hand stroked Cesare's shaft. All too soon, he moved on again. Cesare protested with a soft moan, stifled as the hot grip of Daniel's mouth swallowed him up again, plundering and taking such control of him he couldn't believe he'd ever be his own master again. Cesare knew he'd lost all ability for self-discipline when Daniel changed his rhythm, long slow strokes up the underside of his shaft, and he thrust his hips uselessly, pathetically, against the air, nothing but a beggar under Daniel's touch.

Cesare held his breath when Daniel pulled away for the second time, determined to maintain some semblance of control. Daniel rose to his feet, nude body sculpted by the soft yellow light that fell on his left side from the open window. He looked at Cesare and smiled. Wordlessly, he dipped his hand back into the pocket of his discarded jeans and withdrew lube and a condom, the latter of which he threw to Cesare. Cesare struggled with it for awkward seconds, distracted by the sight of Daniel lubing himself, then by the touch of his hand, cold and wet, helping him with the sheath, then smearing the gel onto his rubber-clad cock. Daniel climbed up onto him, his feet sinking into the very edges of the chair, sliding down behind the cushions as Cesare's hands supported his thighs.

Cesare gritted his teeth as Daniel sank down onto him, feeling himself gripped and welcomed at the same time, feeling Daniel's body adjust around him. Daniel breathed slowly, his lips pursed as he seemingly waited for the soreness to ease. He crossed his wrists behind Cesare's head and leaned forward to kiss him, just the briefest press of lips. As Cesare's cock twitched in him, Daniel began to move, so slowly at first, raising himself up, then rolling forward, down, taking him further with each stroke. Cesare gasped and moaned as Daniel rocked against his pelvis, taking him deep and not letting him go, each movement the crashing of a wave on rocks, claiming more of him.

Cesare's hands tracked the muscles of Daniel's butt, back, and thighs, moving with rhythmic precision. Their breath mingled, both tasting salt and sweat in the hot space between them as the minutes stretched out. Cesare's fingertips skimmed never-ending bare skin, while the rumpled pants and underwear at his feet and the suit jacket and shirt he still wore all felt heavy and clammy, and yet made an oddly pleasing contrast. His hand closed around Daniel's cock, only slightly hard, but heavy and exciting. To feel this man naked against him while he was still partly dressed made him believe he was the one in control, the one with the power... even though each movement of Daniel's hips reminded Cesare that he was completely at the mercy of his body. He growled deep in his throat as Daniel bounced up and down in his lap, riding him harder and faster, breathing hard, his head tilted back, eyes half-closed as Cesare stroked him.

Cesare reached up his free hand to stroke Daniel's jaw, fingers resting instead on the solid curve of his shoulder, somehow resisting the intimacy. The chair creaked beneath them, the room otherwise silent but for the noise of their bodies smacking together and their harsh breathing. He watched Daniel's face, thinking for a moment of how it would be to fuck him a different way, perhaps on his hands and knees, taking all the responsibility, all the control. His thighs trembled as, with a groan of pleasure, Daniel sank back down onto his cock as deep as he could go, working his ass in tight circles, back and forth. Cesare doubted he would be able to hold back no matter what way they fucked, and he whimpered, wriggling in the armchair. Dan's cock continued to thicken in his hand as he stroked it, mesmerized by the dark, glistening head pouting toward him, wet and beckoning.

He wanted to speak but as he watched the pleasure building on Daniel's face, the beads of sweat on his forehead, and the dark red flush along his cheekbones, the words wouldn't come. Cesare pressed himself back against the chair, bracing himself for the climax that he knew would enfold him whether he was ready or not, and tugged harder at Daniel's cock, his free hand trailing down to touch his chest and rub his nipples. His fingers brushed against the roughly scattered curls of hair on Daniel's pecs. Cesare still struggled to believe he'd found him. He bit back another moan, proud of how quiet he'd stayed, how well he'd risen to the unspoken challenge between them. It wouldn't last, though. The orgasm seemed to start from the very center of him, some place he couldn't even identify, dragged up through the pit of his stomach and out through his cock, burning everywhere inside him along the way. As he screwed up his eyes and tried not to yell, Cesare was dimly aware that he wasn't alone.

"Please," Cesare choked out in a strangled whisper, though he couldn't have said what he pleaded for.

Daniel clamped down hard on him, still moving, head flung back, his hand covering Cesare's as his cock jerked and spat, making a mess of the shirt and jacket already damp with both their sweat.

"Fuck, yes! Oh, God…. Fuck!" Daniel cried, strained and panting. His head lolled back to center, and he fixed Cesare with a bleary, half-focused gaze and a self-satisfied smile.

It filled Cesare with a mad, ridiculous sense of power: the strength of what they'd done built-up and shining in him. He palmed his hands up

Daniel's back, lost in the feel of him, the sound of their breathing—still harsh and fast, though it seemed mismatched and louder than ever against the quiet of the room. Cesare's gaze flicked over Daniel's face. Those beautiful blue eyes were closed now, his face flushed and damp, the only expression one of postcoital calm. Cesare leaned forward, careful of the junction of their sensitive parts, and kissed him gently on the cheek.

Daniel nuzzled against him, his skin cooling and clammy, bringing their mouths together.

"I'm sorry," he murmured, as they parted, his fingers tracing the outer edge of Cesare's ear. "I've made a bit of a mess of you."

"*Sì?*" Cesare looked down at his shirt and jacket, and shrugged. "*Niente.* But… I think, at some time, we will have to move."

"Hmm. You could be right."

Carefully, Daniel stood, wincing. He clambered off the chair as Cesare removed the condom, both men trying to avoid each other's gaze. Things seemed more awkward now than they had been before, and Cesare didn't like it. Anxiety rippled through him; had he done something wrong?

His chest tightened with worry. He must have done. The way he'd touched Daniel, looked at him… he'd shown something unspeakable, some fool's hope for an unwise, irrational want. If not that, then it was the waning of a glutted desire. Cesare shuddered at the thought. Was he hideous now to Daniel? The dregs of a banquet once enticing, but one that now turned the stomach—he couldn't bear that idea. Not when Daniel still so effortlessly held his attention with his lithe, easy movement and his devastatingly unpretentious looks, and not with the imprint of his warmth still achingly fresh on Cesare's skin. Not when, with every moment that passed between them, Cesare felt himself more inescapably captured.

Those thoughts snared him like cobwebs, sticky and suffocating. He wished he could sweep them away, but they had so much more weight than normal dreams, and he doubted they would ever fade. No, this whole week would be with him forever.

And maybe that wasn't really so bad.

CHAPTER NINE

ONLY TWO days left.

Dan couldn't shape his mind around those words when he woke. They felt unreal and ridiculous, like fragments of a clouded memory, and they didn't become any more solid as the day wore on. Cesare took him on a boat trip across the Laguna, a paid tour of more strange nooks and crannies the city had hidden away.

He made it impossibly easy to lose hours in his company, and they talked more than it left Dan feeling safe to do. He'd wondered about that when Cesare spilled the story about his sister, all the pain and remorse and the things that bound him to a life he hadn't exactly chosen. At the time Dan had been caught up in it, in Cesare's strange double standards and personal strife. Later, once it had all sunk in, he'd realized what Cesare had done.

He'd changed everything.

It wasn't—it couldn't be—the same now. Dan couldn't help but think of him as a fully three-dimensional person instead of a memory in the making. Utter insanity. He'd known Cesare all of a few days. A fuck. A holiday fling, that's all it would ever be, so there wasn't any sense in getting stupid ideas that couldn't be fulfilled.

Yet, he knew when Cesare looked at him with those wonderfully clear, calm brown eyes and asked if he'd write, that he would. They would stay in touch. And that wasn't a bad thing, it really wasn't… only, as the boat tour spun out the hours and the afternoon sun splintered off the lagoon, Dan knew he'd always be squeezing himself against the sharp edges of wanting more. Had it not been for the beauty of the place and the freshness of the salt air, he'd have resented Cesare for it, turned grumpy and withdrawn and backed away from him, angry with himself and too eager to lash out at others.

As it was, Dan sighed deeply and watched the rippling waves tug at the shore.

He went back to Cesare's room that night, disinclined to invite him into his hotel, however pointless and overdue that show of resistance might have been. An autumnal coolness lagged between them: the sort of glassy, decaying warmth that pervades October sunshine. Every touch seemed laced with sadness.

Nevertheless, as Cesare kissed him by the open window of his hotel room that night, the lights glittering outside in the darkness and the sound of the canal lapping gently far beneath them, Dan couldn't regret any of it.

He stroked his fingers through Cesare's hair, savoring the taste and the scent of him. It was so easy to lean closer, let the warmth of that familiar body erode his resistance… allow everything to fade away except this moment, this man.

A week of being all over each other the way they had been should have served to numb the want, or at least start to deaden the desire they had for each other, but it didn't seem to work like that. Just a few hours in Cesare's company seemed to be enough to get Dan going, as if all the time they spent together was some protracted form of foreplay, just like it had been that first day.

The time had passed in amber, suspended and unreal, and he tried to tell himself the intimacy that existed between them wasn't anything more than that either. False. Misleading… untrue. A familiarity that lasted only as long as his traveler's checks.

He could have believed it too, if Cesare hadn't chosen that night— that last night—to lie on the bed, all warm skin and tousled hair on a sheet as white as an altar cloth despite the abuses it had already suffered, and give him the biggest gift he could think of.

They didn't talk about it, but Dan knew what it meant.

Those perfect hands shook as Cesare spread the pale globes of his ass. His face buried in the pillows, his voice barely more than a whisper, he'd begged to be taken. Dan had obliged, believing he wanted it, that the booze had loosened him up, or that the long hours in the sun and the salt air gave him the right, the ability, to take what Cesare said at face value. He had pretended it was that simple for him too, and he'd known he was cheating himself even then.

The desire died in Dan as he pushed into a tense, unresponsive body. Not a virgin, he realized, but a man used to being fucked far more for his partner's pleasure than his own. It worried him, and he went as gently as he could, expecting the terrible awkwardness of trying to finish the job before losing his hard-on, but Cesare was so open, so vulnerable, and gave him so much. With time and gentle encouragement, he started to relax, melting into the mattress and praising Dan's prowess. In the night's velvet clasp, Dan came, riding deep inside a wave of protective tenderness that confused and disoriented him.

Afterward they lay side by side on the bed, studied the cracks in the ceiling, and tried to ignore the weight of the knowledge that rested between them: that had been the last time.

Dan shot a look at Cesare, his slouching eyes and rumpled hair, the satisfied smile that curled his mouth even at rest…. The desire to touch, to just feel the companionable warmth of holding his body, alarmed Dan. Ordinarily it wasn't something he would have let concern him. He often liked to cuddle. He supposed it had to do with the way he felt after sex: the way the world lengthened itself out around him and allowed him to drift through a landscape of half-remembered dreams, at least until he got hungry. But this… he couldn't allow this.

"Daniel?"

He blinked. "Hm?"

Cesare shifted on the mattress and turned to look at him, head propped on one hand. Inviting musk and warmth stole over Dan, and the muzzy, low-watt lamplight picked out every angle of Cesare's face, each detail rendered anew. A little more than a day's beard growth softened the line of his jaw.

"Thank you," he murmured.

Dan frowned. "Th—?"

"For… all of this," Cesare said vaguely. He lifted a hand, as if he was about to touch Dan's arm, but then he stopped, his fingers left curled in the air. "You make it… very memorable for me. This time. I-I was thinking, perhaps…."

Dan closed his eyes, dreading what might come next. "Mm?"

"Will you maybe come to Italy again? Sometime?"

The question trailed slowly over Dan, threatening a future of disappointments and impossibilities.

"I plan to," he lied. "Yeah, of course."

Cesare gave a sleepy, satisfied sigh. "That's good. Maybe, sometime—"

"Maybe," Dan said. He choked out a small, limp smile. "Yeah."

He glanced across at Cesare. He had to be old enough to know when he'd been let down gently, and Dan was sure he'd take the hint. He couldn't quite make out the look on Cesare's face in the dim light, but there didn't seem to be any discernible change in him, no sudden tension in his body.

"I think," Cesare said after a while, "this is why. You know?"

Dan frowned. "Huh?"

Cesare shifted beside him, that familiar hint of grapefruit on his skin from the shower gel and the warmth of him filled the bed. Dan felt his gaze, but stared instead at the ceiling. One crack, larger than the others, ran the width of it, and he had a strange, incongruous vision of it splitting in two and crushing them both beneath the endless weight of plasterboard and copper pipes.

"Because I know that you leave so soon, *si*? Perhaps this is why I feel…. *Come si dice?* Safe."

Dan searched for something to say and found nothing. No clever phrase that wouldn't wither under the clear brown eyes he could feel burning into his skin. Ridiculous… and he'd end up looking an even bigger idiot than he already did. A brief burst of irritation flared within Dan. He wanted Cesare, yes, but here in this moment, something darker than good honest lust thrashed in his chest.

Tomorrow only the scraps of a few hours would stand between him having to leave Venice, ready to catch his flight, and—by Monday morning—be fully adjusted back to what he was having increasing difficulty thinking of as "normal life."

One more day. What the hell do we do with one more day?

CESARE CAUGHT him thinking about it at breakfast and dosed him up with fantastic coffee and pastries until he smiled, for which Dan was grateful. He couldn't bear the thought of hanging around aimlessly until the time came for him to leave the city, either, and Cesare seemed to sense that.

They made one last excursion, to Torcello. More than a thousand years ago, it had been the lagoon's most important settlement. Now, with the old waterfront silted up, the inhabitants migrating farther into the city, and the dusty, red brick towers of the cathedral attracting more archaeologists than believers, it encapsulated so much of Venice's heavy, stagnant beauty that Dan couldn't believe it wasn't full of aesthetic pilgrims. He marveled at the way bits of ancient culture could be left unkempt and unprotected, baked by the scorching sun and occasionally turned over to festivals and celebrations—brief bursts of life in an otherwise silent place.

"In England the whole thing would be crawling with archaeologists. There'd be a visitors' center and a museum and all sorts of stuff. And in America... well, you know how the Americans get about anything pre-1600. You couldn't have anything like the Cloisters in any other country on earth... ever been to the States?"

Cesare shook his head. "I have been to Monaco, Slovenia, Austria, and Germany. Nowhere more than seventy kilometers across the Italian border. Maybe one day I travel."

Dan grinned, buoyed up by the sunshine, the beautiful wildness of the landscape, and by the way the wind ruffled Cesare's hair.

"Maybe you'll come to England."

Cesare just smiled and said nothing. Dan supposed they were even now.

The five-minute *vaporetto* ride back to the mainland seemed to last for ages. Dan felt his footing on the deck lose its firmness; the water slapped on the boat's hull and he wanted to fall. The pull of something not quite like dizziness assailed him, and the sunlight broke on the waves. It marked the end of everything, and it left Dan hollow.

Leaving would always have been hard. He knew that. You couldn't leave a place like Venice and not expect it to change you. La Serenissima scrawls on the people she touches like a common vandal. He'd be back, of course he would. He said as much to Cesare, but he just smiled, his eyes dim and listless. Dan struggled to find anything to say. He checked out of his hotel, and they had one last lunch together at a café on San Marco.

It seemed like anything he said would sound false, so Dan kept quiet. Any time either of them did try to speak, their words toppled over the other's half-formed sentences, and then they'd both step back, hidden smiles and sore hearts, and neither of them would manage to conclude anything.

They promised to keep in touch, and Dan really wanted to believe it would happen. He wrote all his phone numbers, e-mail, and even his home address down on a napkin for Cesare, carefully folding it before he slid it across the table. Cesare smiled shyly and tucked the napkin into his pocket as if it was a secret treasure. Neither of them were much into social media, but he wrote his own contact information down for Dan in a similar fashion, the broad loops of his handwriting crawling across the paper's soft thickness.

Dan took it, and a little of the self-consciousness he felt melted away into bittersweet acceptance. It was real; he would leave, but he could at least take this with him. That folded napkin gave him the promise of holding on to some of this time, of how it felt to be right there, at that moment, eating a chicken panini to a background thrum of Europop music and clinking cutlery. The breeze rattled at the open window they sat near, and Cesare's gaze was fixed on him, so full of warmth and longing.

After they left the café, Dan could hardly remember the taste of the meal he'd eaten. The whole lunch felt like a succession of moments seared into his brain but impossible to recollect individually. The two of them idled a little while in San Marco, just being tourists together, and Dan wished there could be just one more day, though he couldn't put off the inevitable much longer.

Eventually the time came. Cesare wanted to see him off and wouldn't countenance a refusal, so they headed out together. Despite the things he'd bought, Dan was still traveling pretty light. He hefted his bags and they made their way down to the Alilaguna waterbus stop. The crowds thinned out a little down here; he guessed they'd hit an unexpected lull in the traffic. Cesare shook his hand, looked at him with such pleading in his eyes that Dan couldn't resist.

"Bye," he said, ducking in to press a kiss to Cesare's cheek.

It was almost chaste enough to pass for Continental.

"*Arrivederci*, Daniel. I see you again, I hope. Sometime."

"Yes. Oh, yes… I hope so."

Dan reluctantly withdrew his hand from Cesare's. He had to go. Getting on the boat was the worst part. That, and the snatched glimpse of Cesare waiting on the walkway. He stood, a lonely figure among the crowd, unmoving as the dock receded into the distance.

By the time he got to the airport, Dan had done a pretty good job of convincing himself that the way he felt wouldn't last long. It was the sexual equivalent of a hangover: the payment for the party that gradually would cease feeling terrible in its own right and pall next to the memory of how good what came before it had been.

He wished it would damn well stay that simple.

CHAPTER TEN

DAN SIGHED and stretched, feeling the once-crisp cotton sheets, now smoothed and comfortably warmed by sleep, yield around his body. The blinds rattled softly in the breeze from the open window and filled the room with the rich, slightly earthy scent of the honeysuckle that scrambled up the trellis outside. Dan smiled to himself and wriggled farther down the bed, back into the cocoon of covers, where it still smelled musky and vaguely, deliciously sweaty. Lazy shafts of sun trapped dust and time in stripes of golden light. Perfect. He could feel Cesare's lips on the back of his neck and hear the soft growl of satisfaction dragged from deep in his own throat as the narrow gap between them closed.

He leaned back into the warm, solid cradle of his lover's body, smiling as Cesare's talented fingers continued in their search for his most ticklish spots. So far in last night's hours of exploration, he had found two: one just behind Dan's knee, and the other that spot above his second rib, which he'd broken when he was a kid, riding his bike too fast in the woods. Dan didn't mind if it took Cesare another whole night to find the last one.

He could feel Cesare's—what had he called it?—*uccello*, that was it, his bird, fluttering its proverbial wings, a cock stretching out its neck to crow in the dawn. Dan grinned to himself at the flowery imagery. Italian was full of it, full of strangely vivid words and metaphors. He would have to learn to speak it properly, and he knew where he wanted to start.

"*Facciamo l'amore,*" he murmured, still sleepy and slow, pressing back against the hardening lines of Cesare's body, not caring how terrible his accent sounded, so long as he got thoroughly fucked at least once before breakfast.

Unfortunately, Dan was denied, and he woke abruptly as he fell out of bed.

He sat up and rubbed his forehead. With a growing black mood, Dan surveyed his bedroom floor, the tangled bedclothes, and the distinct absence of both the hazy Italian sunshine and his lazily sensual Italian lover.

"Shit," he said to the world in general.

A cool breeze blew in through the open window, bringing with it a few drops of the misty rain that had started to fall. Dan peered at the glass and the gray London morning beyond it.

"*Shit*," he said once more.

After a couple of unsuccessful attempts, Dan managed to extricate himself from the sheets and stagger to the bathroom. Half-hard, half-asleep—and therefore half still in that wonderful, imaginary dream world of imaginary Cesare and his imaginary bed—he turned the shower on and clambered under the hot spray. He turned the dial up high and let the water pound his back, willing it to wash away the tension, the discomfort, and the nagging ache of unfulfilled desire. A few minutes' particular attention to himself under the water would at least deal with one aspect of that problem.

Stupid. Nothing but dreams... the wisps of things that stuck to him like streaks of dried mud after a run or the tender echoes of bruises that should already have healed. All Venice had done was remind him he wasn't over Paul yet. Anything he thought he'd found with Cesare was surely nothing but a manifestation of that, or so Dan set about convincing himself.

He'd known it hadn't been real, that it wouldn't last, but he'd allowed himself to fall into some ridiculous fantasy, to feel like it represented something it could never really be. Not the way it felt to be quietly held on a lazy Saturday morning, and kissed when you came home from work; not the way it felt to sleep with someone who knew how to make you come and how to make you cry, not because you had some kind of instant animal attraction, but because you'd worked at it slowly, both good and bad.

Paul had never been that man. It had never felt like they had that kind of relationship, whatever Dan had wanted to believe, and it was stupid to think on the basis of less than a week that Cesare had started to fill in the gaps. That being with him had in some impossible way matched up to Dan's hopes. He tugged at his flesh as if he could pull the memories out, banish the things that haunted him, but he just ended up coming too quickly, a jumble of wants and wishes behind his eyes, body sated but unsatisfied.

Dan turned the shower off and dried himself briskly as if he could towel the thoughts away. He couldn't mourn his time with Paul despite the sour spots, but that relationship had been over long before they'd ended it. Besides, it wasn't even Paul he missed, but the *idea* of him—of that one real, steady partner, always in his corner. For everything he'd been, Paul had never been that dependable. And as for Cesare... well, he'd known what that was from the start. Trying to think differently now would just be masochism.

Having got himself into a thoroughly bad mood, Dan cleaned up quickly and, naked but for a towel, padded to the kitchen in search of coffee. He always took Sundays to himself. It was one of the nice things about being single again; he had no obligations, no insistence to share his space and his free time. Working freelance gave him a flexible schedule during the week, but he found it too easy to fill that time and have it spill over the borders into every nook and cranny of life. That was the price for actually getting paid to do a job he loved, he supposed... though he'd have liked to trim the fat off the commissions he took, drop the weddings and the portraits, and just do the work he really enjoyed. Maybe one day.

Or maybe he'd just shelve it with all the other dreams.

Dan made himself a cafetiere of proper ground coffee and pulled a face when he found it didn't taste like the dark roast in the Grancaffè Quadri. He carried it into the other room nonetheless and stood it on the gateleg table while he leafed through the junk mail and bills that had accumulated in his absence. Outside the large window that was the nearest thing his modern, anonymous flat had to a feature, rain drizzled steadily, and the red brick tenement sprawl of Wimbledon frowned under a gray sky.

He didn't have much in the way of messages on his landline. Few people used the number anymore, and pretty much everyone had known he'd be away. Chris had drunk dialed once from some noisy club, yelling above the music that he was going home with a guy whose name he'd forgotten, but that it wasn't important because he had a bum like two hazelnuts in a condom, and was Dan having a good holiday? He'd made a point of saying he was calling the flat because he knew Dan's phone would be with Dan himself in the "Capital of Bloody Romance"... and then laughed uproariously when he'd apparently realized that Dan obviously wasn't in the flat on account of *being* on holiday. But that was just Chris after a few bevies.

Dan deleted the message and made a mental note to ask after Mr. Hazelnuts.

The only other message was from Edith, his sister, and must have come in while he slept. He frowned. He hadn't heard the phone—had he really been so far under? He hadn't slept that soundly in years. Edith was nagging in her nicest manner. He realized he hadn't called her since his return... usually he'd have done that almost as soon as closing the front door behind him.

"All right, Danny? It's me. I thought you'd be back by now. Actually, I thought you were back yesterday, so maybe you're out. Anyway, it's about nine on Sunday morning. Want to come over for lunch? Kids would love to see you. I wouldn't mind either. About one? Give me a bell on your way if you can make it. I'll call back later if I don't hear from you. You know I will! Byesies."

He smiled ruefully. Edith was a lot of things but subtle wasn't one of them.

Dan shivered a little in the cool air. Rain spotted the glass, falling harder now; he had no real desire to go out in that, but it seemed preferable to hanging around the flat all day. His own space, his sacred Sundays off, just didn't hold the same kind of appeal when he felt like this. He swallowed the rest of his mediocre coffee and went to pull on some clothes.

EDITH'S PLACE wasn't far from Dan's, though it slipped over the border into the suburban wilds of Merton instead of true Wimbledon, which still had the cachet of a London address, and marginally better Tube service. He got off the bus at the end of her road and walked past the neatly trimmed ranks of privet hedges and mock-Tudor fronted houses, where gravel driveways crunched beneath the tires of 4x4s that would never see any terrain farther off-road than the local supermarket. At least her ex-husband had left her with one thing worth having aside from the kids.

Dan had liked Greg when they first met. He'd seemed nice, as well as prepared to take good care of Edith, but the cracks began to show after the first couple of years. Dan had hoped things would work out, especially after the kids came along. He and Edith had lived through their parents' divorce when they were respectively five and eight years old and come out fairly unscathed, but he knew how much his sister feared repeating the pattern of her childhood.

Unfortunately wishful thinking didn't save marriages.

Greg had disappeared into the sunset and left Edith with the kids, the mortgage, and the knowledge that six years of marriage somehow didn't match up to an office fling. He'd not even had the balls to put up a battle for either custody or assets, though he hadn't bothered to pay child support either, which had left Edith struggling to make ends meet. She'd remortgaged the place and Dan had helped where he could, and he hoped that just maybe she'd started to come out the other side now, into a clearer future.

He knocked at the front door. Ivy scrambled up the sides of the safety-glazed porch and a child's bike lay discarded on the lawn. A dog barked, muffled, and Edith's shadow moved behind the frosted glass of the door.

"Danny!"

She drowned him in a hug, all sensible dark blue cotton T-shirt and long corduroy skirt, shapeless and far too practical. Her hair had the same mousy tones as Dan's, just lightened to a warmer blonde, and she wore it pulled back from her face in a rather severe knot. It made her look older than she needed to, her skin sallow and papery without makeup.

"Hi, love. You all right?"

"Mm?" She pulled back, one hand automatically smoothing down his hair. "Oh, yes. Yeah, we're fine. Kids are being little horrors, but that's what they do best. Come on, come in. I want to hear all about this holiday of yours, you lucky sod…. Oi, Benson! Get in!"

Edith directed the last part at her golden retriever, who'd barreled cheerfully out of the front door and jumped up to frisk Dan for any potential treats, tickles, or toys. Dan grinned, ruffled the dog's ears, and followed his sister into the house. Benson padded obediently along with them, and Dan breathed a long sigh of something that wasn't quite relief.

Few things felt more irrefutably real than Edith's house. The chipped, faded white paint of the woodwork, the scuffs and smears on the wipe-clean eggshell finish of the walls, their colors outdated and never quite coordinated, all reminded of him of home. The whole place had the sort of lived-in feel that old sweaters acquire after a few years: baggy, comfortable, and a little frayed around the edges. Her kids had no idea just how lucky they'd been, Dan decided. And they wouldn't know until they were older and they could look back on this as the only time in their lives they were completely free, without constraint or limitations.

Not that Edith didn't have ground rules. She could be very strict; he knew that. But she never tried to make the kids fit her ideals or her demands. She treated them as individuals… as real people.

"Coffee or tea?" Edith asked and flicked on the kettle that sat on the old-fashioned opalescent green tiles of her work surface.

"Tea. Please."

Dan peered out of the patio doors to the long, narrow garden beyond and his niece and two nephews careening madly around the lawn with a football. Benson pawed at the glass until Edith let him out to join the kids, and he ran joyfully to chase the ball with them.

"So, what's the matter with you?"

Dan looked up guiltily. "Hm?"

"I'd have thought you'd come home all made up and floating on air. Didn't you like it?"

Dan stared at the cup of tea Edith set in front of him. A few bubbles eddied giddily on the surface where she had stirred in sugar and milk. It was one of the comforting things about family—whether they judged you, harangued you, beat seven shades of shit out of you for being stupid, they still knew how you took your beverages.

"N—I mean, yes, I did. It was… great. I had a great time. Um. I brought presents."

He gestured to the tote bag he'd left by the door, but Edith shook her head.

"Those can wait. Come on. You've got a face on you like a duck's arse and, to be honest, you look exhausted. What happened?"

Dan said nothing, just traced the line of the cup's handle. It was a tall, angular thing, painted with bands of red and orange, and it had a chip on its rim. "No. Actually, it was wonderful."

"So?"

Edith set her own cup on the table and sat down, tossing the dishcloth to one side. Like always, she was straightforward and uncomplicated. Miss Practical. It had been infuriating when they were children.

Dan sighed. "I met this bloke…."

"Oh, God." Edith rolled her eyes. "A lovesick puppy with the holiday romance blues. You didn't do anything stupid, did you?"

"Like what? On second thoughts, don't answer that. I don't want to know how low your opinion of me is." Dan sipped his tea and ignored the look on her face. "Come on, Edie. I was careful. And it wasn't like that, not really. It wasn't… tacky. Well, not much. I didn't go expecting to pick anybody up, but we just—"

"Clicked?"

"Yes. If you really want to put it like that." Dan looked wretchedly at his sister. "It's not how it sounds. Honest."

"No?"

Edith propped her chin on her hand and regarded him with a cool blue gaze. Outside, Benson barked ecstatically, the kids shrieked, and there was a sound rather like a football bouncing off the side of a garden shed with a little too much force. A chorus of giggles followed it. Edith glanced at the patio doors, forever watchful, and probably concerned about her plants. The corner of her mouth pulled back in a sympathetic little curl.

"All right, then. Why don't you tell me what it *was* like? What's his name, for starters? Where's he from?"

"Cesare. Some conservative little village in Tuscany."

"Tuscany? I thought he'd be some silver-haired Venetian count with webbed toes." Edith winked at her brother. "Sorry. Go on."

Dan snorted. But all the same, it helped to tell her. It helped to separate out his thoughts, talk everything through with someone who, while not totally impartial, wouldn't condemn him outright. Edith never did that… not when she could torture him first. He knew he blushed when he told her about how they'd met, how that first day had vanished over the horizon in a slip of warm light and perfect tensions.

"So you screwed him?"

Edith's eyebrow rose when Dan didn't answer. Finally, and somewhat reluctantly, he nodded. He'd omitted mention of Club Commodoro for precisely this reason. She wouldn't approve. In Edith's world, sex didn't happen without several dates and a signed affidavit of sexual health, personal intentions, and financial status. Not since the kids. He admired her for that; they'd grow up knowing they came first, never worrying about their mother's affections being transferred off to some nebulous "uncle" or "friend."

"We played safe. He—"

"So it was all hearts and flowers and kissy wissy till the morning light?"

"No! Look, Edie, if you're going to—"

"All right, all right. Sorry."

"It wasn't like that. *He's* not. It… was sort of a… thing."

He tried to tell her, to explain to her the cool sands of Sant'Erasmo, the shaded walkways beneath the *palazzi* and, most of all, to communicate the warmth and the comfort of Cesare's presence, but it didn't work quite the way he'd intended. Dan traced his fingers over the handle of his cup. He knew the more he talked the worse he sounded, like he'd spun something unreal out of a few fumbled holiday gropes, desperation and loneliness causing him to grasp at sexual straws.

The more real he tried to make Cesare sound, the falser he became. Just some faceless local, with all the allure of summer sunshine and poolside cocktails, fading as quickly as a suntan.

To her credit, Edith stopped teasing. Eventually. She nodded, smiled, and made soothing comments of the kind usually addressed to kids who'd cut their knees. It must have been lovely, he sounded really nice, but at least Dan was home now. He had to get his mind back onto real life, and then he'd soon shake those holiday romance blues.

"'Cause it's not really long since you split up with Paul, eh?"

Dan stared at her. "What?"

"Well, I'm just saying. It isn't."

"Edith…."

Something crumbled a little bit at the edges of Dan's world. While *he* might have considered that, he hated the fact that Edith had so easily leapt on it. It was a private failing, and he didn't want to be that predictable, that transparent… no. It wasn't like that.

He scowled down at his cup, not wanting to look her in the eye and admit she might have a point. She pressed, nonetheless.

"So, maybe… y'know?"

"What?" he said again, his tone dull and argumentative.

She cleared her throat: a gentle reminder that she wouldn't put up with that sort of attitude. Not from any of the kids, and not from him.

"You had some fun… and you miss this bloke because he didn't represent any demands, anything you really had to live up to. Everyone misses being on holiday when they get home and have to get on with life again."

Dan nodded grimly. She didn't understand. She had a valid point, but she didn't understand. All right, so even if it had been real, what kind of a future was there for him with Cesare? The practical problems of visas and foreign countries aside, there were a million things to think about, and all they'd had in the warm Venetian spring would probably be nothing in the cool light of everyday life.

That much might be true, but knowing it didn't change the way Dan felt. He supposed he was being stupid, adolescent, and a dozen other uncomplimentary things, and he knew he shouldn't get snippy with Edith for being sensible. That was what she did, who she was.

Still, sitting here at Edith's well-worn, well-polished kitchen table—the kids and Benson playing outside—made it easier to think about things. He wasn't swayed by Cesare's lips on his, or the touch of his warm, comforting hands. And he'd never ached so much for anyone.

"I didn't think I would, not once I got back and got on with things, but… I do miss him, Edie. I really do."

She took a sip of her tea and looked thoughtful, like some Tibetan mystic engaged in deep contemplation. "Any particular bit of him?"

Dan pulled a face. "You're not funny. That's what I'm saying. It wasn't just about the sex. Not like that. I mean, yes, but… oh, shit. I don't know what the matter is." He sighed. "Thanks for listening, love."

"S'all right. Top up?" Edith nodded to the mug of tea.

"Please."

Dan watched her make the next pot of tea, an ancient and comforting ritual. She looked more like their mother than ever. The clink of the mugs on the tabletop seemed to echo straight out of his childhood. Edith sat back down, elbows on the varnished wood, and blew on her tea.

"Did you get his e-mail address or something, then?" she asked.

"Hm?" Dan looked up guiltily. "Oh… yeah. Yes, we sort of said we'd—"

"Keep in touch?"

"Mm."

"Right." A sardonic smile pulled at the side of her mouth. "Reminds me of that time me and the girls went to Tenerife that summer, for Martina's twenty-first. D'you remember? I sent you that postcard telling you I'd fallen in love with a bartender called Simon."

Dan grimaced. "And you spent six weeks after you got home wondering why he never called or came to visit you, even after he totally, *honestly* said he had family in London. Yeah, I remember. But it's not…."

He exhaled, unwilling to repeat himself anymore. It… well, it could be like any number of things, couldn't it? A holiday screw he'd read too much into. The very fact he'd lain awake thinking about Cesare, dreaming about him, probably meant just what Edith said. What he wanted was the promise of something that had become wonderful in his mind because it didn't have any of the messy complications normal life did.

There wasn't much opportunity to dwell on the thought, though.

A clamor at the patio doors signaled Edith's kids—Lauren, Jack and little Liam—wanting to come in for drinks, biscuits, and the prospect of the presents Dan had mentioned on his postcard.

The family resemblance was strong in all three of them: matching blond mops of hair and blue-eyed little faces, much like Edith had been as a child. Liam pressed his lips to the glass door and blew hard, making a cloud of condensation and a big fart noise. Dan grinned and didn't mind pushing his problems away for the afternoon.

HE GOT home substantially later, worn out with football, runny noses, interminable games of Snakes and Ladders, and more questions about Italy than he was really able to answer. Edith gave him a few knowing looks while he talked, and Dan had to resist the childish urge to pull a face at her. She'd helped, though. Immeasurably. And she did have a point, however much he hated to admit it.

"You're better off," she whispered against his cheek when she hugged him good-bye. "Aren't you, eh? Better off if you don't try to rush into something new. You had fun, but don't try to make it something it's not. I want to see you happy, love. Not chasing things that won't ever happen. You'll only end up miserable."

He'd just smiled, hugged her tight, and gone home. The flat seemed very empty, though Dan relished the quiet. He loved Lauren, Jack, and even snot-streaked Liam very dearly, but couldn't see himself ever quite entertaining the idea of kids under his own roof. Not all the time. Maybe one day, with the right man, he'd find space in his life for a sleek tabby or a furry ginger tom… or maybe he and some faceless, flawless mystery guy would move out to the suburbs and adopt a scraggle-faced, whiskery dog from a local shelter.

Who knew?

Anyway, all the best parts of life were totally unpredictable.

Dan poured himself a drink and put on some music. It drowned out some of the street noise from outside and some of the noise inside his own head. The ends of chores—washing up, laundry, ironing, and all the other getting-home-from-holiday stuff—spread out before him, and Dan sought to put them off for a little longer.

He sat down on the edge of the bed, his drink in his hand, and looked at the brown paper package. Apart from the Customs people, no one had touched it since the gallery owner in Dorsoduro wrapped it. Dan took a swallow of vodka, put the glass down on his bedside table, and carefully started to unwrap the painting.

Colors and sensations colonized his memory; the paper turned to skin beneath his touch, the string and tape giving way as easily as the token resistance of breath in the night. Brown eyes stared steadily into his and two bodies hummed toward the edge of ecstasy. Dan slipped a thumb beneath the next layer of paper. He smiled. Beneath the tissue inside, hot yellows, oranges, and umbers glowed back at him.

He tilted his head, smoothing back the wrappings until he could view the canvas unobstructed. It was a simple thing: bright blue sky, round yellow sun, the blazing colors of parched but fertile earth, all painted with skill but without guile. What the land felt like, not necessarily what it was. Dan ran his fingers along the edge of the picture, and the ridges of paint whispered like flesh under his touch, as sensuous and warm as… everything. The sun on the city's ancient stucco, the harshness of cheap red wine that warmed the belly and burned the throat… the touch of a trembling, eager hand on his skin.

Dan glanced up, through the open bedroom door at the exposed red brick wall on the far side of the living room. He would hang it there. The space had been empty ever since Paul took his Eric Clapton studio prints with him, and the light was right. Every time he saw it, he'd be able to think of Cesare.

He'd think of him so hard the smell of his skin would fill the apartment and, sure, it was going to hurt like hell, at least at first, but it was worth it. The more he thought about it, the more Dan could believe that. It was worth anything just to hold on to those memories and make them feel real again.

CHAPTER ELEVEN

CESARE GOT home late from work, piles of marking stacked in boxes in the backseat of his car, ring binders full of lesson plans, reports, and schedules taking up the passenger seat. A CD of Zucchero Fornaciari's *Greatest Hits* cut off along with the engine and he sat, hands still on the wheel, long enough to luxuriate in a jaw-cracking yawn. Gravagna Montale was far from the center of the known world… just any other tiny, beautiful place.

Light poured down the narrow street, heavy with the dust of a long day, and turned the glass in the windows to molten gold. Cesare stopped to admire the effect and wondered how something so perfect could seem so empty. A stupid thought, he told himself, and one he wouldn't have had but for how tired he felt. He climbed the stone steps up to his apartment, and the scent of the wild thyme that grew along the cracked bases of walls tickled his nose.

Many of the old village houses had been sublet or converted now, and the old farms and villas sold off or left to go to ruin. Most of the places he remembered playing as a boy had gone, and it seemed strange to think of them either replaced by new, faceless buildings, or sunbaked into rubble in the dust.

He let himself into his apartment. It wasn't much, but it was enough: one large room with a kitchen unit, a tiny shower room, and bedroom off it. Outside lay a small concrete terrace on which he could hang laundry and perhaps enjoy the sunshine, overlooking the sleepy street with the distant hum of the autostrada beyond. He didn't need anything more. Close to Mamma for when she needed him, good for transport to work… convenient. The thought that his whole life was one of convenience knocked briefly at Cesare's mind, but he kicked it away. It receded into the shadows, to skitter among the faded, papery memories of Venice. He still smelled the salt when he closed his eyes, heard the water lap against the boats.

There was a message on his phone, and he sat to tug off his shoes as he listened to it: Mamma, demanding his presence for dinner this evening. Gianni was bringing a girl he'd met at the office, so everyone had to be pleasant and make her feel welcome. Cesare curled his lip as her voice continued, segueing just as he expected into the dreaded comparison. *The least you can do is support him. When's the last time you bring a girl home, huh?*

He sighed and, taking a deep breath, dialed her number.

"*Pronto?*"

"*Ciao, Mamma. Come va?*"

"Cesare…!"

Her voice warmed in recognition. That made him feel proud, and he didn't mind listening for a few moments to the minutiae of her day. Cesare clamped the phone between his ear and shoulder and wandered over to his computer, perched on a cluttered desk by the window. He made all the right appreciative and understanding noises while he booted up and checked his e-mail, his heartbeat wild for a moment before the in-box loaded, just in case there was a message from *him*… but there wasn't. And of course there wouldn't be. Cesare *knew* that. It was foolish to pretend, even for a second, that Daniel would contact him.

He deleted a few junk messages and made reassuring promises: yes, of course he would be there for dinner. Yes, it would be wonderful to meet Gianni's new girlfriend. No, there wasn't anyone he would be bringing, she knew that.

"A presto," he finished, listening to her hang up the phone.

He loved her dearly, but she drove him crazy.

Cesare sighed. So much for any plans he might have had for a quiet evening, getting some reports graded and sipping a glass of wine in front of the television. He showered, changed, and set off for his mother's house with a grim but dutiful determination.

THE GIRL, of course, turned out to be very pretty. A freckled, homespun beauty rather than the glacial elegance Gianni normally preferred, but she charmed Mamma. Her name was Silvana, and Cesare's parents occupied most of the meal with probing and chattering at her, drawing out her opinions and views on everything, hearing about her life, her hobbies, and how she had met Gianni. Mamma seemed truly interested—truly animated, which Cesare loved to see. She got into the humor of it all, flicking Papà in the shoulder with the dishcloth she'd used to serve the hot dish of croquettes every time he played too flirtatiously with Silvana. Laughter and smiles long into the night, with a *cena* to remember. Cesare suspected the girl would be back again. He hoped so, from the way Gianni's face softened when he looked at her. It opened up a cold place inside Cesare, and he filled it with wine, a full-bodied but rough Pinot that Papà liked.

He tripped home as he'd arrived, by foot. The streets were mellow—dark and fuzzy, and Cesare felt… what? Loose, free, and maybe a little jealous, he supposed. That Gianni could have such careless joy, such ease with women, while he had never been able to make that choice. Cesare couldn't find it in himself to feel an emotional attraction toward them, though not for want of trying. Their bodies were occasionally beautiful, yes, but they didn't strike at the core of him. They were like strange artworks: mysterious, intricately wrought, and probably best left to people who understood them.

He switched on the light and pulled the curtains. His little apartment let in the dusty glow of the houses opposite at the front, and at the back, the smells of lemon trees and the auto garage at the far end of the street danced on the breeze. Cesare wished he found it easier to put the thoughts of Daniel from his head. He blamed the wine. Too simple to drink and look at this happy family scene, which was so nearly and yet so far from complete because they would never, ever forget those who were missing, and too achingly easy to wonder if there would ever be a time when he introduced a friend to Mamma and Papà.

A man at his side whose hand he might squeeze beneath the table, as Gianni had comforted Silvana, even though he'd thought no one had seen. A man who would look at him and smile, the way she did for his brother. A man like… *no*.

It was all foolishness, and Cesare decided he should not think of it. Not think of it at all. Perhaps that was the better thing. To think of Daniel, to remember *that*, just left Cesare with uncomfortable problems and long nights.

He went to the kitchen, poured himself a glass of wine from an open bottle on the counter, and sat, looking into the ruby depths. Uncomfortable indeed. And lonely. He wanted to do anything to drown out the loops of memory repeating in his head, so he swallowed the wine and retreated to the bedroom—ignoring the mirrors he passed along the way, which looked at him accusingly.

In his bedroom, Cesare reached into the back of the cabinet that held his TV and DVD player. A title selected, he pulled the curtains, set the disc to play, and settled himself on the bed, glass in hand. He fast-forwarded through the movie's unimportant and unappealing attempt at a plot to the section where a black-haired man with a chiseled face and full lips sat in a hot tub, the water pummeling his flawless physique. Another man joined him, very alike, though not so muscular. A quire of dark hair flopped over his brow, making him seem shy. They didn't talk much, which was good because neither had any ability to speak of when it came to acting, but then they began to kiss. The second man's mouth met again and again the smooth, impossibly beautiful face of the first, and his fingertips traced the broad lines of jaw and throat.

His touch held such reverence, as if he was… what? Worshiping? Yes. The word seemed right to Cesare, and he wriggled his shoulder blades back into the pillows, not thinking of anything other than the film. The men, loving, touching… worshiping each other. The water in the hot tub—how would it feel? Soft. Warm. Perhaps the bubbles would burst like kisses against the skin.

The second man straddled the first now, showing the rippling planes of his back for the camera. Strong hands came to caress him, and the water lapped against the very top of his ass, those solid curves hidden from view and taunting with promises and possibilities. As he did every time he watched this movie, Cesare felt mildly disappointed that the model didn't rise all the way out of the tub and show off that beautiful asset. Instead, the first man hiked himself up on the side of the tub and offered his tool for attention.

The camera angle changed, panning around him and lingering on the water that dripped from his body as he leaned back on his hands. A long, trailing shot showed the way his nipples had tightened against the cool air. Slowly, the view tracked south to his improbably proportioned cock, clean shaved and rock hard.

Just like every time, Cesare watched the sequence through half-closed eyes, hand slipping through his open fly to work on his own pleasure as his gaze followed every motion of the man adoring that glorious weapon. And it was a weapon—a beast like that could bring anyone to their knees. Certainly, Cesare would have given anything to be in the second man's place as he worked his mouth around the shaft, lapped at the wide, bulbous head.

When the first man came, splattering the obligatory ropes of semen all over the face of his friend, it slowed Cesare's progress toward his own release just a little. He could never understand why they let it go to waste like that. Breath short and gut knotted tight, he tried to pull the scene from fantasy into something real behind his eyes, tried to conjure the smells, textures, and tastes of how it would be. *How it had been.* He pulled away from that thought, from the memory of the hotel room and Daniel's gentle instruction, no hint of mockery or impatience. The taste of him, salt and ozone and clean sweat, something of the sea and of rough wine. It was much more difficult than the men on the video made it look, he had to admit. But someone like Daniel…. *Maiala della miseria!* Such a man would make it worth studying harder than Cesare ever had before. His lips parted for the remembrance of that fat, hot cock, for the feel of soft, silky skin against his tongue and hard flesh filling his mouth.

Cesare leaned his head back against the bedstead and relished the dark, secret places inside his mind, where thoughts like those could blossom and grow. Where voices called to him from the past, and lips that had never been quite forgotten spoke his name.

Later he fell to the usual patterns of his evenings, the late-night news on the television and his laptop on the bed, e-mails, and lesson plans. Niccolò Misseri was still not doing well in class, still badly withdrawn from the other kids. Cesare scoured back over the same autism support groups, teachers' guides, and information lists that he'd seen a dozen times before, hoping there would be something new, something useful.

Eventually he sighed and readied to turn off the machine, his eyes sore and gritty in their sockets, like two warm marbles. He pinched the bridge of his nose, abruptly and devastatingly discouraged. It wasn't fair. He must speak again with Rosemarie, the English lady who taught at the *scuola*. She said in England autism was regarded very differently; she said perhaps finding an English school or institution to advise would help, and Cesare supposed it would be worth trying. But the rotten core of the thing still remained: that none of it was fair, and that anyone who showed the least spark of difference, anyone who—what? Didn't fit in? No. *Now* he thought more of himself than Niccolò, and that wasn't right.

Cesare sat and scowled at the screen for a few moments, then pulled up an empty e-mail and typed furiously. He reached for his glass of fresh wine, swigged, frowned, and typed some more. Then he deleted everything he'd written and typed again. He shook his head. The English words looked lumpy and misshapen, like rocks sticking out of still water. He tried writing in Italian first and translating, but it still didn't seem to come out right. Cesare sighed and made one last-ditch effort—just a few short, bland words. Bald statement, no frills. He hit the Send button and promptly wished he hadn't, staring at the screen as if it was the black maw of a mailbox into which he should never have deposited a foolish letter.

Daniel would think him an idiot.

CHAPTER TWELVE

"I STILL say I was right," Chris announced.

Dan rolled his eyes. They sat in the Kung Po Kitchen, addressing tempura vegetables and a king prawn dish with mussels and black bean sauce, and if he had to hear one more time what a fool he'd been for letting Paul slip through his fingers, Dan would have to give in to the urge to thump Chris in the head.

"No, really. Think about it." Chris waved a chopstick in the air demonstratively. "He's hot enough to fry eggs on, you had the kind of sex life the rest of us can only envy, he had his own house, car, and career, he—"

"Was distant and emotionally uninvolved," Dan finished for him, chewing a piece of battered aubergine.

"So? No drama. Sounds amazing to me."

Dan pulled a face. No drama wasn't exactly the way he'd have put it, though he wasn't about to say so. "Yeah? If he's so perfect, why don't you go give him a call?"

"Ew, no." Chris wrinkled his nose. "You've been there first. That's gross."

"Weirdo."

"Am not." Chris stuck one chopstick behind his ear, apparently oblivious to Dan's wince, and harpooned a prawn with the other. He pointed the speared crustacean at Dan. "Ultimately, my dear, you just don't know where your bread's buttered."

Dan snagged another bite of tempura. "Don't do that."

"Do what? Speak truth? Ancient philosopher he no say he told you so, *but*—"

"All right." Dan heaved a heartfelt sigh. "You've got a point. But… I don't know. We got so far apart I don't even think he remembered I existed except when he had a hard-on or he wanted someone to complain at."

"Or vice versa."

"Fair point," Dan admitted. "But not the whole story. Did you know he still had loads of his stuff at the house in Lancaster Gate?"

"What, while he was living with you?"

"Yep. *And* he said he was going to let the place out. Turns out he never did. Mary said so."

The swing doors into the kitchen clattered with the passing of a waiter, and spiced, steamy air washed over them. Chris raised an eyebrow.

"Hairy Mary Kilkenny?"

"Stop it. Yes. She's a perfectly respectable artist, and just because she's Irish, you can't—"

Dan shook his head. If Chris wanted to tease, he'd tease. He knew he didn't have a snowball's chance in hell of changing his friend's habits of a lifetime. Whether it was ragging on people like Mary—whose name was Hobart, not Kilkenny—and who wasn't that hirsute to the best of Dan's knowledge either, or remaining convinced in the face of all evidence to the contrary that Paul was the best thing since sliced bread, Chris was going to do what he did best.

"All right. So, you were thinking what? Sneaky love nest?"

"No! Well, maybe. I don't know." Dan bit into another mouthful sulkily. "You wouldn't be saying what a perfect boyfriend he is if he'd been cheating on me."

Chris considered that for a moment, then shrugged.

"I don't know… there's a lot to be said for open relationships. When you make sex something that both parties can enjoy either with each other or with someone else—or all of the above," he added thoughtfully, "then you make the commitment that you share a more honest and intimate one. Sex is just sex, and monogamy can be vastly overrated. I mean, let's face it. Men are dogs."

"Speak for yourself, Rover."

"Wuff!"

Dan groaned. The lunchtime rush had started to abate, the faces of people leaving to go back to their offices and busy schedules a series of flickers in the mirrored panels opposite the table. He thought of the mirrors in the Caffè Quadri, and then wished he hadn't. He sighed.

"Oh, come on," Chris wheedled, popping another prawn into his mouth and pausing briefly to chew. "I didn't really tick you off, did I? Hm?"

Dan shook his head. "No, of course not. But—"

"You know what I'm on about, Danny." Chris glanced down at his lunch, his voice suddenly lower and rather more serious. "I just don't want to see you waste anything."

He stabbed another prawn, and Dan bit back on what he'd been about to say. They both knew what Chris was alluding to; the camp front he put on hid it well, but he'd known loss. What was it, Dan wondered, five years since Garrett's death? Almost, anyway. He frowned at his tempura, unwilling to think back to those times.

Chris had been happy with Garrett. He very rarely showed how much so these days. Dan peered up at his friend, and found Chris looking at him, the traces of an uncomfortable seriousness in his eyes.

"I'm just saying—"

"I'm not wasting anything. And I don't wanna talk about Paul, anyway," Dan said flatly. "That's over and done with."

"Hmm." The tension broken, Chris fished once more among his prawns. "Yes. Your little 'me time' escapade. You've been looking like someone's pissed in your tequila ever since you got back. I *told* you Venice was a terrible place to go on a singleton's holiday. You should listen to—oh, what's this? Was that the flicker of a dirty little secret?"

Dan's eyebrows shot up in immediate and foolish refusal. "No… no, it wasn't. No. I h—"

"It was!" Chris cried, scenting proverbial blood. "I knew it! You blinked, and now you're blushing. Ah, you're rolling your eyes! I *knew* it. C'mon. Tell me everything."

"I don't really want to ta—"

"Dan…!"

Dan frowned. *Cornered. Sod it.* Chris knew him too damn well, and he only had himself to blame.

"All right! Yes, I got laid. Happy?"

Chris's mouth formed a moue of considered unease. "No, I'm not. You weren't going to tell me."

"Damn right!" Dan relented, seeing his friend's slumped shoulders and mock-depressed sigh. "Oh, come on… I don't hear every detail of your love life. Thank God."

Chris sniffed. "No, I'm thankful. Really. I thought I'd have to drag you off to the nearest monastery and throw away the key. So, you had fun? Mucky little pickup somewhere? Find a strapping young gondolier to… punt your canoe?"

Dan pulled a face. He knew Chris meant well. He always did, even if he came on too strong with it, but Dan didn't want to talk about Cesare, didn't want to expose that time, those thoughts, to the glare of judgment. Not to see them wither under Chris's inevitable caustic wit.

Of course, Dan didn't particularly want to tell him about Club Commodoro either. He'd never hear the end of that, and Chris would only take it as carte blanche to start dragging him out on Friday nights again, throwing unsuspecting club boys at him and waiting for something to stick.

It seemed like he had a choice between two evils.

"No. I just… I met this bloke. We had a nice time. That's all."

"Oh! Full-scale holiday fling, eh?" Chris crowed delightedly. "Details, *if* you please. How gorgeous was he? Scale of one to ten? Where'd you find him? Beach or bar? What—"

"Chris, will you just stop?" Dan rubbed his thumb against the knuckle of his forefinger and winced. "It wasn't… well, it wasn't like that. Y'know? Not the sort of bloke who…." He looked at his friend across the table. Chris's eager expression derailed any notion Dan might have had of trying to say what he wanted, so he just smiled and played along. "Yeah. Quiet one, y'know? Looking at him, you wouldn't have thought he'd be up for much, but we started talking in this café thingy, and before I knew it, he'd offered to, er, show me the high points on his itinerary."

Chris cackled. "You slut! I think it's good for you, though," he added, eyeing Dan over the rim of his glass of overpriced mineral water. "Mm, which reminds me—are you going to come to Sada's show tonight? I did tell you, remember. At that manky little gallery off the Edgware Road. You've got to come. I've promised to bring people, and he needs all the moral support he can get, poor git."

Dan vacillated for a few moments. "Well, I—"

"Lovely. I'll pick you up about six. We'll need a stiffener beforehand, I imagine."

"Oh. Goody," Dan said without much enthusiasm.

There went his plans for the evening. Or, at least, they would have done if he'd had any.

SADAHARU SHIGEMITSU had been one of Chris's part-time boyfriends a little over a year ago. They'd met through some mutual friend or other, Chris said, and Dan had liked Sada from the first. He was a good-looking guy, with a ragged shock of overstyled black hair, a wide, expressive mouth, and a glint of humor in his eyes that belied his painfully trendy clothes, though on initial meetings, people were usually surprised by his well-spoken, rounded English, not realizing he'd spent most of his life in Tottenham rather than Tokyo.

To the best of Dan's knowledge, the split had been more than amicable, and friendship had lasted where the attraction—or perhaps Sada's ability to put up with Chris on an everyday basis—had waned. Since then, Sada had become a welcome part of their mutual social circle... although Dan could have done without the periodic enforced attendance of his exhibitions. As far as modern art went, he didn't like to think he'd failed too badly in trying to keep up with fashion, but he just couldn't see the appeal of Sada's work.

They arrived slightly late, electropop oozing out of the gallery's seedy little shop-front windows and pools of neon light seeping onto the pavement. The city buzzed on all around, night buses and squealing car tires, distant music, and passing sirens wailing into the night. Dan took a deep breath and followed Chris inside: *manky* was definitely the word. He'd been here a few years ago, when British art was still clinging hopelessly to the tails of its last rise. Around that time, a man who looked a bit like Charles Saatchi had once been seen perusing one of the exhibitions here, and he suspected the owners hadn't changed a thing since, just in case the gleam rubbed off. Certainly, the concrete steps and dingy stairwell didn't look like it had been painted in decades.

Upstairs, the gallery had a white-cube-and-warehouse-windows vibe to it. The music was louder, and the obligatory table of warm champagne and nibbly things had a crowd of critics around it. He noticed the slew of usual suspects too, the same faces that peppered all these events: Mary Hobart, one of the loudest voices in contemporary textile art, if not necessarily one of the most proficient, and Stuart Glenning, who still looked like an accountant, though he now ran one of the newest and most fashionable PR agencies in the area. Chris said Sada was on the verge of signing with Glenning, though Dan wasn't sure he believed it.

The main draw of the evening was an installation that took up a third of the plain white space. Plaster spheres dotted the floor, each about two feet high. Around them, colored footprints cut from thin plastic sheets led in strange, overlapping, circuitous patterns up to a man's silhouette, freestanding in black cardboard. From the ceiling, mirrors suspended on thin silver wires caught and fragmented both footprints and viewer, so that the twirling swatches of color and motion bounced all around the room, confusing the eye and disorienting the mind.

Sada approached through the crowd, a smile on his face and a glass in his hand. Dan hung back for a moment while he and Chris hugged, trying to tell himself that he was definitely not jealous of that easy intimacy or those snippets of lingering touches.

"Hi, Sada. Great, um, great show."

Sada's grin widened. "Thanks, Dan. Good to see you. I was hoping you'd come—I've got a project idea I wanted to talk to you about."

Dan pricked up his ears. "Oh, yeah?"

"Mm." Sada nodded wildly, pausing for another swig of champagne. "Friend of mine got this arts grant. She's based in Battersea, and she was asking if I knew any good photographers. It's, like, a whole history of life in the area thing. One frame for every step or something, she says. I forget. Local council's all over her. Anyway, I said I'd have a word with you when you got back from… where were you? Venice, was it?"

"Yeah. He was exploring the cultural endowments of the city," Chris put in with a filthy grin.

Dan winced, but Sada seemed oblivious to the smut.

"Really? Wow, I've always wanted to go there. What was it like?"

Dan would have preferred to talk more about the job opportunity, but he could feel Chris positively itching for another chance to say something laced with innuendo, so he just passed off a few innocuous comments about history, light, and architecture and shot a warning glare at his friend when he opened his mouth. Dan thought he'd got away with it, especially when Sada's attention drifted off halfway through, more focused on one of the art critics from the *Times*: a petite woman with a dark red trouser suit, wire-rimmed glasses, and a severe bob, who'd started giving close inspection to the scattered mirrors and transient footprints. Across the room, someone had already set their plastic cup of champagne down on one of the spheres.

Dan wasn't sure whether he liked the piece or not. It spoke too much to him about confusion and fragmentation, too redolent of the tortuously meandering paths he'd taken through Venice's cobbled backstreets.

He blinked, wanting to shake those sticky traces of thoughts out of his head. Would everything remind him of that place now?

His observations were pretty much left to fend for themselves in the ebb of the conversation, and an uneasy quiet settled into the ledge between the three men and the rest of the room. Chris broke it, flinging an arm around Sada's shoulders and gesturing expansively to the installation.

"Well, anyway, this is wonderful," he announced. "Absolutely gorgeous. What's it s'posed to mean?"

Laughter splintered between them, perhaps a way of easing the tension, an expression of comfortable intimacy or, for Dan, an awkward distraction from his current discomfort. He couldn't wait to get away. The part of the gallery not turned over to the installation displayed some black-and-white photography, not entirely unlike the work Dan had once shown here himself. He liked the crisp angles, the sharp contrasts, the view of London's skyline as a postapocalyptic jungle, explored through the fragments of light that hid in the way buildings met above a narrow alley or broken windows held the spiraling dust. Dan moved happily among these frames, secure in his own medium.

He was content to let Sada return to courting his critics, though he observed with interest the fact that Chris followed the artist, lending moral support and the occasional hand on an elbow. The odd well-placed smile too. Was something going on there that Dan had missed?

Dan didn't get a chance to consider it because at that moment an unwelcome jolt of recognition bolted him to the floor.

He knew he'd see Paul again, of course. They still moved in the same circles, still had the same haunts, but... here? Now?

Shit.

He stood on the other side of the room, dangling a cup of champagne in one hand and filling out a midrange designer suit in serious style. That thick, stocky body, like a rugby player without the scuffs and bruises, drew glances from men and women alike and, for a brief moment, obscene, absurd jealousy coursed through Dan. It lasted long enough for Paul to catch his eye, and he cursed inwardly, desperate to pretend his attention was engaged elsewhere, but there wasn't going to be any escape. They did a mutual sort of half grin and continued to edge their separate ways around the room.

The inevitability that they would meet up somewhere around the middle ate away at Dan until he wanted to vault, James Bond style, through the window and into the street below. No chance of that, though.

Paul had started making a beeline for him, bearing through the gaggles of people with that look of determined arrogance he got when he wanted his own way.

"Dan! All right, mate?"

Dan winced and tried to marshal an unwilling smile. He didn't want to have to talk to Paul here, now… in front of Chris, who'd noticed and started waggling his eyebrows and mugging suggestively from halfway across the room. Yes, this moment had been inevitable, but did it have to be right now? Right here?

"Paul. Hi. You look g—" Shit, no. No, he didn't want to say that, however true it might be. "—well. You okay?"

Great. Sounds like a tentative consolation to the recently bereaved.

He shifted uncomfortably and cleared his throat. Paul smiled, and it slipped over Dan like a warm caress, leaving the hairs on the back of his neck standing to attention, and other parts of his anatomy threatening to do the same.

"Yeah, yeah. Fine. Good. You?"

Dan shrugged. "Mm. Thanks. Yeah, I'm—"

"You look good."

Paul moved closer, just a gentle shift of weight, but a big change in the balance of space between them. He still had that cocky grin on his face, all self-awareness and sharp blue eyes. Same aftershave too. Dan fought to stay focused against the wave of unexpected memories that flooded him in a wash of disappointed regret and Paco Rabanne. People moved around them with glasses of champagne and canapés, the buzz of conversation a constant thrum. Dan couldn't have felt more exposed if he'd been naked. All those remembered empty days seemed intensified in every detail, and the open gulf that had yawned between them pressed in on him, renewing his frustration. They'd always been at their best in bed, and that attraction had never fully waned, no matter however much everything else had.

Right now he wanted to grasp at something—anything—an achievement or an anecdote to wave in Paul's face, some statement of independent success, but he couldn't think of a single one.

Dan blinked rapidly. He'd known he'd have to face this moment, but he'd somehow assumed it would be easier, that the things he would remember about his time with Paul would be the crappy stuff. The bursts of drama and passive aggression in between the banality, chafing against the knowledge that what they'd had wasn't getting better.

He remembered it—he *knew* he did—and he remembered how strange that stifling, choked existence had been, pierced by bouts of such intense heat. He remembered trying to make himself believe it was normal, even when he knew it wasn't.

"So, um," Paul began, leaning just that little bit farther in, "these are good, huh?"

He nodded to the photos Dan had been looking at. Dan raised an eyebrow. Working in gallery acquisition, Paul had never really given much of a damn about whether art was good or not, or even whether he liked it: just how well it would sell.

"Not bad." He glanced back at the prints, the high-contrast blocks of light and shadow. Paul's proximity tugged on his senses, feeling so weirdly familiar and yet so strangely foreign. "So, did Sada invite you?"

"Yeah. Coming on well, isn't he? Lots of nice notices about all this stuff in the press."

"Mm," Dan muttered noncommittally, wishing he could get away.

A pair of glazed doors opened out onto a balcony at the other side of the room. Although he knew the air blowing through them would taste of petrol, grime, and chip fat from the takeaway down the road, Dan wanted to be over there, breathing in the nearest thing to cool, fresh air.

"It's good to see you, anyway. I, um, I have missed you, y'know."

Dan's gaze snapped back to Paul's face, though he didn't know what he expected to find there. Paul smiled guilelessly. There was so much clear, hopeful honesty in his expression, and maybe even a little regret. Dan wasn't sure what to say. He was also aware of Chris, lingering by the canapés and champagne, and paying far too much attention to this little interlude.

Dan ignored his friend and cleared his throat. "Yeah, well, it's a little late for—"

"Water under the bridge, though, eh? And of course you've been off on your holidays just recently."

The barb in Paul's tone struck at Dan, and he reacted without thinking. For a moment, it was uncomfortably like old times. "So? I don't think you get a say on that anymore."

"Not asking for one. Just noticed you skipped off to the Continent. Where was it? Rome?"

How the hell does he even—Christ, am I gossip already?

"Venice," Dan snapped, determined not to rise to the bait.

"Ah. We were always going to do Italy, weren't we?"

Dan's jaw tensed. There was a look that could have been mistaken for apologetic regret clouding Paul's eyes... except that Paul didn't really do apologies.

"Yes, we were, weren't we? I guess we never got around to it."

"No. Wish we had. Did you find what you were looking for?"

Paul inched casually closer, too close for anyone but a lover or a combatant, his smile starting to smear into challenge. Dan stood his ground, refusing to move back or admit a thing.

"If you mean peace and quiet, yes."

"And then some, right?" Paul chuckled. "I know you. Bet you had a great time. Meet anyone?"

How the hell d—

Dan fought to avoid shooting an accusatory look across the room at Chris and shrugged instead. He shook his head, but the fat lie he'd intended on uttering didn't quite slip from his lips, and Dan watched the *Times* critic wandering around Sada's installation for what must have been the fifth time, her brow pinched somewhere between concentration and disbelief.

He didn't notice Paul move at first; he made it seem like he was just interested in the photos, but then there he was, sidling round Dan's body, being even more intrusive. His warm, champagne-scented breath grazed the back of Dan's neck, raising hairs and memories of better times. He sniffed, suspicious of Paul's motives and embarrassed at his own reaction.

"If I didn't know better," he managed, "I'd say you were jealous."

"Have I got reason to be?"

Even without seeing Paul's face, Dan knew he'd be smirking. He was the worst kind of arrogant bastard sometimes, and Dan had always thoroughly hated how much of an effect it had on him.

"You weren't when we were together," he muttered. The *Times* critic still circled nearby, involved with the dangling mirrors and fragments of fractured light.

Paul leaned in, lowering his voice until the sound of it just scraped Dan's ear, bypassing all the usual routes of nerves and brain on its way to his groin.

"*You* weren't screwing anything that moved then, Danny."

"I haven't be—Look, it's not even your business, Paul. Forget it." Dan winced, aware that the critic probably wasn't all that out of earshot. "I thought we both agreed—"

"You're right." Paul took a sudden step back, giving Dan his freedom, and it felt like being hit with a blast of cold air. "I'm sorry. I'm out of line."

Dan's eyebrows rose, his mouth quirking into an involuntary grin of disbelief. Apologies came about as naturally to Paul as tap-dancing did to a rock. Dan turned to face him and found him actually looking contrite.

"It's all right," Dan said, though he wasn't entirely sure it was. "I suppose it's… weird, isn't it? It's been a long while."

"It has," Paul agreed, nodding solemnly. "Too long. I wish I'd called you. Talked about it or something. I… I miss you," he admitted, lifting one shoulder in a little minishrug. "Just to talk to. So, um… look… d'you think we could still do that? Talk, I mean?"

"Talk?" Dan echoed dubiously. Why that? And why now?

"Yeah. I feel bad about the way we left it, that's all. I was thinking, how about a drink?"

Dan clutched his tepid champagne defensively. "I've got one."

"Not here." Paul smiled indulgently. "Tomorrow, maybe, or later in the week?"

"Look, I don't know… I might be busy."

"I'll call you, then. How about that? Could I call you?"

Dan made a vague noise of assent, not in the mood to make a scene. "Sure. Yes. I… I'd like that."

He mentally kicked himself for words that could seem like enthusiasm, especially when a grin as warm as sunlight suffused Paul's face.

"Would you really?"

Dan nodded and braced himself for the kiss he could tell Paul wanted to plant on him. That little party trick was always a favorite when anyone with a camera was around, but it didn't come. He wondered if he'd imagined seeing the familiar look in Paul's eye… or whether he'd just wanted to think it was there. Instead, Paul simply smiled again.

"'Kay. I'd really like that. Well, better get back to mingling. It's great to see you, Dan. We'll catch up, yeah?"

"Mm. Bye."

"Bye, then."

He sauntered off, perfection in an overpriced suit, and Dan pretended not to check out the back view as he went.

"I still say you were insane," Chris observed, apparently materializing from nowhere and appearing at his elbow. "If I had that, I'd've chained it to the bed and thrown away the key."

"Tried it," Dan said. "Wasn't that impressed. He kept whining about neck ache."

Chris's guffaw of laughter echoed around the room.

DAN GOT home a little after midnight, woozy with that stuffy-headed feeling of champagne drunkenness and a strong sense of frustrated unease. Seeing Paul had stirred up too much. And why should Paul be interested in talking again now? And why so jealous? After the awkward fizzle out of their relationship, what had changed? Maybe it had been the time apart, the chance to reassess and reevaluate. Maybe, in classic romance novel mode, Paul had realized what he wanted from life and come running back to Dan's side.

Dan scoffed at the interior of his fridge and then tried to remember why he was looking into it. *Oh, yeah… hungry.* He grabbed the makings of a cheese and mustard sandwich and settled himself at the kitchen counter. Thing was, he genuinely didn't care what Paul wanted anymore. He should do, he supposed. They were both still human beings, and the two of them had been close. Once. As he chewed his sandwich, he thought back over those times with maudlin regret. They seemed to him now like faceted glass; what might briefly have had the sparkle of diamonds had never had the depth or fire. The pretty, glittering moments, all subsumed in faceless months of thick, transparent boredom. But he could be good at *flashes* of brilliance, couldn't he? Venice. What had that whole interlude been but a brief splurge of self-indulgent frivolity? Cut glass again. Each second, each kiss, was a droplet from a chandelier, hanging perilously over a sea of time into which, at some point, it would inevitably plummet.

Hah.

It was a depressing thought. Dan wanted to be worth more than moments, but what if he wasn't? What if that was all he'd ever be able to do? He finished the sandwich and sucked mustard off his thumb. He didn't miss Cesare. Not at all. Oh, he missed the sex, because that had been so good and there had been a sad lack of good in recent months, and he missed the fake intimacy. The instant counterfeit of pretending they knew each other. Secrets and dreams that could be shared with someone he'd never see again. Tonight proved that, didn't it? It proved... something, he felt sure. He hiccupped gently. Yeah. Because every time he'd touched Cesare, he'd probably been doing nothing more than reaching out for Paul. It must be that, because less than a week of hotel fucks and strange, snatched moments couldn't leave him feeling like this.

Dan swore under his breath. He should go to bed. He was too tired and full-headed to keep picking over the same old problems. An increasing part of him just felt guilty for what he'd done, taking advantage of someone like Cesare to scratch his itches and plaster his wounds. It had been just that, hadn't it? And that wasn't fair. Even if, thinking back, he doubted Cesare had been any kind of unwilling ingénue. Far from it, of course. He'd been so open, once the sluice gates of his inhibitions parted to let through the tide.

Dan remembered clear brown eyes burning before him, lips bent around that imperfect little O of pleasure, and Cesare's face so full of longing. Gratitude too. So grateful for every touch, even when all it served to do was stoke up the fires that hungered for more... and nothing burned brighter in that man than his potential.

"Bollocks," Dan said, his voice lumpy and loud in the kitchen's late-night quiet. He chuckled at the sound of it and pushed his fingers through his hair. "I'm so fucking drunk."

The squeak of chair on tiles grated at his nerves as he pushed it back and stood up. For a moment dizziness tugged at him, but Dan shook it away and headed to the bedroom. It seemed empty in here tonight. Traces of Paul, of Cesare, of the blond from Club Commodoro, and every meaningless quickie he'd ever had before that all clung to him, trailed after his flesh in every movement and hovered at the boundaries of his vision, but they were only ghosts. He stripped and flopped onto the mattress, burrowing down and away from all of it.

The morning couldn't come soon enough. With the fresh light of a new day, he'd feel better. Well... after a mixed grill and a couple of cups of coffee, maybe.

But the doubts would go. He'd remember—properly, and while sober—how he didn't want Paul back, whatever his groin and his self-doubt said, and how he'd established in a sensible and reasoned manner that just not hearing from Cesare would be better in the long run. It would be easier. He didn't need the drama, and Cesare didn't need the uncertainty.

Right? Right.

Besides, Dan had to get used to thinking for himself again, clear and free in his own life, not tainted by the rustling shadows of other men, their demands leaning on him and their wants and needs snuffling at the edges of every decision he made.

He fell asleep eventually, half dreaming of and half imagining the windswept breadth of the Via Vittorio Emanuele, desolate and lonely in a cloud of needling rain.

CHAPTER THIRTEEN

THE WEEKS eased by. They started slow, an hour-heavy plod of days that never seemed to end, and then it was as if time picked up, remembering it had a job to do. Venice receded, at least a little. Paul called, forcing Dan into a prickly, awkward confrontation of silences and half-empty sentences.

"I thought we could at least be friends. I'd really like that."

Dan sighed. "That's not what you're trying to do, though. Is it?"

"Yes! I mean, I think we split for the wrong reasons, Danny. I really do. But—"

Dan paced the living room floor, phone clamped to his ear and anger rising.

"Yeah, well, I'm sorry. Okay? I'm sorry if you think that, but there's no going back. That's not gonna happen."

"You've met someone, haven't you?"

Paul's voice was rigid with cold irritation. Dan bit back the terse sigh he wanted to give, aware of exactly the chain of recriminations and tantrums it would set off. He opted instead for pale vacillation and instantly regretted it.

"No. It's not.... Well, no."

He heard Paul's breath rasp on the line, just once.

"Oh."

"I haven't met—I mean, it's not because of anything like that."

Dan wished he had the ability to shut up and not dig himself any deeper into this hole, but the words kept coming. He wondered why. Was it some attempt at justification? Why should he feel the need for that? Or maybe apology?

"I just don't want to get back into the way things were, y'know?"

"Fine." Paul didn't sound in the least as if he accepted that. "All right. No, I apologize. I didn't intend to pressure you or anything. I just thought—"

"Yeah. Well." Dan bit his lip. He hated how standoffish he knew he was being and yet hated the fact that he disliked it. The next words to come out of his mouth sounded like conciliation but felt horribly like defeat. "Look… you're not pressuring me. I'm just not sure it's a good idea."

"I'm not trying to pick up where we left off, Danny. You know that. I understand. We let it get bad. But I do miss you. And being friends wouldn't be the end of the world, would it?"

Dan tilted his head back and gazed up at the ceiling. It offered no easy answers, but there was something close to the light fixture that looked like a small spider. He decided to ignore it.

"No, it wouldn't."

"Okay." Paul sounded so pleased. It was treacherously endearing. "So, what d'you think? Let me buy you that drink? For a truce? No pressure, just a drink."

Dan sighed. "All right. Sounds good."

"Great. How about tomorrow lunchtime? I'll be at Sotheby's all morning, but I could meet you after."

"Yes, okay. Give me a bell, I'll meet you somewhere," Dan said vaguely, hoping against hope they could manage to misplace each other somewhere along the way.

He knew he wouldn't be that lucky. When Paul made up his mind about wanting something—whether it was a promotion, a car, or even something as intangible as friendship—he butted, bullheaded, against everything in his way until he got it. Dan supposed he should feel slightly flattered to be the object of such determined attention.

He hung up and swore into the silent air.

He'd go, of course.

THE FOLLOWING morning dawned bright, cheerful, and without much hint of impending doom. Dan went, as he'd known he would. For some ridiculously fatuous reason, not going wasn't an option. It would have been like having an itch in the center of his back and not reaching for something with which to scratch it.

They had the drink at a pretty bistro neither had ever been to before, suggesting Paul's desire for fresh starts and blank slates. He was on his best behavior, all wit and urbane charm and only very mild flirtation, looking the epitome of the City success story in a plain suit and silk tie. Dan couldn't deny he looked incredible. He even *smelled* incredible. He was evasive when Dan asked what he'd been up to at the auction house, not outright refusing to answer questions, just avoiding their existence. Running under the current of his tone was the implication that if Dan really wanted to know, he shouldn't have fucked off in the first place.

It was never said, however, and the whole thing remained genial and pleasant.

That very fact pissed Dan off more than anything, though he had to admit that it *was* genuinely good to see Paul and to spend time with him like this again. It was surprisingly good, in fact. They were actually talking, using words and listening to each other, and it felt great. It felt real, and the contrast to those increasingly hazy days in Venice struck home, stinging Dan with the betrayal of a dream from which it hurt to wake.

They parted on better terms than they'd met, and despite his misgivings, Dan started to think that maybe being on friendlier footing wouldn't be so bad. The fleeting tail of other thoughts, and the dark suspicion that it wouldn't really be either that uncommon or that unforgivable to give things with Paul another shot and see where they went, stalked through his mind. He did his best to ignore them.

Dan didn't want to think of himself as the kind of man who'd jump from bed to bed to soothe his wounds. Nor did he want to believe the entirety of everything that had happened since he broke up with Paul had been about that relationship, in one way or another. Hell, he'd been past adolescence for a long while now, hadn't he? All the same, he remained unconvinced.

He'd been aware just how much he missed it… the way things had been with the two of them, right at the start. Something fresh, new, and vibrant. And despite every logical grain of thought that said he'd already been through this—already mourned the passing and buried the losses—Dan couldn't help wondering what would happen if they did try again.

Paul hadn't exactly suggested that. Not in so many words, though Dan suspected it was on his mind too. He couldn't have said why. The same reasons *he'd* been thinking about it ever since they split up, maybe. Missing him, missing the potential they'd squandered, missing the security of knowing that, even if it was imperfect, he had someone to come home to… who knew?

All he could be certain of was that Paul had seemed genuine. He was good at that, admittedly. He'd seemed so convincing at lunch. So plausible, so familiar, so… well, so *present*. For all his negative points, he still represented something safe, comfortable, and real, or at least the memory of it. Maybe it was wishful thinking or just inconvenient curiosity. Maybe it was fear of winding up alone. Maybe it was a combination of all of those things, muddled up with a fat dose of loneliness, regret, and desperation.

Either way, Dan reminded himself just how stupid it all was. He'd thought he was over this, but the temptations still tugged at him, and spending time in Paul's company again had done nothing whatsoever to improve that.

He even believed what Paul said about the house in Lancaster Gate being left empty due to a fuckup by the rental agent. Paul had told him the story over lunch, explaining with a twinkling smile how it had worked in his favor in the end, because he'd decided to sell anyway, and now he didn't have to worry about getting rid of a tenant.

Dan wasn't sure why he was so ready to believe so many of the things his ex said, though he supposed Paul had no real reason to lie. If he wanted to build bridges, why wouldn't it be genuine? It wasn't as if Dan was his only option in the dating pool, and Paul didn't *need* him… but he might *want* Dan, and that thought was peculiarly empowering.

It wasn't going anywhere yet, though. That much was certain. And, Dan reminded himself, dissecting all of this on the basis of one lunch date was pretty ridiculous.

"I've turned into Bridget fucking Jones," he murmured to himself, not for the first time, as he booted up his laptop and—in the peaceful laziness of an unhurried Sunday morning—checked his e-mail.

When he first got home from Venice, he'd gone through a period of checking it almost obsessively, racing to grab at new messages. He'd stopped that now: the first steps in letting the fantasy die. That was why it was so strange to see Cesare's name in his in-box, and for a moment, Dan didn't believe it could be real.

He opened the e-mail cautiously, read and reread the few simple lines. As text, they were stilted and awkward, clumsy, and uneven. Yet that didn't matter. Hearing the words in his head, Dan fitted them around Cesare's voice, and they had all of his wonderful cautiousness, the tentative English pronunciation that had been so hopelessly attractive and so characteristic of him.

He didn't say much: just that he hoped Dan was well, that he didn't mind this contact. To read Cesare's words, it almost seemed they'd never been more than passing acquaintances, but Dan felt all the unspoken things pressing in, as if the uncertainty and need could seep right through the screen. He got up and made himself another cup of tea, embarrassed at being so affected by such a simple thing… and yet it wasn't simple. Far from it. Reaching out the way Cesare had would have cost him dearly. He'd have needed to screw up a lot of guts to do it, and that protective tenderness pulled again at Dan's chest. He remembered just how much Cesare had to give and how hard it had been for him to do it.

All the same, as he sat back down, blew on his tea to cool it, and looked again at those few, full words, Dan wondered if this really was a good idea. He definitely didn't expect the simple greeting and two lines of text to catch him quite the way they did. Cesare hoped he was well, said *he* was fine although very busy at work… he thanked Dan once more for a wonderful time, closing with the hope that maybe he would write soon. Dan stared at the screen, filled with a curious mixture of doubt and relief. Of course he wanted to e-mail back. He was just worried about what that would mean to Cesare. A friendship would be a wonderful thing. He didn't doubt that, for either of them… but it couldn't be anything more than friendship. Cesare knew that, didn't he? He must do.

Dan chastised himself. The man was closeted, not stupid. All the same, did he really want to risk hurting him? Pedestals could rise a long way off the ground, and he was afraid of falling.

Dan started to write a reply, which he deleted just before sending. He got up, walked around the room a couple of times while he drank his tea, looked at the beautiful, blazing landscape painting on his wall… then manned up, retyped the e-mail and screwed up the courage to hit the Send button, only to suspect he'd done it too soon and might seem desperate. Bloody stupid, because they'd already fucked. He knew the intimacies and delicacies of Cesare's attraction to him, and he knew just how careful he had to be.

Dan cussed under his breath, ran his fingers through his hair, and inspected the irritation he found blossoming in himself. Irritation with Cesare, of all things, for getting in touch… that was stupid, wasn't it? Dan had read the words of his reply over and over before he sent them, checking for ambiguities, double meanings, or turns of phrase that might make him sound too eager, or not eager enough. As if he could be annoyed over this, as if he could blame Cesare for not having English as his mother tongue, for being so easy to potentially damage....

For me worrying so much about doing so.

Dan pushed the thoughts out of his head. Nope. Nothing more than a friendly pen-pal thing, obviously. No sense in admitting the suggestion of anything more than that... why ache so much over contact with someone so far away? Even without the complication of the awkward, exasperating, not-quite reunion he seemed to be edging around with Paul, it wasn't as if any kind of friendship he might manage to sustain with Cesare could develop much. Even if either of them would want it to, which wasn't to say that was a foregone conclusion. Because... well, even if, for the sake of argument, they *did*, then no matter what distance they could cover in miles, Cesare would still have in that awful, ostracizing otherness of his, keeping him somehow forever apart and hidden.

Dan thought glumly of a future filled with brief, blisteringly hot Tuscan summers, and the inevitable returns to dim, English rain. Too depressing for words. He knew what he wanted, and even if he was loath to recall or even admit it to himself, he knew what those stolen hours with Cesare had felt like. Even if that could live outside of Venice's crumbling walls, what was the future in sitting on his dick for three weeks out of every four just for that? It wouldn't be real.

And Dan wanted real... even if it scared him.

THE RESPONSE to his e-mail came a very respectable two days later. Cesare's joy was palpable. His words were still restrained, but they beat with a skittish enthusiasm. Dan replied, irritated by the nervousness he felt, the ridiculousness of sweaty palms and dry mouth, like every word he wrote was a building block of some new friendship. Daft, because what greater intimacy could they have now than what they'd already shared?

Yet for everything that had gone before, Dan came to realize he was wrong about that. What grew out of those first, tentative communications became something entirely different to the islanded time of Venice. The automatic intimacy of coinciding bodies and coinciding needs gave way to a new way of behaving, of thinking about each other. Balanced comfortably on the shoulders of everything they so far knew, each had the option to dig a little deeper, share a little more, secure in the illusion that they were basing it on some long-established kinship. Strangely, in the security of knowing he wouldn't bump into Cesare on the Tube or at a café, Dan found the same kind of peace as he'd found in his arms.

He flattered himself that it wasn't just him, that Cesare also benefited from someone to talk to, even if it wasn't in person. Their exchanges, though growing more familial, also lost the edge of tension they'd had at first. Cesare confided things about work and his family. He ranted against the system, about the autistic boy in his class and the school's convention-bound principal, and provided a few coy, wistful-sounding updates on his brother's developing office romance. They talked about the minutiae of daily life in the same breath as picking apart headlines, observing a fresh political scandal unfold, probing the details of a new Vatican speech, or joking about some inconsequential item in the news.

The only thing Dan didn't feel he could talk to Cesare about was his love life… such as it was. Briefly he wondered why, whether there was some hidden baggage he was trying to ignore, or whether he could get away with telling himself that not talking about it made things easier on Cesare.

Even so, the night he finally ended up in bed with Paul, Dan was surprised to find he didn't feel guilty about it.

He hadn't meant for it to happen. Paul had been texting him ever since Sada's gallery exhibition, and Dan hadn't been as brusque with him as planned. Gradually their relationship had eased over from speaking terms to casual drinks, and somehow Dan had managed to forget exactly *why* he'd been so against that.

There was a long, lazy lunch at a riverside bistro: late spring sunshine with pre-June heatwaves, and all the open promises of summer. Dan had watched the Thames glide greasily by, while the light picked out all the best moments of Paul's smile. It made it easy to wonder why he'd ever wanted to throw any of this away. Had things between them really felt so stale and empty? Or had he just been afraid of the commitment growing too comfortable, perhaps expected some magical recharge of excitement to something they should have fixed themselves?

Whatever the answer, when Paul moved to kiss him in the dappled shade of a plane tree, Dan didn't deny him. They didn't talk about ground rules or meanings, just did their best not to touch too much during the taxi ride.

Paul's place looked much like he'd made Dan's flat look before he moved out. There was the same glass-topped table, and more furniture with clean, modern lines, obscured by piles of magazines and other general clutter. Somehow, the whole effect still managed to seem well tailored, like a study in casual elegance. Paul muttered something about the rental value: that he'd sold the house in Lancaster Gate and was thinking about buying somewhere a bit farther west, but Dan wasn't really listening.

He pulled Paul close, fastening his mouth to those firm, full, occasionally spiteful lips, and ground hard against him, not allowing either of them thought or respite.

The familiarity of it was devastating, like falling back into an old habit with a rush of guilty pleasure. Hands remembered their previous haunts, bodies fitted together as if there'd been no interlude of isolation. It wasn't a reclamation of once-lost territory, but more a return to comforting pastures.

Whatever his intentions had been in trying to forget, Dan supposed they would never have been effective. To say he'd forgotten how good it was with Paul would have been an outright lie. He'd remembered, though the knowledge had faded a little in recent weeks. Now, every touch seared anew, bringing home just how high their tensions ran.

There was no great romantic reunion to it. That didn't surprise Dan—if there'd been no earth-shattering schism in their initial drift, it only made sense to see them loll back together again like sands shifting on a windblown beach. He supposed, though he disliked the thought, he'd struck out for drama in his holiday fling. Silly, really. Back in the living world, the daily grind of normality didn't support things like that, and he'd been aiming at clouds anyway. Why shoot for rainbows when what he had with Paul was uncommon enough?

He recalled Chris's point about the whole hot boyfriend deal and grinned to himself. The sex with Paul was better than it had been in a long, long time. Paul had changed, for a start. He was… unbridled? Yeah, that was the word. There was something immensely liberating about the two of them fucking like machines, without analysis or trepidation, just celebrating the capabilities and extents of their bodies. No baggage, no pulled punches, and none of the awkward easing into something new.

Stripped fast and pushed to the bed, Dan eyed Paul's body hungrily, eager for the way he surged forward into every embrace, like it was something to be captured... taken. He kissed hard, played rough, his hands swift and ruthless on Dan's flesh.

"You want it like we used to?" he murmured, voice scraping the back of Dan's neck.

"Yeah."

A small word, but pretty much all it took. He threw one hand out in front of him, the chrome of Paul's low, modern bedstead cool against his palm, arched his back, and let the world close over him.

They fucked in intense earnest, like always, but Dan wondered if he'd ever realized before how much effort Paul put into showing off. Each change of position, each new maneuver, seemed purposefully performed against the backlight of the lamp. He didn't pause to give it much contemplation; when he rose high enough to crest the same waves, meet every challenge Paul threw him and put down a few of his own, it didn't seem important. All of life's an act, and the people closest to us usually see the greatest number of our disguises.

"Fuck... yes!" Paul murmured when he came for the second time that evening.

Dan considered the tawny head that rested on his chest, breath tickling his skin in warm, damp bursts, and limbs all tangled up around him. He traced his thumb down the unseen muscles of Paul's nape, blond hair soft to the touch.

That was the point he used to say he loved me.

He hadn't often believed it, of course. Though in the lingering seconds of ecstasy, Dan supposed it might have been true in its own way. Moot point, all the same. Paul hadn't even used love as an argument to win him back, which was to his credit. Few things would have impressed Dan less than the indignant whine "but I love you"... as if that made up for everything else. They were just doing what they were doing and not asking questions. Essence of life, really, Dan told himself. Essentially what everyone did. Experience the moment, fret in the quiet hours over its meaning.

Paul raised his head, a fixed sort of half smile curving his lips, and sought Dan's mouth in a loose, limp, but prolonged kiss. The heat of sweat, sex, and interest between them had rapidly cooled, and Dan wondered whether it would be really awful to say he needed to go home, maybe claim some kind of early meeting.

"I did miss you, Danny," Paul mumbled, rolling off and burrowing down beside him. "Really did."

The words trailed off into the changing patterns of his breath, deepening out into sleep. Dan lay still and looked up at the ceiling, counting the cracks and dimples that seemed to dance among the shadows. The bedroom window had been left slightly ajar, and outside, London's usual nighttime symphony of sirens, stereos, and humming traffic played on: just the purr of the city turning over to face the darkness.

Dan sighed and quietly decided that nothing, anywhere, ever really changed.

CHAPTER FOURTEEN

TIME SLIPPED on, and its passing became less noticeable through the interwoven patches of things that seeped their way into Dan's attention.

He wanted to hold back from e-mailing Cesare for a few days after that first night at Paul's place, as if getting back together with his ex was a direct affront to his friend. Perhaps it was, in a sense. Cesare had never really known about Paul, or how long a shadow he cast. Maybe that made Dan a liar, although he shrank from that thought as if it were acid and concentrated on reminding himself that this was just life, and just how things were. And that was okay, wasn't it?

Silence didn't work, though. Dan would catch himself forwarding a news story, or just typing a few lines… curious, for a moment, that it didn't feel strange. Cesare mailed back, of course, bright and cheerful and so eagerly responsive. By text, his English seemed almost fluent, though Dan still imagined each sentence overlaid with that characteristic lilt.

Gradually their e-mail exchanges lengthened, though they always stayed carefully devoid of sentiment, and their friendship deepened. Venice might have receded into memory, but Cesare loomed ever larger and brighter.

The Internet provided an odd kind of intimacy, instant and without pretension. They could be available by e-mail whenever the other wanted, with none of the inconvenience or discomforts of real life, and they could talk about almost anything. They exchanged news both serious and light, and Cesare asked after Edith and the kids, which led to Dan talking a lot about them and the rest of his family, and a great swapping of anecdotes and memories.

Dan told him about the planned art project Sada's friend Miriam wanted to rope him into, though he'd had so little concrete communication from her it was hard to really know where it was heading. Cesare was enthusiastic nonetheless, and it led to some great discussions about photography, art, architecture, and history… that shared delight in discovering the hidden corners of places that had bound them together in Venice.

They would send each other links to interesting exhibitions—a private collection of late Renaissance art going on show for the first time in Padua, a retrospective of an interesting French photographer's work, or a pop-up gallery that had gone viral mostly because it was on a New York subway train—and talk excitedly about them. Sometimes it almost felt a bit like being there with him.

Dan even showed him some pictures of Sada's work, though he knew it wouldn't really be to Cesare's taste. It wasn't, but he still found nice things to say, and Dan could pick up the mild awe and envy he knew would have touched the Italian's words if he'd spoken them aloud. He wondered what Cesare would have given to have a career in art. He said he couldn't paint, that he had no skill or confidence in it and was more naturally an academic than a creator, but Dan was sure there was a grain of wistfulness there. He was right. Another few e-mails later, Cesare was telling him about how he'd tried to paint a little while he was at college, and how the talents of other people he'd known had made him feel inferior and give it all up.

It led back around to talking about work, and Cesare assured Dan that he loved his job. The school he worked at was private, having been taken over some years ago and renovated from a crumbling village elementary into a small but strict institution that sought to pride itself on high standards and traditional values. Cesare seemed to feel that this was mostly lip service, but Dan suspected that might be due to how much of an ass he thought the principal was.

Dan couldn't tell whether Cesare's dislike of the man stemmed wholly or only partly from the arguments they'd had over the autistic boy in his class, but it seemed to be their major battleground. That, and the unfair limits of the educational system. Dan had almost forgotten how impassioned Cesare could be about injustice but of course that theme ran close to his heart, and it must be so much easier for him to fight for others than for himself.

Given that fire-eyed ardor, Dan didn't want to admit to him that, with such casual ease, he'd picked up again with Paul. So easily, so unthinkingly, when that kind of relationship, imperfect as it was and never quite what he'd imagined, was so far removed from what Cesare allowed himself. Part of Dan still thought his masochism ridiculous, though he could understand why Cesare had made those choices and, in a way, he admired them.

His friendship with Cesare seemed so natural and unforced it was hard to remember a time he hadn't been on the other end of the Internet, or when they hadn't been able to chat online late into the night about not very much at all. It was… nice.

Paul remained very much himself. Things on that front were almost back to normal by the beginning of summer. Out of deference to personal space and the treading upon of eggshells, they still retained separate apartments and weren't making a big thing about the time they spent together. Three out of five nights most weeks saw one of them in the other's bed, the weekends filled up with scheduled time together, scheduled time apart, and the occasional visit to someone's relatives or friends.

Chris made a show of being delighted about it, crowing and doing his "I told you so" dance, though he did dip dangerously close to seriousness one evening over drinks at a bar close to his apartment.

They'd come here a lot before Dan got together with Paul the first time, though the place had gone through about five different name and décor changes since then. At the moment, it was going for retro wine bar chic, with a designer wall of reclaimed timbers behind the bar, their cut ends making a palette of different colored wooden bricks that looked striking against the bare white of the other walls.

"You happy, then?" Chris asked, playing with the straw in his drink as he peered up, almost coyly, at Dan. "About him?"

"Hm?"

"Mr. Perfect. Things all right?"

Dan nodded absently. It had been a long day; he'd had an extremely drawn-out wedding consultation with a bride from hell, who seemed to want her wedding pictures to look like a *Vogue* shoot, despite really not having enough to work with in either style or budget.

"Yeah. Of course."

Chris made a thoughtful noise in the back of his throat. "Right. Did he ever tell you what happened with his place in Lancaster Gate?"

Dan took a mouthful of his vodka tonic. He was tired and wanted to go home, but he'd promised Chris at least one drink. He hadn't known it was going to turn into an interrogation.

"He sold it. Didn't I tell you about that? The tenant pulled out at the last minute or something, so he had it sitting empty for a while. The agent fucked up. It put on a bit of value, though, so he decided to sell. Worked out well in the end."

Chris just raised an eyebrow. Dan knew perfectly well what his friend meant, and he sighed, deflated.

"No, I don't think he was cheating on me. I never did, not really. I mean, sure, it *could* have happened, but... nah, I don't think so. It wasn't about that. We just got into such a rut, and we never talked about anything much. We kept a lot private, I suppose. I always thought that was a good way to run a relationship."

"Hmm." Chris pursed his lips into a thoughtful circle. "There's maintaining your independence and being a bloody ostrich, though, isn't there?"

Dan frowned. "I thought you were pleased about us. You never shut up about how wonderful you thought he was, or how I was stupid for leaving. What's changed?"

The evening was wearing on, and the volume of the pop music piped through the bar's speakers was slowly increasing. A headache had started to settle in, throbbing dully over Dan's right eye.

"Nothing." Chris shrugged. "I mean, if you're happy with things. I can't see why you *wouldn't* be. You love him, don't you?"

A gaggle of young women—probably office workers just out from a late meeting, maybe paralegals or something, judging by their smart suits and tired faces—entered the bar, chattering busily. They looked like they deserved a break.

Dan stared blankly at the remnants of his drink. People didn't get back together with their exes months after the breakup unless they loved them, did they?

Love was what made people do stupid things. It was what staved off the loneliness and feeling so very lost, and it was what made people put faith in their partners like packing wet sand into a bucket and turning it out in the hope it would hold its shape.

Paul didn't say he loved him much now. Dan didn't say it either. But it felt like it, didn't it? Like comfort and familiarity and stability, and it was good... so what more could anyone really ask for?

"Yeah," he said. "Course."

"Well, then." Chris grinned. "Lucky bastard."

Dan smiled. He really was.

It surprised him rather that Edith didn't question anything. Back at the very beginning, she'd been wary of Paul, the way she held anyone Dan dated at an initial distance, but she'd seemed to warm to him. He was great with the kids, bringing them presents and taking them out for burgers, and Dan enjoyed those times. It was easy to have fun, all together like that, and Edith never needed to know about the way Paul would collapse on the sofa at home later, letting out a huge sigh and swearing that he never knew why anyone would have kids.

When they went around to her place for dinner, she'd serve lamb chops and potatoes with a smile, and it all felt like old times. Maybe too much so sometimes. Dan wished he knew what the hell was wrong with him. Either he wanted this or he didn't; either he liked the familiarity, or he was afraid of falling back into those well-worn patterns he and Paul had shared.

It had to be one of the two, because he knew he couldn't have everything.

He was perversely pleased to find that they could still fight like they used to: those storms in between the calm. The first came when Paul threw a tantrum about the Italian phrasebooks he found by Dan's bed.

Paul didn't exactly accuse him of anything, but an ominous shadow still fell on their relationship with Dan's nondisclosure of the books' existence… as if Italy or any interest he had in it was somehow a lingering reminder of their problems. Problems that should be put firmly behind them and ignored, perhaps, until they withered away.

Dan was tempted to call him out on that, to demand to know precisely how his twisted logic worked to that conclusion, but instead he simply, coolly, told Paul it was none of his business. His hobbies, interests, or potential holiday destinations were his concern and no one else's and, oddly, that seemed to settle it.

That worried Dan. First, he felt affronted by Paul's readiness to keep compartmentalizing their lives the way they'd always done, despite the fact that *he* had been just as happy with—or just as guilty of—that before. He felt sure there should have been some spark of irritation, some face-off that marked Paul's determination to do things differently, to throw themselves properly into this relationship, if that was what it was truly going to be… and Dan had no idea what that made him. Did he want his independence taken from him? Did he want to goad Paul into something, to make them really face each other instead of dancing this cool ballet of pretenses?

Things weren't quite the same as before Venice.

They hadn't talked about it, but Dan knew it. He was sure Paul did too. Whatever they were doing, it wasn't the same. It was love at a distance: sex and slight mistrust, papered over with the desire to believe in autonomy rather than second chances. They were doing what felt good, what was easy and familiar, and they were doing it because they were a good fit and because they wanted to. It was real, and comfortable, and sensible… but it wasn't the same. Dan couldn't tell if he wanted that to change or just thought he should want it to. Maybe he still wanted Paul to be the man Dan had hoped he'd turn out to be… though he knew by now that was never going to happen. Neither of them was perfect, and neither of them had really changed.

Dan should have told Paul about Cesare. He knew that, just as he knew he should have been more open with Cesare about his love life. He wished he had, but it seemed too late now, and what would he have said, anyway?

It was hard enough to put words to it in his own head, and every time Dan tried, he just ended up feeling guilty and stupid. Spending too long examining any of this whole mess was like shining a light behind the oven in a cheap rented apartment. Everything he saw made him feel less comfortable, but he still had to live with it.

He would have liked to talk to Cesare about it, but Dan couldn't bring himself to pick up the phone, and every attempt he made to write it out ended up sitting in the drafts folder of his in-box, abandoned and incomplete.

Cesare's e-mail the following week, tentatively inquiring whether he was all right, as he'd not been in touch for a while, only served to worsen Dan's sense of utter and hopeless iniquity. He felt like a liar and a fraud, and every negative emotion he had pissed him off all the more because he hadn't done anything technically wrong. He kept telling himself that. He wasn't hiding anything terrible, wasn't *lying* to anyone, exactly… and he needed to keep believing it, because the alternative scared the hell out of him.

Dan replied as breezily as he could, told Cesare he was fine and asked after him. How was he? How about the boy, Niccolò Misseri? The flurry of questions deflected having to mention Paul, but didn't make Dan feel any better.

HE NEEDED something to focus on, so it felt like a blessing when Sada called with news on his friend Miriam's project. Dan had exchanged a couple of introductory e-mails with her soon after Sada's show. He'd indicated his interest, but she was half epitome and half stereotype of the scatterbrained, earnest artist: terrible at planning and eternally hand-waving details away as "something to sort out later." Her messages were explosions of hopeful optimism and lofty yet vague ideas, but somehow she'd secured a sizable chunk of funding for her installation… assuming it ever actually happened.

Ordinarily, Dan would have written the project off as a pipe dream. He didn't do work on spec, particularly when it would involve the kind of time and effort that spending several days walking around Battersea was going to necessitate. However, as Chris had pointed out when trying—probably for Sada's sake—to convince Dan not to bow out of all the nebulous planning, it wasn't that much different from the amount of walking around and aimlessly photographing places that he'd done in Venice. Dan supposed he had a point, though the memory of all those pictures—and the time he'd spent sorting through, editing, and uploading the best of them to his portfolio website—was bittersweet. He wished he'd gotten Cesare to allow him a few proper portraits, instead of just the sneaky candids outside the Chiesa dei Carmini… though Dan still filed those away safely in a folder on his laptop.

It was Chris, who seemed to be becoming ever more instrumental to Sada's career, who finally wrangled an informal meeting between the artists, photographers, and the couple of undergraduate students who were Miriam's excuse for a portion of her funding. She had, apparently, formerly been an art history lecturer at University College London and, according to one of her more cogent e-mails, "youth roots: community history and social conservation" were a big part of the project. Dan was extremely unsure about the whole thing. He'd read Miriam's summary and draft artist statement out to Paul, who laughed at it in a rather unkind way and suggested that this was precisely the reason arts funding was the first thing to get slashed in any budget.

Dan tried to go to the meeting with an open mind. They were meant to be having lunch at the Starbucks just down the road from Sada's place. He was the first to arrive, so he grabbed a latte and a table, and then got what proved to be the first in a series of invective-laced texts from Chris.

Like herding fucking cats! Be a few minutes late.

"A few minutes" turned into several, so Dan got another coffee. Eventually, Sada arrived, looking rather smug, with Miriam and a scowling Chris in tow. They were flanked by three students: a boy with wispy chin hair and a wool cap, despite the sunshine, and two girls, one in printed leggings and a Frankie Goes to Hollywood T-shirt, and the other wearing an oversized leather jacket and clutching a black portfolio case as if it had the longhand draft of an unreleased song by The Cure in it.

Miriam was petite, with a wild strawberry blonde perm and a dark blue crushed velvet tunic that she teamed with a chunky amber necklace and matching bracelet. Somehow this didn't surprise Dan, but he grinned warmly and waved them all over to the table.

Chris looked fit to strangle someone.

"Sorry we're late. We stopped off on the way to have a look at the proposed installation space," Sada said cheerfully, cruel amusement playing in his eyes. "Project HQ for the next few months. There's going to be a local history exhibit, some audiovisual stuff… it'll be fun. Chris has been *amazing* at liaison, *and* he's going to help put the website and e-book together. Literal angel. The way he's organized everything? He's wasted at that magazine."

He winked, and Dan tried hard to stifle his laughter. They both knew how much Chris loved dealing with people who had Miriam's level of whimsical disorganization.

"What can I say? I go where I'm needed," Chris said dryly, sliding into the corner seat.

He shot Dan a look that eloquently expressed just how fed up he was of herding those proverbial cats, and then his gaze flicked briefly to Sada with a distinct note of "I'll get you for this later" passing over his eyes.

They ordered food and more drinks, and settled to discussing the details of the project. Sada had offered to pay, celebrating a modest but recent sale, and, over a vast plate of falafel salad drowned in a bucket of chimichurri, Miriam expounded at great length on her ideas.

"It's going to be a visual time map," she said gravely. "A walk through the past, but *from* the future, bridging the gap between memory and social history, you know?"

The sun caught on the windows, reflected flares of light splintering off Miriam's hair. As if to illustrate the intense importance of what she was saying, she spread her hands wide by her face when she talked, palms out like a mime.

"The installation space is *amazing*. Used to be a coffee warehouse… and we're going to blow all the pictures up so they're completely floor to ceiling, right? Cover *every* inch of wall, get some flats made, stretch canvases over those, maybe have some suspended on wires… Sada's doing a piece that encapsulates, like, the actual overarching concept of time itself. It's going to be in—did we decide that yet? No. I'm not sure if it's going to be 3D printed plastic or if he's going to cast it, but it will hang from the ceiling. But the *photos*… it's one picture for every step. Like a real journey, you know? It's all about the perception, the living environment…."

Dan nodded and smiled. She was making it sound like a harebrained scheme, but the bones of the idea were solid. Across the table, Chris was polishing off a toasted cheese melt and looking slightly less harassed, though Dan distinctly saw him roll his eyes when Miriam uttered the phrase "conceptual illustration of time's ebb and flow."

Not that the project was a bad idea. As a matter of fact, Dan liked the thought of exploring a place and marking it frame by frame, photographing each step of a walk around its grim, postindustrial cadavers and gentrified ruins. Life never stood still. A photograph might be a second caught out of time, but the moment it captured was linked to a million more, both memories and moments yet to come.

Though Battersea had long risen from its days as a smoke-tattered tenement slum and once again become fashionable, Miriam remained more interested in those scars of its past and the grimy glamour of low-rent early-twentieth-century London. She wanted to unearth the last remaining traces of that and capture it for posterity, holding it up to the mirror of the future. Dan saw the value of her vision, even if he had a few doubts about it, but she had undeniable passion… and of course that sizable grant. The possibilities of the project intrigued him, and the prospect of getting paid was a great comfort. Besides, he needed his mind taken off the things he didn't want to dwell on.

When he viewed the world through a lens he didn't think about Paul, or about Venice, or about how lamentably wrapped up in himself he'd been since his return. Like the beautiful white sails of Italian women's bedsheets, caught billowing for an instant against a perfect blue sky, everything seemed safely encapsulated in its own existence, compartmentalized and secured, and it was so much easier to deal with.

Or so it should have been.

MIRIAM'S PROJECT, as Dan soon discovered, involved even more walking than he'd thought it would. She wanted to get started on the photographs as soon as possible, and that meant several long, winding trips around Battersea, foregoing all the recently remodeled parts— including the Tate Modern and the smattering of rather pleasant, if overpriced, cafés it had brought with it—in favor of dank and complex backstreets.

If Dan had realized quite how much legwork would be involved, all accompanied by her chatter and, as a sort of unofficial entourage, by Sada, Chris, and the gaggles of students who seemed to perpetually bob along in Miriam's wake, he might have reconsidered agreeing to take part. It was too late for second thoughts, however, and, like so many other afternoons in recent weeks, Dan now trudged resignedly behind Miriam, with Sada beside him and his camera bag, slung over one shoulder, getting heavier and heavier with each passing hour. They'd lost the latest batch of students a little over twenty minutes ago, as they flagged in the heat of Miriam's ardor and retreated into a nearby pub. She'd shown no signs of calming, though, and determined the rest of the party would plow on to the site of the old Price's candle factory, down near the river.

All the while, over every step of pavement and foot of concrete, with every successive frame that Dan shot, she kept talking in that peculiarly bright, glittery, shrill voice about seeing the passage of years and preserving the city's ancient, beating heart. Dan and Sada exchanged cynical looks but said nothing. *She* wasn't the one carrying the equipment, getting the sun in her eyes, or listening to herself hold forth to a footsore and somewhat beleaguered captive audience.

Chris, however, had found a way of amusing himself, and was in his element as he fluttered at her shoulder, encouraging her terribly and pointing out the particular details of a building's pipework, or the strange beauty of an exterior vent or peeling bricks. He shot a tiger-slick grin over her head at one point, the sun lighting his hair fire-gold, and Sada chuckled dryly.

"He's a bastard, isn't he?"

Dan took a couple of frames of a partially open door; the billowing steam and mingled odors of a Bengali takeaway starting its midafternoon cook curled out from an unseen kitchen.

"Yep. And yet she likes him."

Sada laughed again, the soft and contented sound of a man whose point has been proven. "Yeah. Don't we all?"

Dan slipped him a sidelong glance. "So, you two *are*—?"

"Yes." Sada lowered his gaze and smiled. "Back on again. Really on now, I think."

"Oh." Dan raised his camera and reeled off another series of shots. "Right."

Seemed like he and Paul had started a trend. He wasn't sure what he was supposed to say. Congratulations? Or maybe that he'd guessed as much?

Sada cleared his throat. "Thing is, I wanted to ask you... I mean, I don't know if—"

"If?" Dan echoed, slightly worried.

"Well, it's five years this year since Garrett died, isn't it?"

That brought Dan up short. He opened his mouth, closed it again, and just nodded.

"Mm."

"Yeah." Sada watched Chris and Miriam walk on farther ahead. "I always thought.... You knew him, didn't you?"

"Garrett?" Dan shifted uncomfortably. "Yeah."

He didn't want to get into it, to confirm what Sada must already know. He had no idea if Chris had kept photos—he must have done, though perhaps not on display. That wouldn't have stopped a determined rummage, of course, and few things are more bullheaded than a lover seeking an honest answer. He wished he'd walked faster and not let himself get caught at the back, pinned to the unsettling places this would undoubtedly lead.

"Do we?" Sada asked. "Do I, I mean? Look like...?"

Dan raised the camera to his eye and tried to hold the world away from himself, pushed to the arm's length of a lens. He knew exactly what Sada meant.

"Yeah, I s'pose. You look a bit like him."

Same hair, slightly different style. Same smoothly handsome features, though Garrett's had come from Korean, not Japanese, extraction. If there was a similarity, it wasn't really in the cast or form of eye, nose, or mouth. It was in the sense of fun, the carefree smile and easy joy that Sada had... that Garrett had also had, and for which Chris had loved him. Because love wasn't about ticking boxes or reaching goals, but the intangible essence of completion.

Dan snapped the faded part of a painted wall that had once read Pans Repaired on the side of a building that had presumably been an ironmongery.

He would never have said Chris could be like that with anyone, but to see Chris and Garrett together... he'd been so jealous at the time. Chris kept belittling it, saying they were all too young for settling down, him particularly. Garrett used to dote on all his refusals. He'd raise the issue of moving in together when they were all out as a group, and grin indulgently at Chris flailing his way out of the suggestion, all camp chastisement and bitchy retorts. Then, Dan had considered it the lowest form of showing off. Now, he couldn't begin to imagine how badly Chris missed it.

"I never wanted to be a reminder," Sada said thoughtfully, trampling across the memories Dan had been reliving. "Or a replacement. I don't think I am, but you know. You wonder. D'you think—"

"I don't know." Dan's reply veered further into brusqueness than he meant it to, but he didn't want to have this discussion. Not now, and not like this. "I doubt it. I very, very much doubt it. But I don't know."

"Oh."

He felt bad for not letting Sada get into the matter, not being at least a friend to talk to, if not a shoulder to cry on, but he couldn't feel equipped to deal with it. If Chris had never talked about Garrett, about how he felt, or how he'd coped with the empty years, rife with loss and hurting, how was Dan supposed to know what to say? He didn't want to risk sticking his foot in it and screwing up, bringing back all the pain that everyone who'd known Garrett had tried so hard to bury.

It had been quick, at least. That was something people usually said in a positive sense, though Dan had never been entirely sure why. The car that had screeched out of the night five years ago and wrecked not just his friend's life, but also that of the driver, and the three other people who'd been standing at the same bus stop as Chris and Garrett, had hardly been merciful. Somewhere in the tangle of broken glass and contorted metal, there had been two pedestrian fatalities. Garrett and another man waiting with his wife and young daughter to go home had both died at the scene, while the woman and her child were rushed to the hospital and treated for lesser injuries and shock. The first Dan had known of the accident was being called to go down and pick Chris up from the hospital.

Muddleheaded, half-asleep, and not knowing what was going on, he'd sworn all the way down there. Given who Chris was and the number of times in the past that Dan had been obliged to go and retrieve him from emergency departments at silly o'clock in the morning, he was expecting some stupid drunken prank gone awry or an idiotic accident with a tin opener. Never once to find him standing alone in the hospital car park, his arm in a sling and Garrett's blood still on his shirt.

No. Quick wasn't a mercy at all.

It was numbing, spared everyone the pain and uncertainty of a long, drawn-out death, untenable in its inevitable decline, but there could be no preparation, no softening of the blow. All that was left was the void and the struggle to make sense of anything, to rebuild the shreds of a world blown to pieces. It was why Dan put up with every moment of Chris's snide flippancy and tried not to get irritable with the way he lived now, exaggerating every moment of life. He'd always been full-on, but… who was he to question how the unthinkable had changed his friend's world?

So he pushed Sada away from the topic and shied politely from offering any kind of advice. If there was anything there to fight out, tackle, or be wounded by, then it was better he and Chris do it themselves. As Dan reminded himself, he wasn't precisely Mr. Together in the personal life department right now.

HE MET Paul for a drink after Miriam's tramp around Battersea finished for the day. The same little place they'd gone before: clean slates and new starts, fizzy white wine and open-faced sandwiches drenched with Continental cheese. Thinking about Chris and Garrett had left Dan slightly wrong-footed, like having some sort of mental itch in the middle of his back and not being able to reach it. He didn't relish the memories, either the awful ones or the older ones: decimating destruction next to the remembrance of Chris at the happiest he'd ever been… perhaps the happiest anyone ever could be.

"How was work?" Dan asked, lifting his glass. Bubbles danced in the golden light.

"Not bad. Could have done without some of our *favorite* clientele stopping by. Tell you the truth, I'm sick to the back teeth of all those bloody artists. Had Mary Hobart in this morning, trying to offload the most ridiculous piece of crap. Bloody great textile hanging, embroidered with the word for peace in a hundred and ten different languages…. Arabic, Dutch, Greek, even bloody ancient cuneiform or something. All done with copper foil and God knows what."

Dan twitched the corner of his lip, not willing to join in the dismissal. He knew Mary, and although he might not like everything she did, he'd heard her refer to the working drafts of *Peace Cry* and couldn't help but think that even if the execution wasn't great, the motive behind it had merit. He didn't say so. He wasn't even sure Paul had remembered he knew the woman.

"You didn't take it, then?"

"No! Looked like a sodding Quilters' Guild effort. Something a bunch of middle-aged women might do on a wet Sunday afternoon, and the whole thing was just… no. Oh, damn."

The last utterance Paul addressed to his phone, which had begun to ring. He took it out of his pocket, glanced at the number, and pulled a face. Thumbing the volume down to silent, he left the phone on the table, returned his attention to Dan, and flashed a suave grin.

"Sorry. Bloody work. *Again.* You'd think with the amount of time I spend there, they'd actually be pleased to see the back of me once in a while."

Dan had glanced briefly at the phone when Paul set it down, but the glare of late afternoon sunlight caught on the display and shot any chance he would have had of reading the number upside down. He wondered for a moment why he'd tried to; was it curiosity or suspicion? He picked in mild chagrin at the stem of his glass, working at an almost imperceptible fault in its finish with his thumbnail.

"Still," Paul observed, "at least *you* have the benefits of being your own boss. How's work going? How about that mad Battersea woman?"

"Miriam?" Dan continued to focus on the glass, watching the way the light flared off its curvature as he turned it. "Yeah, she's okay. It's actually not a bad idea. Whole thing's… well, it's good, thanks. Good."

Paul gave him a strange, sideways sort of smile and nodded.

"I saw that spread of yours the other day," he ventured.

Dan looked up from his glass. "Oh?"

"Yeah, you know… in *Calypso*."

"What were you doing reading a women's magazine?"

Paul grinned suggestively. "Well, there was this article about what men secretly want in bed…. No, I just happened to see it, that's all. It was good. The way you caught the light and everything."

"Mm." It seemed odd to Dan that the first thing the reference reminded him of was Venice. His last-minute meeting with the magazine's irritating editor just before he dashed off to the airport to leave all his troubles behind him.

"Some of your best commercial work, I thought. Where'd you shoot it?"

"A hotel in Reading," Dan said absently. "They had a sales convention going on at the time. Had a devil of a time trying to cut the car park out of the shot. Not exactly mad glamour."

Paul laughed softly, and Dan tried not to notice the way the sunlight stroked his hair.

"So, Danny… are you coming back tonight?"

That clear blue gaze was suddenly disarmingly direct. Paul lifted his own glass and took a long sip, supple and inviting. He swallowed, and the pink tip of his tongue just grazed at an errant trace of moisture on his lower lip. Dan grunted noncommittally.

They both knew how the evening would end.

Paul's flat, for all its sleek lines and statements of modern cool, right down to the black-and-white Clapton prints which had lately graced Dan's walls, was pretty untidy. He didn't seem to have settled in well, if at all, with boxes and storage crates pushed up to one side of the bedroom, and no personal touches to speak of. An expensive, wall-mounted TV hung in the main room, but the DVD rack beneath it had yet to be properly assembled, let alone filled. Dan frowned briefly, wondering when they'd last had a movie night. The tendrils of fuzzy, comfortable memories brushed at him, mostly involving soggy microwave popcorn and terrible martial arts comedies, and they intertwined with the feel of Paul's fingers on the back of his neck.

"You smell really good," Paul crooned, each low syllable buzzing against Dan's ear.

He pressed closer, the hard outline of his body full of heat and promise. The muscles of Dan's back tightened, his immediate reaction half desire and half the temptation to run. This familiar tension hadn't felt oppressive before… had it? It seemed to be an eternity before he felt Paul's mouth on his nape, tracking the path his hand had followed, fingers working now to reach forward, unfasten buttons, and break promises.

I will never let you do this to me again.

Dan had said that, not long before they split. He remembered it, when Paul's answer to every disagreement came in the form of caresses, and he'd vowed he would stop looking at things through that blurry, postcoital haze.

All the same, the sheets felt cool when he hit them, Paul burning up around him. More tongue, fingers, and enthusiasm than one person ought to possess, yet with a ruthless determination.

Paul kissed his way down Dan's stomach, freeing his cock from his underwear with swift efficiency and wrapping his mouth around it, burying him in a wet swirl of tongue and a grunt of approval. Dan sucked in a short breath, eyes closed and fingers idly stroking his own nipple, happy to let Paul take charge.

He was good at it, all brisk, firm rhythm and tight suction, but he only kept going until Dan was fully hard. Paul pulled off and grinned up at him, lips wet and eyes bright.

"My go?"

Dan knew what he wanted. He sat up, clambered off the bed, and knelt before Paul, running his hands over the thick contours of his thighs, smattered with gold curls. His skin smelled of a shower gel that matched his aftershave, overlaid just a little with the spicy, warm-leather-and-pine scent that was somehow his essence. His cock craned impatiently for attention and tempted Dan to tease him, pressing his lips instead to Paul's heavy, hot balls. He kissed and sucked, knowing by rote what drove Paul crazy and, he had to admit, enjoying the power trip almost as much as the taste.

"Christ… just fucking suck it, will you?"

Paul's hand, his palm hot, slipped over Dan's nape, fingers strafing through his hair. Dan pulled back, smiled, and glanced up at him, holding Paul's gaze as he slipped out his tongue and so gingerly touched it to the glossy, fat head of his dick.

"Oh, you fucking tease," Paul muttered, his hips giving an involuntary twitch.

His hand tightened on the back of Dan's head, as much a command as a silent plea, and Dan set to work. Paul filled his mouth: hard, salty flesh and sharp heat shuddered against his tongue. Dan, jaw stretched wide to accommodate him, anchored his hands on those thick, warm thighs, and shut his eyes to everything but the hot, solid slide of Paul's cock, wet heat, and inexorable rhythm, a steady beat he couldn't resist.

His breath came hard, short pants of it through his nostrils, echoing back to him in the damp, suffocating nearness of Paul's groin, his own cock stiff and aching for release.

Paul groaned and began to hump back against him, needy little thrusts that fed his dick deeper into Dan's throat.

"God… yeah. Suck that cock, you dirty little f—Christ, Dan…."

His fingers dug into Dan's scalp, and his words scraped across raw, hungry nerves. Dan reached down, fastening one hand around his shaft, the other slipping over Paul's hip to grab the smooth, firm flesh of his ass. He jerked himself hard, mouth full and willing as Paul thrust harder, pulling just a little on his hair. Dan grunted around his cock, wanting more and pleased when Paul obliged.

He fucked Dan's mouth like it wasn't attached to anything, an entirely desensitized, denatured organ, alone and without consequence. Dan surprised himself when he came first, the climax sneaky and underhanded, shooting a jolt of pleasure deep from the pit of his gut. Still pounding his mouth, hot palms on either side of his head, Paul seemed oblivious, but it wasn't long before he was yelling and coming too, rough strokes and dirty gasps that ran close to choking Dan… and were hotter than he'd ever imagined possible.

"Whew!"

Paul pulled out but didn't exactly leave his mouth empty. Dan swallowed and wiped the rivulets of spunk from his chin with the heel of his palm, savoring the dank, musky taste. He licked his lips and grinned when Paul ruffled his hair.

"Nice one, Danny."

He flopped backward onto the bed, propped on his elbows and smiling at Dan, his face flushed and his slick, spent cock resting lazily across his thigh. Dan chuckled and scrambled up to join him, the dull ache in his jaw already becoming little more than a memory.

Paul kicked halfheartedly at the covers and rolled over onto his side. Dan tucked one arm under his head and let the other fall across Paul's waist, fingers trailing against his belly. For a moment, Paul seemed to stiffen, and Dan wondered if he'd move away, but he said nothing and just lay there. The blue-tinged summer evening sky crowded in at the window, and Dan listened to the distant hum of traffic while he watched Paul's shoulder rise and fall with the rhythm of his breathing.

Funny thing, love, he supposed.

CHAPTER FIFTEEN

WHATEVER WAS happening with Paul, it was good. Dan convinced himself of that. It was… fine. So when he and Cesare finally got around to working out schedules and maybe working up the nerve for a phone call, the effect of hearing his voice came as a surprise to Dan. They'd not been e-mailing so often, what with his involvement in Miriam's project, and Cesare apparently drowning in the sea of paperwork that accompanied annual school exams and the presummer holiday rush. He'd mourned the lapse in contact but until he heard it, he hadn't even realized how much he'd missed the lilt of that accent.

"*Ciao*, Daniel!"

Their first live, audible conversation since that last farewell in Venice. Could it possibly have been so long? Cesare's voice ran through Dan like liquid mercury. It almost shocked him; he'd grown so nearly used to not thinking of Cesare that way, keeping the memories tucked neatly in a small, secure box.

"Um… yeah. Hi." Dan cleared his throat, absurdly nervous. "So, um, how are you?"

"Very well. And you?"

"Yeah, good." Dan cleared his throat again, embarrassed at himself. "Wow. It's just… it's been a while. It's good to hear from you. Really hear, I mean… your voice."

Cesare laughed, and it felt good against Dan's ear, shaking loose sunlit memories of worn paths and rounded cobblestones, smooth-edged beneath his feet.

They didn't talk for long, just enough to establish the familiar rhythms of the friendship that had been growing so comfortable, so certain. Cesare's tireless efforts to improve things for the Misseri boy once again proved to be an easy, safe topic of conversation. Dan was able to ask how things were progressing, and they could compare notes on the questions he'd asked Edith about education for autistic children. Though she had no direct experience, she had friends, contacts, people she could ask, and the information he passed along from her about inclusion and support learning all bolstered precious moments of conversation and even more precious moments of hearing the relief and earnest zeal in Cesare's voice. But that was, as Dan realized, the thing about him. Cesare was just so real about everything, so genuinely moved by and interested in other people.

After that, each began to carve little slices of time from his week for the other. Phone calls, e-mails, and instant messaging… all those ways of weaving something of the person into everyday life. Dan ran different questions to and from Edith, dismissing it all as "just for a friend who asked" when she wanted to know the reasons behind his sudden interest in inclusionary education and classroom support. She gave him a very old-fashioned look and pursed her lips, but said nothing.

He didn't want to tell her anything, anyway. Didn't want to acknowledge it, even to himself. Paul might have behaved unreasonably over the Italian phrasebooks, but he'd been right: Dan was keeping secrets, and the pressure of them weighed on him, unwelcome and suffocating. He tried to make himself believe it was the act of lying by omission that made it feel strange; that there was nothing wrong in letting his friendship with Cesare blossom. Maybe that was even true, because it *was* friendship, and it didn't feel like anything underhanded… and yet it wasn't that simple. It had never been simple.

Dan was painfully aware of exactly how it would sound if he tried to explain it aloud. He knew how things looked, and he knew what he'd have said if a friend had come to him with the same dilemma. He couldn't have his cake and eat it, no matter how deliciously tempting it looked, and right now he wasn't being fair to anyone.

Paul hadn't asked him about the new painting in the apartment. It still hung on the wall, right where Dan had wanted it. The simple, vibrant landscape was probably beneath Paul's notice, being too naive and insufficiently sophisticated for the end of the market in which he aspired to deal.

Dan still looked at it every day, though. Still remembered Venice and picking out that representation of the blazing hot Tuscan sun in a tiny gallery with a man whose skin smelled like citrus and who'd traveled a pilgrimage of so many miles just for the chance at a dream.

SUMMER LEANED increasingly over the edges of the days, bearing in with tepid rainfalls, hazy mornings, and long, dusk-smothered evenings full of midges and candlelit barbecues in the tiny North and West London gardens of friends and colleagues. Concrete, charred chicken legs, and tea lights in glass jars. Dan loved it—loved the looks of surprised congratulation and the knowing smiles thrown his way when, for the first time in too long, he and Paul showed up together.

One evening of many at Chris's place, with the pocket handkerchief of a brick terrace clogged with people, and the zinc planters full of ferns and agaves rapidly becoming dumping grounds for cigarette butts and half-finished plastic cups of chardonnay, Dan caught himself imagining this as a future. For once not pushing to expect more, not wondering when it would all magically slot into place, but just thinking of this as the ground from which he might work in the next few years. Maybe he and Paul would move back in together, and maybe the past few months had been the jolt he needed to make him see all his idling through life for the useless prevarication it was.

If, Dan decided, he really wanted something, he ought to stop dawdling around the edges of everything like a first-time ice skater clinging to the rail, and actually make a move.

He foundered on that thought and sat there for a while, cradling a cup of cheap white wine and frowning in the illumination of Chris's tacky outdoor lights. A string of them, all shaped like dragonflies, curled up the trunk of a nearby tree fern and, in their garish, dappled glow, Dan noticed Chris mingling through the press of people. He looked happier than he had in a long time. Genuinely happy, not just grinning and laughing on the surface.

Dan watched, saw how his gaze stayed fixed on Sada even when they were at opposite ends of the crowd. He supposed Chris thought no one really spotted the kiss that slipped between them when they passed, and there was no earthly reason anyone *should* have noticed.

It was brief and subtle, just his lips grazing Sada's cheek, one hand fleetingly resting on his hip, bodies half-turned to each other for that passing second before they parted, both in the middle of doing something else. Just a simple, perfect moment, unconscious and easy.

Dan's frown deepened, and he swigged the remainder of his chardonnay in one long, instantly regrettable swallow.

Strange, he thought, how it was always the smallest things that mattered. The things that are barely noticed at all, yet snowball in their importance the less they're considered, raking up clods of dirt and time around them, like a crab building its shell and hiding within it.

Small thing after small thing batted at the sides of Dan's existence in those weeks. The look on Paul's face when he found the Italian phrasebooks hadn't gone, the stiffness in his posture when, using the freshly cut key he'd been given, he came by earlier than he'd said on a weekday night and found Dan just ending a phone call from Cesare.

Dan didn't really see why it mattered. He waved at Paul in greeting as he was saying his *a presto* and promising he'd relay another question to Edith. Dan smiled as he cut the connection, not quite registering his boyfriend's stone-faced glare.

"Hey, you. You're early. How was your day?"

"Who were you talking to?" Paul demanded.

Dan blinked, taken aback by the pout in his voice. For a moment, his pulse quickened, and that familiar spool of guilt started to unravel in his stomach. He resisted it, reviled it—how dare he let himself be made to feel that way?—and for a while the manufactured indignation was enough to hide behind.

"Just a friend," he said.

"Oh."

Paul stared at him for a moment, with all the imperious judgment of a cat, and Dan felt the world slide out from under his feet a little. It wasn't a lie. He wanted to say that, to shout it out and tell Paul that… or maybe make himself believe it.

In those few seconds, though, if Paul had asked him, he knew he'd have explained. The words were right there on the tip of his tongue.

Someone I met in Venice. My friend in Italy. This guy I met when I was on holiday, he's from Tuscany….

There were a dozen ways to put it. The conversation was right there, mapped out with a hundred routes and at least three possible outcomes.

Dan felt his mouth turn dry, and he both wanted very much and yet did not want at all to talk about it… but Paul just looked bored and annoyed, and asked him where he wanted to go for dinner. The words all dried up and shriveled away, and the phone felt heavy and clammy in his hand.

They went to a sushi bar that night. Dan drank sake until he couldn't feel his tongue, and didn't taste much of anything. He kept waiting for

Paul to say something about the phone call, but neither comment nor interrogation ever came.

AT FIRST, Dan didn't think about the odd things he noticed at Paul's place either. The socks that he was fairly sure belonged to neither of them, stuffed down the side of the dresser drawer. A pen, discarded on the bedside table. They were unimportant things, and of all the gnawing doubts there had been at the back of Dan's mind since getting back together with Paul, pens and their placement hadn't featured prominently. This one wasn't even a particularly impressive example of its kind, but the smallest things can set off the biggest chain reactions.

It was just a pen: a cheap, disposable Biro with no lid and a tiny wad of congealed dark blue ink massed on its nib. The thing was, Dan hadn't noticed it on the bedside table when he left Paul's flat that morning.

Now, while he idled in the bedroom, waiting for Paul to clear the shower and tell him where the dinner reservations were booked, he looked at the thing and frowned. Paul didn't use cheap pens. He had a set of personalized ones and always kept one in his jacket pocket, ready to whip out with a flourish.

He didn't use blue pens either, as a rule. And, if Dan had, he knew he wouldn't have left one here. The more he looked at it, the more the narrow plastic cylinder seemed to stare back. He bit his lip, any further contemplation curtailed by the bathroom door opening. He glanced over his shoulder, appreciating the sight of Paul all clean-scrubbed and damp, a rather inadequate towel knotted around his waist.

"Oh, sod it…. Danny, have you seen my shirt?"

It fractured the moment a little. Dan shook his head, and Paul huffed irritably, pacing off to the airing cupboard. The pen could have come from anywhere. A freebie from some piece of junk mail, the detritus of an emptied pocket… things like that showed up all over the place, all the time. And it wasn't as if Dan had rigorously catalogued every pair of socks Paul had ever owned either. He dismissed the thoughts forcefully and refused to dwell on them.

They meant nothing.

Dinner turned out to be at a quiet, uninteresting little restaurant. For all the lead-up Paul had given it, Dan was expecting somewhere trendy, with square, gray tables and sparse menus. What he got was a small, expensive eatery not far from Russell Square. Ivy scrambled up the exterior, and inside there were smoothly polished, cylindrical brass light fittings on the walls, casting warm pools of fuzzy light on an ugly green carpet. They sat at a linen-covered table close to one of the diamond-leaded windows, a tea light floating between them in a small glass bowl of water. It felt like a golf club carvery, a midrange hotel trying to up its reputation, and the food wasn't great.

All the same, Dan didn't want to complain. Paul seemed cheerful tonight, the snapping and carping of earlier entirely forgotten. Dan was tempted just to sit and watch him, enjoy the comfortable silences and the interplay of eyes and smiles that felt almost as if they were back at their earliest dates again. Water under the bridge since then, though, and plenty of it. He found himself still thinking about the pen on Paul's nightstand and how it had been devoid of any charity or local business logo.

Dan pushed his chicken fillet around the plate and glanced at Paul surreptitiously, watching him eat with that customary hearty efficiency. Every bite big, every mouthful chewed like a step on the way to a goal being reached, hand reaching to his glass of wine before he'd even swallowed. Paul never liked to waste time. He grinned when he noticed Dan looking.

"What? You want to skip dessert?"

"Nah." Dan answered without thinking. "There's raspberry tart on the trolley."

He blinked, aware that hadn't sounded quite as he meant it—or had it?—and cloaked the whole thing over with a smile. Paul batted it back and everything seemed all right, but for the sneaking little voice at the back of Dan's mind that still posed all those horrible, unsettling questions.

Is this what you really *want?*

Dan turned his attention to the watery duchesse potatoes, and looked forward to the promise of raspberry tart.

"So," Paul said, with the clinking of cutlery and the murmurs of polite conversation gnawing at the silence between them. "This Italian friend of yours."

"Mm?" Dan tried hard not to blink, wince, or otherwise incriminate himself, but the words came as a shock.

"The one you were on the phone to the other evening. When I came in. I assume it's a him. Sounded like it, not that I was eavesdropping. Know him from Venice?"

Dan took a deliberate bite of potato and raised his eyebrows. Playing dumb felt silly and disingenuous, but he wasn't sure what else to do. Anxious worms of guilt prickled beneath his ribs, and he wished more than anything that he'd seized that moment when he'd had it in his hands… that he'd told Paul the truth. It would have been difficult, but it would have been easier than this.

"Because I thought you'd never been to Italy before you went there on that holiday, so you must have met him while you were in Venice. I mean," Paul went on in that calm, even tone, as if this was the sort of rational puzzle he'd approached in the same spirit as the crossword, "this is assuming he doesn't live in England. Which I assume he doesn't, because otherwise you wouldn't have all those phrasebooks still hanging around the place, would you?"

"So?" Dan swallowed, the food leaden ash in his mouth. "I didn't realize I had to give a full account of my address book."

"You don't! I'm just taking an interest. Call it idle curiosity," Paul added, smiling tightly.

"Okay, then. Yes. I met him when I was over there. He… knew a lot about the history of the place. The artwork and everything."

Dan wasn't sure precisely why he lied. Cowardice, maybe. Perhaps because it was easier, or he wanted to push Paul, see how far he'd go into conjecture—or just how much he'd already picked up from Chris and other loose-lipped forms of gossip with whom Dan planned to have serious words in the near future.

Dan told himself it wasn't really lying: just not mentioning it, not giving full details. That wasn't mandatory, and in any case, Paul hadn't asked the question. He hadn't, in so many words, wanted to know—

"Did you sleep with him?"

Ah. There we are.

Dan cleared his throat, glanced down at his plate, and then up at the polished brass light fittings. Anywhere but Paul's face.

"Did you?"

"Well… yes, but—"

"I thought so."

The way Paul said it, the exhalation laced with something that sounded just like disappointment, enraged Dan. Like he'd lived down to expectations, proved true something he hadn't even been charged with, and the worst of it was that he found himself wanting to justify what he'd said, words spilling out onto the table without him even seeing them fall.

"We'd split up! Long before that. The whole point of me taking the bloody holiday was to—to take some time out," he corrected quickly, refusing to give Paul the satisfaction of admitting there had been anything to get over in the first place.

"Oh? And that included fu—" Paul bit back on himself, mouth tightening with an obvious view to the public nature of the place.

Funny, Dan thought, because he'd always been so eager to make scenes in the past. Kisses on camera, ostentatious shows of affection... or perhaps possession. He watched the momentary flash of anger pass from Paul's eyes, his voice sliding from ire to whine.

"And now, though? What about now? You're still calling him, and—"

"He's a friend," Dan snapped. "We... we became friends."

"Right."

"Don't look at me like that, Paul. You've got no right to—"

"No right to what? I haven't accused you of anything. I'm simply asking... I mean, have I suggested the slightest thing?"

His injured pride act made Dan want to laugh. "Oh, come on! Like I can't see the bloody great clunking hints. If you want to say it, go on and say it."

"Danny, you're not making much sense."

Dan shook his head, determinedly shutting up and avoiding the temptation to have the row now, right here in front of everyone... and it *was* tempting. Paul would enjoy that, he suspected. Maybe that was more than half the reason Dan didn't say anything, not that he got a chance. Paul's phone rang. Even with the volume set to low, its pseudo-Mozart chirrup was still plainly audible. Paul dragged it from his pocket, glared irritably at the display, and in the briefest of fleeting seconds, Dan saw something in his face that he didn't entirely understand. Paul flicked the phone off, put it by his plate, cleared his throat, and glanced back at Dan, suddenly conciliatory. The corners of his mouth worked around a small half smile, and he leaned forward a little, readying to stand.

"Look, I'm just gonna nip to the... y'know. Won't be a minute."

Dan nodded and watched dumbly as Paul stood, fingers closing on his phone just before he headed off to the gents. He slipped it into his pocket as he walked, but his hand never strayed far from the phone after that, like he was afraid of letting it go, and Dan *knew*.

Strange, because it wasn't an epiphany or anything, not even a thought he could truly pinpoint having. It was more of a whole-body recognition, a breath that changed everything, because in that moment so much made sense.

Cheap pens discarded on tables, odd socks in unfamiliar drawers, phone calls that sounded different even before they were answered... he knew. The echo of someone else's breaths on their life.

He said nothing, though. There didn't seem to be much to say. So Dan waited until Paul came back, and the rest of the meal proceeded without incident. They did the thing they were so good at: talking without saying anything and pretending that the things they *had* said hadn't meant much to start with.

The confirmation came less than a week later, for which Dan was incredibly grateful. He hated what those few days turned him into— snooping in Paul's pockets, sneaking looks at his phone and finding exactly the kind of texts he expected from numbers he didn't know, saved to names that probably meant little. Dan even idly keyed Paul's e-mail address and old password into his laptop, only for the private humiliation of finding he must have changed it since they broke up the last time. He dreaded to think what might have happened if it had all dragged on any longer.

The damn phone bleeping once more, that's all it took.

One more hurried glance at a number Dan guessed was nothing to do with the gallery, then a smirk as Paul read the text message, and a muttered "huh, work." Dan leaned his head back against the top of Paul's sofa; his flat looked a lot more lived-in these days, the DVD rack almost half-full. The evening news plugged on in the background, all mournful reportage and serious faces. Paul started replying to the text, and the clicking of his thumb on the buttons was the most intensely irritating sound Dan had ever heard. He let out a long breath, ire and air sliding between his teeth.

"Funny time for Maria to need you, isn't it? It's still Maria, isn't it? The acquisitions manager?"

"Hm," Paul grunted, still clicking away. His arm stretched out along the back of the sofa, hand resting against Dan's shoulder, he started to rub gently at the juncture between neck and clavicle.

Dan supposed it was meant to be sexy. It wasn't.

"I mean," he went on, "it's half ten on Sunday night. What could she possibly have to tell you she couldn't have done this afternoon? Or even tomorrow morning? Y'know, when you're actually at work?"

"You know what they're like," Paul said, and Dan heard the lacquered layer of complete crap in his voice.

D'you really think I'm a fucking idiot?

He shook Paul's hand away, a little more abruptly than he meant to, and it had the sense of an irrevocable insult.

"Danny? What's the matter?"

"No... what is it actually about, hm?"

He didn't turn his head, didn't look at Paul, but he felt the air change. Paul lowered the phone, his text unfinished.

"What's what about? I don't—"

"Yeah, you do. I, um, I think you do, anyway," Dan finished, his bravado weakening a little. "All this... phone calls. Stuff. You're... I mean, it's not work, is it? Not all of it. I'm not stupid, you know. I... I've noticed."

The news anchor, in her bright red jacket and bright red lipstick, announced the death of a long-retired actor, and the clear colors and smart graphics of the studio gave way to a montage of seventies TV sitcom clips. It made sitting here, not quite accusing his boyfriend of cheating, feel just a little bit less real.

Paul frowned, "You mean...? Oh."

"Yeah. *Oh.*"

No denial, no attempt to dodge anything. Odd, really. Like Paul had been waiting for this as much as he had—and that was an admission in itself.

"Look, I don't know what you think's going on, Dan... but it's not like that at all. Not really."

"Is it not?" Dan said, his voice echoing more as a statement than a question. He just couldn't seem to muster the energy to be angry. "Right, then. Do you want to talk about what it is like, then? Or... I don't know. Has he got a name?"

Silence, and even the playback sitcom dialogue on the TV stopped sounding like real words, just a shapeless parade of noise and the laughter of a long-gone studio audience.

"Stuart," Paul said after a moment.

Dan nodded. That made sense. He knew whom Paul meant, he thought: another one of those besuited heroes, the green-eyed, dark-haired former accountant who used to work at the gallery in Edgware where Sada had shown his installation. Stuart bloody Glenning. It made sense... he'd been there as well as Paul that night, hadn't he? And Glenning now made his living making and breaking reputations, representing all those eager young things only too willing to turn over their commissions—all the things Paul had always wanted to do. All offshoots of the same self-congratulatory, internalized little world, and Dan really couldn't care about any of it.

He tried, unable to understand why this shouldn't bother him, why he felt so dried out and empty, but the whole ugly truth stretched out before him like leather in the rain, crinkled and impermeable.

"Right."

"We're not—" Paul blurted, but broke off just as abruptly. "I mean, it's.... After we split, Stu and I got together a couple of times, but not seriously. We weren't really.... He's just on at me to hook up again. That's all."

Dan bit the inside of his cheek thoughtfully, just to see whether he could feel it.

"Right," he repeated. It did hurt, the biting, but not as much as he'd expected.

"See? So it isn't—"

"And have you?"

The look on Paul's face—that sick, trapped split second before he tried to reply—was all the answer Dan wanted. So much fell into place... the socks, the cheap pens, the little whispers in the flat that spoke of someone else's presence. He wondered why it had taken him so long to see. Maybe he hadn't wanted to. Maybe, whispered the dastardly voice at the back of Dan's mind, *not* seeing had been the only thing keeping him from admitting his own faults and his own cruel, secret lies.

"I...."

"Oh, come off it. You obviously didn't think to tell him that we... actually, no. Hang on. *Did* we get back together? Hm?" Dan looked up sharply, expecting to see apology in Paul's face or at least a bit of regret at having been caught. All he saw there was a spoiled, petulant child, desperately working its way around twisted justifications, clutching at them like the proof of a tarnished innocence. The very worst part of it was that it was like looking into a mirror. "We never talked about it, did we? Not to sit down and say, in so many words, yeah, we're going to give it another shot, and *this* is what we're going to do differently. We didn't plan anything. We just played at it."

Paul actually raised his hand then, as if he wanted to touch Dan's back, gentle comforts and soft apologies. Before he realized he'd moved to do it, Dan reached up and slapped the hand away, hard.

"No. I... I actually don't care whether you're fucking around or not. Y'know? I've had enough, Paul."

He stood, not sure his legs were actually connected to him, not sure the words had really come out of his mouth but supposing from the look on Paul's face that they must have done. He started up in pursuit, and Dan moved faster, not wanting to get caught in a grapple of wills and arguments. Paul snatched at his wrist, he pulled back, and they met in an awkward, tense pressure of flesh, tight breath, and glaring eyes, and then it was all over before it had begun.

Dan almost wished it wasn't, wished that he'd had the momentary pleasure of his fist connecting with Paul's smug visage, smearing that look of wounded pride and disbelief right across his face.

When Paul called his name, echoing after him just once as he grabbed his coat on the way to the door, Dan heard all the archness in his voice, all the narcissistic shock, the inability to believe he was really being walked out on.

"Danny! Dan, you can't just—Where are you going?"

"Home," Dan said, without looking back, and slammed the door with a great deal of rather ignoble pleasure.

That wash of self-satisfied indulgence didn't last long, of course. He barely had the dusk-kissed pavement under his feet again before he was wondering if it had really been the best way to handle things. Part of him thought so, but Dan couldn't shake the feeling he'd regret it. All right, so it hadn't been the huge, romantic reunion that he might have hoped for—what he had to admit he'd *wanted*, even if, in truth, he'd been adult enough to know that wasn't what either he or Paul were after.

They'd lazily stretched out for what they had before, just slipping back into old routines. That much he could acknowledge, but that Paul had consciously made a play for him and, worse, that he'd *let* him do it, and let him succeed, when all he wanted…. *No*. Dan stopped, standing in the dusty, dying light of an anonymous London street, his hand outstretched and a black cab coasting to a reluctant halt two meters along the crowded road.

It wasn't even that.

Betrayal might have had genuine drama to it if he hadn't been so fucking cock-led. Because that's all it had been, hadn't it? He'd felt lost, lonely, and he'd tried to screw his way out of it, grab hopelessly at what he really wanted by latching onto the last thing he'd had.

Definitely not his finest hour.

Dan slouched in the back of the cab, gritted his teeth, and managed the bare minimum of contributions to the driver's insistent conversation about congestion charges, just holding on until he got back to his flat. He tipped well, kept a lid on the desire to take the stairs two at a time, and couldn't wait to shut the door behind him, to just block out the whole day. The whole year, maybe.

He hadn't cleaned up much before he left, not having expected to come back tonight. The photographs, printouts, and sketches he'd left on the coffee table seemed to mock him. They were mostly to do with Miriam's project, plus a few ideas he'd had knocking around for compositions based off the better of the Venice pictures. For a moment, Dan wanted to send them all sprawling to the ground, forgotten detritus and paper scales swept aside in a melodramatic fit of pique.

Of course, if he did that, he'd only have to pick them up again, so he turned away, irritated and chastened by the memories they evoked. Each picture, each step through those days spent with Sada, Chris, and Miriam… how Chris had said he was looking pleased with himself, had asked if he'd found a bit of extracurricular inspiration. And he'd grinned, hadn't he? Grinned like a fool and said maybe… because yes, he'd thought that maybe he had. Just for a little while, he could have started to believe that he was having some of his best ideas, springing from a bedrock which now turned out to be false.

Dan supposed he must have sounded like an idiot because he knew he'd been one. And that presented another problem. How the hell would he face Chris? He wanted to talk to someone, to vent all the anger, hurt, and humiliation before it actually did well up in his throat and choke him to death, but how could he? Just the thought of the look that would creep across Chris's face made him feel sick. No, discretion—as the saying went—would be the better part of survival, if not valor. He hadn't made a big thing out of getting back together with Paul, inasmuch as they technically had done, so why should this be any different? He could drop it into conversation at some later point, some barely important tidbit passed on in fleeting reference. It would be the best way he had of showing he didn't care. Which he didn't. Not really. Not about this. The realization seeped slowly into Dan's understanding. It wasn't the actual act, but the principle of the thing... that Paul had dared to attack his friendship with Cesare, when all the time he—Dan frowned at the dusk-stained living room with all its everyday clutter of life.

All the time, Paul had probably wanted to use it as an excuse to dump him in the first place. Anger stopped Dan from analyzing that idea much further... it might or might not have been true, but he wasn't sure he cared. Hell, had Paul even wanted this? Or had he just wanted to know the truth? It was hard to pick through the muddle in his head, and Dan knew he was probably being unfair. He didn't give a damn, however.

As far as he knew, this whole time had been Paul doing nothing more than marking time until he got where he wanted to be with Glenning. It would be a boost for his career, no doubt. *Typical Paul. Typical fucking....* Dan stopped, sighed heavily, and flopped down on the sofa, thoroughly fed up and tired. He didn't want to be on his own. He wanted an unbiased, nonpartisan friend and—for one foolish, selfish moment—he thought about calling Cesare. That wouldn't be fair, though, would it? Of all the things he regretted, not having told Cesare about Paul suddenly figured higher than Dan had thought it would. He hadn't wanted to, fearing it would be like showing off an expensive wristwatch in the presence of those he knew couldn't afford one, but now it just felt like lying all over again, and the pressure of it was more than he could take.

The whole thing was a fucking mess.

Dan strafed his fingers through his hair and sniffed. Through the open bedroom door, snatches of a Tuscan summer's flaming colors glimmered on the wall, lit through with the grayness of the coming London night.

He shook his head and reached for the phone.

CHAPTER SIXTEEN

DESPITE HER tendency to treat him like he was still fourteen years old, one of the things Dan loved most about his sister was the way she never questioned a person's need. She wasn't a saint, and she did judge—as he knew to his cost—but she never turned someone away when they asked for help. He barely had to say six words on the phone before she told him to come over, and he took the time the cab ride gave him to pretend he didn't want to cry.

Edith's street looked pleasant in the mellowing dark, like all the tall, white-gabled houses were settling down to sleep. Everything seemed suffused with the orange light of streetlamps, shot through with yellowed pinpricks of lit windows and the shadows pooling around hedges and fences.

"Come on in," she said, the door open before he was halfway down the path. "You all right?"

She hugged him, and his body wanted to respond before his brain. Dan took a deep breath, ashamed of how shaky it sounded, and squeezed her tighter.

"Yeah. Yeah, I'm—"

"Come on. I'll put the kettle on."

He followed her inside, grateful for her solid, implacable presence. Benson came out into the hall to greet him, wet nose in Dan's hand and thick-plumed tail wagging against the backs of his knees. Edith made tea, and he sat once more at her scarred kitchen table, looking out through the french doors into a garden filled with soft-lit shadows and secondhand electric light.

"Kids in bed?" he asked, needlessly he supposed, because they must be by now.

"Mm-hm." Edith stood a mug of tea down in front of him, and Dan watched the bubbles eddy on the surface. The smallest things never change, even when the whole world's shaking. "Whether they'll stay there's another matter, of course. So, come on. Do you want to tell me what happened? Other than just the fact you broke up with Mr. Flashy Pants. I mean, wh—"

"He's been fucking around behind my back."

"Oh, Danny."

Edith said it with a disappointed twist of air between her teeth, much as she might tut at a broken cup or a child's bloodied knee, her face a picture of heartfelt compassion. He wondered why saying the words made them feel less hurtful. Could there really be that much distance in them? He'd have thought repeating it—admitting it—would make it worse, but it seemed to do quite the opposite.

Dan contemplated the peculiarity of that as he related the whole thing, from Paul's apparent problem with Cesare to the weird epiphany with the phone. Edith listened and squeezed his hand and made encouraging, sympathetic noises in all the right places, and he started to feel better. They drank more tea and moved from the kitchen to her sitting room, parking themselves on the sofa in front of her coal-effect fireplace. The fire was cold and bare, but the intricacies of the brickwork provided a welcome distraction, and Dan told dirty stories in hushed tones, their cynical, mocking laughter sweeping away the pain. He didn't mean a lot of the things he said about Paul, but nobody, once their name is diminished, can reach out to scar quite so badly from memory.

"D'you want to stay tonight? Crash on the sofa?"

He yawned. It had grown late when they weren't looking.

"Yeah. Thanks. If you're sure it's okay, and you don't—"

"Oh, shush. It's fine. I'll put you to work doing the breakfast run in the morning, make you earn your keep," she added, rising to fetch pillows and a blanket, and pausing to ruffle Dan's hair. "All right?"

He chuckled. "Okay."

Yes, definitely a lot better than his empty flat, and the inevitable prospect of having to deal with Paul again, probably before he was ready. There would have to be that horrible, awkward, surgical disentanglement of their lives, even though Dan had been so careful since the last time to keep them separate.

Despite all his best efforts, there had been overlaps. Keys, CDs, odds and ends of half-finished things. Pieces of paper with Paul's handwriting on them, lists left as uncompleted as their affair… something destined just to be picked at and then abandoned over and over again. He wondered if Paul would get anything serious together with Stuart

Glenning, and, probably for the first time, Dan felt truly jealous. Not for what he'd lost, but for what had never been.

The way of thinking in Venice lapped back at his feet… the dreams of what he'd looked for there and tried to find at home. What had changed to make him throw himself back into it once he returned?

Edith leaned over the back of the sofa and unceremoniously dumped a pillow and blanket in his lap.

"Here y'are."

"Hm? Argh… thanks, love." Dan blinked, face full of cheery pink-and-green fleecy fabric. "Edie?"

"Yes?"

She paused, turning en route back to the hall, to look at him. Her face seemed pale, skin almost papery, in the electric light. He licked his lips.

"Is it really wrong if… well, does it make me a bad person, I mean? If I'm relieved it's over? Does that make sense?"

"No." She smiled. "And yes. It does make sense. Now shut up and get some kip. I'll be out of the bathroom in five minutes, tops. Sleep well, and I'll see you in the morning."

"Night," he answered reluctantly, watching her go.

Settling down wasn't that hard. He'd crashed at Edith's plenty of times in recent years—and not just when he needed her. Since Greg left her, there had been times she needed help too: when one of the kids was ill, or if she was, or, in those early days when the whole thing had still been something of a shock, just when she couldn't face it all on her own.

Oh, she seemed strong now… but everyone wears masks. Layers of them, sometimes.

In the bathroom, Dan found a spare toothbrush and clean towel left folded on the side of the outdated, oyster-colored sink. He switched the lights off on his way back into the sitting room, and the house seemed unbelievably quiet.

He doubted he would sleep much, so he didn't bother to close his eyes, just lay there on the sofa in his boxers and T-shirt, the fleecy blanket mildly itchy against his bare legs, and watched the orange echoes of streetlights dance on the ceiling.

Occasionally, cars passed, distant swooshes and flares of bright headlamps in the dark. He listened to Edith move about upstairs, the creak of floorboards as she checked on the kids, the murmurs of voices as what sounded like Lauren inquired as to what was going on and, presumably, had a shortened version explained to her, with the coda that no, she couldn't go down to see Uncle Dan now, and would have to wait until the morning. He smiled to himself and felt slightly guiltier than he had done for disrupting Edith's routine.

Still, what else was family for?

He stifled another yawn, feeling sleep prowl at the distant ridges of his mind. For some reason, visions of the *Carnevale* masks he'd seen in the shops around San Marco filtered through his head, with their sleekly sinuous designs and painted, glittering rims. Feathers, sequins, and painstakingly applied, delicate layers of gold and silver leaf, all catching the light and reflecting back the echoes of years long past. The smiling, secret, and slightly sinister faces of jesters and devils, and the blank, impassive *bauta*… the masks once made of leather, which nobles would don for both disguise and entertainment.

Dan thought of Edith wearing so many faces conscientiously above her own: mother, daughter, wife and ex-wife, volunteer, teacher, sister, helper, friend… where was the time for her to be herself? But, then, who could say what *self* was, or judge how closely the masks had bonded to it?

He rolled over, the sofa creaking beneath him, and something sharp poked into his hip. He frowned and groped down between the cushions, fingers closing on a hard piece of plastic. Dan pulled it out, peering at his find in the half-light. Apparently part of an action figure, though what part, or what action, he couldn't tell. He leaned across and set it on the coffee table, then settled back beneath the blanket. The night was too warm for him to really need it bunched up over his chin, but it felt comforting, even if it did smell faintly of feet and the back of Edith's airing cupboard.

He'd clutched Paul to him like a mask. Worn the memories and the sad, useless attempt at reconciliation with grim determination, hoping they'd somehow become a part of him. He hadn't been happy. He hadn't been happy since… fuck it, since Venice. And what did that say about him? Dan stared into the darkness, and tried to convince himself that he didn't want to hear Cesare's voice: to believe that, at that moment, missing him wasn't real, and didn't open up an ache in his chest that swelled with every breath.

You're going to have to tell yourself the truth one day. You know you are....

First light came so fast he must have fallen asleep, though he didn't remember doing so and for a while, Dan had no idea where he was or how he'd got there. The memories trickled back gradually, interspersed with noises from outside—car doors slamming, keys jangling and various familiar routines up and down the street running cheek-by-jowl in their packed, intensive chaos. Sounds from upstairs too… feet and doors, water running and the loo flushing.

Dan pulled the blanket over his head and groaned. Respite wasn't afforded for long, however, and he suspected Edith had cruelly prepared the kids to come pouring in and leap on him, which they did, in a tangle of elbows and knees.

"Uncle Dan!" Liam cried delightedly, bouncing frog-legged on his stomach until Dan caught hold of him and held him still, more for the sake of his internal organs than any avuncular gesture. "What you doin' here?"

He peered at Dan from beneath his floppy blond fringe, pale blue eyes serious and nose—as ever—running.

"Did you bring presents?"

"He doesn't always bring you stuff when he comes over, so don't you start trying that one!" Edith called from the kitchen. "And come on—breakfast! Jack, your lunchbox is on the side here, don't forget to pick it up. Lauren, have you found your socks?"

"Yes, Mum," Lauren intoned back, waving her blatantly bare foot under Dan's nose. He caught hold of it, tickled her on the big toe, and when she squealed, released her, threw the blanket off and stood with Liam tucked under one arm.

"Come on, you horrible lot… your poor mother'll go spare."

He shepherded them toward the kitchen, tossing a smile at Edith, rumpled in her mint-green terry toweling robe and spiky morning hair.

"Too right," she said, looking him up and down. "Four kids to deal with today instead of three. Want some toast?"

Dan's grin widened, and he felt more glad of her than ever. "Yeah. Please."

"Okay. Ja—Jack! Jack, what did I say about your lunch? Well, then. Pick it up and put in your bag. Go on. I want to see you do it… thank you. Goodness' sake…."

In barely over two minutes, Dan's morning changed, filled to its brim with local radio chatter, orange juice, and breakfast cereals, complaints about white versus brown toast, shredded marmalade over nonshredded, and whether or not shoes had been cleaned and school ties properly knotted. He marveled at the way Edith dealt with them, like a general marshaling troops or a rancher driving particularly truculent horses, she countered every whinge, nipped every tantrum in the bud, cajoling and occasionally threatening in order to get her own way. In less than ten days, the school holidays would begin, and she'd have all three of them under her feet all day.

Dan had no idea how the hell he'd manage if he was in her position, but then he suspected he lacked her innate ability with kids. Her confidence and firm rule were masks he'd seen her adopt long ago, but they seemed real and natural, while his felt decidedly flimsy, and children can smell fear.

Fond of them all though he was, relief washed through Dan when he watched her parcel the whole pack into the car, ready for the school run. He stood on the doorstep and waved until they were out of sight, and before locking up like Edith had asked, he did a few chores for her. He washed up, tidied a bit, and fed Benson, and the emptiness of the kitchen seemed huge.

HIS FLAT, when he finally sloped home, unable to put it off any longer, wasn't much better. Dan had a shower, shave, and a mug of strong coffee before he turned his phone on, checked messages and endured the inevitable apology from Paul. Well… it started out as an apology, but the thread of whining running beneath the words seemed loud to Dan, like the drone of a mosquito. *Why* had he reacted like that? *Why* had he just stomped off without warning, when they needed to talk things out?

Why not?

Dan checked his e-mail, dealt with some banal professional inquiries, and found a brief, cheerful couple of lines from Cesare. He sounded upbeat, something about a Montessori-derived method of teaching that might help Niccolò, and he closed with such a simple question it made Dan's throat feel heavy.

Just "are you well?"

For the first time in quite a long while, Dan thought about that and realized he couldn't answer it. Not so much the inability to lie and say simply yes, but the inability to really know for sure.

He glanced at the clock, did some brief mental arithmetic, and reached for his phone. His pulse quickened, and he almost had time to wish he hadn't dialed before the ringing tone gave way to the lilt of a familiar voice.

"*Pronto?*"

"Cesare? Hi, it's Dan. Um…."

"Daniel! *Come va?* It's very good to hear from you."

Where he'd sounded tired, Dan heard his voice pick up, and it flattered him a little to think he could do that. It also opened up a fresh wave of regret.

"Yeah, I'm, um… I'm okay. How are you?"

"Fine, *sì*." Cesare paused, seeming uncertain.

Dan searched for something to say, not sure why they weren't tracking through their normal topics of conversation, or why he found it so hard to speak.

"*Scusa*, but… you sound—Did something happen?"

It was the only prompt Dan really needed, and he opened his mouth to find a heavy, tight breath already breaking from it.

"I…. No, not—oh, I don't know. Um. Just that I'd sort of been seeing someone, and he turned out to not quite be… well, who I hoped he was. If that makes sense."

"Ah."

Cesare said nothing more for a moment, and Dan regretted having rung, sure he must have hurt him. He regretted the half-truth too, though the full truth was more complicated than he could get into now. Besides, it meant admitting more than he wanted to. All right, so there was nothing between him and Cesare now, but not for lack of wishing it could be different. If he'd admitted that to himself, then surely even Cesare—with his immense arsenal of self-sacrifice and denial—had done so too. Dan cleared his throat, trying to think of some way to backpedal out of this, to hang up and stop embarrassing both of them.

"Would… would you like to talk about it?"

Possibly the worst thing Cesare could have said. Dan took a deep breath.

"Um. Thanks. It's not… he was an ex anyway. We broke up before Christmas, so I suppose I really should have known better than—"

He stopped, suddenly unable to say anything else as if his mouth had run aground, and he really didn't know what he wanted: forgiveness or distraction. Cesare just made a small, soothing "hm." Silence settled between them, and Dan wasn't sure whether it lasted seconds or hours. He heard a great deal in the things Cesare didn't say: understanding, and an uncomfortable recognition.

"So, not long before you went to Venice?"

He cringed inwardly. "No. Not long."

"I see."

Dan waited, not sure whether he should try to ameliorate the damage he might already have done or just blunder on regardless. Cesare was a grown man, and they'd both been consenting adults, so why did he still worry so much about hurting his feelings?

Cesare cleared his throat, and the sound of it echoed through Dan's ear, like the illusion of the ocean trapped in a seashell.

"Sometimes," Cesare said, apparently with great consideration, "I think perhaps people are not who we think they are, because we have judged them by what we see, not what we feel."

Dan bit his lip. It should have sounded hokey, should have been ridiculous, but it wasn't.

"Yeah," he said softly. "Y'know, you could be right. S'pose it just came as a surprise… I thought I had him figured out. Should have listened to myself."

Partly a lie, he suspected. He should have spent less time lost in his own head, concentrated more on thinking instead of pretending. He didn't want to try and explain that to Cesare, though, and then they were wrapped up in another spasm of that strange, difficult silence.

"So, what will you do?" Cesare asked.

His voice hummed gently against Dan's ear, and there was a note of something he couldn't quite identify in it. Not exactly flirtation, but… expectancy? Hope? He rubbed his thumb along the edge of the desk, pressing hard on the cheap wood veneer.

"Um, I don't…. Well, I mean, I suppose I'd thought about stepping back for a few days. Taking some time out to clear my head. It's kind of an embarrassing situation, y'know? So many friends thought that we were—"

Dan stopped, not willing or perhaps just unsure how to finish the sentence. He didn't want to sound as if he was whining about being heartbroken, nor want Cesare to think he needed sympathy, but... damn it, he sounded like a fool.

"I don't know," he went on, backtracking a little. "Like I say, it's a little bit embarrassing. Seeing all the same people, and, even though we didn't make a big thing out of being back together... I just feel I've ended up with egg on my face. So I can't deny it'd be nice to hide for a while. Not have to see all the sympathetic expressions everyone puts on. Like it's a bereavement or something."

"*Sì*. Maybe you should just step away from everything. As you say."

Something Dan couldn't quite identify lingered in Cesare's tone. Almost a sense of hunger, a tentative pull toward what he realized they both wanted more than anything.

"Yes." Dan bit his lip. "Perhaps I should."

"If you wanted to."

For a moment, Cesare almost managed to sound unconcerned. He cleared his throat, and Dan could just picture him—the way he'd stand, the way he'd look, so uncertain as he tried to wad up the courage to say what he wanted to.

"*Ehi*, perhaps you should come to Italia again, eh? Had you thought about coming back?"

Dan shut his eyes, the other man's image an imprinted negative on the backs of his lids. "Mm... it's something I'd considered," he said, trying to keep his tone casual but, all the while, hating himself for saying it at all.

He wasn't doing it again, he told himself. Definitely not. Cesare didn't deserve to be used as a plaster, a pick-me-up on the rebound. He had no automatic carnal rights to this man, simply on the strength of what had happened in Venice, and no matter how much it sounded like Cesare wanted him there right now, it couldn't happen.

Life wasn't like that, and it didn't allow for inconveniences.

Besides, did he want to be the kind of man who ran away from everything?

It could become a nasty habit, Dan supposed: fleeing for the Continent pretty damn quick, as Paul had said. Yet he didn't care. He just wanted somewhere to lick his wounds, somewhere unscarred by the mess he'd made and undamaged. He stared up at the painting on the wall and smiled.

"Definitely considered."

"You should," Cesare said quickly, as if he'd been aching for those words. "You should come. Maybe… think about it, *si*? Maybe I see you while you're here."

"Maybe," Dan agreed.

They spoke for a little longer, no further mention of the plan, but the conversation still plagued him long after the call ended. Every time Dan's gaze caught the painting on his wall, those blazing Continental colors, he thought how stupid it was. So very fucking stupid, that those memories of Venice—his naughty holiday fun, in all the tacky glamour he'd couched it—should have been more honest, more real, than the man he'd wasted nearly four years of his life on.

He knew, deep down, he didn't mean that. Wasted. That word sprang out of hurt, not reason, and he'd pull himself together soon enough and start thinking rationally about it all again. Not just yet, but soon enough. In the meantime, he wanted to swear and stomp and call Paul seven kinds of bastard, but he didn't want to do it here or alone. He wanted peace, and quiet… solitude. A friend, unbiased and nonpartisan.

If he tried very, very hard, Dan could almost believe that was what Cesare was.

CHAPTER SEVENTEEN

"*EHI… ERRE, Niccolò, è una rana, sì?*"

The boy turned to stare sullenly out of the window, ignoring the flashcard and the small plastic frog on the table in front of him. The frog lay, forlorn, beside the exercise book and pen with which he was supposed to write out the simple sentence Cesare had transcribed for him to follow, but he wouldn't even acknowledge it.

Cesare eased a low breath of frustration out between his teeth, determined not to show anger. Niccolò Misseri was not a stupid child. He knew this. Niccolò's parents knew it. There were reports from doctors and psychologists that confirmed it… yet if Cesare couldn't help the boy improve his grades, connect with the work and with the other children, he would be irreparably branded subnormal, perhaps unable to pass the school year, his future stained by the school's failure to help him.

Of course, the principal, Signor Alvisio, didn't see it that way. He was of the opinion that Signora Bianchi, whose one day of attendance at each school in the area was supposed to provide sufficient coverage for every child with special needs, was more than enough of a concession. He disagreed with Cesare on the need for anything more and had blocked attempts to secure a referral for Niccolò to any other teacher, citing what Cesare believed to be the ridiculous and ultimately bullshit excuse that this would "divert funds and attention" from the other children. Signor Alvisio, in Cesare's opinion, was a Grade A bastard. Cesare knelt before the boy and picked up one of the rounded plastic letters that sat in a box on the wooden table. A new idea from Daniel's sister, this. To help Niccolò feel the words, not try to understand them as written shapes. Autistic children often thought in images, not words, apparently. The memory of his English friend's voice drifted through Cesare's mind for a moment, and he smiled, turning the little shape over in his fingers. Niccolò, hunched up in his chair, away from the threat of contact, mumbled and kicked the leg of the table.

"*Basta, Niccolò. Ehi, ecco, sì? R… rana. R.*"

He frowned but seemed interested in the letter. Cesare put it down in front of him and watched the boy pick it up, chasing the smooth edges with his fingers, mouth moving over the sound it made.

"*R... r... r....*"

"*Sì!*" Cesare's smile widened. "*Sì, bene. Molto bene, Niccolò! La...? La rana. Sì?*"

He took up the plastic frog, made it hop along the edge of the table. Niccolò's face wrapped around a shy smile, intense concentration on this new object. He kept rubbing his palm over the rounded letter *r*, so Cesare helped him lay out the rest of the word, showing him where the letters went, how they spelled out sounds.

Gradually, Niccolò's stuttering, rolling *r* sounds lengthened out and became half, then almost the whole word. He consented to take up his pen and wrote the first part of the sentence Cesare wanted him to follow. His writing was still terrible, but he seemed to show a better understanding of the letters, to engage with the words more. Cesare supposed that could have been his imagination or perhaps wishful thinking, but with the afternoon wearing on and the warm summer sunshine trickling through the open window, it felt like a breakthrough.

At the sound of Signor Misseri's car on the gravel drive outside, sharply cutting the sticky, late afternoon air in two, Cesare smiled and sat back on his heels. His knees were killing him, squatting down on the floor like this. He didn't begrudge a minute of the time spent here at the family's home, the summer lessons, and the extra help... but if none of it did any good, what was the next alternative? The Misseris were not wealthy, and there was no provision for additional tutors or more specialized schooling.

"*Signor Eveschi?*" Angela Misseri poked her head around the door of the study—the makeshift lesson room—her eyebrows raised.

Cesare glanced round, the little plastic frog still in his hand. He smiled, nodded at her, cast a quick look back at Niccolò. Any other boy would at least have acknowledged his mother's presence, surely. Not Niccolò. He just sat, rubbing the plastic letters in his hand and now looking out of the window, staring at the sky.

Cesare showed her what the boy had done, how hard he'd tried. She smiled, delighted, and her face lost a great deal of the tight-lined worry it held—just for a moment. He said good-bye to Niccolò, flushed with pride at the small wrinkle of fingers and part-smile he got from the boy, and talked for a short while with Angela on the landing. Cesare could do little for her in the way of assurance or comfort, but her gratitude touched him.

Downstairs, he passed a few brief words with her husband, Ugo, terse and businesslike as ever. He was a rather short, stocky kind of man, with thick black hair and brows drawn down over his nose in a permanent embryonic scowl. Still, Cesare had once thought him a little attractive, just for that sense of masculinity he carried, and he was never entirely sure what to say to him. At one time he had seemed intimidating, as if he could somehow look at Cesare and see everything he was. All his… failings, though he no longer thought of them like that.

He shook those thoughts away and talked about Niccolò's improvements in speech and writing. Ugo offered him a coffee, but Cesare declined and bade them farewell until next week. He left the small, comfortable house and walked out to his car, an irresistible feeling of cheerful glee bubbling up inside him. The school holidays were still quite new, their sacred time stretching away before him over the summer, and today had been perhaps the first of many small victories. If Niccolò could continue to improve as he had been doing, then the next school year would not be as great a problem for him as they'd feared.

Cesare pulled away from the quiet suburban cul-de-sac, heading back into town, and from there, for the autostrada back to Gravagna Montale. Birds singing, traffic not too heavy… and more reasons than that to feel good. Yes. Perhaps, more than any other thing, because of what lay ahead, nestled at the foot of the next week, ready for anticipation and delicious hopes.

Daniel was coming.

Cesare's little Fiat puttered gently along the widening roads, leaving the suburbs behind him and enjoying the town sluicing past. They were fantasies, of course, all the ridiculous romantic pictures that clouded his mind. But perhaps it did no harm to dwell among them, for just a little while, to imagine the bliss of Venice recaptured.

His lover, returned.

The thought simultaneously excited and terrified Cesare. Of course he hoped they might, in some way, continue where they had left off—he was of the same weaknesses of all flesh and had the same needs and wants, however deep he buried them. Yet after the time that had passed, the friendship that had grown between them, the last thing he wanted was for Daniel to think ill of him, or to ruin things by pushing too hard.

After all, while Cesare might remember him as a lone traveler, he now knew Daniel had other baggage. His… ex. The man he had gone to Venice to forget, Cesare supposed. He tried to ignore the momentary stab of jealousy and reached out to put the radio on, letting a burst of music wash over him and—almost—brushing the feeling away.

Easy, for a man like Daniel. Easy to have friends, lovers… partners. The thought of the word stuck in the back of Cesare's throat, sharp and metallic. He reflected on his own romantic history, pallid and shameful in its shriveled, pathetic nonexistence. Discounting the fumbles of adolescence, the long-running, one-sided boyhood infatuation with football *capitano* Carlo Antonelli, and that lovely but all-too-brief affair during his teacher training, what had there been? One, two men, perhaps. Tito, with his sharp little prick and his hard, angry words, poking and poking and everything always being about politics, about power. Never real love. Cesare, loath though he was to admit it, had been glad when Tito left for Rome, yet he still bore the guilt of what the man had done to his wife and children.

He had considered, very briefly, trying to help them, but… she had her own money, her own career. What would his sudden presence have done? *Buongiorno, signora, I am the man your husband fucked.* No. No good. And so Cesare's retreat back into lonely nights with the company of books, magazines, and DVDs had seemed logical, had seemed all he was really worth.

He'd experimented, once or twice. His ill-fated weekends in Padua and Bologna, his first and only visit to a sauna. Pretense upon pretense, until the lies tried to choke him. He paid for an escort once. A beautiful young man named Marco. Cesare found his website, looked at it every day for six months while he put aside the money, and then when he finally took the plunge, it had been nothing like he imagined. The boy was too businesslike, too impatient, and too intimidating, and the encounter had lacked all the things he'd wanted from it. He returned home a great deal poorer, and chastened, determined to leave his desires in check, simmering below the surface. Even if he couldn't believe what the church said about the sinfulness of certain acts, he chose to accept that they were not for him. That such a life, such freedoms, weren't meant for him.

Or, at least, he had done.

Now, Cesare navigated the narrower roads that led home. The hilly, bare fields and ancient traces of Gravagna Montale—with its sunburnt gaggles of old stone houses interspersed with more recent buildings: industrial units and ugly, squat blocks of flats—were strangely calming. Day to day, coming back to this, Cesare usually felt at least a little trapped. Yet, the sun was shining and his head was full of silly, romanticized, pretended notions, so nothing seemed to touch him.

Daniel is coming.

He knew he shouldn't let the knowledge affect him the way it did, but he couldn't help it. Just the thought made him giddy, breathless, *alive*... as if the wealth of bursting sunlight opened up in his chest and flowed from there, filling him right down to the ends of his toes. It pulsed within him as he drove, every building that rolled past and every waft of thyme and petrol in the air infused with its reflected glory. Daniel was coming. To see *him*.

All right, so perhaps that was not entirely the whole reason. They had talked about it on the phone: how he did want to get away, after the recent events; the breakup with the man whom Cesare did not really wish to think about; and how Toscana would be a great choice.

Cesare hoped he hadn't sounded too desperate. With the first suggestion, he hadn't thought for a moment that Daniel would agree... he'd just meant to say that he thought the landscape here would appeal to his photographer's eye. The rolling hills, the bright, rich sunlight, and the old buildings that still shrouded the place with their veils of years.

Cesare had just suggested that he think about coming to Tuscany. Nothing more. But he could tell Daniel liked the idea from the way he sounded like he was smiling when he said yes... the way Cesare just knew he himself must have looked when he asked where he should stay. Cesare had surprised himself by asking. He would never have thought he would be brave enough, or forward enough, but Daniel brought all those things out in him. Just like he had in Venezia.

Stay with me?

He'd said yes. He sounded as if he really wanted to, as if he were looking forward to it.

The light washed through Cesare anew, red shadows behind his eyes bursting in blissful anticipation. He would come... and it would be wonderful.

Probably.

Of course there was no guarantee that anything would happen. He had to acknowledge that. They were in Venice no longer, and all his dreams were dreams only and nothing more... but he enjoyed them nevertheless. The memories of Daniel's kisses, of his body, the way he made love—they were branded deep in Cesare's mind. He'd missed it so much. Not just the closeness, the comfort of another human being—though he'd gone without that for a long time—but just being with Daniel.

It would be good to see him again. To dream, just for a little while.

Naturally, the waiting proved hard.

Every day inched by, the weeks stolidly refusing to pass. Each loose page wavered on the calendar, fighting doggedly against the impulse to fall, while Cesare pivoted from excited anticipation to total terror and back again.

What if Daniel came but things were not as they'd been before? Venice had been a place out of time, out of mind.... Daniel had gone back to his life since then. To his other man—and Cesare mocked himself for thinking that. *Other* man. As if *he* was anything like the man Daniel had been seeing, as if he meant anything more than the brief, fleeting release he'd provided. That gave rise to the other fears he'd known: Had he made a fool of himself? Would he? Perhaps it hadn't been wise to arrange Daniel coming here. It could place too heavy a burden on their still-young friendship, and that would be a terrible thing.

Besides, here Cesare had a life too. People who knew him, a reputation and a presence in the village that he would still have to keep up once his English friend had gone home. What if people guessed? Would it be obvious just from looking at his face what they had done together? What he was?

All of these thoughts he pushed from his mind in the daytime, and the light made it easier to keep them away. He was being ridiculous, *certo*. He was a grown man, as was Daniel. His affairs were his own—whatever village gossips might or might not pretend—and, in any case, there would never be anything more between them than what had been in Venice. And *that* was unlikely to be happening here. Daniel had clearly moved on, as the phrase went. Cesare should appreciate his friendship and expect nothing more. And he didn't *expect*, as such... but all those hours, gilded with the sea spray and the pearlescent light of La Serenissima, were difficult to forget.

He tried hard not to think too much about it, not to plan ahead one-sided imaginings of things that probably wouldn't even happen the way he pictured them, and just accept that—whatever *did* happen, and however it occurred—it was good and enough. He went to Mass with his parents and sat in the old wooden pew, the smells of beeswax, pollen, and sanctity tickling his nose while the priest spoke.

His mother looked frail for a moment, just when he chanced to catch sight of her during the service. A wan shaft of light reached along the nave and touched the gray hair, neatly combed beneath the black lace veil that covered the top of her head, and Cesare felt a sudden and overwhelming wave of guilty sadness. It was wrong that he should have spent so much time thinking about himself, about the things he dreamed of, the things he wanted in such silly, frivolous ways.

After Father Morassutti finally finished, leaving the congregation to mill back out into their daily lives, he went back to his parents' place for a late breakfast. There was sunlight, tinged with the dusty promise of a long summer to come, and scalding hot coffee. He let Mamma wheedle more information out of him about this English friend he had coming to stay. He'd told them, of course; there was no way the whole village wouldn't hear about the English photographer man within the first hour of Daniel's arrival. She had it in her head somehow that he was related to or maybe knew Rosemarie, the teacher at the *scuola* who was also English, as if that entire country sat around the table every afternoon for tea and muffins.

Nevertheless, Cesare was not about to disabuse her of the notion. It suited him well to let her think there was a connection to the school or some other sphere of his life far removed from the truth. Duplicitous, perhaps, but easier on all of them. He smiled, drank his coffee, and nodded.

"You must bring him over," she said, topping up his cup. "Eh? We can all say hello. Have a nice *cena*, all together."

Cesare's smile stiffened, and the coffee thickened in his throat. He caught his father's gaze across the table and forced out a noncommittal reply. Perhaps he would. He liked the idea, in the safe and controlled confines of his imagination. Daniel would fit well into this comforting, warm room, with its outdated décor and the rimed traces of his childhood all over the place. Like the great *palazzi* of Venezia, the ancient waterways, and museums, there was a heartbeat of history here, though a much smaller, more private one. Not as grand, not as interesting for many, though as he downed his second coffee, Cesare thought what a great deal it meant to him.

WHEN THE day finally came, it didn't feel real. Cesare rose far too early, the nerves it annoyed him to be so riddled with churning his stomach. He watched the early morning broadcast of an American news channel on cable, his lips moving in time with the words as he tried to remember how to think in English… but he couldn't think at all. Nothing in his head but memories of a man who wasn't going to be as handsome when Cesare met him today as he would be in the confines of imagination. Nobody could be so perfect, so flawless. All the same, his pulse skittered. Cesare was almost afraid to shave, thinking he would have to meet Daniel with great sheets of toilet roll stuck to his face, a welter of scabs and dried blood.

He took a deep breath, clung to the sides of the sink, and went slowly. So slow… like the touch of gentle hands on his skin. More memories washed through him, irresistible and pervasive.

Maiala della miseria!

He needed to stop this. It was becoming ridiculous. He was a grown man, and they were only friends. Cesare reminded himself of that, over and over, like a mantra or a prayer. He had no right to expect anything else from the man. Just friendship.

He cleared his throat and fixed the soap-laden reflection in the mirror with a solemn glare.

Yes. He must stop it and be sensible.

That resolution lasted as long as he looked himself in the eye. By the time he had dressed and jogged down to his Fiat, insidious remembrances were already creeping back into his head. Cesare tried to block them out. He turned the key in the ignition, switched on the radio, and glanced at his watch as a bland pop track bounced around the inside of the car. Not long now. Daniel's train would arrive at Pontremoli within the hour. He had sent a text message earlier in the journey, confirming he had made the connection and was running on time—a feat in itself for Italian rail travel and, Cesare suspected, quite possibly some kind of sign from heaven. The few simple, abbreviated words had made Cesare's pulse quicken, and he almost had to say the words "he is coming" to make them feel real.

Now his breathing deepened again, his palms slick on the wheel. He muttered a cuss and backed the Fiat out onto the road. The sun was already high, bright with the promise of another hot day. It would be a good summer, by the looks of things.

The streets slipped by, the smells of warm stone and the wild thyme that popped up defiantly in every crack, in every path, marking out the old byways of the village houses, giving way to the grit and fumes of the autostrada. Cesare rolled his window a little way up and let the music play on as he drove and tried not to think about what awaited him.

Pontremoli Station was rarely busy, and today the sun touched the low collection of buildings delicately, as if afraid to wake them from some slumber. Cesare parked, conscious of how stiff and stale he felt after the drive. Did he smell all right, look all right? He locked the car and then made his way down to the platform, annoyed with himself for thinking about the speed of his gait. Was he walking too fast, seeming too eager? Cesare cleared his throat, took another of the deep breaths that barely calmed him.

The train was coming.

Signals changed, a bell clanged, and the nasal, crackling announcement came over the speakers. The tracks rattled and Cesare stopped breathing, stopped blinking, the grit in his eyes and the taste of the diesel fumes at the back of his throat as nothing next to the weltering excitement in him.

The ear-splitting wail of brakes calmed, and passengers began to disembark. Cesare stayed where he was, lingering by the wall of the waiting room, beside a large, glossy, mobile phone company advertisement, which had been fly-billed with peeling posters for local youth bands. He waited, scanning the loose knots of people and the milling bodies.

He must be here... surely.

Cesare looked down the length of the platform, far more restive than he'd hoped to feel, and all those nerves jangling afresh. Where the last time he'd seen Daniel they had been strangers, bonds of a different intimacy now joined them. All those calls, texts, and messages, despite the illusive intimacy of the Internet, had made something real and undeniable between them. The thought that he might somehow let that down, topple from the precarious edge of his pedestal—or worse, find that Daniel slipped in his own eyes—was suddenly and acutely terrifying. Cesare tried to push the ugly fear away, wanting to banish anything cold or imperfect from touching this sun-streaked little patch of concrete, but the worries stuck all the same.

He reached out a hand, his palm touching the cool wall. The textures of paint, paper, and wood seemed to blot out the warmth of the sun, the smell of the train, as if his body wasn't equipped to deal with more than one sensation at a time. So much wretched expectancy, filling him up like a cup, overflowing and pushing everything out ahead of it.

Then, yards away, there was a familiar glimmer of light brown hair. Cesare's stomach tightened, and he caught himself actually leaning forward, tensing into the moment of recognition. It was Daniel. The same easy confidence, the same lean, rangy frame... he was here. And he hadn't changed.

He'd thought Daniel would look different somehow: as if his recollections had been imperfect, or he'd constructed some false memory in the time they'd been apart. Cesare took in the sight of him slowly, not quite daring to breathe. He'd had his hair cut. His clothes seemed a little smarter, town garb rather than the relaxed wear of a man on vacation, though he still wore that same tan leather blazer. Cesare stifled a shiver at the memory of how it smelled.

A beam of sunlight broadened out across the concourse. Cesare smiled and started forward. Daniel looked up, saw him, and grinned.

The complicated moment of reaching Daniel seemed both to draw out and pass too quickly, the seconds sliding together, yet the ground yawning ever wider as Cesare tried to cross it. Daniel was moving too, coming to him, grinning and laughing. They met halfway, more awkward excitement than Hollywood embrace, though Cesare couldn't help but grin like a fool at the feel of his arms. The moment of greeting him, the first smile of recognition, extended into a drawn-out, paceless thing, full of Cesare's fast-beating heart and their overlapping laughter. The brush of his lips on Cesare's cheek, the warmth of his body, and the enticing deliciousness of his scent... he wanted to hold each sensation divided and complete, but they all mixed together, colliding and mingling in the fractured beauty of the embrace.

Cesare didn't want to let go, though he knew he would have to. Daniel filled his arms, his lungs... everything. He squeezed tighter.

"Ah, *mi sei mancato*, Daniel. You have a good journey?"

They parted, still smiling foolishly at each other.

"Yeah, not bad. Good, really. It's… bloody hell, it's good to see you."

Cesare nodded fervently, a little reluctant to actually take his hand away from Daniel's shoulder, the leather of the blazer sun-warmed and smooth beneath his fingers. He looked so good, smelled so good… even the sound of his voice touched something at Cesare's core, roused things he wasn't used to feeling. He suspected the ridiculous grin would be plastered across his face indefinitely, but he didn't care.

Right now there was nothing but sunshine and his friend.

They talked on the way out to his car, exchanges of pleasantries, news, delight at the week ahead. Daniel had very little with him—just one small rucksack and a bag that, from its shape and padding, Cesare supposed carried his beloved camera equipment.

He unlocked the Fiat, pausing for a moment with his hand on the dusty gray paintwork.

"It's not very far, to go home, but before we go, do you want to go anywhere, or you need to…?"

Daniel shook his head and grinned, the bright air playing around the tousled gold of his head. "Nope. I'm all yours."

Cesare smiled broadly and folded into the driver's seat. Very beautiful words, even if he didn't wholeheartedly believe them.

CHAPTER EIGHTEEN

IT WAS strange country. Dan had been expecting rolling cornfields, stubble baked to burning by an unrelenting yellow sun. Instead they drove through the back end of a town that might have been almost any other. Industrial units, small shops, and the square, gray shapes of disused buildings gave way as they passed through the parts of nature that had been allowed to butt up to the sprawl. Green fields edged the roads, their grassy patchwork filled with sheep, cows, and the occasional horse switching its tail.

It was oddly English.

They didn't speak much after Cesare pulled onto the autostrada, settling instead into a companionable silence. Dan watched the tarmac and concrete spin by, only knowing from the wide azure streaks of sky and the bright, golden quality of the light that this was Tuscany. A smile spread across his face—not just at that thought, but at that reality of all of this. He was here, and free from everything for a few days. All the responsibilities, the pressures... the things that gnawed at his mind in the dark hours. The mess he'd made of things with Paul, the ever-present necessities of work and everyday life, and in fact the whole grinding machine of London, with its grayness and constant motion, seemed to fade into insignificance here, next to this.

Next to Cesare.

He settled back into the Fiat's upholstery and watched the urban sprawl veer back to lush hills and primal greenery. Gravagna Montale must be located in a beautiful part of the region, that much was obvious. Dan had taken the time to read up a little bit too, though there was precious little actually in English on the Internet, seeing as this place was so far off the tourist track. There was history here—centuries of it. He could see the footprints of years in every bend of the landscape, in each little daub of a village painted in hot flashes of yellow and red against the ancient hills, dropped like careless splashes of paint against an undulating canvas.

It seemed almost unreal to come to this so soon after the mundanity of the autostrada, the grim colors and the boring austerity of the journey. Dan snuck a look at Cesare, surprised when he glanced back right away, a smile already on his face.

"You will like, I think, the village. It's very old, in some parts."

"Your family's not been there long, though?" Dan said, grappling for something to throw into the conversation that didn't betray the sudden lurch he'd felt in the pit of his gut… like he was going to Venice all over again.

"No." Cesare turned his attention back to the road. "Not, uh, not very long."

He talked a little more, reeling off place names Dan couldn't even begin to spell, much less locate on a map. It was hard enough mentally adjusting to the Italian system of regions, provinces, and all the complicated places in between. Yet to listen to Cesare felt like being embraced by the warm, comforting pages of a history book, a narrative crafted with such affection that it made the words spring to life in Dan's mind.

He spoke of the way the region was constructed and briefly of his childhood, his parents' house, and the different parts of Italy they'd come from. Dan knew he was missing out on idioms and hidden meanings, but it didn't seem to matter too much. A faint smell of wild thyme perfumed the air, beneath the grit of the road and the car exhaust fumes, and outside, the village of Gravagna Montale rose up before them.

Nestled into the ancient landscape, the proud arches of venerable trees painting flashes of dappled green across the parched yellows of the fields, Gravagna Montale was strikingly beautiful. Gorgeous old buildings dotted the hillsides, some patched with the retouched mortar and ramshackle extensions of decades of continual use, and some crumbling and degraded by long years of neglect.

As they neared the roads, the buildings grew more utilitarian, and, once they got into the village itself, a very strange combination of grim, gray modernity and ancient, mellow stone greeted Dan. It seemed as if the handsome, time-worn houses, still leaning across the street to gossip with each other like old women at fences, had been sleeping and woken to find themselves surrounded by this new age of concrete and steel. He pictured the town creeping out, seeping meter by meter to usurp the land, both changing and preserving the character of the commune: leaving the buildings essentially untouched, but choking off the air supply of the place. It wasn't hard to see that once, much more of this place must have been rural, agricultural land. Now, Dan supposed that, like Cesare, more people needed the town and the services and jobs it offered to sustain themselves. All the life of this beautiful little place—a history stretching back centuries—and yet it seemed as if it was reaching out in its last gasp for survival, its plaintive breaths mingling with the sound of traffic on the autostrada beyond.

He blinked, aware that socioeconomic ponderings weren't really what was expected of him right now. Cesare had parked in front of a small house on a corner plot, its thick stone walls the color of buttercream, roofed with worn terra-cotta slates. Two sets of steps, in the same mellow stone, led up to separate doors, and Dan realized the house had been divided into flats some time ago. The traces of running repairs to the façade were evident, with patches of discoloration to the mortar and pointings, and the small pots of bright red geraniums resting beside the base of the walls could not disguise the mild air of decay.

Even the pavement had a camber to it that could have been worn down by centuries of foot traffic, and as he got out of the car and crossed to the foot of the steps, Dan smelled the scents of thyme and citrus on the air, leavening the edges of the stale and gritty summer warmth.

"Welcome," Cesare said, all nervous geniality as he unlocked the front door and ushered Dan inside and up a narrow flight of stairs.

The place was definitely small and not exactly the pinnacle of modern design. Dan's brief glance took in the neutral palette, its careworn shades of beige and oatmeal scuffed and outdated by a good ten years. A small glass-topped coffee table, worn sideboard, three-seater sofa, and two recliners occupied one end of the room, with a beech-effect bookcase and lower midrange sound system close by, while a desk and elderly desktop PC stood at the other end. The furniture all seemed mismatched and acquired for necessity rather than aesthetics. Two doors led off, Dan assumed, to the bedroom and the bathroom, while the small, open-plan kitchen appeared to have been tacked onto the design as something of an afterthought. A tiny mosaic-topped table and two folding metal chairs provided scant space to eat, though he could make out the sleek lines of an expensive coffee machine on the black, granite-effect worktop.

Despite the flat's limitations of size, natural light did flood in through a pair of french doors on the far wall, by the kitchen, affording—even in the hazy peach-yellow dusk—glimpses of a miniscule roof terrace and the suggestion of views across the buildings and hills beyond.

"It's beautiful," he said, meaning the roof terrace and the sudden, inexplicable visions of shared breakfasts out there, with warm toast, soft grapefruit, and the mellow sound of Cesare's laughter. The praise sounded extravagant, however, and he tried to backtrack. "I mean, it's… no, it's nice. Everything you need, right? And, um, I bet the building's pretty old."

He glanced upward, at the only thing distinguishing this place from any host of cheap, purpose-built starter hutches. Cesare's apartment being on the top floor, it had all the benefits of the original ceiling, with wooden beams and vaulting. Much of it had been painted over at one time or another, and some parts boxed in to accommodate either taste or perhaps modern plumbing, but it still presented a neat encapsulation of the union in this place between old and new, tradition and progress.

It couldn't have suited Cesare better.

Cesare moved awkwardly around the space, obviously wishing he had more to offer, and talking about how the building was relatively quiet, the noise of the road muted, and the village still a very traditional place. Dan shed his jacket, allowed Cesare to make him comfortable, and allowed him his litany of self-deprecation. He talked even while he went to put coffee on, the lift in his voice revealing his nervousness.

"Would you like…?" Cesare paused en route back from the kitchen and gestured to the bottles on the sideboard. "I have grappa."

He said it with a smile, and the shared memory of a hotel room seemed even closer now than it had when Dan got off the train. He cleared his throat.

"Uh, yeah. Great. Thanks."

Cesare poured the drinks. The metallic spin of the lid, the sound of the bottle clinking on the rim of each glass in turn, and the splash of liquid all settled awkwardly in the air. He passed Dan one glass and their fingers briefly grazed against each other.

"Thanks. Um. *Salute.*"

Cesare settled into the chair opposite him and raised his glass. "*Salute.*"

It tasted just as good as Dan remembered: strength and warmth in liquid fire. And Cesare's proximity too… he'd missed that scent, that sense of solidity. Dan blinked. No, he wasn't here to start thinking like that. Though right at this moment, with the way Cesare's gaze touched him over the sparkling rim of that glass, it would be easy to seduce him again, but Dan knew he'd never forgive himself if he tried. It would be wrong, wouldn't it? Being so cavalier with someone so vulnerable. Especially when he doubted he could trust his own judgment... know whether he wanted this for himself or out of some misguided attempt at reconstructing his own failures, reacting to his own private screwups. Yet they were both consenting adults, and maybe he only kept casting Cesare as vulnerable from the fear of admitting that he wasn't really that fragile. And with the way he kept looking at Dan, who could truly be sure who was seducing whom?

The kettle boiled. Cesare fetched tiny cups of scalding black coffee and set them down on the table, the *chink* on the glass top loud in the sudden quiet.

Dan cleared his throat again, forced their conversation around to the continuances of things they'd talked about in e-mails, the threads of a friendship picked up anew, though the shifted balance of it couldn't be ignored. They knew each other better now, yet being in the same room still cast a dangerous light between them, coloring the edges of every glance, every laugh. Dan almost wished it wasn't so, that he could just regard Cesare as a good friend, and nothing more.

The crux came when Cesare mentioned sleeping arrangements. There was only one bedroom, so he proposed to loan it to Dan and take the couch himself.

"No, I can't kick you out of your own bed! I'll be fine on the sofa, really."

Cesare wouldn't countenance the protests. He held up his hands, a gesture of placation and innocence. "No, is all right, Daniel. Please."

"Okay." Dan relented, the power of those dark eyes too great. "If you insist. Thank you."

Cesare's smile seemed to light up his whole face.

They took the evening slowly, Cesare giving him plenty of time to recover from a journey that really hadn't been arduous enough to warrant any kind of special treatment. Although he was admittedly a little tired, part of Dan wanted to protest that it was okay, and there was really no need to worry, but Cesare's attentions were enjoyable, and he decided not to argue. It was just so nice to be with him, to just *be*, and Dan couldn't help contrasting how easy that was to the stagnant tensions he'd had with Paul.

He kept his phone off as much as possible. Apart from the initial
flurry of phone calls from Chris and Edith's stalwart coping—with a side
of "I told you so"—there hadn't been much fallout from Dan's second
split with Paul, although the occasional snide text about a lost book or
DVD did pop up, and he didn't want to be bothered with those.

In a way, he was pleasantly surprised by how little drama there had
been. Maybe they'd gotten it down to a fine art and didn't need to bother
with histrionics. Maybe Paul was too busy fucking Stuart Glenning and
telling him what a terrible boyfriend Dan had been. Dan found he really
didn't care. There was nothing more to say and no more time to waste.

Things were easier with Cesare. Infinitely so, and Dan wondered
if that was just novelty value. He hoped not, because it felt so good.
The conversation flowed as naturally as if they'd been in each other's
company for hours, as if there had never been miles or time between
them, or as if no years had ever passed when they hadn't known each
other. Dan couldn't help but think what a curious thing that was, and
how strange the bonds between people were, that some should feel so
unbreakably *right*, and others should never reach that place, even with
years of effort.

Cesare had cooked dinner—a simple pasta dish that Dan devoured
gratefully, sitting at the tiny bistro set. After they'd eaten, he opened the
french doors, letting the soft night sweep in, and they followed the meal
with more coffee and more grappa. They talked for a long while, ranging
from the little nothings of travel and weather to the camera equipment
Dan had brought with him and the differences in technique and style
wrought by the seismic changes in digital photography.

He tried not to watch Cesare's lips when he spoke or when the
grappa they returned to drinking after the coffee wet his mouth, leaving
the full smoothness of his lower lip glossy and inviting. It wasn't what
he was here for. It wasn't fair.

Eventually, Dan couldn't stifle his yawns any longer.

"Oh! Sorry, long day. I think it's finally catching up. Do you, um,
do you have plans for the week? Anything I need to—"

"Not at all." Cesare shook his head. "Well, there is… there is plenty
of time for that. I thought perhaps I show you some of the places near
here, the old houses. There are some that would make good pictures for
you, I think."

"I'd love that," Dan said. "Thanks."

"*Niente.* My pleasure. This is as much a holiday for me as… ah, but there is time, *si*? Plenty of time. For now, you have some sleep. *Vieni.*"

They stood, Dan trying to pretend his joints didn't crack as he did so. Cesare was such a gracious host, so eager to make him comfortable and put him at his ease. There wasn't far to go to the bedroom, but he let Cesare lead the way anyway. He showed Dan the bathroom, which was small, with an old-fashioned but very well-scrubbed suite, and then opened the bedroom door.

Just like the rest of his home, Cesare's bedroom betrayed little of his personality. There was a double bed, a cheap television standing atop a low chest of drawers, and a narrow wardrobe. All the furniture seemed to be of some variation on cheap natural pine and MDF, while the bedcovers and curtains were plain, neutral… almost like a hotel. Dan guessed Cesare must have tidied his entire life away in preparation for his visit, because it barely looked as if anyone lived here at all.

"Here you go."

Cesare's voice buzzed against the back of his neck, and Dan tried not to notice it. He turned, finding himself uncomfortably close, those dark eyes holding his gaze, unwavering.

"Th-thanks. Are you sure you don't mind—"

"Not at all. You will be more comfortable, and if you need anything, I am just… here."

He gestured vaguely over his shoulder, back toward the sitting room, though his gaze didn't leave Dan's. His face held that same fearful anticipation, that same pent-up, tense desire he'd been so full of in Venice, and the paper-thin pretenses they were hiding behind seemed to Dan so stupid, and yet so insurmountable.

"Thanks," he repeated hoarsely. "I'll, um, be fine. It's very kind, all this. 'Preciate it."

"Ah, *è niente.*" Cesare shrugged, and it seemed to break the tension a little. "I will see you in the morning. Sleep well, yes?"

"Yeah. You too."

A smile, awkward but immensely endearing. Dan wanted to leap on him, rip him to shreds on the spot. He held back; anything now had to come from Cesare, or it was no movement at all. It made watching Cesare shuffle backward in the direction of the bathroom, retreating ever away, torture.

Dan shut the bedroom door once he heard Cesare go into the bathroom, and cussed under his breath. So stupid. He either had to get this out of his mind or out of his system. Preferably both.

He glanced around the room. Cesare appeared to favor neutral colors and bare pine furniture... or perhaps that just happened to be what his budget ran to. Either way, the bed, wardrobe, and chest of drawers were all pine, and so was the curtain pole. Mushroom-colored curtains framed a window looking out onto the houses on the other side of the narrow street, their soft, mellow stone glimmering in the mingled light of the moon and streetlamps. The space beside the TV, on top of the chest of drawers, was empty. Dan supposed, prior to his visit, it would have housed odds and ends of clutter... coins and pocket detritus, maybe. Alarm clock, diary, or whatever else Cesare kept close by him, the loose edges of life and the grease that turned its cogs. He sniffed, detecting the traces of furniture polish on the wood and fabric conditioner on the bedding.

It felt good to have this much fuss made over him.

Dan stripped down to his undies, rooted through his luggage for his washbag, and listened for Cesare to vacate the bathroom. The lavatory flushed, water ran, and Dan heard the door handle turn. He waited for Cesare to call out that he'd finished, but no sound came. Instead, there was the soft motion of footsteps on carpet and a knock on the bedroom door. Dan opened it and found Cesare a little closer than he'd expected, as if he wanted to push right through the wood, not even waiting for it to open.

Dan supposed he just wanted to say the bathroom was free, but Cesare didn't speak at all. His face was so solemn, his expression complex and shifting, like sunlight broken over waves. Part terror, part hunger, part defeat, and part utter, desperate intensity, he looked at Dan as if he was the hope and the failing of everything. Dan made to speak, intending some cheerful, flippant "all done, then?" type comment, but his mouth was dry and his lips rubbery, and he managed barely a murmur.

It was a silly, awkward moment, but right at the center of it, Dan could see one simple, terrible truth—one way to make everything so clear.

Cesare's gaze slipped south a little, and it seemed to burn its way over his bare skin. Dan took a short, shallow breath, almost like a gasp of surprise, though he wasn't sure why. It seemed to take a terribly long time, as if the whole world had slowed down to see what they planned to do next.

Cesare's head tilted just a little to the side, his body inclining to Dan's, and Dan barely registered his own response, hardly aware of moving because it was just so natural to do. So much like breathing just to put his hand here, his mouth there, and the whisper of assent that passed between them was no more than a simple, flickering glance. Cesare kissed him hard, full, surge after surge of it, hands hot on Dan's bare back, his shoulders, his arms.... Small, hoarse sounds broke from Cesare's throat, bursting in Dan's mouth and vibrating through his whole body, and he was only vaguely aware of, for once, being just as sloppy and noisy a kisser as Cesare.

They were mistimed, though. As he started to run out of breath and nerve, Cesare picked up his rhythm, and Dan struggled to keep up. Words he didn't know but could make a pretty good guess at understanding sluiced over him with all the hypnotic shapes of a foreign language, and Cesare's mouth cleaved to his, kisses briefly exhausted. His smell and his taste, all mixed up, wrapped Dan in toothpaste wintergreen, cloves, and citrus, and he felt the warm, solid breadth of Cesare's palm on his neck, then his jaw.

"I'm sorry... so sorry, Daniel. I—"

"Shh."

"You don't want this," Cesare began, though he'd made no attempt to move away. Still clinging on and still hazy with want. It rolled off him in waves and he shook, just a little, when he stroked his thumb along Dan's cheekbone. "You don't—"

"Yeah," Dan murmured, lips still bound up with his, Cesare's skin so incredibly warm to the touch, like he could sink into it or something. "Yeah, I do. I really do. If you—"

"*Da morire! Dai....*"

The words were barely out before Cesare was on him again, mouth mauling everything in its path, hands roaming every available quarter of Dan's flesh. He felt himself being backed to where he judged—he hoped correctly—the bed might be, but it was easier than he'd imagined to give himself over to Cesare's guidance.

They tumbled to the sheets and he tore at Cesare's shirt, unmistakably and confusingly glad to see and touch once more that scattered thatch of dark hair, the firm planes of muscle padded with that little bit extra, the flesh that spoke of good health above obsessive fitness, intermittent exercise over gym membership. It was real and wonderful.

Both down to their underwear now, equal and desperate, they ground against each other, inch by inch, kisses renewed. Dan pulled away first, short of breath and slightly dizzy, intent on fixing his mouth to a greater prize. Cesare let him, legs dangling partially over the edge of the bed as Dan knelt above him. He grinned as he peeled down Cesare's underwear and that familiar friend peeped out to greet him.

Beneath Dan, Cesare's chest rose and fell with increasing urgency, making it clear that he couldn't last long. He was already so hard, the dark, fat head of that beautiful cock wet and beckoning. Dan pressed his lips to the shaft, inhaling that delicious sharp, hot scent. Crushing his cheek to the crisp curls of hair at the junction of Cesare's thighs, Dan let his tongue tease a path along the underside of his lover's length, lost in the sensations of silk-smooth skin and hard flesh. Cesare groaned, the low rumble rising to a yelp as Dan took him deep, wanting to taste all of him, to waste no more time playing around each other, teasing and tempting beyond endurance.

He heard Cesare swear, and fastened his lips into a tight ring around his shaft, bobbing and plunging with relentless enthusiasm until the inevitable occurred, a bright corona of pleasure bursting from Cesare's center.

"Ah… too fast," he murmured, or something very like it, hands pawing at Dan and body tightening before a series of convulsive tremors ran through him, words once again abandoned.

Dan didn't care. He delighted in every messy, explosive second of it, in Cesare's sweat and his spice, the spontaneity and lack of control. It felt like absolute possession, like a psychological as well as a physical victory, but he didn't have much time to dwell on it. Cesare, still gulping at the air like a drowning man, rolled them both over, fumbling for Dan's cock.

"Fu—oh, God," Dan murmured, reaching for him, fingers buried in the head of dark hair that he'd missed so much more than he knew. "Take it slow, yeah?"

Cesare wasn't listening, attacking with all the vigor, all the energy he must have been saving just for this moment—or perhaps that he hadn't known he was saving at all. Dan could hardly argue, not when it was this good. He came somewhere in the midst of wrestling bodies and straining positions, Cesare's hands, mouth, and heat wrapped around him and burning him through to the core, ripping every last shred of pleasure out of him.

"Fuck," he muttered as they collapsed in the general vicinity of each other, breath scraping at dry lungs. He stretched out his fingers, brushing their tips along what he thought was Cesare's thigh. "You all right?"

Cesare's response was a mangled mixture of heavy breathing and an Italian affirmative of a vaguely blasphemous nature, if Dan's phrasebooks had served him as well as he thought. He cranked himself up on one elbow and peered down the length of the bed, unsure whether the flush on Cesare's face was due more to sex or embarrassment. Cesare blinked, his mouth bowed around a half smile, and looked away, suddenly shy.

"I...."

He moved to get up, forgetting his underwear was still tangled somewhere around his knees and Dan's legs were still partially over him, and the whole thing culminated in a muddled jumble of flesh and laughter. Dan pulled himself around to face Cesare, hand resting companionably on his stomach, thumb toying with the sparse curls of coarse dark hair he found there.

"Look...."

Christ, is there a way to make this nonawkward?

Cesare's eyes followed him closely, flickering beneath the bars of his lashes. As Dan was still groping uselessly for something to say, the gentle pressure of Cesare's hand slid over his, then traveled farther up his arm to curve around the point of his shoulder, trailing aching, complex things in its wake. Cesare leaned in and his kiss was gentle, questioning. Dan supposed there really wasn't much point in pretending anymore, so he let the kiss deepen into what it wanted to be, his fingers threading their way into Cesare's hair, and those very solid, very real arms wrapped tight around him.

It scared him a little, with its depth and its solemnity. Yet he couldn't argue with how right it felt, how easy it was to let Cesare slowly, deliberately wear away at every last grain of the resistance he'd thought he needed.

This was no delicate flower, no child prisoner in a fairy-tale castle. Sure, so they were both old enough to know better, but if Cesare wanted it, wanted *him*, then he wasn't going to stand back and pretend there were principles involved.

Cesare broke the kiss, lowering his head to the region of Dan's neck. Slowly, methodically, his wide, hot mouth traced the line of Dan's throat, words and the tiny bursts of kisses prickling against the skin.

"*Mi sei mancato tantissimo, sai?* I have missed you."

His voice, low and warm, seemed to work its way right into Dan's blood.

"*Anche tu,*" he agreed and made Cesare laugh as much with his horrible pronunciation as the attempt to answer him in his own language.

Dan gazed up at the patchy, faintly yellowed ceiling, enjoying the feel of Cesare's breath on his skin. Thoughts batted against his brain like moths, but they were the same old, tired questions. What the hell did he think he was doing? What on earth was he thinking…? He chose to ignore them. For now.

After so long, so many months of telling himself that there was no possibility of anything even remotely serious with this man, here he was, once again. And it felt right. Cesare kissed his neck, and Dan melted slightly into the mattress.

A little later, once they'd shed the last remnants of clothes, content to share the bed and the night in its entirety, Dan lay still, looking up at the shadows dancing across the ceiling.

Cesare had gotten up, opened the window a crack, and sheepish but smiling, picked up both sets of clothes and deposited them on a chair before coming back to bed. They hadn't spoken. Dan wasn't sure why; maybe it would have broken the spell, disrupted whatever it was that had happened tonight.

He didn't know, but he didn't want to question any of it. So he just lay in the dark, listening to the rhythms of Cesare's breathing change. He'd soon be asleep himself, but he'd rather lie awake. A strange sort of irritation colored that, which he regretted. Still, he'd never gone looking for drama… not for any of this. He didn't want it. Too many complications, too much to go wrong.

Beside him, Cesare turned in his sleep, the pattern of his breathing shifting again. Dan wished he hadn't had those thoughts, that he hadn't given them free rein. He moved his arm, adjusting his position so that their bodies didn't touch, so he wouldn't take what he was afraid of having. Cesare looked so peaceful, so comfortable.

Tenderness tugged at the base of Dan's throat, nudging him with the urge to just fold himself against that broad, solid frame and forget that anything else mattered except feeling safe and warm. As if this was just another holiday, a break from real life.

Unfortunately he doubted he could make himself that blind. Not now. Too much had happened that he couldn't ignore—chief among those things the look on Cesare's face when he closed the gap between them. His hunger, his desire. It scared Dan. Not the intensity, but the thoughts that plagued him once the ardor cooled... once he had time to wonder what they were going to do next. He regretted ever feeling like he should have stopped, discouraged Cesare or somehow been the adult in the situation. Who was he to assume Cesare didn't know what he was doing, that all the same fears and cold, lonely realizations didn't strike at him in the empty night? If only they'd seen where it would lead, that first day at the pizzeria.

Dan lay carefully back against the pillows, still trying to maintain his distance, and gazed into the dim room, recalling that moment's meeting. Yes, an attraction... he'd recognized that, but had he felt it? *Really* felt, known it was different?

He wasn't sure. Not sure of anything now—anything at all.

Beside him, Cesare fidgeted in his sleep, one foot edging across to nudge Dan's leg, and the weight of his body shifting to roll closer. He murmured something Dan neither heard properly nor understood, and settled again to his quiet, still sleep. Dan looked down at his face, so tranquil in repose. Sable lashes shaded his cheeks, and his mouth was relaxed, the corners curled into a slight smile. His rumpled hair smelled warm, like coffee and cotton, and Dan fought the urge to touch it, kiss it....

It would be wrong to wake him. He'd just lie here and watch Cesare a little while longer, and there wasn't anything wrong with that, was there? Dan folded his arm beneath his head and settled down, drawing the covers up over the pair of them.

Time to stop lying, he supposed. For one of them, at least.

Chapter Nineteen

THE MORNING came before either of them was really ready for it. Dan woke, blinking in the cool, early light, and for the first few moments, he wasn't fully aware of Cesare's presence. That fact, and the memories that accompanied it, washed over him with a sudden, mangled sense of panic, relief, and above all, pride. He wasn't sure what it said about him as a person, but recalling the tide of Cesare's pleasure last night, that desperate contact so yearned for and yet so forbidden, left Dan feeling smugly triumphant. That, and a little bit of something else that he wasn't sure he was prepared to examine right now. Certainly not without a coffee.

He blinked at the ceiling, gaze tracing the hairline crack that ran across the middle of it, toward the paper light shade. Beside him, Cesare shifted in his sleep, and Dan glanced across the bed. Little was visible of him but the top of one arm, a shoulder, and the nape of his neck, topped with that thatch of dark hair. Though prepared for the wash of tenderness that tugged at him, Dan didn't expect its intensity. His throat tightened and his breathing grew just a bit faster as he tried to rein it in, to get a handle on just how and when he'd allowed himself to start feeling this way.

There wasn't much use in denying it, he supposed. He reached out, let his splayed fingers run tentatively, so very gently, up Cesare's arm, until the point of his shoulder was nestled in Dan's palm. From there, it felt good to curl his hand around that broad curve, to touch him just enough to feel the rhythm of his breath, but not enough to wake him.

Dan rested his head on his crooked arm, and lay still for a while. His sleepy cock tented the boxers he remembered pulling on at some point last night when he got up to go for a piss, and he was tempted to let it ease its way out of the fly. Cesare would probably enjoy waking up with that rubbing lazily at his ass, but Dan restrained himself. Too much. Too like an expectation, a demand that it wouldn't be right for him to make.

He slipped out of bed before Cesare woke, picked his jeans from the floor, sneaked a clean shirt from his case, and got himself through to the bathroom as quickly and quietly as possible. Dan grimaced at his reflection, not enjoying the shifty look he found in his own eyes or the remnants of pouchy, papery skin that the long journey, lack of sleep, and—he had to admit it—rather large amount of grappa had bestowed upon him.

When he opened the bathroom door, he realized that Cesare must have got up, because the kettle was boiling and the TV was on, cycling through the litany of morning news. Dan gravitated to the tiny kitchenette and found Cesare, still sleep rumpled and clad only in underwear and a dark blue dressing gown, pouring water into a tall cafetiere. The smell of ground coffee spiraled into the air, delicious and enticing. He looked up, caught sight of Dan, and his lips curled.

"Good morning. You sleep well?"

"Very." Dan nodded, aware of the meanings and shared smiles behind their words.

Cesare turned his attention ostensibly back to the coffee, sorting teaspoons and mugs. He glanced at Dan once more, quickly, like the coy flirtations of a stranger, and the faint suggestion of a blush shaded his cheekbones.

"Um...."

Dan regretted it as soon as he opened his mouth. The word hung, half-finished, and he had no idea what should follow it. Assurance, or the attempt to diminish the importance of what had happened... to pretend it didn't mean much. That was stupid. Cesare was looking at him, though, so he felt he had to say something. He wet his lips and wished his head hadn't suddenly grown quite so empty.

Cesare smiled, the warmth of it irresistible. Setting down the cup he held, he turned to Dan and held out his hand. Dan was still searching for the words he wanted. They didn't come, but it didn't seem to matter. He crossed the few bare feet of linoleum and Cesare met him halfway, eased him into a clumsy embrace. His lips were warm, his mouth gentle but insistent.

He kissed away Dan's lingering nervousness, kissed away the clumsiness and the ineptitude, and held him. Dan found his arms sliding around those broad shoulders, his body pressing close... his forehead just resting against Cesare's once their mouths slipped apart.

It felt natural. Right, as if there was nothing either of them needed to say. No justification, no admission or apology. Nothing but this.

They ate breakfast beside Cesare's tiny balcony. It wasn't quite wide enough to sit out properly, but with the french doors open and the table and chairs pushed close, it was possible to pretend. The sun was already quite high, the breeze scented with the distant traces of citrus and the rumbling fumes of the autostrada. Cesare said a lot of thyme grew wild locally, like weeds. He talked of playing up on the hills as a child, and of the sunbaked grass and the smell of the herbs, and of how the thyme would sprout between the paving slabs and in the cracks of the village streets. There were lemon trees too, and olives. Great gnarled things. A farm with grove upon grove of them used to run above the village, one of several that had once patchworked the landscape in these parts, but had gone under years ago.

An English couple had bought the old house that stood right at the top of the hill, looking out over the valley. It was derelict when they came and, because they had all the optimism of foreigners where official planning permits and building regulations were concerned, a ruin when they left, far beyond saving.

Yet there were still beautiful places. Even in decay, and even in the face of the modern buildings that forever encroached: the unsympathetic conversions of old houses to apartments, the industrial estates, and the cheaply built prefabricated sprawls. As they ate, they made plans for the day, for the week, with Cesare talking about the places worth visiting, things worth seeing. He seemed to have given it a great deal of thought, and Dan enjoyed the sense of his arrival having been so keenly awaited. Arrogant, he supposed. Though it could just have been Cesare thinking of things to keep them occupied in case the reunion didn't go as… what? Planned? No, that wasn't quite right.

Last night hadn't been planned, not in so many words. Inevitability wasn't planned. The whole point of it was that it just happened. Dan glanced up over his second cup of coffee, watching Cesare's face in the golden light. So handsome. So easy to be with, so easy to—

Fuck, why was the word so hard even to think?

It was what this was, wasn't it?

THAT FIRST day was wonderful. Ridiculously so. Cesare took him up into the hills of which he'd spoken, and they did smell of lemons, of thyme, and of the sunbaked stubble of dry grass and old trees. Dan shot more frames than he could keep count of, capturing vibrant skies with the shapes of fallen, disarrayed masonry against them, lighting the black starkness of trees with the wonderful gold light that seemed to bounce straight up from the ground. The views were amazing.

Cesare sat on a block of stone that had once been part of the old farmhouse's westerly wall, and watched him, a broad smile on his face.

"I saw you work before," he remarked. "In Venice."

Dan turned and reeled off a shot of him sitting there before Cesare had time either to move or argue. He didn't seem to mind. His smile didn't falter and he didn't tense up; he simply accepted the moment, his gaze meeting the eye of the camera evenly and looking straight past it to Dan himself.

Between the light, the backdrop, and the smile on his sitter's face, Dan was pretty sure it was going to be one of the best pictures he'd ever taken. It certainly felt like it. He lowered the camera and squinted, his vision streaked with neon on shade.

"Is it work?"

Cesare just shook his head and laughed.

They talked as easily as they had online: about his job and the ongoing difficulties with Niccolò Misseri, to whom Cesare had devoted so much of his spare time.

"You're still teaching him? In the holidays?"

"*Sì*. Routine is good for him. To go all that time, with nothing, he would forget too much. More than the other children. And... *ehi*, I don't mind it. Maybe, if I can help him, he catch up a little more, do better in class."

The midday sun blazed above them. Dan raised the camera once more and took another shot of Cesare, his face still touched by that look of optimistic empathy.

Gorgeous.

"*Basta!*" Cesare grinned and raised a hand, ineffectually shielding his face from the camera.

Dan relented—no more pictures. Cesare was still looking at him, though, so full of... what? Desire, but something more than that. Such warmth, such comfort. Right here, right now, amid all the wonderful smells of lemon, thyme, and scorched grass, Dan wanted nothing more than to drag him up off that block of stone and pull him close. They could probably make love right out here in the open and never get caught.

Judging by the expression on Cesare's face, Dan guessed he'd probably like the idea, but he doubted he'd really go for it.

Maybe it'd be worth trying....

Dan wanted to suggest it, but Cesare spoke his name before he'd marshaled the idea into a coherent proposition, and it blurred things for a moment, made Dan blink and, though he was surprised to realize it, sent a small, pleasurable prickle down the back of his neck.

"Mm?"

Cesare looked up at him from his perch on the block, adorably reticent.

"A question. My, uh, my mother wants me to bring you to the house for dinner." He colored a little and gave Dan a small, embarrassed smile. "You don't have—"

Holy shit. Meet the parents?

It disconcerted Dan, but he choked down the surprise and the sudden, unsettling changes to what had been such a tranquil afternoon.

"No, not at all. That'd be… um. You told your family about me, then?"

"Of course not." Cesare shook his head. "Not to say… I mean, they know I have an English friend who is coming to see me. I, ah, I let her think it was to do with the *scuola*."

Dan said nothing. *Of course not.* Well, he couldn't pretend he'd forgotten about Cesare's secret double life thing, but he hadn't expected it to irritate him so much. Cesare seemed to need something from him, though, so he folded his mouth around a tight smile and searched for an appropriate response.

"Oh. That's… nice."

"If you would rather not, then—"

"No, it's okay. It's fine. Actually, I'd love to meet your family. I didn't expect to be doing it right now, that's all." As Dan caught sight of the tension in Cesare's face, he bit back a defeated sigh. "All right. When did she plan for us to go?"

Cesare seemed to relax, and he shrugged.

"Any day, is not a problem. They are very good people. I think you will like them."

"Mm." Dan nodded. "But they don't know that you're—"

"No."

Cesare let the word fall with uncharacteristic sharpness, the fact that no great revelations would be forthcoming this week clearly indicated in his voice. His expression softened a little, and Dan tried to remind himself that it wasn't his place to judge.

So he just smiled, said that he'd look forward to it, and then he turned his face toward the beautiful blue expanse of sky and pretended it didn't matter.

Not long after, they went back to Cesare's place and, once the door was shut and the curtains in his bedroom were drawn, he touched Dan gently, like a plea or a prayer, and it was impossible to deny him. The clothes were peeled away, taking that strange, dusty heaviness with them. Cesare opened out on the bed beneath him, fingers spread wide like cobwebs as he reached for Dan, his lips parted and his eyes shining with such indelible delight.

They screwed for a long while, the way they'd done that first time in Venice, though it was slower now, the desperation put away in favor of a more subtle union of bodies and desire. Making it last, making the most of every touch, became a point of principle. Dan plunged between Cesare's thighs over and over, as Cesare's half-choked, dry rasps of breath scraped the sheets. He finally lost himself in it and came with his mouth pressed to that thick mass of dark hair, Cesare arching back into him and every curve and hard angle of his body seeming to whisper a promise.

CHAPTER TWENTY

THE EVENING sun flared through the windows of Cesare's bedroom, turning the glass to wet gold and catching on the mirror by the door. Dan glanced nervously into it and reached up to fiddle with the collar of his shirt.

"Are you sure I look all right? I should have shaved."

From behind him, Cesare put his hands on Dan's shoulders and smiled at the uncertain reflection.

"You look wonderful, *caro. Sei tanto…* sexy."

Dan grinned lopsidedly, enjoying the feel of those strong fingers rubbing the tension out of him, even if it didn't much bolster his nerve for the evening ahead. Cesare wanted this so badly, he knew, but he wasn't sure how it was meant to work. Were they supposed to walk in side by side, their solidarity a statement of affection? Or was it to remain hidden rather than just unspoken, all cloaked with the innocuous language of friendship? Maybe Cesare wanted to break it gently, let Mamma and Papà Eveschi work things out for themselves without any of the drama he so feared. If they ever did.

God. Has he done this before?

He'd wanted to ask but found it too awkward to really do so. For every vision of Cesare introducing his beloved parents to some nebulous "friend," Dan found within himself a new understanding of what their potential rejection would do to their son.

Fair enough, then, he supposed. Keeping quiet.

All the same, he didn't like it. Lying by omission was still lying, and that was a stain that remained painfully recent for Dan. He felt guilty enough about how he'd played things with Paul, and he didn't want to repeat those… well, not even mistakes. Callous, stupid things he *knew* he should never have done. It didn't matter if Paul had been cheating or not—if he'd ever been faithful—when Dan had been so wrapped up in his own deceits.

Besides, he'd never met anyone so wonderfully transparent as Cesare. It seemed such a shame he was prepared to ruin all that honesty with this one streak of falsehood. But despite it all, Dan couldn't bring himself to really hold a grudge. He would go, sit through whatever discomfort this little plan caused, and hope that they got home again in one piece.

Dan's smile widened at that. *Home.* Yes… this did feel like it, didn't it? These vaguely shabby rooms, with their painfully functional, mismatched furnishings, and the faint smell of citrus on the air.

This man.

Cesare squeezed his shoulders.

"Are you ready?"

"Mm-hm. Let's go."

THE BUILDING must have dated back hundreds of years in its oldest parts. It had been extended and updated in various forms, though its bulging walls and crumbling mortar held the same mix of butter-rich, sandy tones as Cesare's place, with the same earthy red-brown tiles on the roof. It stood as one of a row of four, all nestled close to each other, windows small and wooden shuttered, except for the house at the end, which boasted rather 1980s white UPVC frames. Curving away around the corner, two very similar rows lined a steep cobbled street, reminding Dan strongly of childhood holidays in Suffolk and the Cotswolds, where the tide of architectural progress had been forcibly held back for the sake of a tourist-driven economy.

It was beautiful, though.

They'd walked the short distance from Cesare's place, the autostrada never more than a distant thrum beneath the birdcalls and gentle breeze of the coming dusk. Cesare had been talking about the village, about the area, and Dan hadn't been sure whether it was to hide his nerves, or to fill the insatiable hunger Cesare seemed to assume he had for history. Not that it wasn't interesting, Dan supposed, while allowing himself an inward smile at the incorrigible desire of a teacher to, well, teach.

Cesare was still going now, the sound of his voice and the slanted, rich accents he put on English words weaving a warm, comforting sling beneath Dan. The house just around the corner had been a café once. Apparently, there was a story in one of the local history books about the owner having been in the Resistance during the war and, so it was said, shot by the Germans. An alternative account suggested the man had fled to Switzerland, but Cesare said he didn't know whether it was possible to prove either version.

"This is Italia." He gave Dan a rueful, sidelong smile. "We're not so good at keeping records. Only generating paperwork."

Dan grinned. "Oh, I don't know. England's pretty good at bureaucracy too. We might even beat you lot."

Cesare chuckled and his footsteps slowed, echoing into the dimming street. He cleared his throat.

"Well," he said, glancing up at the third house in the row, its façade all sand-colored stone and thick lintels. "This is it."

They stood almost close enough for Dan to reach out and squeeze Cesare's hand, which, for one brief, absurd moment, he desperately wanted to do. He choked down the impulse, knowing it would be unwelcome, and simply nodded instead.

"Right."

Pots of geraniums festooned the windows and door, salmon pink to deep, clashing red. Dan couldn't help himself wondering if the ones outside Cesare's door were cuttings or something; mothers did that, didn't they? When Edith had moved into her first flat, Dan remembered their mum bringing pots and pots of young plants down in the car. Tomatoes, busy lizzies, marigolds… all culled from her own garden and all apparently necessary to brighten up the new abode.

He shook the speculation, assuming he must be at least as nervous as Cesare for his mind to be running off like this, and almost flinched when the dark wood front door began to open.

"*Ahhh, ma guarda! Ciao!*"

The voice was not unlike Cesare's, but deeper, older… perhaps already thinning with the sharp sound of old age, though the man who emerged to greet them still looked hale enough. He was fairly tall, and in his youth he must have been broad-shouldered and probably running to burly; these days, he carried most of his weight in his girth. His clothes were of the comfortable kind, his face was ruddy, and his gray hair was a little untidy. Warm light spilled out from the hallway behind him, though the day was not yet over.

He lifted his hands, caught for just a second in Dan's eye like some Roman emperor of revels, and beamed happily before dragging Cesare into a warm hug. They spoke too quickly, too idiomatically, for Dan to follow, but then Cesare turned and introduced him.

"Daniel, this is my father, Luca. Papà, this is—"

"*Bah, sì, sì.... Daniel! Come va? Prego, prego....* It is a pleasure to meet you."

He shook Dan's hand warmly, stretching a wide, smiling mouth around English words he clearly wasn't accustomed to using.

"A-and you," Dan managed before being swept into a tumult of words, gestures, and above all, into the warm, brightly lit little house.

He remembered Cesare telling him about the old family home, the place he'd grown up and where so much had happened—both good and bad, life and loss—but he wasn't sure exactly when the Eveschis had relocated to Gravagna, or how long they'd been in this house. It had the lively, chaotic feel of a well-loved home, but Dan supposed the photographs that lined the walls must all date from another place, another time.

He glanced at them as he passed, looking for snippets of Cesare's backstory, and was rewarded with a few brief swatches of memory. Cesare as a bony-kneed boy in his football kit, grinning broadly and standing between his two brothers, or posing reluctantly in graduation gowns, clutching his degree. A long time ago, Dan supposed.

Now he caught a glimpse of Cesare from the corner of his eye as Luca ushered them into the kitchen. Just a smile, a slight nod of his head, but it spoke of so much more. The look on his face was both imploring and delighted, as if Dan had done more by simply being here than Cesare had ever dared to expect from anyone, and Dan supposed that was his secret weapon.

For those fleeting few seconds, he realized just how much he would do without question, how much he would withstand, to be on the receiving end of a look such as that.

He turned his gaze away quickly, already annoyed at himself for his guardedness, and followed where Luca gestured.

The kitchen was, like the rest of the house seemed to be, small but cozy and full of light. It spilled out, golden yellow, from wall-mounted uplighters, their opalescent ceramic shades scalloped at the edges, high-wattage bulbs burning at their centers like bright pearls. Rather outdated, though well-polished, pine kitchen units ran around the edges of the room, framing a checkerboard floor of terra-cotta and cream quarry-type tiles. The smells of warm bread and something cooking in a rich, tomatoey sauce wafted temptingly through the air, and the whole room seemed to halo the slim, petite woman at the center of it.

Mamma Eveschi's jaw-length hair, gray but artfully washed through with a hint of ash blonde, was cut to flatter a slightly long, oval face. Her large, hazel eyes were deep set, and her wide mouth—very like Cesare's—looked as if it should always be smiling. Deep frown lines on her forehead and lines tracking from her nose to her chin suggested that this wasn't so, but as she reached out to shake Dan's hand she did smile, and it was beautiful. All of Cesare's easy charm and grace, he thought, but feminized, made more delicate and homey. She kissed his cheek and insisted that he call her Luisa.

"You are very welcome, Daniel," she told him in heavily accented English as she ushered him up to the table and introduced him to people who Dan realized, with a momentary flash of dread, must be Cesare's brother and his... what? Wife?

Somehow Dan hadn't expected to be slotted in so neatly: dinner guests two by two, couples seated beside each other, either side of the table. He'd imagined, perhaps stupidly, that it would just be him, Cesare, and the parents—and that thought had been daunting enough.

"My son, Gianni," Luisa said, smiling proudly, "and this is Silvana."

Dan smiled awkwardly. *He* definitely bore a distinct family resemblance. Same shape to his face, same nose as Cesare and Luca, but a harder, darker jaw, trimmed with a scruff of artful stubble.

Gianni flashed Dan a brief, not entirely sincere grin.

The girl—Silvana—wasn't what Dan expected from Italian women, inasmuch as he'd had expectations. She was rather pale-skinned, dusted with freckles, and her hair was a light, reddish brown. Hanging in loose curls, it brushed her bare shoulders and, next to the printed cotton dress she wore, splashed with blotches of color that appeared to be in the pattern of field poppies, gave her a thoroughly charming, georgic, English look.

She smiled and shook his hand, rattled off something in Italian, her accent hard for him to adjust to, and he found himself just beaming idiotically and nodding.

A bloody tourist, all over again.

The initial burst of horror segued through anger at Cesare for dumping him into this and then quickly into shame. He was being stupid. It wasn't a test, a trap... and why had he assumed he would be the only guest? There purely to be asked questions and poked, prodded, interrogated?

That would probably have been worse, anyway.

Dan sat, and the family were, for the most part, so welcoming and natural that he quickly began to forget his discomfort. Cesare, in the chair to his left, shot him one small, grateful glance. It held so many warm, hidden things that Dan almost missed a breath.

Luca poured wine—a rough but full-bodied red—while Luisa served the food. She did tell Dan what the dish was called and explained what it was, but he struggled to keep up. All he knew was that it was some kind of meat, minced and seasoned, with thick gravy, layered over polenta, and it tasted great.

The whole of the meal passed slowly on that count. Dan, aware everyone was making an effort for him, wasn't sure how to tell the family their English wasn't as good as they thought. Wading through the heavily accented words, laced with idiomatic phrases and rapid bursts of laughter, he got lost and found himself reduced to just sitting there, grinning like an idiot.

Still, they seemed like nice people.

Cesare's parents asked him questions, just as he'd thought they might. All smiles and stilted, rather old-fashioned English. Where was he from in England? Cesare said he was a photographer and how very interesting it sounded: was it for newspapers, or was he an artist? Did he still use film, or was he into this modern digital stuff? Had he ever been to Italy before? The list ran on.

Dan answered everything as best he could, providing plenty of information, but sticking to the parameters of the prearranged backstory he and Cesare had agreed on the night before. Dan had almost laughed at him for putting so much effort into it and suggested that maybe he was making it more complicated than it needed to be.

They had met in Venice. At a museum. He had encountered some language barrier problems; Cesare had assisted. They had talked, discovered a common interest in arts and antiquities, their friendship developed from there… and, Dan suspected, if Cesare's parents believed that, they'd believe anything.

For a moment, it had made him so angry. He'd wanted to say something, to slap sense into Cesare, somehow, because it seemed too impossible that his family shouldn't know, shouldn't suspect. But Dan had pulled back.

After all, it wasn't his country, his life, or his rules.

He'd looked thoughtfully at Cesare in the dusty, lemon-scented light of his tiny balcony, seen how anxious he was that this should happen, and that it should be *right*, and he'd caved. In a heartbeat.

Sure. Whatever you want.

Even now, Dan warmed a little bit at the recollection of how Cesare had smiled when he said those words.

I don't know why on earth I put myself through this....

The thought was a lie, of course.

Nevertheless, if anyone doubted the backstory, there was no outward sign of it. The meal, the wine, and the chatter all kept coming, until Dan was beginning to feel exhausted by it.

Gianni's girlfriend talked a lot, he noticed. Her English was the best of the bunch, and she seemed to be a pretty cosmopolitan kind of girl, eager to chat and to ask her own questions about London.

He obliged as best he could, suspecting she was rather disappointed with his obvious lack of high-fashion-and-celebrity anecdotes. Just as the English tended to think of the whole of Paris as one big bohemian flat-share, Silvana seemed to assume Dan was on intimate terms with every hotspot from Voyage to the Met Bar. He almost wondered how she'd take hearing about Chris, Sada, Miriam, and that whole cheap-shoes-and-champagne art scene, but he knew it wouldn't have been politic. Besides, for the briefest of moments, thinking about friends and home brought back memories of Paul and the whole mess of the past few months... and Dan didn't want to dwell on that or to taint this evening with it.

He nodded, smiled, and found his gaze shifting to Cesare. He was smiling, saying something to his father that Dan didn't understand, but he wanted to smile too, all the same. He wanted to catch Cesare's eye and hold it for just a little longer than he should, like that first day overlooking the Canale—and that was impossible.

Cesare did glance at him after whatever joke or jibe had passed between him and Luca faded away, and Dan tried not to feel hurt by the close-guarded walls in his face. Oh, there was warmth there, but he could see how hard Cesare was holding back, and that stung.

Luisa got up and fetched ice cream, with the promise of dark, bitter coffee to come, and Dan turned his attention to Gianni. He didn't talk as much as his brother, and Dan couldn't help wondering whether he was imagining the tension between them. He wasn't sure. Oh, the man was cheerful enough, friendly enough, but there seemed to be something in the way Gianni looked at Cesare… a certain hardness in his expression.

It could have been no more than sibling rivalry, yet Dan couldn't shake the suspicion that, somehow, he *knew*. The thought itself annoyed him, and he tried to ignore it, but it kept recurring, like a sneaking and insidious paranoia.

Inwardly, Dan cursed himself. He shouldn't think like that. He *didn't*, usually. It was probably Cesare's influence: that perpetual terror of being discovered, so alien to the way Dan lived life. The man's parents clearly loved him, and anyone could see Cesare meant as much to them as they did to him, so what the hell would it matter?

So stupid….

Dan remembered the choking panic of coming out to his own family, of course. His frustration with Cesare wasn't a lack of understanding— though maybe the benefit of hindsight colored over much of his sympathy. Dan recalled all too well the look of faint amusement on his mother's face when he'd finally screwed up the courage to utter the crucial words.

Gay? Is that all? Oh, poppet… as if it matters!

He supposed, despite all the obvious affection in his family, it wouldn't be like that for Cesare. In all honesty, Dan doubted it was that simple, even in the man's own mind.

Still, he struggled to put the thoughts out of his head, at least for the rest of this evening, and fought to remember that this wasn't his choice to make. Dan dipped his spoon into the bowl of rich, thick ice cream before him, savored the taste of mixed berries and mascarpone, and resisted the urge to check his watch.

AFTER IT was all finally over, they walked home through the stuffy, overheated night. Memories of the family's well-meant kisses still grazed Dan's cheeks, his lips stiff from smiling so much and his hands almost raw with hearty shaking. Yes, of course he would keep in touch, no, he was not in Gravagna for long at all… yes, he would see as much of the area as he could before going home, and no, he hadn't decided yet whether or not to travel farther down country before he went home.

They had all been charming, warm, lovely people, but they'd exhausted him. Even now, Dan noticed the way Cesare kept his distance— long after they were out of sight of the house. Dan wondered if he really believed there were faces behind every shuttered window they passed, peering out at him in the dark.

Did anybody truly care, though? Would anyone even see if he reached out now and touched his lover? Despite being tempted to jump him just to find out, Dan resisted.

Instead he watched Cesare's face as they walked, the shadows stained with the light of infrequent streetlamps, and the guilty sliver of a yellow moon picking at his skin. He looked ahead, his hands in his pockets and his body hunched slightly forward. Dan wanted to say something, break the silence, but he wasn't sure how to do it. Somewhere a game show played on a television, canned laughter from an open window. A car door slammed.

"D'you think it went well?"

He blurted the words out, thick and heavy into the space between them. Not what he really meant either.

D'you think I passed?

Cesare glanced around, the momentary confusion in his eyes broken by a smile.

"*Sì.* Very good. They liked you. And you were...."

"What?"

Cesare shook his head, not clarifying whether he lacked the English word he wanted or had just chosen not to voice it. Mildly irritated, Dan said nothing, and they walked on again in silence.

CESARE LOCKED the door behind them, once again so thankful for his sanctuary and his private space. If Mamma had had her way, he would still be living with them, and that didn't even bear thinking about.

Daniel moved to the kitchen area, automatically throwing himself into those very English rituals. Kettle on, cups, and spoons.... Cesare smiled, moved by the sheer intimacy, the tiny domesticity of it. Such a strange people, the English. All full of pomp and circumstance and stiff emotions, yet they needed to feel safe in the worlds they created, the edges defined by the comforts of home.

He had been wonderful tonight.

Cesare wanted to tell him that, but putting words to it would mean Daniel asking what he meant, and potentially him having to explain, and... *no*. What could he say that would not somehow be in danger of ruining this perfect time, this precisely balanced moment?

He had been wonderful because he had been himself. Just a man, a friend, and nothing more complicated than that. Smiling, laughing, talking—making such a good impression on everybody. What was it Mamma had said, when Daniel was chatting with Silvana? That he was such a charmer, this *inglese*, and Gianni should be careful.

Che simpatico!

The sound of the water pouring into cups, the *chink-chink* of the spoon made him look up, and Cesare could not prevent the smile that slipped across his face.

Meraviglioso.

Daniel returned it, so full of light and warmth. He padded across the floor, set the cups down on the coffee table, and straightened up, standing close enough to be both a temptation and a prize.

He didn't resist when Cesare reached out—no, not even a reach, just the laziest lift of a hand, brushing the bare skin of Daniel's arm where his shirtsleeves were rolled back. Fingers followed where their tips grazed, and Cesare let his hand trail down, the weight of the action carrying it to Daniel's knuckles, then palm.

Two hands, Cesare mused, each the other's twin. Alike in every way and yet so very different. He squeezed gently, allowing his fingers to thread their way between Dan's, and never more delighted than when the returning pressure came, and his wonderful man smiled.

He leaned in, a silent question, and a soul-deep shiver of pleasure rippled through him at just the gentlest touch of Daniel's lips. Cesare had almost fooled himself into thinking that a chaste, innocent kiss was all he wanted when a small, shallow moan eased its way into the space between them. He didn't realize at first it had come from him, barely cognizant of raising his other hand to Daniel's jaw, trapping his mouth in a deeper entreaty.

"Well, honestly." Daniel chuckled softly as they broke apart. "Still got an appetite, even after dinner?"

"For you? *Per sempre.*"

The words danced in Cesare's head, batting against the inside of his skull like moths. So much he wanted to say—to explain and promise— but he couldn't. English was a complicated, lumpy language, too full up with missed meanings and misunderstandings.

He just let them part once more, allowing his smile to look like one of embarrassment, as if he was shamed by his lust.

Little could have been further from the truth.

CESARE CERTAINLY didn't seem to be in much of a mood to let the evening go.

They sat on the sofa in a mellow pool of lamplight, drinking the coffee Dan had made and touching in the most casual of ways—just relaxing, as if it was the end of any normal day. All the tension that Cesare had carried earlier, before the meal, was gone... any kind of tension, in fact. Dan couldn't remember him being this relaxed. He was tempted to make the most of it, maybe even ask a question or two, but that could ruin things, he supposed.

Would you ever tell them?

It was simple enough to answer. Either Cesare would, or he would not. Either he could see a future in which he was open and honest about himself, or there was nothing more to come but more of the same. Lying by omission and carrying on in impossible, circuitous patterns.

Dan tried to let the thoughts die, crumpled up in the back corner of his mind, but they wouldn't rest. That one stupid, insistent little voice of practicality kept going on and on, demanding to know how he thought any of this would ever work out, and what the hell he was doing here anyway... and, at first, he barely even noticed Cesare's caresses growing more focused and the hand shifting stealthily up his thigh.

"*Facciamo l'amore, sì?*" Cesare murmured, leaning closer to kiss his neck.

The combination of warm breath, warm lips, and rough stubble, added to the rather promising sentiment did a better job of dispelling Dan's least comfortable ponderings than he'd managed himself.

"Mm," he mumbled, eager to be convinced.

Cesare stood up, tempting him toward the bedroom with an attractively rumpled smile, and held out his hand.

"*Vieni, amore.*"

Dan allowed himself to be pulled up from the couch, surprising Cesare by putting a little spring into the movement and ending it far closer than he'd expected, with a firm, unyielding kiss pressed to that smiling mouth. Warm breath brushed his lips, mixed up with a soft, eager chuckle.

"*Ah, monello! Ti desidero*, eh?" Cesare pulled back a little to look at him, his expression suddenly deep and solemn. "You know... I want you. *Sì?*"

Dan nodded, aware of the weight behind the question. Cesare exhaled, seeming almost relieved, and together they backed down the narrow corridor toward the bedroom door. It was awkward, neither really wanting to let the other go, and neither being completely able to see where he was going. They laughed and it punctured the tension a little.

Cesare didn't bother to shut the bedroom door. He left Dan's side long enough to flip on the bedside lamp and to draw the curtains, then turned to face him again, unbuttoning his shirt.

Dan stood in the open doorway, just watching.

"Nice."

Cesare let the shirt fall and stood there, bare-chested, fingers resting clumsily on the fly of his crumpled trousers. The lamplight threw two smudged bands of shadow across his frame, highlighting his broad shoulders, his firm waist and the whorls of dark hair so vivid against pale skin.

Slowly, Dan crossed the room, already working on the strictures of his own clothes. So easy to toss them away, like they didn't matter, like he'd never need them again.

Cesare didn't quite manage to keep up that brave elegance when it came to pants. There was the inevitable hopping from foot to foot to shuck off socks and undies until, finally naked, they tumbled to the covers, playful and hungry. Another embrace, another kiss, and Dan could already feel Cesare's hardening cock rubbing against his belly.

"Daniel... please, *amore*. Let me feel you. Put it inside me. Please."

Cesare's hands skimmed over Dan's shoulders, neck, and biceps, his legs already lifting and parting, begging to receive what he wanted. It was an impossible picture to resist. Dan kissed him, full, hard, and wet, and took hold of his thighs. Crisp curls of hair tickled his palms.

"Come on. Wriggle forward. Edge of the bed, love. That's it."

Cesare slid to the edge of the bed, his thighs lifted and clasped to Dan's sides. Dan backed off the bed and put his feet to the floor, leaning over Cesare, palms placed flat on either side of his head as he bent closer and planted a long, wet kiss on his mouth. Cesare moaned, knees pulled up tight and his arms stretched out, fingers scrabbling in the folds of the sheets. Dan kissed harder, leaned closer, and rubbed his hardening cock against Cesare's asscheeks.

"Daniel... please?"

Dan ground tighter against him. Cesare pushed back, hungry, yearning.

"You sure?"

"*Sì.*" His eyes fluttered closed, one last wriggle of his hips reaffirming his desire. "Please."

Dan reached for the lube and condoms, leaving Cesare to flex against the sheets while he prepared. A squeeze of the cold gel, and he touched his fingers to Cesare's cleft, seeking out his center.

Two spots of color bloomed in Cesare's cheeks. Eyes closed, his dark lashes dropped bars of shadow beneath them, that wide mouth bending around a series of whispered words that Dan didn't understand.

He pressed firmly but gently, sliding his finger a little way in, giving Cesare time to adjust, enjoying the way he pulled that sharp breath across his teeth.

"*Ah... sì. Così dai....*"

Dan stroked himself with his free hand, conscious that he mustn't rush this, however tempting it was. His balls churned with the desire to fuck hard and fast, push Cesare right to the limit of what he could take, but he had to wait—and it was agonizing.

Cesare gave a small, surprised grunt when Dan added a second finger, pumping them with firm, short strokes. His thighs dropped out wide, toes clenching on the air as the shapeless ends of words slipped between his lips. He was tight, but Dan could see how badly he needed it. He withdrew his fingers and gradually, carefully, guided the head of his cock to Cesare's pucker, rubbing slowly against the entrance.

Cesare moaned low in his throat, lips pressed tight together. Dan pushed gently. The head of his cock sank in, passing first one ring of muscle, then the second. There was resistance—though far from virginal, Cesare clearly still found it hard to give in, however much he wanted to, and Dan tried to ease his discomfort by going as slowly as he could.

Cesare groaned, his eyes screwed shut and teeth gritted. Dan reached for his cock, stroked him a little as he continued to push in with steady pressure, but no more than Cesare could take.

"You're okay?"

"*Sì... ah, sì, amore.* Please. Fuck me. Ah! You're fucking me, Daniel...."

He said it as if it were a revelation, an achievement. Dan gave one slow thrust, driving home just a little more, dragging a rough, hungry moan from Cesare. He was beautiful like that: filled up and lost to pleasure.

They traded long, loose kisses, tongues dueling and breath panting. Greedy, eager noises broke from Cesare—low, rough sounds born deep in his chest—and his face and neck flushed a dark red. Dan pulled his hand from the covers, laced their fingers together, and wrapped those twined digits around Cesare's pouting cock.

"C'mon." He squeezed gently. "Let me see you touch. Yes?"

"Touch," Cesare echoed, the word thickly accented in his mouth, his eyes barely starting to open.

He stroked himself, slow at first, needing Dan's encouragement. Dan bent over him; more kisses, more of those wonderful noises of his, and then he was doing it. Touching. Taking it. So hot, so tight... so open. Dan stroked Cesare's hair as they fucked, his jaw, fingers moving ceaselessly with the urge to feel more of him, to communicate all the things that he didn't have words to say. A hotter kiss than before fused them, Cesare lifting up a little from the sheets, his tongue a thread of fire and his teeth scraping Dan's bottom lip.

"Fuck me harder," he whispered, his gaze unfocused. *"Forte. Scopami forte, col tuo cazzo, il tuo bel... di più, ehi? Dai."*

Dan hoisted Cesare's legs just that little bit higher and obliged. His cock crashed against the last of Cesare's defenses, his momentary cry of pain replaced by a succession of other noises... enjoyment, fulfillment, then ecstasy. Dan angled his hips to hit that last secret spot, striking just the right combination of strength and subtlety to turn Cesare to jelly. Cesare's hand stilled on his cock, rhythm lost and grip erratic in the face of this new assault on pleasure, so Dan took control. He wrapped his hand around Cesare's cock and stroked in time to the smart pace of his thrusts, pumping over and over. The sound of his balls slapping Cesare's wet cheeks mixed with the damp suction of cocks, hands, holes, and ragged, broken breaths to make one whole, desperate ballad.

He wished he could keep it up forever and that there would never be anything more complicated than this perfect, natural bliss, but it wasn't to be. Dan's orgasm built with terrible, inexorable intensity, however hard he tried to push it back, to wait for Cesare to come and let him have his own time.

"G'na… 'na c'm," he muttered, slamming harder into Cesare's ass, his guttural cries only lessening the time it took.

Cesare loosed a phrase he didn't understand and squeezed him tight with those thick, muscular thighs, one hand on the back of Dan's head and the other on his shoulder. As Cesare stared up at him with a blurry look of bliss, Dan came, hard and breathless, gazing into those clear brown eyes. It flooded him with more than pleasure. He didn't remember ever feeling so vulnerable, so—

"*Amo tutto di te, Daniel! Sì, sì… tanto. Ti amo tanto!*"

He was still fucking, still pumping like an automaton, except the rush of it, the tingling heat and sensitivity, made him dizzy, the roar of blood in his ears disorienting. Dan loved how much of a talker Cesare could be in bed, but sometimes it was hard to keep up, and he struggled to be sure of what he'd heard. The look on his face, though… the way his lips flexed around the ends of half-spoken words. Cesare's fingers stroked clumsily against Dan's jaw as he started to tumble into his own climax.

"*Ti amo,*" he whimpered once more, and there was no mistaking it this time.

Cesare's first spurt of semen hit Dan's chest, then his stomach and, lastly, a spray of pearly droplets graced the dark curls around Cesare's navel. Dan held on to him tightly, his hands digging into the warm skin of thigh and waist, his palms stroking Cesare's flesh, sharing comfort and warmth as he coaxed him through it all. It was a sight he could have watched for a thousand years.

"Ah!" Cesare gasped, a small twist of laughter lost somewhere in the sound as, sated, he fell back against the covers, his hands over his face and the breath whistling between his palms.

"*Ti amo,*" Dan murmured gently, though Cesare wasn't looking at him anymore. He rubbed a circle on Cesare's thigh, desperate not to lose the sense of contact, of shared communication between them. "*Ti amo,* Cesare."

Funny how the words were even smaller and scarier than in English.

Dan knew he had to pull out and get rid of the rubber, but his legs had turned to mush, and it was all he could do to stay upright. He was shaking too, he realized. And sweating. A shower was definitely in order… but perhaps not yet.

Cesare lifted one hand from his eyes and touched Dan's shoulder gently. There was a look of such tender awe in his face.

"Daniel, *sei*... ah! Y-you are too much."

Dan frowned, worried he'd caused pain, but Cesare's languid smile seemed to belie that. Dan eased himself out and dropped the condom in the bin beside the nightstand.

"Ah," Cesare groaned again, and Dan wasn't sure if it was relief or regret.

He crawled back into bed beside him, already fighting sleep and wanting the warmth of someone next to him when it came.

"*Ti voglio tanto bene, caro*," Cesare whispered, wrapping an arm around him and dropping a kiss to Dan's hair.

Dan pressed close, surprised by how much he needed the contact and how far down below him the world seemed to stretch. He laid his cheek against Cesare's chest, enjoying his scent and the intimacy of resting in the mess they'd made together.

"I love you too."

CHAPTER TWENTY-ONE

THE WEEK passed ridiculously fast. For Dan, it felt like some incredible weight lifting from him, and he was so glad of that. Too glad, possibly.

He knew it was his fault, the fact they hadn't talked about what was happening. All those e-mails and phone calls, those weeks and months of friendship... never once referring back to Venice or how they'd met, or mentioning sex at all. They'd skirted too carefully around it, tried to make believe that, if they closed their eyes, there would be nothing there but what they wanted to exist, like the imagined worlds of children.

All the same, if Cesare actually wanted to talk about it, he hid the fact well. Dan caught him looking sometimes, just little glances from the corner of his eye, and, from the expression on his face, supposed that he was waiting to be told just what it was that they had. What to expect, maybe, or how long it would be until it all went wrong.

Faced with thoughts like those, Dan couldn't bear even starting the conversation.

It had been wonderful, though. Cesare drove him out to several of the old, ruined landmarks of Gravagna's past, and took him into Pontremoli itself, showing him the cathedral and the beautiful bridges. Dan found it incredibly inspiring—the colors, the shapes and compositions of this wonderful, strange place. Like Venice, the crumbling stones and ancient walkways seemed to whisper to him, weaving stories and promises into the scented air.

He saw the other side to the place too: the new buildings, the faint attempts at progress in an area whose population had been in steady decline since the war. It was somewhere he could imagine coming back to, he thought, though he wasn't sure how far that was wishful thinking and the lure of Cesare beside him.

Maybe not totally that, though. He'd had a little while alone in the town, time to wander at leisure and sample the coffee shops when Cesare went to keep his appointment with the Misseris. Dan smiled at the memory of how uncertain he'd been, and how he'd had to promise

Cesare it was okay for him to go and give Niccolò his lesson, and that he didn't need to spend every minute looking after Dan.

Cesare had smiled, looked very much as if he wanted to kiss him, and gone to keep the scheduled meeting. They had lunch after he'd finished, and he looked so bright and excited when he told Dan all about how the boy was doing and how much he seemed to be improving.

It had been a good day. They had all been good days, full of Cesare smiling and laughing, and that wonderful, comfortable feeling that Dan got when he did. In truth, Cesare hadn't seemed to stop smiling since that night after dinner at his parents' house.

Dan knew they'd have to talk before he left, but it was so easy to push back that inevitable blackening of this perfect time.

On Saturday morning they lay in Cesare's bed, the covers long since pushed away, the air warm and a dry breeze curling lazily through the open window.

"I don't think I can get up," Cesare announced. "You have killed me."

Dan, idly playing with Cesare's toes, raised himself up on one elbow and peered critically at their owner. "You look all right to me. And you were definitely alive a couple of minutes ago."

He blushed and Dan grinned.

"Anyway, do you *want* to get up?"

Cesare appeared to consider this for a moment.

"No," he said eventually. "Not very much."

Dan laughed. He loved the way Cesare was opening up to sex, to the fun of it, the way he looked when he got sucked, touched, fucked: the way he got so much out of it and responded—like a cat being stroked, like a compass needle swinging to north—but still stayed so humble, so unassuming, as if he'd never expected it to be... what? Good? Or just never expected it at all, Dan supposed. He let that thought trail away from him, happy to leave it undisturbed.

Instead he pressed a kiss to Cesare's foot and swung his legs out of bed.

"I'm going to make a drink. What would you like?"

The bits of Dan not used to being quite as athletic as he'd been last night creaked in protest. He grimaced and tried to ignore them.

"Tea, please, *caro*."

Dan managed to get to his feet and bowed. "Your wish is my command."

Cesare laughed and stretched out against the mattress. As promised, Dan went and made tea, then brought it back to bed, snuggling up to Cesare to drink it, despite the heat of the morning.

He wondered, briefly, if he would still be making these trips when the weather was cold enough for log fires and hot chocolate. Maybe they'd have tired of the arrangement. Dan tried to squash the thought, the images it put into his mind. Cockroach-like, they scurried stubbornly around his brain, obstinately avoiding the thick-soled boot of rational thinking.

"Are you all right?" Cesare asked. "You are very quiet."

"Just thinking," Dan said, trying not to.

He leaned his head on Cesare's shoulder. A week or so, a handful of times a year. The odd weekend or short break in between, slipped in for quick fixes and desperation. Perhaps more than that if he was careful, didn't take any other holidays, and worked like a dog when he was at home. Self-employment was great for giving a man a flexible schedule, but it was a bastard on the bank account.

Still, it could be done, couldn't it?

It *could*, but it was no life. And it would put Cesare in a terrible position. Too indebted, too obvious. All the time burdened with the fact that Dan would remain his guilty, dirty secret.

Dan wondered if he could live like that. Looking over his shoulder, making sure not to break the rules, always staying within the lines. It would be easier for him, if it came to it, wouldn't it? His life in London wouldn't have to change. He could just have… something a little extra waiting for him under the hot Mediterranean sun.

Yeah, right.

The thoughts were bitter and ugly in his head, and he wished he hadn't had them. He was a fool for ever getting involved: a fool for thinking he could play this game, because the only thing he wanted was the one thing he couldn't have.

"So. Where do we go from here?"

Dan knew it was his voice, though it didn't sound like it. The words felt thick and rough, loud against the room's quiet. Cesare's mouth stilled on his hair.

"*Prego?*"

He didn't want to talk about it. Dan knew that with the same painful clarity that told him he couldn't put this off any longer. He reached up, sliding his hand over Cesare's, their fingers twined together on his chest.

"You know. I mean… what are we doing, hm? Really doing?"

Cesare pulled away, drawing his knees up and propping his arms on them, the bedclothes rumpled around his waist. Dan turned his head, watching him carefully, but Cesare just looked down at the covers, his face caught in profile against the morning light. That high forehead, the fuzzy, untidy mop of hair, his long, straight, nose… and that wide, supple mouth, tight and bowed in apprehension.

Dan regretted hurting him. The pain he'd caused before, now, and all the pain he was likely to cause in the future. He wanted to reach out and touch Cesare's back, skin to skin, a comfort and an assurance that it was all right, that he did… care. Yet he sat still, didn't do it, and didn't speak. There had to be a resolution, if not an answer.

"What happens next, *sì*?"

Cesare sounded weary, resigned. Dan sighed.

"Yeah. Yeah, I suppose. I mean, is it just gonna be long weekends and holidays? Your English friend who comes to stay?"

He heard the bitterness in his tone, faintly surprised by it, and a little embarrassed. Cesare glanced at him, eyes guarded and cool.

"Daniel…."

"Well, how else? You're not exactly out."

A frown pinched Cesare's brow, and Dan regretted that low, unkind blow. He thought back to the *trattoria* in Venice, the night Cesare had told him about his sister's death: how so much had devolved upon him, how his loneliness had been a conscious choice, a path he had taken, knowing the price.

It wasn't a coward's way out, a decision made for the sake of an easy life—Dan had known that then, and he knew it now, but it still felt like a terrible, painful betrayal. It felt as if Cesare was ashamed of himself, ashamed of *this*… and Dan couldn't stand it.

"Would you tell them?" he demanded, pushed by that needling, uncomfortable jealousy. "Because you'd have to, wouldn't you? If we—"

A muscle twitched in Cesare's jaw, his expression uncharacteristically hard. "If what?"

Dan shrugged and looked away. Those silly, fanciful notions of hot chocolate and log fires danced once more through his head. As if they could really keep this up indefinitely. This… *thing* they were doing. It wasn't possible, it wasn't right, it was—

"If we made something of this," he heard himself say, no idea where the words had come from. "If we were going to be together."

He studied the cool cotton of Cesare's bedspread, a pale, neutral color with a thin line of dark brown piping running parallel to its left edge. Very sleek, very modern. Had he really just said that?

"Daniel…."

Cesare's voice held a dark, raw edge that hurt to hear. Dan wondered why he'd introduced himself like that on that first day… why hearing Cesare use the full form of his name gave him that small, deep pulse of pleasure every single time.

Had he known, that day beside the Canale, that he wanted to be someone different?

"I want to, *caro*. My God… I want to. But—"

"Then do it," Dan said, still staring stubbornly at the covers. "Do it. Let's just… fuck everybody, right? We could—well, I don't know exactly how, but—"

"I can't."

"—the important thing is," Dan continued wretchedly, refusing to listen, "that, I mean, it's not impossible, is it? It's really not that far to travel, probably there are people who do longer weekly commutes, and—"

"Daniel, I can't. I am sorry. *È assolutamente impossibile.*"

Dan blinked, his throat heavy and choked, but the words still finding their way out all the same. "We could… I mean, we can do *something*, can't we?"

Cesare laid his hand on Dan's wrist: just a gentle pressure, the weight of his fingers probably meant as some kind, reassuring gesture.

"You know the way it is for me. *Mi famiglia*, my work—all of it, *caro*. I can't. I told you."

"But if you wanted—"

"Is not 'want,' Daniel. I cannot."

Cesare sighed deeply and took his hand away. Dan felt the loss keenly and looked up, trying to catch his eye. It hurt to see the expression on Cesare's face, so full of pain and regret.

"Yeah, but—"

"Please… don't."

Dan exhaled, deflated. "Then what are we doing? What's the point?"

He knew he sounded angry. He *was* angry, despite being painfully aware of how stupid, useless, and generally unflattering that reaction was.

They'd talked about this before, in Venice. At the time, Dan supposed it had been an interesting theoretical abstract—he hadn't really believed that there would be anything remaining after those pleasant, islanded days except good memories and maybe a trace of beard burn.

It all seemed very different now.

He'd seen how much so the other night at dinner, and he'd known then how impossible Cesare's stupid "don't ask, don't tell" thing was... hadn't he? Dan couldn't live like that, he was certain. He wouldn't want to. Trouble was, where did that leave them?

Nowhere much, and it was all his own fault.

"Well, you've got to make some kind of decision, haven't you?" he demanded, lashing out rather than admit that he wished he'd never spoken. "You've got to choose."

It was a clumsy ultimatum, and Dan knew he wasn't going to get anywhere with it. He scowled at the bedcovers, not willing to see the look of hurt on Cesare's face.

"You don't know!" Cesare said, as close to angry as Dan had ever heard him. "You don't understand, Daniel. *Mi famiglia...* my whole life here.... It is not easy to change everything. Even for you."

Dan said nothing. There wasn't really a way of expressing the dull ache that pounded in his chest, and he wasn't sure he trusted himself to speak anyway. Cesare muttered something that was probably not very complimentary under his breath and swung his legs out of bed, heading for the bathroom and leaving Dan to contemplate where, exactly, they did go from here.

He winced as the bathroom door closed, the sound hollow and final, reverberating through the flat's thin walls. He should have explained, he knew it. Somehow. There should have been words to show Cesare what he meant, to lay out for him the fact that—no matter how many trips— Dan would always be happy to make them, but that he needed to know his journey would end *somewhere*. Not just another indefinite, numbing path through an unchanging life.

Not again.

They picked at it a little over the rest of the day: torn remnants of references and half-dropped hints. Cesare apologized, of all things, which left Dan feeling like even more of an asshole. When Cesare asked, earnest and serious, if he would come again, it was hard to keep from jumping him on the spot. They were walking down by the old village square, so Dan knew he couldn't, but even that reminder of the constraints placed on their relationship didn't seem to matter.

He just nodded, said "of course," and walked a tiny bit closer to Cesare, bumping his shoulder with his own. Cesare grinned, and the meaningful looks that danced between them—heavy in the purple-smeared dusk—cloaked everything with such a veneer of comfortable reconciliation that Dan almost couldn't remember being pissed off.

Almost.

In the morning, Cesare asked if he wanted to come to Mass. Dan supposed he should have said yes, should have gone and sat beside him, maybe even tried to see the face of a benevolent and loving God somewhere in the fractured, dusty light of stained glass windows and shadowy recesses.

He just shook his head and mumbled something about it not really being his thing. It made him feel like crap when Cesare nodded, his mouth folded around a small smile that seemed to say "I thought so."

He told Dan to make himself at home in the apartment, and kissed his cheek before he left. Dan looked down from the little front window and watched Cesare go. He walked briskly, brightly, as if he had everything in the world to be pleased about, the breeze ruffling his hair and whispering across the shoulders of his one good, uncrumpled suit.

Dan shook his head and swore to himself. He remembered the concert Cesare had taken him to see in Venice, in the church of Santa Maria Gloriosa dei Frari. It had been a secular event, sure, but it had still felt weird to watch how Cesare looked at it all. Like he really believed… but it was more than belief, Dan supposed. It was more like belonging— and that unsettled him.

After Cesare left, Dan spent the few hours he had to himself mooching around the apartment. He was disinclined to venture off into the local wilds without Cesare, even though he still felt burdened with the lingering sourness of their not-quite fight. It wasn't wrong to look through some of Cesare's things, Dan told himself. Not like he was snooping, which he wasn't. Just a mild curiosity about the kinds of things he had on his bookshelves, the CDs he liked… that kind of stuff.

There were a lot of books: some art and coffee table books, along with popular novels, mysteries, thrillers, and translations of classics. Most of them were in Italian. A few were in English but not many. Cesare's music collection sat jumbled on one shelf of the beech-effect bookcase. Dan flicked through the CDs, finding mostly light classical pieces and compilations of composers' best-known works, though he smiled at the handful of corny '80s power ballad and rock discs, interspersed with ten- and fifteen-year-old Italian pop albums.

He liked the thought of Cesare as a younger man, lost in dreams of tight blue jeans, motorcycles, and soaring three chord power riffs. Had he ever wanted to leave this country behind? Move away, perhaps, start a whole new life somewhere else?

Dan shook his head. Stupid thoughts. Cesare wouldn't change; he'd never leave, at least not while his parents were still alive. Even if it could have been technically possible for him to spend time in England, or anywhere else in Europe for that matter, teaching Italian or working as a tutor, or whatever else his qualifications might fit him for... he wouldn't leave them.

Dan padded back into the bedroom, and it was *the* bedroom, not Cesare's bedroom, because they'd abandoned the plan of Cesare sleeping on the couch in the first couple of days. The vague thought of packing his bag pulled at Dan, though he really didn't want to do it, however much he knew he should. He'd be going home on Monday morning: train, then plane, and then back in London by late afternoon.

Funny how it could be so simple.

He didn't mean to go riffling through anything. It was just a matter of opening a drawer at random, not really with any particular goal in mind... and there it was. Cesare's secret life. A few battered Donald Strachey mysteries, some cheap gay romcom movies, and a tiny stash of the most vanilla porn Dan had ever seen in his life. He stared blankly at the covers, and a depressing array of full-lipped, raven-haired, finely chiseled hunks stared back. They all seemed to look pretty similar, and Dan couldn't help but notice he didn't resemble any of them. For a moment, that gave him a twin glimmer of pride and insecurity, and he wondered whether these anonymous, cookie-cutter studs were what Cesare wanted or what he wanted to be.

Psychology aside, the titles were all pretty similar. No whiff of fetishes or naughty secrets: just hot guys screwing in various locations. Like the novels and the tacky films, they were just normal, simple things. Nothing more esoteric than that… which was probably the saddest thing about it.

He should have stopped looking then. He knew that: he was rooting around in things that weren't meant for him. Somehow, though, it was too easy. The small sheaf of letters that lay beneath the novels had been pushed to the back of the drawer but not apparently overtly hidden. Dan told himself that flicking through them was okay, because it wasn't as if he could read Italian well enough to make out what they said.

A couple were crumpled, as if they'd been screwed up and then carefully smoothed out again. The paper was good quality and the writing rather round and florid, though the notes were short. A Polaroid snapshot was tucked in between them, and a familiar piece of scenery immediately caught Dan's attention. He'd recognize the colonnades of the Piazzetta di San Marco anywhere, but he didn't much like the look of the man in the picture. Leaning against one cream wall with the backdrop of the distant lagoon behind him, he sneered at the camera as if he thought he meant more than the crowds of people milling around behind him.

Judging from the epithet, *Tito a San Marco*, scrawled across the bottom of the picture, and the fact that Cesare had kept the snapshot at all, maybe he *had* meant that much. Dan wasn't sure how he felt about that. So this was Tito, with the wife and daughters and clandestine affair conducted from his apartment in Castello? He looked like a man whose middle age had leapt out of the mirror one morning and frightened him, and wound him up with the desire to take it out on everyone else.

Dan found himself wondering what the letters said and why Cesare had kept them so carefully, but he felt bad about snooping already… though not *quite* bad enough to stop him from taking a peek at the other papers in the drawer.

If the nice stationery had belonged to Tito, these were the work of someone else. They seemed pretty old, and the handwriting was different: scribbled lines wandering haphazardly over yellowing sheets of lined A4, like the kind torn from school exercise books. Most of it was illegible to Dan, although he did make out the enthusiastic *mille baci* signature at the bottom of one page, spattered with boldly drawn kisses.

There were another two photos tucked in between the pages, and they made Dan's chest ache. They were old-style six-by-four-inch prints, showing Cesare as the younger man Dan so often wished he'd met. He was adorable: young, handsome, floppy-haired and wide-eyed, and standing with his arm around the neck of another young guy… much better looking than Tito. If the scribbled love letters were to be believed, Dan assumed his nickname had been Naldo. Going by how young Cesare looked in the pictures, this must have been the "friend" he made during his time away for teaching college.

The guy had midbrown wavy hair, an infectious smile, and a black leather jacket. They were both holding glasses of beer, and the intimacy between them could have passed for friendly: students in high spirits and nothing more. At least, until you looked at the expression on Cesare's face.

It was a glimpse of another time, an ocean of possibilities and freedoms that he should have had, and he looked so happy, so free. Just an out-of-focus snapshot, but it held a whole world within it and a void of bittersweetness.

Dan closed the drawer, regretting ever having gone poking about in the first place.

CESARE WALKED back from the church at a leisurely pace, enjoying the light breeze and the birdsong in the trees. Father Morasutti's Masses were good, but they still left him more appreciative of sunlight and fresh air than he'd been before he entered the church.

Mamma had asked where his English friend was; she'd wanted them over for breakfast after the service. He hadn't minded making Daniel's excuses. No one really expected him to go, except perhaps Mamma, and Cesare supposed he was grateful for that, really. It would have made Daniel uncomfortable, in his funny, stifled, English way. Strange, he thought, how a man as uninhibited, as passionate as he was could be so awkward about some things.

Inevitably, Cesare's mind drifted to some of the more memorable demonstrations of that passion, and the recollections warmed his cheeks. His beautiful man… and there was something to that now, wasn't there? *His.* What there had been in Venezia had not been a never-to-be-repeated aberration, and Daniel's friendship over the past months had not been born out of pity. It was something true, tangible, *real*.

Of course, it carried the thrill of danger. That scent of mischief pounded hard in Cesare's blood, echoing in every footstep. Right here, against the decaying medieval walls and the decaying medieval minds of

Gravagna, he held tight to his chest a searing, powerful secret. It was his own, and no one could wrest it from him. *Certo è vero*, Signor Eveschi, the man who went nowhere, did nothing, was no one, had kissed, touched, loved the body and soul of a wonderful, vibrant, talented man. A friend... a lover. Someone who shared the most intimate secrets with him, and accepted his secrets in return, or at least understood them.

Daniel wanted more than secrecy, and the memory of that uncomfortable conversation lingered bitterly on Cesare's mind, though he believed, truly *believed*, that it would be all right. He would explain to Daniel how much the bond between them meant and how all that mattered was what they shared between them. It affected no one else. It was a private covenant, easily as potent a gift as the wafer and wine that had lately passed Cesare's lips—though he suspected Daniel would not like the comparison.

Cesare remembered long hours spent on his knees in church as a boy, gazing up at the terrible, sweet sadness on the face of a sculpted Christ, his body torn and bleeding upon the cross. It had moved him then, in ways he didn't completely understand, nudging his spirit not toward shame and mortification, but a deep ocean of compassion, the desire to comfort and hold... and to be held.

There was no shame. There had never been shame.

Daniel would perhaps understand that one day. He could, couldn't he? He was an intelligent man. He noticed beauty in the world, in all the small and perfect things that marked God's communion with mankind, and if he could see that, surely he could be open to the tide of peace and love that washed around Cesare now, in the corn-gold sunlight that touched the worn road.

It felt like a blessing. It *was* a blessing, and he knew that was more than the silly, giddy excitement he felt talking. He just wished he could explain it to Daniel.

As he approached his front door, Cesare glanced up at the window, half expecting to see a face there. He did not, but his pulse quickened all the same, and he smiled at himself for his foolishness.

What was this thing, to feel so stupidly invincible? Light and free and full of joy that seemed to ripple beneath his skin. He should be far more worried, he knew. He should be thinking of how badly wrong things could go—of what might happen if people discovered what Signor Eveschi and his English friend did with the curtains drawn.

Cesare started up the stairs to his apartment, trying for a moment to picture the looks on his parents' faces, if they knew. Their horror, revulsion, disappointment, embarrassment… he had enacted it a million times before in his head, but the images seemed somehow duller now. So strange, like trying to recall things seen in a dream that faded on waking and grew clouded, burned away like mist. Did that mean he was braver or simply not thinking clearly?

He didn't know, but it wasn't important because then he was entering the apartment and Daniel was there, smiling and looking so natural in this place, as if he had always been here. He had been sprawled on the couch, reading one of the paperback mystery novels with which Cesare tried to improve his English. Now, he let the book fall closed and he stood up, handsome as ever in his customary jeans and T-shirt.

Cesare shut the door behind him, aware he was grinning like a clown, his chest tight with the urge to hold this man close to him, to press kisses and promises to every inch of his skin.

He didn't know how to say that, how to ask for what he wanted, and just marching straight over there and grabbing Daniel didn't seem like the way to do it. He would think either that Cesare could not go less than an hour or so without him or, perhaps worse, that going to church got him horny… which would not be good.

"Well, I'm all packed," Daniel said, cutting through Cesare's deliberations.

It was a dark cloud over an otherwise lovely moment.

"*Sì.*"

Because he would leave, wouldn't he? Tomorrow morning, and who knew how long it would be before the next visit, the next snatch of time, hidden away from everything else. Cesare felt the smile slip from his face, his mouth sagging into uncomfortable disappointment, and he cleared his throat.

"You, uh, do you want to do anything tonight, Daniel? Go somewhere, or—"

"Nah, not really. I'm happy here."

So much still separated them, Cesare thought, this terrible acreage of space. *Happy.* Was he? Did he have that within him, to make this man happy?

"All right," he said.

"Unless you wanted to—"

"No... here is good."

Cesare smiled and wondered if he was imagining the mild awkwardness that had descended with the mention of Daniel's leaving. Maybe he was; maybe he wasn't. Either way, it didn't last all that long.

Daniel offered to make coffee, and buffered once more by that odd English ritual of kettle and spoons, the unease soon passed. They sat on the little balcony, as Daniel seemed to like to do, and Cesare tried not to think of how hard it would be to be without him.

"So," he began, thumb rubbing the white ceramic handle of his coffee mug, "wh-when you think, perhaps, you will come again?"

He didn't quite dare look up, not wanting the uncertainty of watching Daniel's face before he heard the answer. It was silly. He would come, Cesare was certain. He wanted to—he'd said as much, hadn't he?

I mean, is it just gonna be long weekends and holidays? Your English friend who comes to stay?

The uncomfortable memory of that challenge flickered through Cesare's head but paled next to the meaning it had veiled. Daniel wanted to be more than an occasional visitor.

The thought filled him with an ecstatic, impossible glee, tempered with flashes of sheer terror. It would work in some way because it had to, because there could be no possibility of it not working, but as to the *how*... that was another matter.

"I don't know."

Cesare frowned. That did not sound encouraging. He glanced at Daniel, watching that clean, clear profile, sharp against the bright sky. His eyes were narrowed, and he squinted down over the parched, red roofs, toward the road.

A cold, sharp fear locked itself around Cesare's throat. Could that really be anger in the tightness of his lips, the shortness of his voice?

"Prego?"

No, it must be that he didn't know because of work. Something like that. Cesare supposed it was easier for him than it was for Daniel, at least in that way—he had all the certainty of knowing what his schedule was for virtually the whole year ahead. The dates of the school's holidays and semesters remained essentially the same, year in, year out, whereas Daniel had to make his own timetable, his own living. Yes, that must be it.

Daniel shook his head. "I dunno… I'll have to work something out. I mean, we… *we'll* have to, won't we?"

He stopped abruptly, lifted his mug, and took a long sip of his coffee. Cesare looked at his own mug and the wisps of steam rising from the dark surface of his drink, escaping into the empty air.

"You… you can come any time, Daniel. You know, *sì*?"

Daniel swallowed and the sound of the mug when he set it down again on the little bistro table seemed loud.

"Yeah, it's not, um, it's not just the practical side of it, though. Is it, hm? I mean, I'm all for taking things slowly—don't get me wrong. I don't want to rush anything, and I don't want to push you. But, end of the day, I need to know what…."

His words trailed off into a terse exhalation, part sigh and part just a breath of annoyed frustration. Cesare didn't understand—was this his fault? He looked away, fixing his gaze on the gently swaying boughs of a slim, pale ash tree that grew in a garden at the end of the street. Some days, the woman who lived there hung her laundry out on a line beside it, and her children played in the tree's shade.

"I just don't know how you can do it," Daniel said quietly.

Cesare stared at the distant tree, that one small, slim flare of green in among the crowded, dusty press of houses. The ripple of the foliage in the breeze was soothing, and he tried to match his breathing to it.

"*Pre—*"

"No, you know exactly what I mean. Needing a cover story just in order to have dinner with your family. Pretending that… well, I don't even *know* what you're pretending. I just don't know if I can do it. And, if I can't, I want to say so now, because I would really, really rather not hurt you. I—"

Daniel bit the word off quickly, as if it was something he hadn't wanted to say. Cesare glanced questioningly at him, surprised by the look he found on his friend's face. It was a mix of anxious unease, anger, and something altogether softer, more tender—and it was beautiful.

"Daniel…."

"It's this 'don't ask, don't tell' crap!" he snapped, glaring at Cesare with an unexpected fire in those calm blue eyes. "I don't know how you can do it. And I don't know what you want me to—"

"*Niente,*" Cesare blurted. "Just you. *Tu sei tutto ciò che voglio.*"

He reached across the table, not aware of the intention to do so… not aware of much until his fingers grazed the back of Daniel's hand. Daniel sighed, though the stiffness in his face did not lessen.

"So I go, do I? And I come back, and we do this all again? You pretend I'm just some daft tourist you met on holiday, and we're friends, and the only reason you live alone is because you haven't met the right girl yet, yeah? It's… it isn't fair."

Cesare blinked and withdrew his hand. "You know how it is, Daniel. I told you—in Venezia, I told you. We talk about all these things before. You said—"

"That was different. Everything was different then."

Cesare clenched his jaw. *Sì*, all different. No consequences then. No real life. And who was this man to say what was fair? He had thought Daniel was intelligent enough to understand, at least to see how hard he had worked to build this careful, sheltered life… *certo*, it wasn't perfect, but it was enough. And if he tried every single day to remind himself why the choices he had made were the right ones, it was possible not to go crazy, and to leave himself just enough room to function.

Daniel had to see that. He had to understand. Cesare needed him to understand.

Things here weren't simple. His life had never been simple, and turning it all upside down for this man, however wonderful he was and however much Cesare ached for the fulfillment of all the dreams he promised… it was a step into a terrible abyss. The ground fell away from him when he thought about it, and fear coiled in his throat, catching him between feeling as if nothing in the world could vanquish him and as if this awful sense of vulnerability could choke him where he sat.

Yes, Venice had been another place. It had held Cesare's secrets before. And yes, he'd known secrecy so many times beyond that. It wasn't the worst thing in the world. Sometimes it felt a little like it, but it wasn't truly so bad.

They could make it work. Daniel could see that, couldn't he?

Cesare gazed imploringly at him across the table. The days they'd spent in the hills around the village and traipsing through the streets of Pontrémal, had lent Daniel's face a slight ruddy tan. His hair seemed a little lighter than it had been back in the spring too, shot through with threads of gold. He looked too much at home here, too natural a part of life to cause that kind of pain.

"Maybe not so different," Cesare said softly.

That light, faint summer breeze whispered between them, scented with lemons and the hot grit of the autostrada.

Daniel bit his lip. "Cesare, I don't think it's a good idea."

No... he couldn't say that. He couldn't take all of this back to England with him, deny everything that they had done, everything they'd been... that they *were* to each other.

"Daniel! *Non dire così!*" Cesare heard the note of begging in his voice. It wasn't flattering, but he couldn't regret it. He could not afford to be that proud. "You don't want to come back, to...?"

He raised his eyebrows, leaving the details unspoken.

You don't want me?

"I'm sorry." Daniel broke his gaze, turning away to look out once more at Gravagna's stale, stifled houses. "I want to, you know? I... do want to. Of course I do. But you need to tell me what's going to happen, before we... y'know. Before this goes too far. Because I can't be your secret. Not forever."

Cesare pressed his lips together, unwilling to say what he might soon regret. So easy to make demands, huh? So easy to lay down rules, say what must and must not be.

"This week's been fantastic," Daniel said, his voice calm and clear, all honesty and affection, not wheedling or apologetic. Cesare closed his eyes, letting it wash over him. "It really has. I've had an amazing time, and I... I have faced up to the fact I care about you. A lot. You know that."

A thousand Roman candles burst in Cesare's chest: silent, but nonetheless potent for it. He said nothing, just holding this moment close, in all its complex, contradictory brilliance. Yes, his wonderful man was an Englishman through and through, but Daniel loved him. Cesare had heard the words from him, and he believed them... even though he wanted so much to hear them again, in the daylight this time.

He opened his eyes, looking at the uncertainty in Daniel's handsome face. There was a silence between them, and in it hung promises. Cesare tried to will his lover with a silent question, afraid of speaking. The corner of Daniel's lips twitched, and he smiled in a small, sad kind of way.

"I love you, then. That's better, isn't it? That's... more honest."

Cesare nodded warmly. "*Sì.* And I love you, Daniel. *Tanto.*"

It felt so good to say it: exhilarating, giddying, and yet so comfortable and calming, all at the same time. He loved what it did to Daniel and the soft, sweet look that welled up in his eyes.

"*Tantissimo*," Daniel said, grinning.

He was achingly endearing when he tried like that. Cesare smiled and would have given the world to kiss him, but Daniel's grin was already ebbing, and his face grew so much more serious.

"So, I need to know what you want to do."

This was Daniel's last day. He would be leaving first thing in the morning. Cesare had wanted nothing more than to have one last afternoon with him—and one last night.

"Cesare?"

"You know what I want, Daniel."

"Then make a choice."

Cesare fought back a mirthless smile. Ah, he made it sound so simple! He shook his head, ashamed at his own irritation. He wanted today to be so sweet, but the shade of this problem hung over them, darkening everything like the threat of a summer storm.

"Are you afraid?" Daniel demanded. "Is that it? You said to me once before that if you told your parents, you believed they'd still love you. You sounded confident. You *said* the only reason you didn't tell them was because there was no one in your life."

"*Non capisci*," Cesare muttered.

Must he make this so hard?

"Well? I didn't take you for a coward."

The word cut into him, and a blinding peal of rage flared before Cesare's eyes.

"*Codardo? Come osi? Non dire cazzate!* You don't know, you don't understand… what I have to do, what my life is. Everything I would lose. My job, my—"

He broke off, unwilling to escalate this into a full-blown argument. Below, the ash tree still swayed in the breeze.

"They couldn't do that to you," Daniel said, shaking his head.

Cesare did not reply. He wanted to be angry, to shout and yell at Daniel that he didn't understand… but, he supposed, shouting would not help him to do so. Daniel loosed a small, defeated sigh, and the sound scared Cesare all over again.

It was too much like a farewell.

CHAPTER TWENTY-TWO

THERE WAS no real comfort in coming home.

Dan landed at Heathrow on Monday afternoon and was met with the typical gray, dismal downpour of an English summer.

He traipsed out of the airport, his bag over one shoulder and his hair plastered down with rain before he even managed to hail a cab. It seemed strange to think that one week should have changed so much.

When he'd arrived in Pontremoli, he'd still been able to believe that there wasn't anything between him and Cesare but friendship or, at the very outside, the kind of chemistry that, powerful though it was, they could keep casual and undemanding. But that wasn't true, and it hadn't been true for a long time.

Dan slouched in the back of the cab and tried not to remember the crunch of dry grass beneath his feet, or the feel of Cesare's lips on his skin.

He shouldn't have picked that fight on his last day. It didn't feel totally real, even now—had he really called Cesare a coward? It seemed like a kind of low, underhanded cruelty Dan hadn't thought he was capable of, but he distinctly remembering doing it. For the briefest of seconds, it had actually felt good.

He'd apologized, of course. They'd made love one more time, on the Sunday night, and it had been a bittersweet, complicated thing. At the time, the feelings had been cloying and almost too much, but of course he missed it now: lying in that rumpled bed, holding Cesare against him, legs clamped around those thick, broad thighs, hips flexing as they slid their slick cocks together. Cesare had dug his fingers into Dan's back, holding on so tight the muscles had felt bruised this morning.

Just touching, nothing more than that. It was all it had been. Kisses, caresses, simple human contact… lying still once it was over, wrapped up in each other and not quite daring to speak. Eventually, Dan had spoken. He'd promised he'd come back, whispered the words into the darkness, and felt Cesare fold against him, warm breath skating across his chest. No other words. No explanations.

God, it was such a fucking mess.

Dan stared sullenly out of the car window, willing the rain to keep falling and falling, and wash the whole world away with it.

When he finally got in, the flat looked exactly the same as it had when he'd left, which wasn't surprising, though it smelled musty, all choked up with stagnant sunshine and airless days.

Dan flung open windows, unpacked his things, and checked his messages. There wasn't much. Nothing from Paul, which was a blessing. After all the initial tantrums, everything seemed to have gone very quiet there, for which Dan was extremely grateful. There was one from Miriam, saying that the first canvases were ready for the installation and asking if he wanted to come down and take a look. She sounded pleased, and Dan was curious as to how the final project would turn out, so he jotted down the address. He gave Edith a quick ring, just to let her know he was back, and was grateful for the fact she didn't probe into the minutiae of exactly where and why he'd gone.

"So," she asked, her voice only a little tight, "did you have a good time?"

"Yep," he answered. "It was nice, y'know… just having the few days away from things. Clear my head."

Another outrageous lie. Dan's head was so far from clear it felt like it might explode. Edith didn't push him, though. He spoke to the kids. They were on their summer holidays now and rampant with enthusiasm, so Dan promised that they'd find something fun to do later in the week.

Chris was next on his list. A brief text just to say he was home and to ask if he had time to meet up later for a drink. Dan didn't know why he asked that but found his fingers stuttering over the keys nonetheless.

He tossed the phone on the bed and went for a shower, suddenly feeling slightly chilly.

DAN ARRANGED to meet Chris at a lounge bar about ten minutes' walk away from the installation space Miriam was so excited about, which meant he had time to pop in and see the pictures first.

The space was good, he had to admit. The warehouse's Victorian brickwork and heavy glass windows belied a fresh, modern renovation job to the interior, even if it was only half-done. The Arts Council funding sign, swirly green logo on white plastic, sat propped up on a chair near the front door, probably because no one had got around to fixing it up on the wall yet. On the lower floor, an exhibition of paintings done by inmates in a local prison took up most of the space that wasn't wreathed in dust sheets, and everything smelled of fresh paint. Sada's "concept of time" piece wasn't due for another few weeks, but some of the cables that would support it already dangled from the ceiling, and a plexiglass case for the archaeological exhibit stood in one corner, still partly swathed in plastic wrappings.

Miriam waved at him from a steel-and-glass staircase just next to the lavatories, and Dan greeted her with a smile.

"Hiya. How's it going?"

"Oh, it looks *wonderful!*" she cooed, her chunky jewelry swinging and her heels clacking on the steps as she led him upstairs. "Your pics look fabulous. Just what we wanted. Ready? Ta-da!"

She ushered him into their space, a temporary, windowless, rectangular structure created from flimsy stud walling in the center of the warehouse's upper floor. It was dark, and smelled of sawdust, but Dan could see the effect she was going for, although the piece was still in the extremely early stages of assembly.

Huge, moveable, lightweight timber frames stretched from floor to ceiling, set in pairs all the way down what would eventually be an aisle. It gave Dan a brief frisson of pleasure to see his photographs blown up to just over life-size, the streets and edges of buildings brought right from those hazy, long treks around Battersea to this new, recreated reality.

"...getting the audiovisual component in on Thursday," Miriam was saying, "and then it's just a case of synching everything up so it loops over properly, and we're good to go for the launch. It's going to be very intense, I think. Loved working with you, darling."

"Yeah," Dan said absently, craning his head back, as if he really expected to see the buildings towering up above him. "You too."

He let her talk a bit more and promised to show up for the opening, before finally excusing himself and leaving for the bar.

It was still reasonably early, though an entire day spent between various forms of public transport had Dan yawning as he sat in the dim, self-consciously hip, blue-and-purple interior, waiting for Chris.

He'd settled himself at the corner of the bar, just on an angle so he couldn't catch unexpected sight of himself in the mirror that ran along the back wall, and ordered a pint. The barman looked like a student and had an unfocused expression, bitten fingernails, and a soul patch that didn't resemble facial hair so much as an unfortunate dribble. He slid the drink across the bar, and Dan nursed it gratefully.

Apart from the black leatherette barstools, most of the seating was in the form of booths with white tables and blue and purple banquettes. At the edge of Dan's eyeline, a staircase led up to the next floor and, at the foot of it, a giant cheese plant in a blue-and-white ceramic pot seemed to be on guard, like some horrific triffid.

Somewhere in the bar's funky chrome bowels, Amy Winehouse's *Back to Black* album was being piped through speakers, providing a slightly muffled background noise to the ambient chatter and clink of glasses.

Dan was about halfway down his pint when Chris turned up, brown-skinned and sun-kissed in light cotton jeans and a short-sleeved shirt, mirrored sunglasses pushed up onto the top of his head.

"Blimey, you look like you've had a good week," Dan observed.

Chris waved a hand dismissively, ordered a gin and tonic with lime, and sat down across the corner of the bar from Dan, giving a theatrical huff.

"Hi, love. Busy like you wouldn't bloody believe. Honest. We scarpered at the weekend, went down to Brighton. That was mad too, but at least it wasn't work."

Dan nodded. "You and Sada?"

The barman pushed Chris's gin and tonic toward him, and Chris flashed the man a dazzling, faintly flirtatious smile as he forked over his change. It dropped abruptly from his lips when he turned back to Dan, replaced with something rather like sheepish avoidance.

"Mm-hm," he said, lifting his glass.

"Oh."

"Anyway." Chris swallowed. "How are you? You're back, obviously."

"Yep."

"And…? You darted off to foreign climes again in bit of a hurry, after all that business with Shit-For-Brains."

Dan smiled. "I thought you liked Paul."

"Sacrilege!" Chris wrinkled his nose. "I always said he was a wrong'un. Never good enough for you."

Dan's grin widened, and he laughed. "Daft sod."

"I mean it!" Chris took another sip of his drink and dropped the playacting. "You all right, though? Really?"

"Yeah. Thanks."

"If you say so." Chris disentangled his foot from the barstool and prodded Dan in the calf with it. "So, I assume you flounced off into the arms of your exotic Latin lover?"

Dan winced. "Don't."

He'd come clean, in the end, and told Chris more about Cesare than he'd wanted to. It came from needing someone to talk at, if not to, and, though Chris still made fun of him, he was at least more sympathetic than Edith. Of course, exactly how much Dan had told him was a slightly different matter.

"Well?" Chris raised his eyebrows. "Didn't you? I thought that's why you were going. Talk about getting back on the horse! We should get you leather chaps. Maybe a pair of spurs, and then you can—"

"Ugh, no. No! I mean, it isn't like that. It's… well…." Dan sighed and glared down at his beer as if it was somehow responsible.

"Oh, spit it out, please. The suspense is killing me."

"All right." Dan grimaced. "Yeah, I stayed with him. We…. Well, it's kind of getting complicated."

"Really? Doesn't sound all that complicated to me. Rampant shagging and a willingness to rack up frequent flier miles… I'd say you've got a long-distance thing going. And good for you! Fuck Paul. Or not, obviously, as the case may be…."

Dan glanced sharply up at him, and Chris's expression softened a little. He took another swig of his gin and tonic.

"Is that what this is about? Someone needs a serious chat?"

"Kind of, yeah." Dan swigged his beer, and then watched the froth slide down the inside of the glass. It was easier than looking Chris in the eye. "I've screwed up a bit, I think."

"Well, we know *that*," Chris said, though his tone was only gently teasing. He folded his arms on the bar and leaned close, his hair-gel-and-aftershave scent tickling Dan's nose. "This is the stuff that started in Venice, isn't it?"

Dan nodded. Despite the front he put on, Chris could be a good friend when he tried. For example, he knew when Dan didn't want to be the one to put words to things.

"I thought something was… different. I could see it when you came back. This bloke… he was why you gave it another spin with He Who Shall Not Be Named, yes? Come on, no sense fibbing. I see all."

Dan nodded again, another smile bursting through his tiredness. "Yeah."

"Mm-hm. And you think…? What? You fell in lust on the rebound? Or—"

"I think it's complicated," Dan cut in, raising his glass to his lips again. He swallowed heavily, the beer bitter and grounding at the back of his throat, pulling him back to reality. "I think I—I think he's in love with me. He's just this… amazing, honest, generous person, and I kept telling myself I could walk away, but…."

"Whoops. Rocked the boat, did we?"

"Yeah, you could say that." Dan gave a small, embarrassed chuckle. "Shit, I'm a mess."

Chris snorted. "Been saying that for years."

"Fuck off."

"Oh, be nice." Chris grinned, then reached out and squeezed his wrist. "Look, you want my advice? You just have to ask yourself the questions and listen hard for the answers. You know what I mean."

Dan exhaled, aware that his friend's flippancy was there for a reason, like all the sturdiest walls usually are. He scratched his head, hating to ask what he wanted to of Chris, but too much in need to skip the query.

"How did *you* know, then? With Garrett. Tell me to get lost if you don't wanna… y'know."

He glanced nervously at Chris and found him staring at the bobbing wedge of lime in his G&T, mouth a tight line. The corner of his lips twitched before he spoke.

"About a month after we met, I s'pose. Or the first minute I saw him. Maybe both." He extended a long, careful finger, stuck it into his glass, and gave the lime wedge a savage prod. It wobbled erratically, like a dinghy on rough waves. "Yeah. I suppose about a month. I couldn't stand to be more than two feet away from him. I knew how he felt without even looking at him. He was just as bad. We were… connected." Chris smiled, his face softening with the memories as he sucked the gin off his finger. "Typical honeymoon period, really."

Dan quirked an eyebrow. "Was it?"

"'Course not." Chris scoffed. "I was still just as head over heels in love with him when he died. So you can believe it *does* happen, Danny-Boy. Whatever anyone thinks."

"Mm." Dan downed the rest of his beer, slightly regretting having raised the issue. "Thanks, mate."

"Are you, then?" Chris prompted.

"Hm?"

"About to run off to Italy? Buy up some dilapidated olive farm and devote yourself to a life of blissful Tuscan sunshine?"

Dan smiled mirthlessly. "No."

"Tell Auntie the truth, dear."

"Stop it. No. I just.... Fuck." He sighed. "I know all the reasons why it's stupid, and all the reasons I shouldn't, but... I really like this bloke. I *really* like him. I just don't know if—I mean, he's not out. He's Catholic, he has this traditional family that he thinks he can't be honest with, and I don't know if I can deal with all that. All the... baggage. You know me. I'm not good with baggage."

He glanced up, hoping for some kind of amelioration, some kind of boost to his flagging confidence. Chris just cocked an eyebrow and looked at Dan over the rim of his glass.

"Nope. You're not."

"But I want to be," Dan blurted. "I want to be someone who can help him, who can be there for him. I... I don't *want* to be his dirty secret. But I would be, if he asked. I know I'd bloody do it—and it's really pissing me off."

The truth didn't seem so bad once it was out. Chris just smiled at him, looking ever so slightly smug and triumphant.

"Yeah, love's a fucker, isn't it?"

Dan stared at his friend. He wasn't sure what else he'd expected—to be chastised for being a fool, or simply told what to do? No, because that would mean there *were* clear, obvious answers, and Dan knew that wasn't the case. Either he got down off his high horse and admitted that, for anything to work between them, he would have to accept Cesare's limitations, or he rode off into the sunset and didn't look back.

Chris was right. He knew the answer.

Bastard.

Dan looked gloomily into the depths of his empty beer glass. The bar was beginning to fill up. The volume of the semidistant Amy Winehouse album was increasing and, just past the potted triffid, a gaggle of office girls, fresh out of work, were settling themselves at a table, each clutching what Dan suspected was probably a shooter with a humorous name.

"Anyway," Chris said brightly, swishing the last half inch of his gin and tonic in the glass, making the partially melted ice cubes chink. "I'm glad we could catch up. I was going to call you. Got some news, and I wanted you to… well, actually, yeah. You *are* the first one I'm telling."

Dan frowned, confused. "Telling what?"

Chris knocked back the rest if his drink in one gulp and swallowed hard. He gazed into the empty tumbler as if he was avoiding meeting Dan's gaze.

"What, Chris?"

"Sada and I are getting spliced."

Dan stared, mouth hanging open. Chris glanced up at him, expression uncharacteristically solemn, and after a beat of silence, he burst out laughing.

"Oh, Danny! Dan, your *face*…!"

Dan shook his head. "Bastard. What—Is this a windup, then?"

"No. Honest, we are. We—" He stopped, looking as close to bashful as Dan had ever seen him, and bit his lip. "I asked him at the weekend. On Brighton Pier. He said yes."

It was all too easy to imagine. The salty sea air, the sunshine, the look on Sada's face…. Dan caught himself wondering if Chris had actually bought a ring and got down on one knee. He wouldn't have put it past him. He blinked, realizing that he was supposed to say something at this point, but finding his mouth completely dry.

"Um…."

"Congratulations," Chris prompted dryly. "That's generally what you, y'know… say."

"Yeah. No. Yeah… um. Congratulations," Dan managed, still reeling. He cleared his throat, embarrassed.

"I really do actually love him, you know," Chris said, lowering his voice. "Since we're talking mushy stuff tonight."

"Yeah." Dan smiled, finding at least the ghost of his voice at last. "Yeah, I know."

Chris looked away again, fingering his empty glass. "Not the way I—I mean, not like how it was with Garrett. It'll never be like that. Just… me and Sada feel right, you know? It's comfortable. Secure. I want to show him that. I want him to know he's stuck with me. And I want him with me too. Guess… like, when it feels right—when it feels real—you've got to take that and hold on to it, haven't you?"

He shifted his gaze back to Dan abruptly and raised his eyebrows as if he wanted reassurance, though he seemed totally at peace with what he was saying. Dan still couldn't believe it. Chris, of all people, talking about marriage? *Chris*? He realized how loud the silence between them sounded, despite the music and the chatter of other people, and he licked his lips hurriedly.

"Um. Well. Right, yeah… congratulations, I mean. Really. That's… that's great. Surprising, but… great."

He knew he should be able to sound more convincing. It was good news—important news. Something profound and life-changing for Chris and for Sada, and he should… he should be happy for them, shouldn't he? Only, all that Dan could find in himself was a dark, apathetic void.

It wasn't that he didn't care. Far from it. He was… jealous? He blinked, trying to pin the feeling down. It thrashed around inside him, spiteful and selfish, a tendril of bitter anger.

"When, um, when are you going to… do it, then?"

Chris flashed him an awkward smile. "Dunno, really. Soon. We want to do it soon. Y'know. Before he has a chance to change his mind."

He grinned, laughed nervously, and Dan supposed he'd be hearing that joke a lot in the coming weeks and months. He nodded.

"Right."

"You'll be there, won't you? For me?"

"For both of you. Yeah. Of course."

"Thanks." Chris looked relieved. "You never know, you could bring your Italian stallion."

Dan grimaced. "Don't call him that."

"Oh, come on. Lemme have my fun."

"Fine. Whatever…." Dan shook his head. "Does Sada know what he's getting himself into?"

Chris just beamed, for once totally devoid of any smartass comment.

DAN WAS still mulling it over when he got home. Chris and Sada. He'd seen it coming… seen *something* coming, anyway, and he was glad for them, though Chris's dedication to an official commitment was a bit of a surprise.

It annoyed Dan that part of him wanted to call Cesare and tell him, if only for the fact that it would illustrate a point he felt he needed to make. He made himself a cup of tea and wondered precisely what that was—some bollocks about honesty and openness, probably. Another instance of him trying to force Cesare to do what *he* wanted, with little or no consideration for the fact that his life was very different from Dan's.

Dan flopped down in an armchair to drink his tea and check his messages. He was expecting something from Edith or one of the kids about the promised excursion to Hampton Court at the weekend, but that wasn't what he found.

"*Ciao*, Daniel. Is Cesare."

Dan's tea stopped halfway to his mouth and he held his breath. Something didn't sound right—Cesare's voice didn't normally have that thickness to it, that sense of weary resignation.

"*Ehi*, I wanted to know you are come home safe, and… I will speak to you soon, I hope. *Ciao*."

The message crumbled a little at the end, as if Cesare had fumbled the phone. Dan didn't waste time; he was already setting his mug down and scuffling for the international dialing code.

"*Pronto?*"

"Hiya. It's me."

"Oh." Cesare sounded relieved. "Daniel. Is nice to hear your voice. You have a good journey?"

"Yeah, not bad." Dan settled himself back in the armchair, the phone clamped to his ear. He supposed he could try and make Cesare laugh with anecdotes, and he had several to choose from: the bossy flight attendant on his trip back, the cab driver with the Pakistani accent and the militant views on immigration, and even his quick visit to Mad Miriam's installation space. He was tempted, but he wasn't sure Cesare was in the mood to laugh.

This sounded like something other than just the moping of missing someone. It seemed serious.

"Is, um, is everything okay?"

There was a pause, a beat of silence on the line, full of nothing but Cesare's breathing, and Dan waited for him to speak.

"Ah, I had a phone call today," he said eventually, his voice low and just a little close to shaking. "Signor Alvisio, the, uh, *come si dice*, the head at the *scuola*? Preside."

"Oh." Dan frowned, reaching for his mug of tea.

"I am not to go back, in the new term. I have been, uh, *licenziato*. Fired."

"Oh my God... *why*?" Dan closed his eyes. "Why? I mean, they can do that? Just like that? Doesn't he have to give you a reason, or...?"

Cesare sighed, and it crackled on the line. "Unofficially, he says it is because of Niccolò. I have been providing too much extra help."

"What?" Dan rocked forward in his chair, almost spilling the tea. "Because you *helped*? That's ridiculous! They can't do—I don't understand."

"The classes are inclusionary. All the children are supposed to be treated equally. Signor Alvisio say I was wrong to give Niccolò extra help in term time, and is a breaking of contract to tutor him in the holidays."

Cesare sounded beaten, defeated. Dan loosed a short, terse sigh.

"I don't believe it. Well, you have to appeal, don't you? Like... unfair dismissal or whatever. Niccolò's parents would speak for you, surely. What about your union? You have a union, surely? And you say he said 'unofficially' it was that? What the hell was the *official* reason?"

He tried to take a breath and calm down; his barrage of questions wasn't helping. Cesare sucked in a long breath and cursed softly.

"Officially? Unofficially, officially... everything is lies. *Cazzo*. What they will put down on the papers, they will say I failed to mention something when I apply for the job. That I have lied." The anger was mounting in his voice, and he spat bitterness into Dan's ear. "You know what they find? Fucking Arcigay. The rally at Roma. Is years ago, it means *niente*! Signor Alvisio says I did not disclose the arrest. The *carabinieri* held me for less than an hour, Daniel! It is nothing. I know what it is. This is not about Roma. This is about Niccolò, about me... about the fact that man has always hated me!"

Cesare broke off abruptly, and all the anger in his voice seemed to have transmuted back to that tone of weary hopelessness.

"Signor Alvisio says what I did was too much. I made the governors—the school—look bad. 'Inadequate,' he say." Cesare scoffed. "He was very clear about that. He also said that, if I appeal, it will not be well for me."

Dan frowned. Silence filled everything, and he held his breath, afraid to speak. All the horror stories and injustices that they'd talked about before, the kind that had no place in a modern world, played out behind his eyes. At the time he'd thought it was just Cesare's anxiety, that vague paranoia he hid behind. Even his run-in with the *carabinieri* in Rome had been less dramatic than it first sounded, and somehow Dan had never believed there would be real repercussions. Not this way. Even if he'd admitted the existence of that kind of prejudice, he hadn't believed it would happen. Not to them.

Eventually, Dan bit his lip and forced the words into action. "You mean... it would all be made public? The arrest, and why you were there, and—"

"*Sì.*"

"Did he actually say that? The principal?"

"Not... *come si dice*? He did not say in so many words," Cesare said dryly. "But I was not in any doubt."

"Oh, hell. Is it... is it because of me? Because of us?"

Cesare murmured something in Italian that Dan didn't catch, but the sound was oddly comforting. "No. Not you, *caro*. Not your fault. I think Signor Alvisio has wanted an excuse for a long time to be rid of me. But I think perhaps, yes, there is... some little bird singing, you know?"

"Who?"

"I don't know. I don't think it matters."

Cesare sounded as if he really believed that. Dan bit his tongue, knowing he shouldn't argue. Of course it mattered that somebody would do that to him, couldn't he see that?

The memory of dinner at Cesare's parents' house drifted through Dan's mind, and he recalled the hardness he wanted to think he'd imagined in the face of Cesare's brother Gianni. *No, surely not.* He pushed the thoughts away. It would be too ironic if, all that time, the family Cesare wanted so badly to protect was to blame for dumping him in the middle of all this. If they'd done something so spiteful, so cruel, to someone who was supposed to be one of the closest to you in the world.

Dan cleared his throat, glanced at his watch and wondered how much money he had left on his credit card.

"Look, I can be there in... well, I don't know when the soonest flight is. But I can find out. I'll—"

"You don't have to, Daniel. Is no need."

"But—"

Dan pinched the bridge of his nose, the phone hot and uncomfortable against his ear. He wanted to, he realized. More than he'd thought possible.

The flat, the whole bloody city, felt like nothing more than a cardboard prison, as fake as Miriam's timber-and-canvas backstreets, and he was sure he'd explode if he didn't get out.

Dan peered up at the window, watching the rain patter the glass, sliding down the pane in complex, twisting rivulets. If Cesare didn't want him to come back, why had he told him?

"What are you going to do?" he asked, though it felt like a stupid question.

Cesare wouldn't *do* anything. If he wouldn't take his parents aside and have a quiet word with them, he was hardly likely to fight a very public battle over unfair dismissal in both the courts and the press. It would bring everything out into the open, and it was all Dan's fault.

He supposed he should feel guilty, but that was hard to do, in among all the blinding, burning anger.

"*Non so*," Cesare said. "*Non c'è niente da fare…* I can do nothing. I-I am sorry. I don't know why I tell you. Not today. I…."

"Do you need a reason?"

More silence, but it felt softer, tempered with acceptance. Dan wondered if he was kidding himself to think Cesare really understood.

"No," Cesare said eventually, his voice barely a whisper. "I… I call because…."

A full, ragged breath trailed over the words he seemed to want to say. Dan sniffed.

"Yeah. Well, I'm coming back, okay? I'll let you know as soon as I have a flight, and—" He screwed his eyes shut for a second, hating himself for what he knew he had to say, the boundaries that needed to be in place. "—a hotel, or something."

Cesare didn't reply at first, and for a moment, Dan worried that he'd read the man wrong. Perhaps he wanted not just comfort and company, but a palpable demonstration of something, a defiant stand against the world.

"*Sì*," Cesare said quietly. "Thank you. I think that is… for the best, yes? You don't need to come, but—"

Dan clenched his jaw. He'd known. He'd known all along how Cesare played things, and there was no point in being angry at him now—

not when he needed a friend more than anything else. All the same, that knowledge didn't stop Dan wanting to throw the phone across the room and possibly punch a wall or two.

"Yeah," he said. "But I will. I want to. You and me, right?"

CHAPTER TWENTY-THREE

CESARE TRIED to concentrate on the road, to lose himself in the action of driving and the hazy band of blue that wavered where the tarmac met the sky. The acid greens and parched yellows of trees and grass edged his narrow view of the world, and the Fiat's windshield was spotted with the corpses of insects and the dusty grit of the day's stale, hot air.

He had not slept last night. There had been nothing in his head but Signor Alvisio's thin, wheedling voice, over and over again, telling him that he did not need to return to the *scuola*.

Unprofessional conduct, he had called it. Behavior that had placed him, the school, and Cesare himself, in a difficult and untenable position. The law stated that children with special needs like those of Niccolò Misseri were, once properly assessed and integrated into the classroom, to be included and treated like all the other pupils. Was there not classroom support available? Did the child not have a weekly hour's lesson with a woman contracted by the Education Department to provide special learning support?

Cesare had pointed out that, although that was technically true, Signora Bianchi was not particularly good at her job, and her infrequent visits had not helped Niccolò improve his work in the slightest.

He should have stayed quiet, he knew. That much had been clear from the hardening of Signor Alvisio's tone, and Cesare could just picture the man's sharp, sour face turning red as he tried to contain his anger. His skin always seemed slightly oily, his mouth a thin-lipped straight line a little too wide for his face, and framed by two large folds that formed an almost perfect triangle between his pointed chin and the tip of his long, angular nose.

The children had a handful of unpleasant but fairly amusing names for him. Cesare especially liked the one that compared him to a bald, old yowling tomcat; it was just unfortunate that this particular cat had the power to remove him from his job.

The principal had been furious. Cesare had imagined his thick, dark-framed glasses steaming up from the inside, and had been forced to bite back the absurd impulse to laugh at the notion.

But there was no laughing. Nothing funny.

Perhaps there are other considerations, hm? Personal issues.

The words were clear but subtle.

If... certain things come to my attention, Signor Eveschi, it is my duty to act upon them. You understand, yes?

As the world collapsed around Cesare, the whole of his life falling in upon him until nothing existed but the cold, dark stream of panic in his head. Signor Alvisio's voice kept droning on. There was to be no argument, no resistance. No appeal.

Cesare sat down after the principal rang off, feeling light-headed and queasy. It hadn't felt real. Surely it hadn't truly happened, had it?

His thoughts fell to the week before and to Daniel. He should, perhaps, have felt angry, resentful... this was his fault, wasn't it? There must have been some point, some incriminating moment, where they hadn't been as careful as they thought, where someone, somewhere, had seen Cesare and his English friend, and known what they were.

He should blame the man, he supposed. Or blame himself, and all the stupid, foolish, idealistic arrogance that had made him think he could get away with it. Oh, one night, one weekend, one small, snatched piece of time, in Venezia, Padua, or Bologna—that was different. That was not brought back here, brought under the cruel lamp of everyday life, and examined, picked apart....

Yet he could not be angry. There was no rage, no guilt, no terror: just an irresistible wave of numbness sweeping over him until Cesare could no longer deny it and relented into the feeling. He'd always known it would happen, somehow.

Perhaps he should be relieved. Daniel would think that, wouldn't he? So full of all that pride and bombastic refusal to compromise. He had wanted nothing more than the truth, and now here it would be... spilling out all over the place, changing everything before it as water turns sand to mud.

Nothing would be the same, Cesare had realized, and he had sat in the quiet of his apartment and cried for the loss.

He wasn't entirely sure how he had come to telephone Daniel. It was simply addressing a need, as thoughtless as eating to ease hunger, drinking to slake thirst… just hearing his voice and knowing that, as long as he was listening, Cesare was not alone.

He had not expected him to turn around and leap straight back onto another plane, but he hadn't even needed to ask—not that he *would* have asked.

It was confusing. Cesare wasn't even sure he wanted Daniel here. There were so many ways things could happen now, and he didn't know what to expect. Anything from people whispering and laughing in the street to rocks through his windows, or *Mamma e Papà*…. He foundered on that thought. They would find out. The only question was how.

There would be gossip—perhaps there had already been gossip, and he had just been so wrapped up in Daniel's visit, in falling in love all over again, that he hadn't noticed.

Stupido!

He had poured himself a brandy, drunk it too quickly, and tried to think his way through the labyrinths ahead of him. Maybe there was sense in denial, but for how long? If Signor Alvisio stuck to his version of events and continued to claim that this was all to do with Niccolò Misseri, then that was fine, and Cesare could do the same, but would he do that?

Cesare doubted it. And, besides, at some time, some place, there would still come the gossip. The whispers. The sidelong looks and hidden smiles on the faces of strangers.

An open secret was still a secret. Daniel had taught him that.

Now he tried not to think. He just wanted to drive.

He had spent the morning at the Misseris' house, explaining as best he could at least a portion of what had happened. After all, whatever changed in his life, Niccolò's was going to alter drastically too.

Angela had cried, said she didn't understand, especially when, without Cesare, the boy would not have passed to the next grade. He pushed her praise gently aside and tried to assure her that there would be another teacher, someone who could help Niccolò just as much, if not more than he.

It didn't seem to help. He had promised to call back when Ugo was home, to help them as best he could and, in the meantime, continue Niccolò's lessons. A stable routine was always best.

Cesare took the first turn on the right, not familiar with the direction in which he was heading but not really caring if he got lost.

The hotel was a little way outside of Pontremoli. It was not set in as advantageous a location as many of the places popular with tourists. They tended to prefer the converted villas or bits of old *castello* buildings, which were so dramatic and impressive against the rolling landscape. That didn't matter, though. Cesare had choked down his fill of drama.

Today he was grateful for anything that was understated.

He had been on the road by the time Daniel texted him to say he'd arrived, and they had arranged to meet in the lobby. The dry weight of tears he had no energy left to countenance prickled behind Cesare's eyes, and he blinked hard, forcing the asphalt and the metal barriers back into focus. That his man should do this for him, unasked; that he should refuse all arguments, all protests, and just come to be beside him... it was more of a gift than Cesare knew how to accept.

It wasn't hard to find the place, to park his car, and push through every action on autopilot, though everything felt the way it did in dreams—loose and jumbled, just a series of unconnected moments sleeting by him, barely noticed until they had already passed.

The hotel seemed nice. It was a big, square building, built of red brick and designed to look as if it was older than it really was, the exterior festooned with ivies and wrought-iron plant holders. A board near the entrance carried a message for attendees of some kind of sales conference, and Cesare supposed that, here, that was how the place got the majority of its business. Travelers, salesmen, people from out of town. People who didn't want to be recognized, didn't want to be seen.

Suddenly he wished he'd asked Daniel to come and stay with him, almost choked by the desire that they should be together in his apartment, just the way they had been until last Sunday night. Not here, in this place lost along the autostrada, where secrets were kept and promises broken.

Cesare couldn't dwell on it, however, because movement across the lobby caught his eye. Daniel. He had been sitting in one of a small rank of beige-upholstered chairs by a low glass table littered with magazines. To the left, the concierge's desk was being staffed by a bored-looking girl in a dark blue blazer, apparently more interested in filing her nails than observing his arrival. She didn't matter. Nothing else mattered.

Daniel smiled, moving uncertainly toward him. He looked exhausted, his blue shirt was crumpled, his hair more tousled by travel than intentional effect, but Cesare barely noticed the imperfections. The lobby's dark gray carpet seemed to slip from under his feet, the whole place fading away, and his arms were around Daniel, his chin pressed into the firm warmth of his shoulder, his scent filling up everything. Yet there was no pressure from Daniel, no forwardness in his touch. It was nothing more than a simple hug, though it was tight enough and strong enough to make things seem just a little bit more bearable.

But for all the strength, all the importance, it could have been nothing more than an embrace between friends. A certain hesitance lingered in Daniel's face as they parted, and Cesare guessed he was unsure as to whether a kiss on the cheek would pass for Continental friendship. Those blue eyes, red-rimmed and bleary, searched his for an answer, and Cesare determined that he would give one.

Slowly, deliberately, he brought his hand to Daniel's jaw, and the feel of warm skin and stubble against his palm was so natural, so right. The flicker of confusion in Daniel's face was quickly quashed as, without waiting for permission or protest, Cesare leaned in and kissed him, chaste but full. He marveled at the way his lips seemed so perfectly molded to Daniel's, a total union of flesh and breath. It could have lasted seconds, minutes, or hours, Cesare decided, and he would not have been able to tell the difference.

They parted, and he noted the slight flush across Daniel's cheekbones, the sheepish look in his eyes, and the curl of his lips.

Pride had, perhaps, conquered timorous caution.

Cesare glanced across the lobby and caught sight of the girl on the concierge's desk, staring at them. He stared back, amazed at his own actions, as if he actually wanted her to say something, to dare her into speaking. His heart thudded wildly. He'd never felt like this: such an intense, irrefutable anger, like a fire that could be poured out at will, pointed in any direction and left to lay waste to all it touched, all that dared stand between him and the world of which he had a right to be part.

The girl said nothing, but she kept staring. Eventually, Cesare became aware of Daniel touching his arm, just a firm but gentle pressure on his sleeve.

"Come on. Come and tell me what's going on, yeah?"

Cesare blinked, suddenly light-headed and disoriented.

"*Sì*," he murmured, content to let Daniel lead him out of the back of the lobby, through a pair of double doors, and onto a thickly carpeted, bland staircase, lit with square fluorescent lights.

The doors swung shut behind them, and Daniel let out a short, dry bark of laughter.

"God!" he breathed. "What the bloody hell was that all about?"

Cesare shook his head, not even sure himself whether he was pretending to misunderstand or just unable to answer.

"*Non so*," he said. "I... I don't know."

Daniel smiled disbelievingly at him. It was contagious; Cesare couldn't help smiling too, though he hadn't the faintest idea why. He wanted to kiss Daniel again, he knew that. As if perhaps the past twenty-four hours could be washed away by his touch and never need to seem real.

"C'mon." Daniel nodded at the flight of stairs ahead of them. "I'm up here. Two-thirteen."

IT HADN'T been easy to book the flight or the hotel on such short notice, but it had definitely been worth it. Dan could still feel the echo of Cesare's kiss on his mouth and, whatever else was about to change irreparably, he was reasonably sure that at least some elements of it would be for the better.

He didn't like the way Cesare looked, though. He seemed worn out, stretched thin by worrying. As he entered the hotel room, such a familiar ritual for them, he let out a long, tense sigh. He barely seemed to resemble the relaxed, smiling man Dan had grown used to seeing.

"Sit down," he said. "Tell me about it."

The twist of a small, grateful smile curled the side of Cesare's mouth. There was only one chair in the room; straight-backed, it stood in front of the dressing table, upholstered in a rather faded green fabric. Cesare crossed the room and sat heavily on the edge of the bed, hunched forward with his arms propped on his knees. He looked up at Dan, pale-faced and seeming so tired, so utterly defeated.

"*Sei arrabbiato con me?*" he asked.

"What?"

Dan pulled the chair out, swung it around and straddled it, his arms crossed over the back. It felt stupidly formal, like this was an interrogation or something, and he wished he'd gone to sit immediately at Cesare's side. Trouble was, that would have made it too easy to pull him close and too easy to avoid the questions that had to be asked.

"I mean," Cesare corrected himself, "are you… angry at me?"

It was a stupid question. He knew that, didn't he? Dan's throat tightened and he shook his head.

"No. Of course not."

"I think you were right, what you said before. I should have been honest. If I had just—"

"Well, there's no point in what-ifs now, is there?"

Dan didn't mean to sound brusque, but he couldn't watch Cesare descend into self-pity and hopelessness. Not now. He listened while Cesare retold the story, relaying everything the principal had said, every innuendo and cloaked threat. He knew, which meant the secret was out. The entire business with Niccolò was little more than another convenient smokescreen, something to hide personal prejudice and bitterness behind, and to Dan it seemed just as gutless as the trumped-up accusation of Cesare's lying by omission in the first place.

It was unthinkable to Dan: something archaic and medieval, stumbling blind and unwieldy out of a bygone age. This was supposed to be the dawn of a new century… though he knew it was true that things never changed fast enough. He wished he'd been more sympathetic all those times that Cesare had said coming out would change his whole life. It didn't seem so much like an excuse anymore.

"So," Cesare said finally, his voice husky. "*È finita.* That is it. *Mi sono stancato.*"

"No." Dan shook his head. "I mean… I understand you don't want to make a big appeal, you won't go public about it, but—"

"It wouldn't help." Cesare steepled his fingers, their tips pressed to his lips, and closed his eyes, almost as if he were at prayer. "Not me, not Niccolò, not… not anybody."

Dan sat heavily on the urge to argue. He knew, in Cesare's place, he would have acted differently. He'd have been ranting, railing, calling every newspaper he could and launching the biggest public appeal the country had ever seen… but it wasn't his fight, and he wasn't in Cesare's place. He was just sitting here, watching the man he'd never meant to care so deeply about suffer.

Dan hadn't thought it was possible to be so coldly, agonizingly furious and still be able to function. He wanted to run out into the street or up onto the rooftop and just bellow his anger and frustration at the sky. Obviously that wouldn't be much use to anyone, but he'd feel better.

He cleared his throat.

"Um… look. So far, all that's concrete is that you won't be working at the school anymore. Right?"

Cesare glanced up at him, a frown lodged between those dark, pen-stroke brows. He nodded.

"Right." Dan bit the inside of his lip. "Then… if the principal's not going to, uh, make any big declarations, you don't have to either. It makes sense, doesn't it? You just say it was a disagreement over policy, and… stick with that. As far as everyone's concerned, including your family, that's all it is. And if you don't push for unfair dismissal, it stays that way. Fine for everyone."

He blinked rapidly and looked away, abandoning Cesare's gaze in favor of the hotel carpet.

"You're angry with me," Cesare observed.

"No." Dan shook his head. "Not with you. With…. This is ridiculous, you know? You shouldn't have to—They can't do this to you, and you shouldn't let them. You should—"

He broke off sharply, hearing the way the words sounded. It wasn't his right to tell Cesare what to do. He knew that, but knowing it didn't make the thing any easier to swallow.

"Fuck," he muttered, standing up and pushing away from the chair.

So much of the time they'd spent together had been in bland, square little rooms like this. Right now it didn't seem like there'd ever be anything else to life, and Dan hated it. He craned his neck back, staring up at the patchy ceiling, feeling the stretch in his cramped, sore muscles.

He'd do it. That was the worst thing. He knew he would. If Cesare wanted, Dan would play it his way. Hotels, passing visits, and charades of innocence performed against a conspiracy of silence. It wasn't much of a life, but he'd take it—and that was about as uncomfortable as truths got. There wasn't much alternative, was there? Dan couldn't see Cesare ever leaving his parents, not after everything he'd done for them, and what options would he really have in London?

Dan got by in the capital, but only because he'd been incredibly lucky financially. His mother had helped him buy his first flat, and his work supported him, so long as he kept costs down. The trip to Venice had been the biggest expense he'd lavished on himself in years, and *this* trip was going to leave a serious dent in his credit card. European Union membership might mean that, if Cesare came to live with him, immigration would be a relatively surmountable possibility, but would he be permitted to work in England? Neither his English nor his qualifications would be acceptable for general teaching, Dan assumed, but could that change?

Maybe they could find him training or some other kind of work. Teaching Italian, perhaps, or private tutoring? Dan felt as if he was jumping the gun, but they were questions that would have to be asked, even though he knew Cesare was unlikely to entertain the prospect of leaving his family behind.

"No," Cesare said.

Just one word, soft and simple, but it seemed loud in the blank, quiet little room. Dan frowned and looked at him, confused.

"What?"

"If I do that, I am still lying, still pretending... as if I had done something wrong. No more. Is not wrong, Daniel. Not me, not you—not what I did to help Niccolò. None of it. Also, I think that people will still talk. Is better now to be honest, to tell the truth, than to have anyone I care about hear these things from someone else." He took a deep breath, the panic evident on his face. "I am going to do it. Besides, if I don't, what life for us, eh?"

"Us...?"

Cesare looked beseechingly at him, so much unsaid in his face.

"I don't want to move too fast, Daniel, but I don't want a life that does not include you. So, no more hotels, no more smiling and saying nothing when Mamma ask me, 'you going to bring home a nice girl?'. No more. No more for me, and no more for us. I want something better than this, you understand?"

Dan nodded weakly and tried to swallow past the lump in his throat. He couldn't look Cesare in the eye. And to think this was the man he'd accused of cowardice. He blinked and studied the arrow of flesh at the top of Cesare's shirt, that solid column of a neck that bore so much. The pulse seemed to beat faster there, and the muscles of his jaw twitched.

"I love you," he said quietly.

The words slipped out without Dan meaning to say them, just a small, calm assertion of fact. He forced himself to meet Cesare's gaze, finding his face strangely blank, as if he hadn't heard or understood.

"And I think you're brave. Anything you want," Dan added, his tongue almost stumbling, his lips feeling numb and loose. "I'll… I'll be here. Anything you need. Any way I can help."

Cesare's expression softened just a little, his mouth curling into the promise of a smile.

"I love you too, Daniel," he said quietly, warmth filling his eyes. "*Grazie.*"

Dan exhaled, not sure why he felt so dizzy, like the floor was trying to pitch him off-balance. All the same, he needed to speak now, to say anything just to break the silence.

"Are you hungry?" He could hear how falsely bright his voice sounded, but he plugged on anyway. "We can get something to eat. There's a carvery or something downstairs… no idea if it's any good or not."

Cesare nodded again, and Dan saw how important the talking was for him—just the sound of someone else stopping the empty air from closing in on him. He kept talking, aware that most of it was rubbish.

"My sister worked in a hotel kitchen once, in London. Quite a posh chain. She was only dishwashing, but some of the stories she told me… I'm amazed I ever actually eat out, even now."

Cesare gave a small, dry chuckle and stood up slowly, moving as if every muscle ached.

"You are funny," he said, smiling. "And I love you very much, Daniel. You make me a lucky man."

Dan looked away, stupidly embarrassed. The still-fresh memory of that strange, intense kiss Cesare had planted on him in the lobby played across his lips, and he stifled a smile.

"*Andiamo,*" Cesare said, crossing the room and reaching for the door handle. "And, perhaps, after dinner… I can stay tonight?"

He peered shyly at Dan from under his lashes, and Dan almost wanted to laugh. Only Cesare could ask that and seem as if he genuinely needed to be told the answer.

"You'd damn well better."

DINNER WAS a simple, pleasant meal. They wandered down to the hotel's mediocre restaurant, ordered from a mediocre a la carte menu, and split a bottle of fairly substandard Pinot, all while exchanging musings on the sales conference attendees and the scatterings of other guests.

Cesare loosened up a bit with the wine and smiled properly for the first time since Dan had met him here. They laughed, joked, talked about normal, everyday things—and the world didn't appear to stop turning.

"Oh, damn... 'scuse me," Dan said, midway through dessert, as his phone beeped a text alert.

He checked the message and grinned before shutting it off, causing Cesare to raise an inquiring eyebrow.

"My friend, Chris. He's asking whether I think he should suggest Jamaica, Paris, or Italy for a honeymoon. He's getting married," he added. "They haven't set a date yet."

Cesare smiled encouragingly, and Dan paused before tacking on any further explanation, not sure how Cesare would take it.

"When I say 'they,' I mean he and his boyfriend."

He watched Cesare's expression slowly change, slipping from genial interest, through disbelief, to coyly prurient curiosity.

"They're both nice guys," Dan added, and gave Cesare a brief summary of how he knew Chris and Sada, and the chaotic, tangled, beautiful mess of their relationship. "Remember? I showed you the pictures of his installation. The one with the—"

"Balls?" Cesare supplemented to Dan's vague gesticulations.

They both grinned, Cesare's smile widening as he realized the double entendre he'd made. He gave a little shrug, indicating as politely as possible that Sada's plaster spheres were a tiny bit ridiculous.

"That's the one. Yeah."

Dan watched him for a while, unable to wipe the smile from his lips. He'd wondered if bringing up Chris and Sada's impending nuptials might be a bit like running a lab experiment on Cesare, just to see how he reacted, but Dan felt more comfortable about it now. So comfortable that he couldn't help his mind wandering into strange, glittering fantasy realms.

Could he see his own future stretching out like that? Him and Cesare? Snatched scenes flickered through his head of all the things they might be, say, do... city breaks in Prague and Amsterdam, lazy holidays on pristine beaches, maybe even some commitment more permanent than shared travel plans.

They weren't the sorts of things Dan usually found himself contemplating comfortably. But for once the thoughts weren't intimidating. They were just maybes and possibilities, cobwebbed together in a string of potential futures. He reached for his wineglass and let his knuckles brush the back of Cesare's hand, pushed to a shy smile when he didn't pull away.

I love you.

The words stayed unsaid, yet the meaning seemed to shimmer in the air between them. The corner of Cesare's mouth curled into a knowing smile, and he lifted his own glass, mirroring Dan in a toast.

"*Salute.*"

"*Salute,*" Dan echoed.

Cesare smiled.

UPSTAIRS, DAN didn't bother to turn the light on. He swiped his key card through the lock and shivered at the feel of Cesare's warm breath on his nape.

They didn't speak. Dan supposed they either didn't need to, or they were both too tired. Though the mundane crap of air and rail travel, as well as the drama of the past few days, had really caught up with him, Dan kind of hoped it was the not needing to option, rather than the exhaustion one. Achy back and gritty eyes notwithstanding, he wanted the assurance of Cesare's body close to his, skin on skin, and hot mouths searing away the uncertainties.

Cesare seemed to be thinking along the same lines because he pressed a kiss to the back of Dan's neck and squeezed his bicep through his shirt.

"*Mi fai impazzire, amore.* You know that? You drive me crazy. I want you."

Dan smiled. He wasn't so tired he couldn't think of a dozen things he'd like to do to the owner of that sexy purr. He wondered briefly how long they'd have to spend with each other before the edge got worn off their sex life—certainly, last week hadn't been long enough.

"You can have me," he murmured in response to Cesare's words. "*Bisogno te.*"

"*Ho bisogno di te,*" Cesare corrected as they backed into the room, Dan then wheeling him around against the door for a long, wet kiss.

He tasted of wine and spice, and the rules of grammar had rarely been less important.

"Whatever," Dan muttered, breaking long enough to peel off his shirt.

Cesare laughed and claimed his mouth again. His hands traced Dan's arms and back over and over, just delicate whispers of touch as if he thought too much contact might wake them both from some transient dream. Dan dealt with the buttons of Cesare's shirt, slipping his fingers into the dark thatch of hair on his chest that he always seemed to miss so badly. Crisp curls tickled his palms as he pushed the fabric away and tackled Cesare's fly, wanting them both naked as fast as possible.

Shirts were dropped to the ground, and the dim, blue-tinged light painted both their bodies. Cesare stepped back toward the bed, his fingers twined into Dan's, and gazed at him, his eyes looking almost black, the dusk-smudged shadows softening the lines of his face. He pulled Dan close, his touch more decisive now, strong fingers trailing a path down his torso, pausing to toy with his nipple.

One last kiss, and Cesare sat on the coverlet, letting go of Dan's hand and focusing on unbuttoning his jeans for him. Dan held his breath, his cock achingly hard, straining against the confines of pants and underwear as his lover worked slowly on his fly. He let his hand fall to Cesare's head, running his fingers through that dark shock of hair, his body tightening with the anticipation of that full, hot mouth. Cesare eased the jeans down, pausing to kiss his stomach and trace the swells of muscle and flesh, his breath a ticklish graze against Dan's skin as he fumbled his way to his prize.

Dan exhaled slowly as the air hit his cock. He was already nearly fully hard, and Cesare wasted no time in pressing his lips to the shaft, running chains of warm, wet kisses along his length. His broad palm cupped Dan's balls, juggling them deftly as, with a soft grunt of pleasure, Cesare took him into his mouth, tongue dancing an intoxicating swirl on the underside of his head.

"Fuck," Dan murmured, his grip on Cesare's hair tensing.

The man was getting seriously good at this.

Cesare made another small, deep grunt of amused delight and began to suck him: slow, measured strokes that soon had Dan rocking his hips to their irresistible rhythm. The room was silent except for the wet suction of Cesare's mouth and the gulps of his breathing overlapping with Dan's soft gasps.

"Oh… can't hold out if you do that," he warned, as Cesare quickened his pace.

In answer, Cesare just looked up at him, those dark eyes so full of affection, gratitude, and lust. Next to the flare of his cheekbones, skin drawn tight and lips stretched around Dan's slick shaft, it was impossibly erotic.

Dan let his hand slip from Cesare's head, sliding down so that his palm rested against the side of his lover's face. His thumb on Cesare's cheek, Dan felt the movement of his dick within that hot, willing mouth, each bobbing thrust taking him closer to a star of ecstasy that swelled ever greater, until it threatened to fill up everything.

He was nearly there when Cesare pulled away, and the loss was a visceral one.

"Ah!"

"I'm sorry. Daniel, I want to… uh…."

Cesare's hand ran up the outside of Dan's thigh, his expression pleading as he tried to find the word he needed. Dan felt strong fingers rub the curve of his ass, and understood.

"Sure," he said, still somewhat breathless, but impressed by Cesare's newfound assertiveness. "Have you got a condom?"

A look of intense pain flickered across Cesare's face, and he swore blasphemously. It fractured the intensity of the moment, and Dan spluttered with laughter, stroking his cheek once more before he stumbled to his suitcase and the possibility that he hadn't yet unpacked the rubbers and lube stashed in the end pocket from last week.

Relief washed through him as his fingers closed on the essentials, and he turned back to Cesare, triumphant.

"Ta-da!"

It occurred to Dan there was something faintly ridiculous about saying that as he stood there in the semidarkness, naked and still with most of a hard-on, brandishing a pump of lube and a brightly wrapped condom. He supposed there must be, because he started to laugh again, and then Cesare was laughing too, and the whole thing seemed incredibly, hysterically funny.

It was catharsis of a kind, and it lasted until Cesare got up, pulled him into a hug, and kissed him, hands tenderly cupping his jaw.

"*Ti amo tantissimo*," he murmured, his voice throbbing straight from Dan's ear to his groin. "So much, I can't say."

His hard cock grazed Dan's, their bodies pressed close together, and Dan was tempted to grind against him, latch on and not let him go until they were both done, writhing and coming in a jumbled ecstasy of bodies and limbs.

But that wasn't what Cesare had asked for, and if he wanted Dan's ass, he was going to get it.

"*Fallo,*" Dan whispered, tugging Cesare's wrist as he edged him back toward the bed. "That's right, isn't it? Do it. *Facciamolo.*"

Cesare gave him a wolfish, lustful grin, and Dan decided there were definite benefits to studying foreign languages.

It was different from the way they'd done it before. Dan lay on his back, welcoming Cesare between his legs, no reticence at all now in the loose, hungry kisses they traded, so changed from that first time, that first day in Venice. It didn't matter that Cesare was unused to the position and the role. Clumsy but eager, he let Dan guide him in, showing him how to smooth the path with fingers and lube, until his thick cock entered with surprising ease.

"*Ah, cazzo!*" Cesare murmured, his head lolling forward, his bottom lip caught between his teeth.

Dan reached up and lazily rubbed his shoulder, luxuriating in the hot burn of that cock filling him, slow and insistent. He wrapped his free hand around his own shaft, wanting all at once to stroke himself off fast and to let the pleasure last forever.

"C'mon," he urged, spreading his legs wider, his heels against Cesare's ass. "Fuck me."

Cesare moaned low in his throat, leaning down over Dan as he began to thrust, and seeking his mouth. He kissed long and deep, the breath catching between them as he tried to strike a rhythm. Dan wrapped his arms around Cesare, hands skimming the smooth, warm skin of his back, veering up to knot impatient fingers in his hair.

Cesare's cock stroked deep inside him, the weight and the friction of his body above Dan heightening every sensation. He let himself make some noise, not caring if the other rooms on this floor were occupied or whether anyone could hear them. It seemed important to let Cesare know that he was doing well—that his every touch was like a searing line of bliss—and that he was wanted, desired, needed, and loved.

"Fuck!" Dan groaned again, tugging on Cesare's hair.

Practice might make perfect, but enthusiasm counted for a hell of a lot, and Cesare was pounding him harder, hunched over his body and surging in wave after wave, panting and sweating. Every thrust struck Dan's prostate, pleasure pooling at the base of his spine and heat flooding his limbs. He jacked his own cock faster, wetting Cesare's belly with his precome, the boundaries between them rapidly blurring. His hand, Cesare's hand… fingers winding around him, skin touching skin, and hot, hard flesh stroking faster within him, striking at his most tender, secret spots.

Cesare's mouth latched onto his once more, the two of them squeezed tight together. Cesare's hips bucked ever more erratically and cry after escalating cry echoed through the damp, hot slivers of space between them. It had never felt so open, so intimate.

Cesare leaned his forehead on Dan's shoulder, the weight of his body increasing as his arms gave way, his climax intense and unstoppable. He cursed and roared, and perhaps even more—Dan was too close to his own peak to stop and examine him closely, but those dark eyes did seem a little wet. He came with Cesare's lips on his neck, Cesare's hand on his dick, and Cesare's cock still embedded in his ass, the two of them as near to one body as they could get.

Afterward, neither of them seemed able to do much except lie there tangled up in each other and totally enervated. Cesare loosed a small, soft laugh, and without looking, Dan raised a hand and ruffled his hair, a satisfied grin slipping across his face. Cesare caught his hand and pulled it down to his mouth for a kiss before letting it go and wrapping his arm around Dan's waist.

Dan could feel sleep creeping up on both of them, at once an unwelcome thief and a delicious prospect. He yawned.

"*Come va?*" Cesare's fingers flexed just above Dan's navel and gave him a gentle tickle.

Dan smiled. "*Va bene.* That's right, isn't it?"

"*Sì.* Very good."

He snorted. "My Italian's rubbish. It's a good job I've got other talents, isn't it?"

Cesare chuckled sleepily. "*Ehi*, I don't know…. We are all learning, *amore. I* am learning, with you."

He kissed the point of Dan's shoulder and laid his head back against the pillow, his breaths already lengthening out and every ounce of tension apparently gone. Dan thought about the sentiment for a moment and supposed it was true. They were learning, both of them. So much. Certainly, he could see now the way things would have to be, the choices and the sacrifices that would have to be made.

They were at the start of a long journey and not an easy one.

Still, Dan wasn't deterred. He couldn't remember wanting anything more.

CHAPTER TWENTY-FOUR

OVER BREAKFAST they tried to talk out a plan of action, but Dan worried the daylight had burned away some of Cesare's resolve. He looked white and pinched at the prospect of speaking to his parents and started to backpedal, saying he didn't even know how many people in Gravagna were talking about him.

"Does it matter?" Dan asked. "You said the point was being honest. That's the only thing that stops the rumors having power."

Cesare scoffed and muttered something about rumors being powerful enough to cost him his job. Dan sighed.

"Yes, but if you don't want to appeal that...."

"I know. I know. *Va bene.* I don't want to, but... ah. Is hard."

"Yeah." Dan deposited a glob of jam on his croissant and looked gloomily at it as it seeped stickily over the edge of the pastry. He still wasn't sure whether the preserve was supposed to be raspberry or strawberry. "Have you thought about who it might have been?"

Cesare shook his head.

"Someone who saw us during the week, maybe," Dan volunteered, wondering if it was really a good idea to put words to his suspicions. "Or someone who knows you very well...."

"Eh?" Cesare frowned. "You think, what, is—? You think they already know, they are—"

His voice rose in pitch, anger flaring his face somewhere behind the fatigue and fear. Dan hated seeing it, and he wrinkled his nose, trying to dismiss the argument before it started.

"I don't know. I'm just thinking aloud. I mean, who's to say it's even one person? You said yourself how whispers go."

Cesare's mouth twisted ruefully. He poured himself another cup of coffee from the cafetiere that sat between them on the white-clothed table, and said nothing. Across the dining room, a few of the sales conference guests were tottering in, all clad in shiny pinstriped suits and dreadful ties, to broach a small repast. For hungover middle-aged men, their voices were loud and obnoxiously jovial, and Dan wished the ground would open and swallow them, and maybe take the whole hotel with them.

He was so fed up with hotels. He'd done it for Cesare, though. A gesture of compassion, not compounding everything that seemed to be going on in Gravagna, not "giving people reason," as Dan remembered his own mother putting it when he was younger. Not that she hadn't always been supportive of him—she had. But, when he was a stupid, arrogant, self-conscious, and ragingly hormonal teenager, and had wanted to do stupid, hormonal things like bleach his hair, and pair tacky jewelry with cheap, crude T-shirts emblazoned with cock jokes, she'd eased back on her unconditional acceptance.

Don't make people uncomfortable, she'd said, *and it won't come back on you, love*.

He hadn't understood what she meant then, and it had led to one of their very few blazing rows: him yelling that he didn't have to apologize for anything, her losing her temper and saying he was still under her roof and her rules… just like any other family, he supposed.

The point was, there *wasn't* anything to apologize for. Dan knew that, but he knew now that subtlety wasn't necessarily apology. It wasn't necessarily hiding, or lying. It was about not having to make the statement in order to be accepted, because that acceptance should not have to be asked for.

He bit into the croissant and wished he was religious enough to pray that Cesare's parents could think that way too. He suspected Cesare had prayed this morning—there had definitely been distinct murmuring in the bathroom.

Dan supposed it was mildly disheartening that the nearest he'd got to beseeching for divine intervention was texting Chris with a quick explanation of what was going on and asking him to wish them luck. He'd had a message back almost immediately. Typically Chris, typically flippant, and almost enough to leave the weight of tears behind Dan's eyes.

Told u love's a fucker. Knew u lied abt the olive farm. xxx

Now he looked across the table at Cesare and shook his head at the memory. He did love this man, and he wanted not only Cesare's safety, security, and happiness, but the promise of something they could both depend on.

If that meant changing his own life too, so be it.

THEY DROVE out to Gravagna Montale later that morning, Cesare still worryingly tight-lipped and quiet. He surprised Dan by picking a fight in the car, snippy and irritable until he got to the crux of what must have been bothering him.

"This make you happy now, huh?"

"What?"

Dan frowned, no idea what he was talking about. Cesare scowled at the road ahead. The sky had grayed, the hint of a summer cloudburst threatening above them.

"Is what you wanted that I should do, isn't it? All along."

Cesare didn't take his eyes off the road, but the words hung heavy between them nonetheless. Dan held the tip of his tongue in his teeth for a moment before answering, aware that it was up to him not to let Cesare do this to himself.

"No," he said, keeping his voice calm despite the urge to give in and snip right back at him. "I didn't agree with you hiding who you are, fair enough. But I see why now. And I'd never have wanted it to happen like this. You know that."

Cesare snorted and mumbled something in Italian, the meaning of which Dan decided not to guess at. It irritated him, and he felt a flicker of fear at the thought this thing could break them. After all, it could, so easily. Cesare might end up resenting him, not for any part Dan had played in this sudden and ugly turn of events, but just for his very existence. He'd been the wrong man in the wrong place at the wrong time, and maybe that was all it would need to sour how Cesare saw him.

Dan hoped it was only irritation that made him think like that, although he suspected there might be a little truth in there too. In any case, whether he was right in suspecting Gianni or not, those wonderful hazy days last week, strolling around the sunbaked hillsides and cobbled streets, had probably been the catalyst that started this whole thing.

It pissed Dan off immeasurably to find himself combing through the memories, trying to pick out any moment, any incident, when he'd looked at his lover the wrong way, let himself slip and betrayed them both with an affectionate smile, a casual touch.... No. He wasn't prepared, even in the privacy of his own head, to attribute any of this as his fault—or Cesare's fault, come to that. Neither of them had done anything wrong.

The first drops of rain began to patter against the windshield as Gravagna's rolling hills rose up either side of the road, dotted with the crumbling remnants of old farmhouses and homesteads. Dan had wound his window down a crack, trying to leaven the hot, dry air inside the car with a breath of wind, and now rain streaked the glass, the air outside smelling of that familiar combination of grit, scorched grass, and lemons.

Dan glanced at Cesare, pleased at least that he'd stopped mumbling. His lips still moved occasionally, silent genuflections that might have been traces of prayer or half-remembered words to an old song. There was so much tension in his body, his arms locked and his shoulders hunched as he drove, barely blinking. Not for the first time that day, Dan wished they could just drive and keep driving, never stopping until they got so far away that nothing else would matter.

"So," he said. "What's the plan?"

"*Non so,*" Cesare murmured, shaking his head. "I-I don't know what to do."

They'd talked about it a little last night over dinner. For all the fantasies he kept to himself about whisking Cesare off to London and a magical life of freedom and opportunity, Dan had tried to be sensible. He'd asked what the likelihood might be of Cesare successfully applying for a job at another school, and it had seemed hopeful. Apparently, although Dan was still slightly confused by the convoluted system of government, there were seventeen *comuni* in the province of Massa-Carrara, and it would be possible—should he find no other employment in Pontremoli—for Cesare to apply to somewhere nearer Villafranca di Lunigiana, or Fivizzano, or perhaps even farther afield.

He hadn't sounded enthusiastic, though, and Dan guessed that was to do with more than just the inflated commute time.

Dan settled back into the Fiat's uncomfortably warm upholstery and watched the village draw closer, disliking the thick, foreboding silence that filled the car, but unable to find anything that would break it.

THE STREET itself was quiet when Cesare parked a few yards down from his apartment building, though the shrieking laughter of children echoed on brickwork somewhere close by. He glanced at Dan for a moment before he got out of the car, and he seemed as if he wanted to say something, but what it was Dan did not discover.

He got out and followed Cesare up to the warm, buttercream stone of the building's frontage, and waited while he grabbed a handful of mail from the peeling, green-painted box on the wall. Dan pretended not to peer over his shoulder, half expecting some crude scrap of paper with a foul message of abuse scrawled across it, or maybe an unwrapped condom or skillfully disguised dog crap concealed in a twist of plastic. Any one of those tasteful touches that lets a guy know he's welcome in the neighborhood.

There wasn't anything, though—at least nothing worse than what appeared to be bills and utility statements. A motorbike engine fizzed a couple of streets away, and Cesare's back tensed, his shoulders rising a good half inch. Dan had already started to raise his hand, reaching out to him before he caught himself and, bitterly, supposed the gesture was not welcome.

Anger at that, at Cesare, at his own reaction, and—right now—at pretty much everything, churned in his gut, but Dan clamped down on it. All he had to do was get Cesare through this, day by day, until things were clear enough to see where they were going.

After that, the hard choices started.

He breathed in, the scent of the potted geraniums by the door sharp and clean against the thick air, and followed Cesare up to the apartment.

Once inside, safe again in his own space, shut away from the world, Cesare seemed to relax a little, though he still looked pale and drawn. He tossed his car keys down and ran his hand over his hair, giving a long sigh that sounded so defeated it made Dan want to hit him. Instead he just cleared his throat.

"Hey," he said quietly. "Come here."

Cesare looked at him, seemingly confused until Dan held out his arms. In that instant his face softened, and none of the carping and the argumentative spikiness mattered.

"*Non ne posso più*," he murmured, his body hitting Dan's in an urgent collision of need, face pressed to his neck, arms locked around him. "*Come posso…?*"

"It's okay," Dan soothed. "*Va bene*, yeah? It's gonna be okay."

They stayed like that for a long while. Dan didn't count the seconds or minutes; he just held on, waiting to feel the tension start to slip from

Cesare's frame. Eventually it did begin to happen. His breathing slowed, and the warmth of the embrace seemed to loosen the tightness in his muscles. He pulled back a little, enough to press a clumsy, needy kiss to Dan's mouth, full of hope and gratitude.

Dan cupped the back of Cesare's neck, his other arm around that broad waist, and returned the kiss, deeper and fuller, not letting Cesare move away until they were both out of breath.

No excuses. No room for doubts.

They parted, and Cesare gave him a small, shy smile, though the look in those dark eyes was anything but bashful.

"You know I'm never more than a couple of hours away, don't you?" Dan said softly, fingers still toying with the hair on Cesare's nape. "Any time you need me."

"*Sì.* I know. *Grazie, amore. Grazie di amarmi,*" he added, the words cloaked with another fond smile. "Would… would you like a drink? I think maybe I have one before I call Mamma."

As soon as it had appeared, that heartening calmness began to dissipate again, the same signs of anxiety tucking the corners of Cesare's mouth and eyes, and pulling his dark brows together.

"It's probably something you should be sober for," Dan said, not being entirely serious, "but you've got a point. Anyway, it's always five o'clock somewhere."

Reluctantly he let Cesare go and stuck his hands in the pockets of his jeans. Never more than a couple of hours away… well, it was something of an exaggeration, but the basic point was there. Dan wandered to the french doors and opened them. Heated by all the stonework and brick, the wall of warm, humid air that assailed him from the balcony was like the inside of an oven.

Still, the rain had stopped. Dan had predicted it would be only the briefest of summer showers. He gave one of the wrought-iron chairs a cursory mop with his sleeve before lowering himself to the seat. He didn't feel as if he'd ever been away. Sure, it had turned out to be a pretty brief snatch of time between getting home and leaving again, but it wasn't just that. Dan had a strange, unsettling sense that somehow nowhere else was ever going to feel as familiar as this again.

He looked out over the red roofs and mellow walls, the sloping angles of houses and streets all packed in together and making for an unorganized, jumbled mess of life. Here and there tiny flickers of individuality could be seen: the damp flapping of someone's laundry, caught in the rain, or the nodding foliage of a tree or shrub in a garden. They were small details, but they fitted in among the whole, like puzzle pieces within a bigger picture.

From inside, Dan could hear Cesare checking his messages; a series of different voices played, too muffled and too rapid for him to even try to understand. Cesare muttered something, and the sound was followed by footsteps, then the creak of a cupboard opening, the clink of glasses and the glug of a bottle. Dan didn't turn his head when Cesare came out onto the balcony, edging past the tangle of chair and table legs. It really was too small for two people to sit comfortably out here. He set a glass down before Dan, and about an inch and a half of Bassano grappa washed the sides of the tumbler.

Dan smiled. Cesare let out a short breath as he settled into the other chair, his fingers loosely caressing the sides of his glass. The bottle stood between them, refracted veins of light glinting on the liquor inside.

"Everything okay?" Dan asked cautiously.

"*Sì*. A few people have already heard I lose the job." He shrugged. "News travels fast. Mamma wants me to call her."

"Ah."

Cesare took a long sip of his drink.

"I think," he said slowly, "that I may try to find work as a tutor. Work privately, you say, yes?"

"S'a good idea." Dan considered the notion, unable to stop the brief thought flashing through his head that it was a kind of work which could be done almost anywhere.

One day, maybe. The time wasn't right to have that conversation, but he fancied that he read the hint of possibility between Cesare's words.

"Is flexible," Cesare said. "I could be like you, come and go when I want, not just in holidays. *Angela e Ugo—i signori Misseri*—they say they want me to stay on, keep teaching Niccolò. They can't pay much, but it's a start, and they are very happy with how he has done so far."

"I'd think so." Dan nodded. "I mean, you told me the kid improved enough to move up at the beginning of next term. Sounds like that's all down to you."

"Ah…. Niccolò worked hard." Cesare curled his lip dismissively. "It was just a matter of giving him the time. It always is. With patience, all things come."

"Yeah. I suppose so."

It sounded like a promise.

Dan raised his glass, smiling at the smell of the grappa, so redolent of another place and time. All those months ago, he couldn't have pictured for a second that he'd be sitting here drinking it again now with Cesare.

As the fiery liquid wet his lips, Dan tried to imagine life in another four, five, even six months' time. Would it still feel like this? Would there have been pain and drama, and would they have weathered it together, or would everything have changed again?

Even if it did, and all that was left was the past, Dan wondered if he would be able to remember all this with fondness: a perfect spool of memories caught forever in amber. He hoped so.

It was more than that, though, he realized. More than hope. He believed in it. Believed in *them*. Not that Chris had been right—it was far too soon to run off into the sunset, waving his passport and crowing excitedly about emigration. But... well, it was worth daydreaming about, wasn't it?

He'd thought about it, in the still, dark reaches of the night. About coming out here to be with Cesare, even if the worst happened and his family rejected him, and how, in those fuzzy, fantastical dreams, they could go somewhere else, somewhere more open and accepting. Modena, Padua, La Spezia... even the names sounded faintly magical.

Oh, sure, there would be so much to consider, organize, plan for. It was hard to know where to begin. Dan's first thoughts had been for Edith and the kids, his mother, and his friends. He'd miss them all incalculably—and he'd be missed too. On the other hand, Italy wasn't the other side of the world. Regular visits would be possible and probably unavoidable, he realized, easily able to imagine Chris rescheduling his entire summer out here.

There would be other hassles, if he chose that path. He knew that. Work, tax, the inevitable mountains of paperwork and bureaucratic insanity. Nevertheless, Dan rather liked the idea of being a dissolute expat, living a life of sun-drenched leisure... even though he didn't believe for a second it would really be that way, no matter how good this moment felt right now.

If Cesare lost everything, he'd blame Dan. Maybe not at first, and maybe not even consciously, but the resentment would fester, swelling until it finally exploded, leaving nothing behind it but the ragged remains of what they might have had.

Even if things *did* work out now, Dan reminded himself, it was no assurance of a stable future. Three months from now, or three years, they could still decide the distances and the differences were too great, and call it a day. Or—just maybe—they'd still feel this way in three decades' time, and even when the hill farms and the last olive groves were all concreted over, they might look back and say that this had all been worth it.

Yet for the first time in his life, that didn't worry Dan. The possibilities, the open-ended trails of things that might be, seemed exciting and wonderful—not for what might lie at the end of them, but just for the fact they were there.

He glanced across the table at Cesare and realized how much he'd learned from him… and how much there was still to be learned.

They drank the grappa in silence, just content to sit and take pleasure from the moment's tranquility. After he'd finished, Cesare stared morosely into the bottom of his empty glass and sighed.

"I will go and call her. I think… I go for a *cena* tonight, I can talk to them and, maybe, is not so bad."

Dan nodded. "I'll wait for you."

"Oh." Cesare held his gaze for a moment, then blinked and looked away hurriedly. "I thought, perhaps—"

"What, you want me to come with you?"

He hadn't expected that. He'd assumed it was something Cesare would want to do alone—something Dan shouldn't trespass into. Yet there was no denying him, not when he turned on those sad eyes and gave Dan such a solemn, vulnerable look.

"Please?"

"Sure." Dan sighed. "I mean, if you don't think it's…. If it's not going to be awkward."

Cesare shook his head. "I want you with me, Daniel. Please."

"Okay."

The word was a shallow scrape against the air, and Dan looked away, burying his nose in his glass and knocking back more of the grappa than he knew he should have in one mouthful.

THE WAITING was probably the worst part and not only because there had been too much of it in recent months. As the gray, rain-washed afternoon gave way to the start of a blurry dusk, Dan was convinced that nothing could possibly happen that would be any worse than the myriad of horrible fantasies he'd pictured.

In his mind's eye, anything and everything went wrong from tears to violence and back again and, by the time Cesare was changing his shirt and checking his appearance in the bedroom mirror, Dan was sure they must be as nervous as each other.

"Ready?" he asked, one shoulder propped against the bedroom doorjamb.

Cesare glanced at him and nodded, looking pale and sweaty.

"*Sì. Andiamo.*"

Dan gave him a weak smile and, as Cesare passed him in the doorway, he touched his arm.

"Hey. Just remember to breathe, all right?"

Cesare frowned, probably not fully understanding.

"I mean, um... *stare calmo, sì?*" Dan tried.

Cesare smiled and nodded, his pallid nervousness broken through for a moment with something that looked a lot like gratitude.

"*Sì. Ehi...* I like when you speak *italiano*. Is very sexy."

Dan laughed. His body close like this, Cesare still smelled of oranges, cornfields, and musk, and he leaned in, pressing a brief, sweet kiss to Dan's mouth.

"*Andiamo.*"

"Yeah."

He followed Cesare down to the street, and they walked slowly through the softening lines of the old houses, a light breeze rippled at the edges of the day's discarded warmth.

Lights burned in the Eveschi house, though it was still too early to really need them, and the red and pink blooms spilling from Luisa's window boxes and planters seemed incongruously bright against the thinning light.

"*Maiala della miseria,*" Cesare murmured, apparently to himself.

Dan doubted whether he'd get through the evening at this rate and wished he could reach out and touch his lover's hand... any kind of small, innocent gesture that could just let him know he wasn't alone.

There wasn't time for it, though. The well-polished door opened and Luisa stepped out to greet them, all smiles and cheek kisses. Her perfume reminded Dan of starched sheets and spring flowers, and he almost wished they could have been here with no other motive than a nice, peaceful meal.

"It is very nice to see you again, Daniel," she said, smiling warmly at him. "I am pleased you come back."

"Pleased to be back," he croaked. "Nice to see you again."

She squeezed his arm before turning her attention to Cesare. Her critical glance seemed to take in every inch of him from head to toe, and her smile dropped a little when she spoke—too rapid for Dan to catch, though it sounded like a question.

"*Non è niente, non è niente, Mamma,*" Cesare said, his words peeling away into a stream of Italian that Dan didn't understand.

He followed them indoors, meek and silent, and let Luisa usher him into the kitchen. It took him a while to adjust to her quick-fire, slipshod English, a curious mix of old-fashioned phrases, strange word orders and intonations, and disorientating slides back into Italian when she couldn't find the word she wanted.

Luca rose from his chair at the kitchen table to greet them, pumping Dan's hand enthusiastically before turning to hug his son. Cesare looked queasy and tight-lipped, and Dan felt equally off-balance, as if the whole thing was some dizzy, surreal trance. Sweat prickled at the base of his spine.

The meal hadn't been planned in advance, so there was no hearty Tuscan cooking this time, just a chicken salad that Dan was invited to share. He sat gratefully and wondered how the hell he was supposed to eat anything.

He picked dutifully at the food nonetheless. Balsamic vinegar and black pepper laid sharp and sickly on his tongue. Cesare and his parents were still talking, and Dan could pick out enough to realize that Luca had mentioned the school. His thick, gray brows drew together, that face that was so much like Cesare's clouded with a tension that seemed to run close to annoyance.

Cesare's voice grew tighter, and Dan watched him talk, wishing he could keep up with the words. Cesare definitely referred to Niccolò Misseri, and Signor Alvisio, and Dan heard the outraged passion in his tone as he seemed to be recounting at least one version of what the principal had said.

"Ah! *Non ci credo!*"

Luca threw his hands up and rattled off a string of words that Dan guessed, from the way Luisa pursed her lips, were probably not in most phrasebooks. She put her hand on her husband's wrist and looked at Cesare, a terrible disappointment and sadness in her face.

Dan glanced nervously at Cesare, aching with the desire to touch him the same way, just some simple gesture of comfort, and feeling ever more useless. He didn't understand most of the conversation, couldn't make any contribution, and wished fervently that Cesare hadn't wanted him here.

Luisa took that moment to meet his gaze, and she smiled awkwardly. Dan's pulse thudded, a stupid, fleeting terror slipping through him.

"Daniel… you please to can help me *un momento?*"

She held out one long, slim hand, palm toward him, gesturing to the coffeemaker on the cluttered kitchen worktop. Dan knew a sizable hint when he saw one.

"*Mi piacere,*" he said, and she smiled, rather like someone encouraging a not terribly bright child who's just learning to talk.

The kitchen was not large enough for Luisa's ploy to get them out of earshot, but it did put a little space between them and whatever was going on between Cesare and his father.

It sounded, if not like an argument, then at least a very excitable exchange, and Dan could barely focus on the things Luisa asked him to do. Open the canister of ground coffee, fetch a filter for the machine…. His fingers felt numb and fat, his brain stuck in a circle of cursing himself for being bad enough at this stupid language that he couldn't even wade in on Cesare's defense—couldn't even tell if he *needed* defending.

He managed to get the coffee from the can to the machine without spilling it, and Luisa leaned across him to turn it on, a shop-bought box of Cantucci di Prato in her other hand. The coffee machine began to hum and burp quietly to itself, and she blinked, staring down at the box of biscotti she held.

"*Quanto…,*" she began, the slight frown on her brow partially obscured by her hair until she reached up and tucked the pale strands behind her ear. "Ah. No. I-I am pleased, Daniel. Truly."

She glanced up at him, and the world seemed to lurch very slightly on its axis. Dan swallowed, his mouth dry and his tongue rough against the roof of his mouth.

"Um, I'm sorry. I don't—"

"Pleased you come back to Toscana," she said.

"Oh. Right." Dan fought the urge to lean against the counter for support. "Well, it's… it's very beautiful here. I—I like it. A lot."

"*Sì*." Luisa gave him a strange, small smile. "I see that."

His stomach tightened into a cold, hard ball. She knew… she must do. This was one of those awkward "saying things without saying things" exchanges, and Dan hated them. He was never sure whether he was not-saying the same things as the other person wasn't. He wondered how long she'd known, what he should say, whether Cesare knew that she knew, or—

"*Conosco i miei polli*," Luisa said with a shrug, her delicate fingers ripping open the top of the box of biscotti.

"Er.…"

The idiom was lost on Dan. Wrong-footed, he was trying to work out what she meant. Was that something about chickens? He noticed the way she was looking at him then and slowly became aware of what she'd really said.

She smiled at him, her face caught somewhere between kindness and concern, curiosity and suspicion, and he supposed she *should* be suspicious of him. Who was he but an interloper in her son's life? A stranger at the feast who served no purpose but to mess up the seating arrangements and make everything awkward. He tried to smile back and wished fervently that he was braver, and stronger, and better at this.

At the table, things between Cesare and Luca went suddenly and ominously quiet. Dan glanced across, hoping against hope to catch Cesare's eye, and was struck cold at the look on his face.

He's said it, hasn't he? Just like that.

He looked back at Luisa, still adrift and confused. She turned her gaze from Cesare back to Dan, and she didn't smile or give him any soft-eyed, poignant look of understanding. If anything, she seemed harder than she had when he'd come into the kitchen.

That horrible, sickly, taut moment seemed to stretch on into infinity, full of unspoken things and hidden words. Dan sought some kind of hint from Cesare and found a weird peace in his expression as those dark eyes met his. Cesare inclined his head, just once. A muscle tensed in his jaw and the corner of his mouth curled a little, as if he wanted Dan to know it was okay.

It didn't feel okay, but Dan resisted the urge to react. He stood there, numb, silent, and stupid—and waited.

Eventually, Luca blew out a long breath, like a great gust of relief, and sat back in his chair.

"*Non è così importante*," he said, looking at Luisa.

She shook her head but didn't even glance at Cesare. Dan bit his lip, unable to unpick the strange, complex threads strung between the three of them. The coffee machine beeped, and Luisa turned abruptly, dealing with the small practicalities of cups and spoons.

Dan helped her, setting all four cups down before taking his seat back at the table, beside Cesare. It felt different sitting next to him now. Somehow. Two sets of eyes seemed to follow every move, every breath. Dan couldn't deal with it, choked by the claustrophobic sense of being judged, evaluated, and picked apart.

Beneath the thickly varnished, scarred pine of the table, he reached out, zoning in on Cesare's fingers and grabbing hold. Dan squeezed his hand, surprised yet elated to find Cesare responding, his damp palm crushed to Dan's with a desperate, answering pressure.

Just remember to keep breathing.

The silence was deafening. Dan didn't know what to do, what to say, how to react... and then Luisa just leaned forward, the plate of biscotti di Prato in her hand.

"*Ehi, Daniel*," she said with a smile. "*Mangia!*"

He blinked, assailed by a sudden urge to laugh.

"Er... *grazie*."

And that seemed to be all there was to it. He took one, she offered the plate around, and they all sat there, eating biscotti and, before long, chattering away in that muddled mix of Italian and English, as if nothing had happened.

Perhaps nothing had. Dan wasn't sure anymore.

But, he supposed, it made sense. It was how things would be, wasn't it? Whether or not Luisa and Luca had always known, whether or not they liked it, Cesare remained their son. It would be something the family worked around. Tacit acceptance of a thing not spoken of, not outwardly acknowledged.

The thought filled him with cold horror edged with disbelief.

They left eventually, Dan's head ringing with all the questions about photography he'd been asked. It had definitely been a mistake to try and explain Miriam's installation to them, and his nerves were hanging in tatters. Luisa kissed him on both cheeks, Luca did too, and the rain had begun to wash the street outside.

Dan stood there in the dimming evening, waiting as Cesare's parents took turns to hug him, and his cheeks stung with kisses and fine, needling raindrops alike.

Cesare turned to him, smiling beatifically, and the electric light from the hallway caught on the rainwater, the fine mist of it outlining him in a fizzing gold corona.

The front door closed behind them as they started to walk, quietly but firmly. Dan glanced over his shoulder and saw Luisa's face in the cloudy little window beside it. He smiled, and she smiled back, raising her hand and flexing her fingers in an awkward, but—he thought, at least—genuine wave.

Cesare didn't see. He was walking a couple of paces ahead, his hands in his jacket pockets, his head tipped back and his cheeks puffed out as he sighed at the sky, eyes closed against the gentle rain.

"Hey," Dan said, the edges of his voice lined with the echo of Gravagna's ancient stones. "Still breathing?"

Cesare turned his head, and the anxious terror had finally dropped from his face, though he still looked pale. He smiled, a weak but warm curl of his lips, and nodded.

"*Sì*. Yes. I… I am breathing. You were… ah. Wonderful."

He pulled his hand from his pocket and held it out to Dan, fingers slightly crooked, his palm a cup that caught the splintered reflections of moonlight and shadows in it. Raindrops spattered against his skin. Dan looked at him for a moment, thinking of the last time they'd walked down this street in the dark, and how he'd wondered if Cesare really was terrified of eyes behind the shutters. Somewhere, somebody's television was blaring out the tinny soundtrack to a film with car chases and gunfire.

Dan reached out and took his lover's hand, threading his fingers through Cesare's and allowing himself to be pulled near, moving across those last few feet that separated them as if the space didn't exist. Dan walked close to him, breathing in that scent of cloves and citrus, delicious against the crowded night air.

He smiled to himself. Was this really the same man?

"What did you say to them?" he asked.

Cesare shrugged. "Just the truth. That I am… who I am. And I am happy. You were right—I think Gianni was our little bird."

Dan frowned. "What makes you say that?"

"Something Papà said. *Ehi*, it doesn't matter. Gianni and I… we always had our troubles. I don't know if he meant for all of this to happen. Maybe not."

Another shrug. Dan suspected it cloaked a greater degree of pain than Cesare admitted to, and he didn't want to push for details… but it was hard to ignore.

"So, wait… he told the school about what happened in Rome?"

"No!" Cesare shook his head. "What, you think I am an idiot? *Mi famiglia* never knew about that." He curled his lip ruefully. "You know, the bad thing is that, if I *had* tell everyone about that in the first place, it would never have hurt me now. If I had been open from the start…."

Dan said nothing. The irony wasn't lost on him, but it seemed better to let Cesare talk. He appeared to need it, and platitudes weren't going to help.

"No… I think Gianni has just been saying things to his girlfriend, Silvana—you remember her? *Sì.* 'Ah, Cesare, he's too shy, he never goes with women, he never brings home a girl.' He has always said those things, always made me out to be a nobody. Papà asked me if I had told Gianni, if he knew about me. I said no. Now I wonder… I don't know if he ever guessed. But I think he has told Silvana all the places I like to go, and I think he make all he jokes he always like to make about me… and she tells her father. I suppose they have very boring lives, if they have to talk about me."

Cesare's voice was too bitter, despite his attempts at hiding it, for Dan to smile. Still, he privately noted that Gianni's sense of humor probably left a lot to be desired too.

"So, why would that matter? Who's her father? And has your brother really always been like that?"

Cesare wrinkled his nose. "Gianni takes a lot of interest in other people, *caro*. Always, he thinks he could live their lives better than them. Silvana, maybe she is the same way, and her crazy father. Mamma says her father plays golf with a friend of Signor Alvisio." Cesare smiled mirthlessly. "A man on the school board. *Importante.* And I thought they all talk about important business on the green. Not who kisses who. *Stupido*, eh?"

He laughed dryly, and Dan smiled with him.

"That is the only thing I can think of. The only way Signor Alvisio could have known. From there, I think he started to go looking. Try to find something on me. A parking ticket, a library fine... I don't know. *Ehi*, maybe Silvana's father is from Roma. Maybe she has a cousin in the *carabinieri*? *Non so.* I don't even think it matters anymore. People have their whispers. They try so hard to hate. And he couldn't bear me making him look a fool any longer."

All around them, shards of sound slipped from open windows, and somewhere a dog was carrying on a repetitive, high-pitched bark. The misty rain carried the day's warmth with it as well as the dim burr of traffic on the autostrada, not quite distant, yet not quite close enough to truly impinge. The air still smelled of lemons, but the scent was sallow now, lost with the cinders of the night, and perfumed with a hint of wood smoke.

"If Gianni's always said stuff like that," Dan began hesitantly, unsure how far he wanted to push the thought, "did your parents ever... you know? Didn't they suspect, or—?"

Cesare sighed softly. "Maybe. They didn't say so, but then you see how they are. They would never have said anything. Maybe *I* am the stupid one, eh? The only one who was ever hiding it."

Dan opened his mouth to protest at the accusation of stupidity, but Cesare squeezed his hand, seeming to anticipate the words.

"I know, *amore*. I am not stupid. But I was afraid for a long time. They... they don't approve," he added, sounding out the word slowly, as if it weighed heavily on him.

Dan supposed it must do. It must hurt like hell.

"I thought it all went pretty well, though?"

Cesare shrugged again. "*Sì.* Better than I hoped, I suppose. Maybe it wasn't such a shock to them after all. They don't approve, they don't *like* it, but they will be all right. They love me... and they like you."

Dan allowed himself a hint of pride. "Yeah? I like them. And you," he added, nudging Cesare's shoulder with his own. "I like you a lot."

Cesare laughed: not so bitter this time.

"They will pretend it's not there," he said. "Accept it, but not name it. And it will take time, for them. You understand?"

"I think so."

"I am sorry, *amore*. I know you don't want to be, how you say, my 'English friend.'"

"Oh, I don't know." Dan wrinkled his nose. "I can probably live with it."

"*Sì?*"

"Yeah. For you. For now."

Cesare said nothing, but the warmth radiated off him in waves. Leaning close, he kissed Dan's cheek, his lips cold from the fine haze of rain.

Dan smiled. They were nearing Cesare's apartment, and with it the security of four pale walls, within which anything could happen. In time, maybe they even would. He hoped so. He knew things would change, albeit more slowly than he'd like. It would take time, but time was something they could craft between them: perfect, islanded moments strung together like beads of amber, whose secrets were never whispered aloud or opened up to cruel scrutiny. What had begun in that dreamy, languid city of light and water had already grown into something Dan had never imagined he'd just stumble into this way, and it was only just beginning.

For now, though, they had the night, and possibilities gleamed in it like stars.

GLOSSARY OF ITALIAN WORDS AND PHRASES

a presto—See you soon.

amo tutto di te, Daniel! Sì, sì… tanto. Ti amo tanto!—I love everything about you, Daniel! Yes, yes… a lot. I love you so much!

anche tu—You too.

andiamo—Let's go.

angelo mio—My angel.

arsenalotti—Shipbuilders.

bambino, pl. bambini—Child, boy, baby boy.

basta—Just (only).

basta, Niccolò. Ehi, ecco, sì? R… rana—Just, Niccolò. Hey, here, Yes? F… frog.

bauta—Name of a type of mask/costume.

bigoli con l'anara—A Venetian pasta specialty.

bisogno te—Need you.

buongiorno—Good morning.

calle, pl. calli—A narrow street.

campo, pl. campi—A square, literally, a field.

capitano—Captain.

carabinieri—The Italian paramilitary police.

Carnevale—Carnival.

castello—Castle.

castraure—Purple artichokes.

cazzo—Fuck.

cena—Dinner.

centrale—Central.

certo—Sure, certain, definite.

certo è vero—It is certainly true.

che bellissimo—How beautiful.

che bello… fammi sentire quanta voglia hai di me, sì?—How lovely…. Let me hear how much you want me, yes?

che simpatico—How nice.

che volpe!—That fox!

che volpone!—That sly fox!

chiesa, pl. chiese—Church.

ciao—Hello.

cicheti (chiefly in Venice)—Savory snacks or small side dishes, typically served in a bar or informal restaurant.

codardo? Come osi? Non dire cazzate!—Coward? How dare you? Get the fuck out!

colombina—Columbine.

come si dice—How do you say?

come posso—How can I?

come va?—How are you?

comune, pl. comuni—Town council, municipality.

conosco i miei polli—I know my chickens.

conversazione—Conversation.

così! Così, dai…. Daniel, sei tanto bello! Non fermarti, è meraviglioso—So! So, come on. Daniel, you're so nice! Don't stop, it's wonderful.

così dai—Like that.

croissant con crema—Croissant with cream.

croissant con marmellata—Croissant with jam.

da morire! Dai—To die for! Come on.

diavoletti—Imps, little devils.

diavolo—Devil.

donna italiana—Italian woman.

dottore—Doctor.

è amore—It's love.

è assolutamente impossibile—It is absolutely impossible.

è finita. Mi sono stancato—It's over. I got tired.

eccitazione—Excitement.

ehi—Hey.

era bello—It was nice.

era incredibile—It was incredible.

erre, Niccolò, è una rana, sì?—Look, Niccolò, it's a frog, yes?

facciamo l'amore—Let's make love.

facciamolo—Let's do it.

fallo—Do it.

famiglia—Family.

fermo! Oddio… mi ucciderai! Ehi, sei venuto?—Stop! Oh God… you're killing me! Hey, did you come?

forse è il destino—Maybe it's destiny.

forte. Scopami forte, col tuo cazzo, il tuo bel… di più, ehi? Dai—Hard.

Fuck me hard, with your cock, your beautiful... more, Hey? Come on.

fra le coscie—Between the thighs.

frocio del paese—The local fag.

gondolieri—Gondoliers.

grazie—Thank you.

grazie di amarmi—Thank you for loving me.

Ho bisogno di te—I need you.

ho tanto bisogno di te, caro—I need you so much, dear.

il tuo bell'uccello—Your beautiful cock.

importante. Come posso spiegarmi?—Important. How can I explain?

inglese—English.

le tue mani sono dolci. Sei bellissimo—Your hands are sweet. You look so handsome.

licenziato—Fired, dismissed.

losanghe—Lozenges.

ma guarda—But look.

maiala della miseria!—Holy crap!

mangia!—Eat!

meraviglioso—Wonderful.

mi chiamo—My name is....

mi dispiace—I'm sorry.

mi fai impazzire—You drive me crazy.

mi piacere—I was pleased.

mi sei mancato—I missed you.

mi sei mancato tantissimo, sai—I've missed you so much, you know.

mille baci—A thousand kisses.

moeche—Softshell crabs.

molte grazie—Many thanks.

monello—Brat.

musica antica—Ancient music.

naso—Nose.

naturalmente—Naturally.

nel culo—In the ass.

niente—Nothing.

non capisci—You don't understand.

non ci credo—I do not believe it.

non dire così—Don't say that.

non è così importante—It's not that important.

non ne posso più.... Abbracciami, amore—I'm exhausted. Hold me, love.

non parlo molto italiano—I don't speak much Italian.

non so. Non c'è niente da fare—I don't know, there's nothing to do.

ospedale—Hospital.

osteria—An Italian restaurant, typically a simple or inexpensive one.

palazzo, pl. palazzi—Palace.

panino, pl. panini—Sandwich.

pastissada—A ragù of horsemeat.

per sempre—Forever.

Piazzetta, pl. piazzette—Little square, from piazza, square.

piume—Plumage.

prego—You're welcome. But also used in other ways, such as: no problem, don't mention it, please, hello (on answering the phone).

preside—Principal.

prima colazione—Breakfast.

prometto—Promise.

pronto—Ready.

quanto—How much.

ristorante—Restaurant.

salute—Bless you, cheers! (toasting).

scuola elementare—Elementary school.

scusa—I apologize; I beg your pardon.

scusi? Posso prendere in prestito il vostro giornale, prego?—Sorry? May I borrow your newspaper, please?

scusi. Può aiutarmi? Dov'è il negozio più vicino? Panettieria? Salumeria?—Excuse me. Can anyone help? Where's the nearest shop? Panettieria? Salumeria?

sei arrabbiato con me?—Are you mad at me?

sei così bello—You're so beautiful.

sei tanto—You're so….

sei troppo bello… dio mio, Daniel! Come mi tocchi—You're too nice… my God, Daniel! As you touch me….

sei un diavolo—You are a devil.

sestiere—District.

sgroppino—Dessert made with lemon sorbet and Prosecco.

sì—Yes.

Sì, bene. Molto bene, Niccolò! La…? La rana. Sì—Yes, good. Very good, Niccolò! The…? The frog. Yes,

signor—Mr.

signore—Sir.

signorina—Young lady.

stare calmo—Stay calm.
stiamo insieme stanotte—Stay with me tonight.
stupido—Stupid.
tanto—A lot.
tantissimo—So much.
ti desidero—I desire you.
ti voglio—I want you.
ti voglio bene—I love you.
ti voglio tanto bene, caro—I love you so much, dear.
Tito a San Marco—Tito in San Marco.
trattoria, pl. trattorie—Tavern.
tu sei tutto ciò che voglio—You're everything I want.
tutto il tuo corpo, sopra di me—All your body, above me.
un momento—Just a moment.
un poco—A bit.
uomo bellissimo—Beautiful man.
va bene—All right.
vacanza—Vacation, holiday.
vaporetto—Water taxi.
via, pl. vie—Street.
vieni—Come.

M. KING resides in a damp, verdant corner of southwest England, where she may usually be found behind a keyboard and a vat of coffee. Her work features flawed and fascinating characters, vibrant storytelling, and worlds to lose yourself in time and again, with titles ranging from horror to fantasy, humor to romance, erotica to tear-jerking drama... and more.

On the rare occasions she isn't writing, M. King enjoys taking long, muddy walks with her dogs—otherwise known as the hairy chaos monkeys—reading, dabbling in her herb garden, and falling off horses. Just not all at the same time.

Visit her website at www.thenakednib.com. You can contact her at mkingauthor@gmx.com.

FILTH
M. KING

Does gender really matter?

For Kel and Toni, life is precarious. Kel turns tricks for cash and works hard to stay clean, while Toni seeks absolution in a bottle of Mexican hormone pills. Their love is raw and obsessive, but as Toni struggles with anxiety and gender identity, Kel fears the reality of Toni pursuing male-to-female transition, and questions his motives for doing it.

While Kel grapples with his worries and the attentions of regular client Michael—otherwise known as the Sherbet Pervert—Toni faces different problems. Her best friend, Danielle, a transgender woman, thinks Kel is a bad influence and pushes Toni to leave him. Toni holds off, aware that deep down, she's not like Danielle, however much she wishes she could be. Hell, sometimes Toni can't even get comfortable with one set of pronouns.

Things are already complicated, but one terrible day forces Toni and Kel to confront some frightening possibilities when they're shown just how easily their harsh little world could crumble.

www.dreamspinnerpress.com

BREAKING FAITH

M. KING

Brett Derwent thinks he has life all planned out. With the freedom of college life just months away, Brett's eagerly awaiting some fun and independence… until he meets Tommy Hawks. Over the course of one northern Montana summer, an intense romance blooms between the young men, but Tommy has a painful secret—one that even first love can't mitigate. Continually brutalized by his violent father, Tommy is pushed to the edge, torn between the desire to protect his mother and four siblings, and his fear of losing the love he never expected to find.

When the unthinkable happens and Tommy's father is found dead, Brett is afraid to learn the truth. Appalled to think that his lover may be responsible, Brett must face impossible questions: how much of his life—of his youth—is he willing to sacrifice for Tommy, and will having faith in him be enough?

PASSING
SHADOWS

M. KING

Sequel to *Breaking Faith*

After serving six years for murdering his abusive father, Tommy Hawks is released from prison. He moves back in with what's left of his family and tries to negotiate a new life with them and his partner, Brett, who has stood by him through everything. But moving on isn't so easy.

For six years, Brett Derwent sacrificed any chance of a normal life: he spent his college fund on defense lawyers, drove hundreds of miles to visitation days, and had his love letters read by strangers and his phone calls monitored by jailers. Now he and Tommy are faced with the monumental task of starting over as adults when they hardly had the chance to begin together as teens.

Resentment simmers just below the surface, but so do gratitude and guilt. Brett and Tommy need to give each other the time and space to discover who they are individually, and Tommy especially needs the opportunity to stand on his own—even if that means another separation.

www.dreamspinnerpress.com

Also from Dreamspinner Press

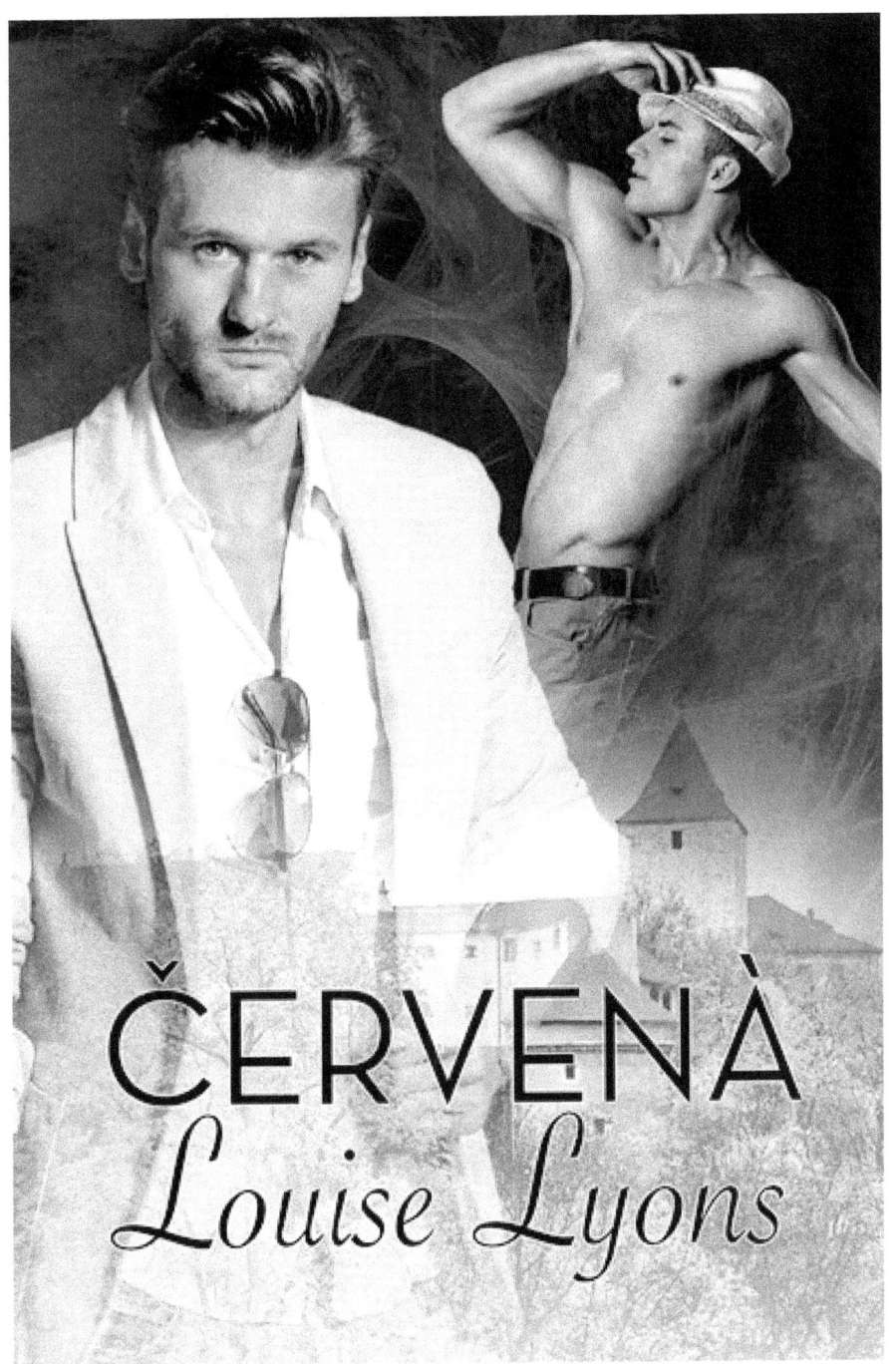

ČERVENÀ
Louise Lyons

www.dreamspinnerpress.com

www.ingramcontent.com/pod-product-compliance
Lightning Source LLC
Chambersburg PA
CBHW070046030726
47506CB00002B/376

* 9 7 8 1 6 3 4 7 7 4 5 8 1 *